Cattleman's Pride
by Diana Palmer

"You smell of roses, Libby," he murmured deeply.

She could feel the sudden tautness of his lean body against her, the increasing warmth of his embrace. She tried to pull away, but he wouldn't let her.

"Don't fight this," Jordan said gruffly. "You haven't stopped wanting me."

"I want hot chocolate, too, Jordan, but it still gives me a migraine, so I don't drink it."

His dark eyebrows lifted. "Let's see if you can convince me."

He bent, drawing his lips slowly, tenderly, across her mouth in a teasing impression of a kiss. He was lazy and gentle, and after a few seconds her traitorous body betrayed her. She was lost. Her arms wreathed around his strong neck. She gave in to the delight of his ardent touch, to the mastery that she'd only guessed at before.

"I can't get enough of you, Libby!" he whispered hungrily.

She nuzzled closer, drowning in the pleasure of being close to him. She shouldn't be letting this happen. But she couldn't help herself…

Wild in the Moonlight
by Jennifer Greene

She'd Been Hurt. She'd been lonely. She needed.

And maybe those were secrets she never meant to reveal to a stranger, but she never told him anything. She just kissed him back, wildly, freely, intimately.

Cameron thought he was a man who took gutsy risks…but Violet was the brave one, the honest one. Something in her called him. Something in him answered her with a well of feeling he'd never known he had.

He raised his head suddenly. "I never meant—"

She gulped in a breath. "It's all right. I didn't think you did."

"It was the moonlight."

"I know."

"I *need* you to know you can trust me."

"I'm thirty-four, Cameron. Too old to trust someone I barely know. But also way too old to make more of a kiss than what it was. We'll just call this a moment's madness and forget all about it."

Easier said…

Available in March 2005 from Silhouette Desire

Sin City Wedding
by Katherine Garbera
and
Scandal Between the Sheets
by Brenda Jackson
(Dynasties: The Danforths)

☙ ❧ ☙

Cattleman's Pride
by Diana Palmer
(Texan Lovers)
and
Wild in the Moonlight
by Jennifer Greene
(The Campbell Sisters)

☙ ❧ ☙

Private Indiscretions
by Susan Crosby
(Behind Closed Doors)
and
The Long Hot Summer
by Rochelle Alers
(The Blackstones)

Cattleman's Pride
DIANA PALMER

Wild in the Moonlight
JENNIFER GREENE

SILHOUETTE®

Desire™

First published in Great Britain 2005
Silhouette Books, Eton House, 18-24 Paradise Road,
Richmond, Surrey TW9 1SR

The publisher acknowledges the copyright holders of the
individual works as follows:

Cattleman's Pride © Diana Palmer 2004
Wild in the Moonlight © Alison Hart 2004

ISBN 0 373 60194 8

51-0305

Printed and bound in Spain
by Litografia Rosés S.A., Barcelona

CATTLEMAN'S PRIDE

by
Diana Palmer

Dear Reader,

As I write this letter, I celebrate another wonderful year at Silhouette Books.

I went to the Romance Writers of America convention in New York City in July of 2003 and was privileged to meet so many of you, my terrific readers. I also enjoyed meeting other authors and making new friends. I had some wonderful meals with my editors at Silhouette, Harlequin and MIRA Books.

I got to tour Harlequin's new Manhattan office, have tea at the Plaza Hotel with a contest winner from Savannah and had supper with my editors, my friend Ann and my son Blayne at the Bull and Bear Restaurant. I went to the Black and White Ball at the Waldorf Astoria Hotel wearing a ball gown and an orchid. Our Harlequin Enterprises President and CEO, Donna M. Hayes, our Vice President of Editorial, Isabel Swift, and my own editor, Tara Gavin—also the Editorial Director in the New York office—presented me with a Tiffany silver heart necklace to mark my one hundred books for the company. I attended the RWA luncheon, where I got another wonderful surprise with two bestseller awards (one for *Desperado* and one for *Lionhearted*) by the wonderful and supportive people at Waldenbooks.

What a trip! I will never forget the experiences or the joy of being with so many nice people.

As I enter my twenty-third year as a Silhouette author, I must tell you that the best part of my job is the people I work with. When I had appendicitis in Chicago in 2001, Isabel Swift and Tara Gavin stayed in the emergency room with me all night—along with my best friend, Ann—and didn't leave until I was out of surgery. To do that, they sacrificed a wonderful meal and some important business activities where they were needed. I know of no better description of true friendship than that; I know of no better job on earth when I do it with people like that.

I wish all of you my very best. Thank you for your years of loyalty and friendship. You are the reason I do the job.

Love to all,

Diana Palmer

To Amy in Alabama

Chapter One

Libby Collins couldn't figure out why her stepmother, Janet, had called a real estate agent out to the house. Her father had only been dead for a few weeks. The funeral was so fresh in her mind that she cried herself to sleep at night. Her brother, Curt, was equally devastated. Riddle Collins had been a strong, happy, intelligent man who'd never had a serious illness. He had no history of heart trouble. So his death of a massive heart attack had been a real shock. In fact, the Collinses' nearest neighbor, rancher Jordan Powell, said it was suspicious. But then, Jordan thought everything was suspicious. He thought the government was building cloned soldiers in some underground lab.

Libby ran a small hand through her wavy black hair, her light-green eyes scanning the horizon for a sight of her brother. But Curt was probably up to his ears in watching over the births of early spring cattle, far in the northern pasture of the Powell ranch. It was just barely April and the heifers, the two-year-old first-time mothers, were beginning to drop their calves right on schedule. There was little hope that Curt would show up before the real estate agent left.

Around the corner of the house, Libby heard the real estate agent speaking. She moved closer, careful to keep out of sight, to see what was going on. Her father had loved his small ranch, as his children did. It had been in their family almost as long as Jordan Powell's family had owned the Bar P.

"How long will it take to find a buyer?" Janet was asking.

"I can't really say, Mrs. Collins," the man replied. "But Jacobsville is growing by leaps and bounds. There are plenty of new families looking for reasonable housing. I think a subdivision here would be perfectly situated and I can guarantee you that any developer would pay top dollar for it."

Subdivision?! Surely she must be hearing things!

But Janet's next statement put an end to any such suspicion. "I want to sell it as soon as possible," Janet continued firmly. "I have the insurance money in hand. As soon as this sale is made, I'm moving out of the country."

Another shattering revelation! Why was her stepmother in such a hurry? Her husband of barely nine months had just died, for heaven's sake!

"I'll do what I can, Mrs. Collins," the real estate agent assured her. "But you must understand that the housing market is depressed right now and I can't guarantee a sale—as much as I'd like to."

"Very well," Janet said curtly. "But keep me informed of your progress, please."

"Certainly."

Libby ran for it, careful not to let herself be seen. Her heart was beating her half to death. She'd wondered at Janet's lack of emotion when her father died. Now her mind was forming unpleasant associations.

She stood in the shadows of the front porch until she

heard the real estate agent drive away. Janet left immediately thereafter in her Mercedes.

Libby's mind was whirling. She needed help. Fortunately, she knew exactly where to go to get it.

She walked down the road toward Jordan Powell's big Spanish-style ranch house. The only transportation Libby had was a pickup truck, which was in the shop today having a water pump replaced. It was a long walk to the Powell ranch, but Libby needed fortifying to tackle her stepmother. Jordan was just the person to put steel in her backbone.

It took ten minutes to walk to the paved driveway that led through white fences to the ranch house. But it took another ten minutes to walk from the end of the driveway to the house. On either side of the fence were dark red-coated Santa Gertrudis cattle, purebred seed stock, which were the only cattle Jordan kept. One of his bulls was worth over a million dollars. He had a whole separate division that involved artificial insemination and the care of a special unit where sperm were kept. Libby had been fascinated to know that a single straw of bull semen could sell for a thousand dollars, or much more if it came from a prize bull who was dead. Jordan sold those straws to cattle ranchers all over the world. He frequently had visitors from other countries who came to tour his mammoth cattle operation. Like the Tremayne brothers, Cy Parks, and a number of other local ranchers, he was heavily into organic ranching. He used no hormones or dangerous pesticides or unnecessary antibiotics on his seed stock, even though they were never sold for beef. The herd sires he kept on the ranch lived in a huge breeding barn—as luxurious as a modern hotel—that was on property just adjacent to the Collinses' land. It was so close that they could hear the bulls bellowing from time to time.

Jordan was a local success story, the sort men liked to tell their young sons about. He started out as a cowboy long before he ever had cattle of his own. He'd grown up the only child of a former debutante and a hobby farmer.

His father had married the only child of wealthy parents, who cut her off immediately when she announced her marriage. They left her only the property that Jordan now owned. His father's drinking cost him almost everything. When he wasn't drinking, he made a modest living with a few head of cattle, but after the sudden death of Jordan's mother, he withdrew from the world. Jordan was left with a hard decision to make. He took a job as a ranch hand on Duke Wright's palatial ranch and in his free time he went the rounds of the professional rodeo circuit. He was a champion bull rider, with the belt buckles and the cash to prove it.

But instead of spending that cash on good times, he'd paid off the mortgage that his father had taken on the ranch. Over the years he'd added a purebred Santa Gertrudis bull and a barn, followed by purebred heifers. He'd studied genetics with the help of a nearby retired rancher and he'd learned how to buy straws of bull semen and have his heifers artificially inseminated. His breeding program gave him the opportunity to enter his progeny in competition, which he did. Awards starting coming his way and so did stud fees for his bull. It had been a long road to prosperity, but he'd managed it, despite having to cope with an alcoholic father who eventually got behind the wheel of a truck and plowed it into a telephone pole. Jordan was left alone in the world. Well, except for women. He sure seemed to have plenty of those, to hear her brother Curt talk.

Libby loved the big dusty-yellow adobe ranch house Jordan had built two years ago, with its graceful arches and black wrought-iron grillwork. There was a big fountain in the front courtyard, where Jordan kept goldfish and huge koi that came right up out of the water to look at visitors. It even had a pond heater, to keep the fish alive all winter. It was a dream of a place. It would have been just right for a family. But everybody said that Jordan Powell would never get married. He liked his freedom too much.

She went up to the front door and rang the doorbell. She

knew how she must look in her mud-stained jeans and faded T-shirt, her boots caked in mud, like her denim jacket. She'd been helping the lone part-time worker on their small property pull a calf. It was a dirty business, something her pristine stepmother would never have done. Libby still missed her father. His unexpected death had been a horrible blow to Curt and Libby, who were only just getting used to Riddle Collins's new wife.

No sooner was Riddle buried than Janet fought to get her hands on the quarter-of-a-million-dollar insurance policy he'd left behind, of which she alone was listed as beneficiary. She'd started spending money the day the check had arrived, with no thought for unpaid bills and Riddle's children. They were healthy and able to work, she reasoned. Besides, they had a roof over their heads. Temporarily, at least. Janet's long talk with the real estate agent today was disquieting. Riddle's new will, which his children knew nothing about, had given Janet complete and sole ownership of the house as well as Riddle's comfortable but not excessive savings account. Or so Janet said. Curt was furious. Libby hadn't said anything. She missed her father so much. She felt as if she were still walking around in a daze and it was almost March. A windy, cold almost-March, at that, she thought, feeling the chill.

She was frowning when the door opened. She jumped involuntarily when instead of the maid, Jordan Powell himself opened it.

"What the hell do you want?" he asked coldly. "Your brother's not here. He's supervising some new fencing up on the north property.

"Well?" he asked impatiently when she didn't speak immediately. "I've got things to do and I'm late already!"

He was so dashing, she thought privately. He was thirty-two, very tall, lean and muscular, with liquid black eyes and dark, wavy hair. He had a strong, masculine face that was dark from exposure to the sun and big ears and big feet. But he was handsome. Too handsome.

"Are you mute?" he persisted, scowling.

She shook her head, sighing. "I'm just speechless. You really are a dish, Jordan," she drawled.

"Will you please tell me what you want?" he grumbled. "And if it's a date, you can go right back home. I don't like being chased by women. I know you can't keep your eyes off me, but that's no excuse to come sashaying up to my front door looking for attention."

"Fat chance," she drawled, her green eyes twinkling up at him. "If I want a man, I'll try someone accessible, like a movie star or a billionaire...."

"I said I'm in a hurry," he prompted.

"Okay. If you don't want to talk to me..." she began.

He let out an impatient sigh. "Come in, then," he muttered, looking past her. "Hurry, before you get trampled by the other hopeful women chasing me."

"That would be a short list," she told him as she went in and waited until he closed the door behind him. "You're famous for your bad manners. You aren't even housebroken."

"I beg your pardon?" he said curtly.

She grinned at him. "Your boots are full of red mud and so's that fabulously expensive wool rug you brought back from Morocco," she pointed out. "Amie's going to kill you when she sees that."

"My aunt only lives here when she hasn't got someplace else to go," he pointed out.

"Translated, that means that she's in hiding. Why are you mad at her *this* time?" she asked.

He gave her a long-suffering stare and sighed. "Well, she wanted to redo my bedroom. Put yellow curtains at the windows. With ruffles." He spat out the word. "She thinks it's too depressing because I like dark wood and beige curtains."

She lifted both eyebrows over laughing eyes. "You could paint the room red...."

He glared down at her. "I said women chased me, not that I brought them home in buckets," he replied.

"My mistake. Who was it last week, Senator Merrill's daughter, and before her, the current Miss Jacobs County…?"

"That wasn't my fault," he said haughtily. "She stood in the middle of the parking lot at that new Japanese place and refused to move unless I let her come home with me." Then he grinned.

She shook her head. "You're impossible."

"Come on, come on, what do you want?" He looked at his watch. "I've got to meet your brother at the old line cabin in thirty minutes to help look over those pregnant heifers." He lifted an eyebrow and his eyes began to shimmer. They ran up and down her slender figure. "Maybe I could do you justice in fifteen minutes…."

She struck a pose. "Nobody's sticking me in between roundup and supper," she informed him. "Besides, I'm abstaining indefinitely."

He put a hand over his heart. "As God is my witness, I never asked your brother to tell you that Bill Paine had a social disease…"

"I am not sweet on Bill Paine!" she retorted.

"You were going to Houston with him to a concert that wasn't being given that night and I knew that Bill had an apartment and a bad reputation with women," he replied with clenched lips. "So I just happened to mention to one of my cowhands, who was standing beside your brother, that Bill Paine had a social disease."

She was aghast, just standing there gaping at his insolence. Curt had been very angry about her accepting a date with rich, blond Bill, who was far above them in social rank. Bill had been a client of Blake Kemp's, where he noticed Libby and started flirting with her. After Curt had told her what he overheard about Bill, she'd cancelled the date. She was glad she did. Later she'd learned that Bill had made a bet with one of his pals that he could get Libby any time he wanted her, despite her standoffish pose.

"Of course, I don't have any social diseases," Jordan said, his deep voice dropping an octave. He checked his watch again. "Now it's down to ten minutes, if we hurry."

She threw up her hands. "Listen, I can't possibly be seduced today, I've got to go to the grocery store. What I came to tell you is that Janet's selling the property to a developer. He wants to put a subdivision on it," she added miserably.

"A what?" he exploded. "A subdivision? Next door to my breeding barn?!" His eyes began to burn. "Like hell she will!"

"Great. You want to stop her, too. Do you have some strong rope?"

"This is serious," he replied gravely. "What the hell is she doing, selling your home out from under you? Surely Riddle didn't leave her the works! What about you and Curt?"

"She says we're young and can support ourselves," she said, fighting back frustration and fury.

He didn't say anything. His silence was as eloquent as shouting. "She's not evicting you. You go talk to Kemp."

"I work for Mr. Kemp," she reminded him.

He frowned. "Which begs the question, why aren't you at work?"

She sighed. "Mr. Kemp's gone to a bar association conference in Florida," she explained. "He said I could have two vacation days while he's gone, since Mabel and Violet were going to be there in case the attorney covering his practice needed anything." She glowered at him. "I don't get much time off."

"Indeed you don't," he agreed. "Blake Kemp is a busy attorney, for a town the size of Jacobsville. You do a lot of legwork for him, don't you?"

She nodded. "It's part of a paralegal's job. I've learned a lot."

"Enough to tempt you to go to law school?"

She laughed. "No. Not that much. A history degree is enough, not to mention the paralegal training. I've had all the education I want." She frowned thoughtfully. "You know, I did think about teaching adult education classes at night...."

"Your father was well-to-do," he pointed out. "He had coin collections worth half a million, didn't he?"

"We thought so, but we couldn't find them. I suppose he sold them to buy that Mercedes Janet is driving," she said somberly.

"He loved you and Curt."

She had to fight tears. "He wrote a new will just after he married her, leaving everything to her," she said simply. "She said she had it all in his safe-deposit box, along with the passbook to his big savings account, which her name was on as well as his. The way it was set up, that account belonged to her, so there was no legal problem with it," she had to admit. "Daddy didn't leave us a penny."

"There's something fishy going on here," he said, thinking out loud.

"It sounds like it, I guess. But Daddy gave everything to her. That was his decision to make, not ours. He was crazy about her."

Jordan looked murderous. "Has the will gone through probate yet?"

She shook her head. "She said she's given it to an attorney. It's pending."

"You know the law, even better than I do. This isn't right. You should get a lawyer," he repeated. "Get Kemp, in fact, and have him investigate her. There's something not right about this, Libby. Your father was the healthiest man I ever knew. He never had any symptoms of heart trouble."

"Well, I thought that, too, and so did Curt." She sighed, glancing down at the elegant blue and rose carpet, and her eyes grew misty. "He was really crazy about her, though.

Maybe he just didn't think we'd need much. I know he loved us...." She choked back a sob. It was still fresh, the grief.

Jordan sighed and pulled her close against his tall, powerful body. His arms were warm and comforting as they enfolded her. "Why don't you just cry, Libby?" he asked gently. "It does help."

She sniffed into his shoulder. It smelled nice. His shirt had a pleasant detergent smell to it. "Do you ever cry?"

"Bite your tongue, woman," he said at her temple. "What would happen to the ranch if I sat down and bawled every time something went wrong? Tears won't come out of Persian carpet, you just ask my aunt!"

She laughed softly, even through the tears. He was a comforting sort of man and it was surprising, because he had a quick temper and an arrogance that put most people's backs up at first meeting.

"So that's why you yell at your cowboys? So you won't cry?"

"Works for me," he chuckled. He patted her shoulder. "Feel better?"

She nodded, smiling through tears. She wiped them away with a paper towel she'd tucked into her jeans. "Thanks."

"What are prospective lovers for?" he asked, smiling wickedly, and laughing out loud when she flushed.

"You stop corrupting me, you bad influence!"

"I said nothing corrupting, I just gave advance notice of bad intentions." He laughed at her expression. "At least it stopped the cascading waterfalls," he added, tongue in cheek, as he glanced at the tear tracks down her cheeks.

"Those weren't tears," she mumbled. "It was dew." She held up a hand. "I feel it falling again!"

"Talk to Kemp," he reiterated, not adding that he was going to do the same. "If she's got a new will and a codicil, signed, make her prove it. Don't let her shove you off your own land without a fight."

"I guess I could ask to see it," she agreed. Then she winced. "I hate arguments. I hate fights."

"I'll remember that the next time you come chasing after me," he promised.

She shook her head impotently, turning to go.

"Hey."

She glanced at him over her shoulder.

"Let me know what you find out," he said. "I'm in this, too. I can't manage a subdivision right near my barn. I can't have a lot of commotion around those beautiful Santa Gerts, it stresses them out too much. It would cost a fortune to tear down that barn and stick it closer to the house. A lawsuit would be cheaper."

"There's an idea," she said brightly. "Take her to court."

"For what, trying to sell property? That's rich."

"Just trying to help us both out," she said.

He glanced at his watch again. "Five minutes left and even I'm not that good," he added. "Pity. If you hadn't kept running your mouth, by now we could have…"

"You hush, Jordan Powell!" she shot at him. "Honestly, of all the blatant, arrogant, sex-crazed ranchers in Texas…!"

She was still mumbling as she went out the door. But when she was out of sight, she grinned. He was a tonic.

That night, Janet didn't say a word about any real estate deals. She ate a light supper that Libby had prepared, as usual without any compliments about it.

"When are you going back to work?" she asked Libby irritably, her dyed blond hair in an expensive hairdo, her trendy silk shell and embroidered jeans marking her new wealth. "It can't be good for you to lie around here all day."

Curt, who was almost the mirror image of his sister, except for his height and powerful frame, glared at the woman. "Excuse me, since when did you do any housework or cooking around here? Libby's done both since she turned thirteen!"

"Don't you speak to me that way," Janet said haughtily. "I can throw you out any time I like. I own everything!"

"You don't own the property until that will goes through probate," Libby replied sweetly, shocked at her own boldness. She'd never talked that way to the woman before. "You can produce it, I hope, because you're going to have to. You don't get the property yet. Maybe not even later, if everything isn't in perfect order."

"You've been talking to that rancher again, haven't you?" Janet demanded. "That damned Powell man! He's so suspicious about everything! Your father had a heart attack. He's dead. He left everything to me. What else do you want?" she raged, standing.

Libby stood, too, her face flushed. "Proof. I want proof. And you'd better have it before you start making any deals with developers about selling Daddy's land!"

Janet started. "De…developers?"

"I heard you this afternoon with that real estate agent," Libby said, with an apologetic glance at her brother, who looked shocked. She hadn't told him. "You're trying to sell our ranch and Daddy hasn't even been dead a month!"

Curt stood up. He looked even more formidable than Libby. "Before you make any attempt to sell this land, you're going to need a lawyer, Janet," he said in that slow, cold drawl that made cowhands move faster.

"How are you going to afford one, Curt, dear?" she asked sarcastically. "You just work for wages."

"Oh, Jordan will loan us the money," Libby said confidently.

Janet's haughty expression fluttered. She threw down her napkin. "You need cooking lessons," she said spitefully. "This food is terrible! I've got to make some phone calls."

She stormed out of the room.

Libby and Curt sat back down, both angry. Libby explained about the real estate agent's visit and what she'd overheard. Curt had only just come in when Libby had put the spaghetti and garlic bread on the table. It was Curt's favorite food and his sister made it very well, he thought, despite Janet's snippy comment.

"She's not selling this place while there's a breath left in my body," he told his sister. "Anyway, she can't do that until the will is probated. And she'd better have a legitimate will."

"Jordan said we needed to get Mr. Kemp to take a look at it," she said. "And I think we're going to need a handwriting expert to take a look, too."

He nodded.

"But what are we going to do about money to file suit?" she asked. "I was bluffing about Jordan loaning us the money. I don't know if he would."

"He's not going to want a subdivision on his doorstep, I'll tell you that," Curt said. "I'll talk to him."

"I already did," she said, surprising him. "He thinks there's something fishy going on, too."

"You can't get much past Jordan," he agreed. "I've been working myself to death trying not to think about losing Dad. I should have paid more attention to what was going on here."

"I've been grieving, too." She sighed and folded her small hands on the tablecloth. "Isn't it amazing how snippy she is, now that Daddy's not here? She was all over us like poison ivy before he died."

"She married him for what he had, Libby," he said bitterly.

"She seemed to love him…."

"She came on to me the night they came back from that Cancun honeymoon," he said bitterly.

Libby whistled. Her brother was a very attractive man. Their father, a sweet and charming man, had been overweight and balding. She could understand why Janet might have preferred Curt to his father.

"I slapped her down hard and Dad never knew." He

shook his head. "How could he marry something like that?"

"He was flattered by all the attention she gave him, I guess," Libby said miserably. "And now here we are. I'll bet she sweet-talked him into changing that will. He would have done anything for her, you know that—he was crazy in love with her. He might have actually written us out of it, Curt. We have to accept that."

"Not until they can prove to me that it wasn't forged," he said stubbornly. "I'm not giving up our inheritance without a fight. Neither are you," he asserted.

She sighed. "Okay, big brother. What do you want to do?"

"When do you go back to work?"

"Monday. Mr. Kemp's out of town."

"Okay. Monday, you make an appointment for both of us to sit down with him and hash this out."

She felt better already. "Okay," she said brightly. "I'll do that very thing. Maybe we do have a chance of keeping Daddy's ranch."

He nodded. "There's always hope." He leaned back in his chair. "So you went to see Jordan." He smiled indulgently. "I can remember a time not so long ago when you ran and hid from him."

"He always seemed to be yelling at somebody," she recalled. "I was intimidated by him. Especially when I graduated from high school. I had a sort of crush on him. I was scared to death he'd notice. Not that he was ever around here that much," she added, laughing. "He and Daddy had a fight a week over water rights."

"Dad usually lost, too," Curt recalled. He studied his sister with affection. "You know, I thought maybe Jordan was sweet on you himself—he's only eight years older than you."

"He's never been sweet on me!" she flashed at him, blushing furiously. "He's hardly even smiled at me, in all the years we've lived here, until the past few months! If anything, he usually treats me like a contagious virus!''

Curt only smiled. He looked very much like her, with the same dark wavy hair and the same green eyes. "He picks at you. Teases you. Makes you laugh. You do the same thing to him. People besides me have noticed. He bristles if anyone says anything unkind about you.''

Her eyes widened. "Who's been saying unkind things about me?'' she asked.

"That assistant store manager over at Lord's Department Store.''

"Oh. Sherry King.'' She leaned back in her chair. "She can't help it, you know. She was crazy about Duke Wright and he wanted to take me to the Cattleman's Ball. I wouldn't go and he didn't ask anybody else. I feel sorry for her.''

"Duke's not your sort of man,'' he replied. "He's a mixer. Nobody in Jacobsville has been in more brawls,'' he said, pausing. "Well, maybe Leo Hart has.''

"Leo Hart got married, he won't be brawling out at Shea's Roadhouse and Bar anymore.''

"Duke's not likely to get married again. His wife took their five-year-old son to New York City, where her new job is. He says she doesn't even look after the little boy. She's too busy trying to get a promotion. The child stays with her sister while she jets all over the world closing real estate deals.''

"It's a new world,'' Libby pointed out. "Women are competing with men for the choice jobs now. They have to move around to get a promotion.''

Curt's eyes narrowed. "Maybe they should get promotion before they get pregnant,'' he said impatiently.

She shrugged. "Accidents happen.''

"No child of mine is ever going to be an accident,'' Curt said firmly.

"Nice to be so superior,'' she teased, eyes twinkling. "Never to make mistakes…''

He swiped at her with a napkin. "You don't even stick your toes in the water, so don't lecture me about drowning."

She chuckled. "I'm sensible, I am," she retorted. "None of this angst for me. I'll just do my routine job and keep my nose out of emotional entanglements."

He studied her curiously. "You go through life avoiding any sort of risk, don't you, honey?" he mused.

She moved one shoulder restlessly. "Daddy and Mama fought all the time, remember?" she said. "I swore I'd never get myself into a fix like that. She told me that she and Daddy were so happy when they first met, when they first married. Then, six months later, she was pregnant with you and they couldn't manage one pleasant meal together without shouting." She shook her head. "That means you can't trust emotions. It's better to use your brain when you think about marrying somebody. Love is…sticky," she concluded. "And it causes insanity, I'm sure of it."

"Why don't you ask Kemp if that's why he's stayed single so long? He's in his middle thirties, isn't he, and never even been engaged."

"Who'd put up with him?" she asked honestly. "Now there's a mixer for you," she said enthusiastically. "He actually *threw* another lawyer out the front door and onto the sidewalk last month. Good thing there was a welcome mat there, it sort of broke the guy's fall."

"What did he want?" Curt asked.

She shook her head. "I have no idea. But I don't expect him to be a repeat client."

Curt chuckled. "I see what you mean."

Libby went to bed early that night, without another word to Janet. She knew that anything she said would be too much. But she did miss her father and she couldn't believe that he wouldn't have mentioned Libby and Curt in his will. He did love them. She knew he did.

She thought about Jordan Powell, too, and about Curt's

remark that he thought Jordan was sweet on her. She tingled all over at the thought. But that wasn't going to happen, she assured herself. Jordan was gorgeous and he could have his pick of pretty women. Libby Collins would be his last resort. The world wasn't ending yet, so she was out of the running.

She rolled over, closed her eyes, and went to sleep.

Chapter Two

Janet wasn't at breakfast the next morning. Her new gold Mercedes was gone and she hadn't left a note. Libby saw it as a bad omen.

The weekend passed with nothing remarkable except for Janet's continued absence. The truck was ready Saturday and Curt picked it up in town, catching a lift with one of Jordan's cowboys. It wasn't as luxurious as a Mercedes, but it had a good engine and it was handy for hauling things like salt blocks and bales of hay. Libby tried to picture hauling hay in Janet's Mercedes and almost went hysterical with laughter.

Libby went back to work at Blake Kemp's office early Monday morning, dropped off by Curt on his way to the feed store for Jordan. She felt as if she hadn't really had a vacation at all.

Violet Hardy, Mr. Kemp's secretary, who was dark-haired, blue-eyed, pretty and somewhat overweight, smiled at her as she came in the door. "Hi! Did you have a nice vacation?"

"I spent it working," Libby confessed. "How did things go here?"

Violet groaned. "Don't even ask."

"That bad, huh?" Libby remarked.

Mabel, the blond grandmother who worked at reception, turned in her chair after transferring a call into Mr. Kemp's office. "Bad isn't the word, Libby," she said in a whisper, glancing down the hall to make sure the doors were all closed. "That lawyer Mr. Kemp got to fill in for him got two cases confused and sent the clients to the wrong courtrooms in different counties."

"Yes," Violet nodded, "and one of them came in here and tried to punch Mr. Kemp."

Libby pursed her lips. "No. Did he have insurance?"

All three women chuckled.

"For an attorney who handles so many assault cases," Violet whispered, "he doesn't practice what he preaches. Mr. Kemp punched the guy back and they wound up out on the street. Our police chief, Cash Grier, broke it up and almost arrested Mr. Kemp."

"What about the other guy? Didn't he start it?" Libby exclaimed.

"The other guy was Duke Wright," Violet confessed, watching Libby color. "And Chief Grier said that instead of blaming Mr. Kemp for handling Mrs. Wright's divorce, he should thank him for not bankrupting Mr. Wright in the process!"

"Then what?" Libby asked.

All three women glanced quickly down the hall.

"Mr. Wright threw a punch at Chief Grier."

"Well, that was smart thinking. Duke's in the hospital, then?" Libby asked facetiously.

"Nope," Violet said, her blue eyes twinkling. "But he was in jail briefly until he made bail." She shook her head. "I don't expect he'll try that twice."

"Crime has fallen about fifty percent since we got Cash Grier as chief," Violet sighed, smiling.

"And Judd Dunn as assistant chief," Libby reminded her.

"Poor Mr. Wright," Mabel said. "He does have the worst luck. Remember that Jack Clark who worked for him, who was convicted of murdering that woman in Victoria? Mr. Wright sure hated the publicity. It came just when he was trying to get custody of his son."

"Mr. Wright would have a lot less trouble if he didn't spend so much time out looking for it," came a deep, gruff voice from behind them.

They all jumped. Blake Kemp was standing just at the entrance to the hallway with a brief in one hand and a coffee cup in the other. He was as much a dish as Jordan Powell. He had wavy dark hair and blue eyes and the most placid, friendly face—until he got in front of a jury. Nobody wanted to be across the courtroom from Kemp when a trial began. There was some yellow and purple discoloration on one high cheekbone, where a fist had apparently landed a blow. Duke Wright, Libby theorized silently.

"Libby, before you do anything else, would you make a pot of coffee, please?" he asked in a long-suffering tòne. He impaled a wincing Violet with his pale blue eyes. "I don't give a damn what some study says is best for me, I want caffeine. C-A-F-F-E-I-N-E," he added, spelling it letter by letter for Violet's benefit.

Violet lifted her chin and her own blue eyes glared right back at him. "Mr. Kemp, if you drank less of it, you might not be so bad-tempered. I mean, really, that's the second person you've thrown out of our office in a month! Chief Grier said that was a new city record...."

Kemp's eyes were blazing now, narrow and intent. "Miss Hardy, do you want to still be employed here tomorrow?"

Violet looked as if she was giving that question a lot of deliberation. "But, sir…" she began.

"I like caffeine. I'm not giving it up," Kemp said curtly. "You don't change my routine in this office. Is that clear?"

"But, Mr. Kemp—!" she argued.

"I don't remember suggesting anything so personal to you, Miss Hardy," he shot back, clearly angry. "I could, however," he added, and his cold blue eyes made insinuations about her figure, which was at least two dress sizes beyond what it should have been.

All three women gasped at the outrageous insinuation and then glared at their boss.

Violet flushed and stood up, as angry as he was, but not intimidated one bit by the stare. "My...my father always said that a woman should look like a woman and not a skeleton encased in skin. I may be a little overweight, Mr. Kemp, but at least I'm doing something about it!"

He glanced pointedly at a cake in a box on her desk.

She colored. "I live out near the Hart Ranch. I promised Tess Hart I'd pick that up at the bakery for her before I came to work and drop it by her house when I go home for lunch. It's for a charity tea party this afternoon." She was fuming. "I do not eat cake! Not anymore."

He stared at her until she went red and sat back down. She averted her eyes and went back to work. Her hands on the computer keyboard were trembling.

"You fire me if you want to, Mr. Kemp, but nothing I said to you was as mean as what you were insinuating to me with that look," Violet choked. "I know I weigh too much. You don't have to rub it in. I was only trying to help you."

Mabel and Libby were still glaring at him. He shifted uncomfortably and put the brief down on Violet's desk with a slap. "There are six spelling errors in that. You'll have to redo it. You can buzz me when the coffee's ready," he added shortly. He turned on his heel and took his coffee cup back into his office. As an afterthought, he slammed the door.

"Oh, and like anybody short of a druggist could read those chicken scratches on paper that you call *handwriting!*" Violet muttered, staring daggers after him.

Libby let out the breath she'd been holding and gaped at sweet, biddable Violet, who'd never talked back to Mr. Kemp in the eight months she'd worked for him. So did Mabel.

"Well, it's about time!" Mabel said, laughing delightedly. "Good for you, Violet. It's no good, letting a man walk all over you, no matter how crazy you are about him!"

"Hush!" Violet exclaimed, glancing quickly down the hall. "He'll hear you!"

"He doesn't know," Libby said comfortingly, putting an arm around Violet. "And we'll never tell. I'm proud of you, Violet."

"Me, too," Mabel grinned.

Violet sighed. "I guess he'll fire me. It might not be a bad thing. I spend too much time trying to take care of him and he hates it." Her blue eyes were wistful under their long, thick lashes. "You know, I've lost fifteen pounds," she murmured. "And I'm down a dress size."

"A new diet?" Libby asked absently as she checked her "in" tray.

"A new gym, just for women," Violet confessed with a grin. "I love it!"

Libby looked at the other woman with admiration. "You're really serious about this, aren't you?"

Violet's shoulder moved gently. She was wearing a purple dress with a high collar and lots of frills on the bodice and a very straight skirt that clung to her hips. It was the worst sort of dress for a woman who had a big bust and wide hips, but nobody had the heart to tell Violet. "I had to do something. I mean, look at me! I'm so big!"

"You're not that big. But I think it's great that you're trying so hard, Violet," Libby said gently. "And to keep you on track, Mabel and I are giving up dessert when you eat lunch with us."

"I have to go home and see about Mother most every day at lunchtime," Violet confessed. "She hates that. She said I was wasting my whole life worrying about her, when I should be out having fun. But she's already had two light strokes in the past year since Daddy died. I can't leave her alone.''

''Honey, people like you are why there's a heaven,'' Mabel murmured softly. ''You're one in a million.''

Violet waved her away. ''Everybody's got problems,'' she laughed. ''For all we know, Mr. Kemp has much bigger ones than we do. He's such a good person. When Mother had that last stroke, the bad one, he even drove me to the hospital after I got the call.''

''He is a good person,'' Libby agreed. ''But so are you.''

''You'd better make that coffee, I guess,'' Violet said wistfully. ''I really thought I could make it half and half and he wouldn't be able to taste the difference. He's so uptight lately. He's always in a hurry, always under pressure. He drinks caffeine like water and it's so bad for his heart. I know about hearts. My dad died of a heart attack last year. I was just trying to help.''

''It's hard to help a rattlesnake across the road, Violet,'' Mabel said, tongue-in-cheek.

Libby was curious about the coincidence of Violet's father dying of a heart attack, like her father, such a short time ago. ''Violet could find one nice thing to say about a serial killer,'' Libby agreed affectionately. ''Even worse, she could find one nice thing to say about my stepmother.''

''Ouch,'' Mabel groaned. ''Now there's a hard case if I ever saw one.'' She shook her head. ''People in Branntville are still talking about her and old man Darby.''

Libby, who'd just finished filling the coffeepot, started it brewing and turned jerkily. ''Excuse me?''

''Didn't I ever tell you?'' Mabel asked absently. ''Just a sec. Good morning, Kemp Law Offices,'' she said. ''Yes, sir, I'll connect you.'' She started to push the intercom button when she saw with shock that it was already depressed. The light was on the switch. She and Libby, who'd also seen it, exchanged agonized glances. Quickly, without telling Violet, she pushed it off and then on again. "Mr. Kemp, it's Mrs. Lawson for you on line two." She waited, hung up, and swung her chair around. She didn't dare tell poor Violet that Mr. Kemp had probably heard every single word she'd said about him.

"Your stepmother, Janet," Mabel told Libby, "was working at a nursing home over in Branntville. She sweet-talked an old man who was a patient there into leaving everything he had to her." She shook her head. "They said that Janet didn't even give him a proper funeral. She had him cremated and put in an urn and there was a graveside service. They said she bought a designer suit to wear to it."

Libby was getting cold chills. There were too many similarities there to be a coincidence. Janet had wanted to have Riddle Collins cremated, too, but Curt and Libby had talked to the funeral director and threatened a lawsuit if he complied with Janet's request. They went home and told Janet the same thing and also insisted on a church funeral at the Presbyterian church where Riddle had been a member since childhood. Janet had been furious, but in the end, she reluctantly agreed.

Violet wasn't saying anything, but she had a funny look on her face and she seemed pale. She turned away before the others saw. But Libby's expression was thought-provoking.

"You're thinking something. What?" Mabel asked Libby.

Fortunately, the phone rang again while Libby was deciding if it was wise to share her thoughts.

Violet got up from her desk and went close to Libby. "She wanted to cremate your father, too, didn't she?"

Libby nodded.

"You should go talk to Mr. Kemp."

Libby smiled. "You know, Violet, I think you're right." She hugged the other girl and went back to Mabel. "When he gets off the phone, I need to talk to him."

Mabel grinned. "Now you're talking." She checked the board. "He's free. Just a sec." She pushed a button. "Mr. Kemp, Libby needs to speak to you, if it's convenient."

"Send her in, Mrs. Jones."

"Good luck," Mabel said, crossing her fingers.

Libby grinned back.

"Come in," Kemp said, opening the door for Libby and closing it behind her. "Have a seat. I don't need ESP to know what's on your mind. I had a call from Jordan Powell at home last night."

Her eyebrows arched. "Well, he jumped the gun!"

"He's concerned. Probably with good reason," he added. "I went ahead on my own and had a private detective I know run a check on Janet's background. This isn't the first time she's become a widow."

"I know," Libby said. "Mabel says an elderly man in a nursing home left her everything he had. She had him sent off to be cremated immediately after they got him to the funeral home."

He nodded. "And I understand from Don Hedgely at our funeral home here that she tried to have the same thing done with your father, but you and your brother threatened a lawsuit."

"We did," Libby said. "Daddy didn't believe in cremation. He would have been horrified."

Kemp leaned back in his desk chair and crossed his long legs, with his hands behind his head. He pursed his lips and narrowed his blue eyes, deep in thought. "There's another thing," he said. "Janet was fired from that nursing home for being too friendly with their wealthiest patients. One of whom—the one you know about—was an elderly widower with no children. He died of suspicious causes and left her his estate."

Libby folded her arms. She felt chilled all over now. "Wasn't it enough for her?" she wondered out loud.

"Actually, it took the entire estate to settle his gambling

debts," he murmured. "Apparently, he liked the horses a little too much."

"Then there was our father." She anticipated his next thought.

He shook his head. "That was after Mr. Hardy in San Antonio."

Libby actually gasped. It couldn't be!

Kemp leaned forward quickly. "Do you think Violet is happy having to live in a rented firetrap with her invalid mother? Her parents were wealthy. But a waitress at Mr. Hardy's favorite restaurant apparently began a hot affair with him and talked him into making her a loan of a quarter of a million dollars to save her parents from bankruptcy and her father from suicide. He gave her a check and had a heart attack before he could stop payment on it—which he planned to do. He told his wife and begged forgiveness of her and his daughter before he died." His eyes narrowed. "He died shortly after he was seen with a pretty blonde at a San Antonio motel downtown."

"You think it was Janet? That it wasn't a heart attack at all—that she killed him?"

"I think there are too many coincidences for comfort in her past," Kemp said flatly. "But the one eyewitness who saw her with Hardy at that motel was unable to pick her out of a lineup. She'd had her hair color changed just the day before the lineup. She remained a brunette for about a week and then changed back to blond."

Libby's face tightened. "She might have killed my father," she bit off.

"That is a possibility," Kemp agreed. "It's early days yet, Libby. I can't promise you anything. But if she's guilty and I can get her on a witness stand, in a court of law, I can break her," he said with frightening confidence. "She'll tell me everything she knows."

She swallowed. "I don't want her to get away with it," she began. "But Curt and I work for wages..."

He flapped his hand in her direction. "Every lawyer

takes a pro bono case occasionally. I haven't done it in months. You and Curt can be my public service for the year," he added, and he actually smiled. It made him look younger, much less dangerous than he really was.

"I don't know what to say," she said, shaking her head in disbelief.

He leaned forward. "Say you'll be careful," he replied. "I can't find any suspicion that she ever helped a young person have a heart attack, but I don't doubt for a minute that she knows how. I'm working with Micah Steele on that aspect of it. There isn't much he doesn't know about the darker side of medicine, even if he is a doctor. And what he doesn't know about black ops and untimely death, Cash Grier does."

"I thought Daddy died of a heart condition nobody knew he had." She took a deep breath. "When I tell Curt, he'll go crazy."

"Let me tell him," Kemp said quietly. "It will be easier."

"Okay."

"Meanwhile, you have to go back home and pretend that nothing's wrong, that your stepmother is innocent of any foul play. That's imperative. If you give her a reason to think she's being suspected of anything, she'll bolt, and we may never find her."

"We'd get our place back without a fight," Libby commented wistfully.

"And a woman who may have murdered your father, among others, would go free," Kemp replied. "Is that really what you want?"

Libby shook her head. "Of course not. I'll do whatever you say."

"We'll be working in the background. The most important thing is to keep the pressure on, a little at a time, so that she doesn't get suspicious. Tell her you've spoken to an attorney about the will, but nothing more."

"Okay," she agreed.

He got up. "And don't tell Violet I said anything to you about her father," he added. His broad shoulders moved restlessly under his expensive beige suit, as if he were carrying some difficult burden. "She's…sensitive."

What a surprising comment from such an insensitive man, she thought, but she didn't dare say it. She only smiled. "Certainly."

She was reaching for the doorknob when he called her back. "Yes, sir?"

"When you make another pot of coffee," he said hesitantly, "I guess we could use some of that half and half."

Her dropped jaw told its own story.

"She means well," he said abruptly, and turned back to his desk. "But for now, I want it strong and black and straight up. Call me when it's made and I'll bring my cup."

"It should be ready right now," she faltered. Even in modern times, few bosses went to get their own coffee. But Mr. Kemp was something of a puzzle. Perhaps, Libby thought wickedly as she followed him down the hall, even to himself.

He glanced at Violet strangely, but he didn't make any more comments. Violet sat with her eyes glued to her computer screen until he poured his coffee and went back to his office.

Libby wanted so badly to say something to her, but she didn't know what. In the end, she just smiled and made a list of the legal precedents she would have to look up for Mr. Kemp at the law library in the county courthouse. Thank God, she thought, for computers.

She was on her way home in the pickup truck after a long day when she saw Jordan on horseback, watching several men drive the pregnant heifers into pastures close to the barn. He had a lot of money invested in those purebred calves and he wasn't risking them to predators or difficult births. He looked so good on horseback, she thought dreamily. He was arrow-straight and his head, covered by that wide-brimmed creamy Stetson he favored, was tilted in a way that was particularly his. She could have picked him out of any crowd at a distance just by the way he carried himself.

He turned his head when he heard the truck coming down the long dirt road and he motioned Libby over to the side.

She parked the truck, cut off the engine, and stood on the running board to talk to him over the top of the old vehicle. "I wish I had a camera," she called. "Mama Powell, protecting his babies..."

"You watch it!" he retorted, shaking a finger at her.

She laughed. "What are you going to do, jump the fence and run me down?"

"Poor old George here couldn't jump a fence. He's twenty-four," he added, patting the old horse's withers. "He hates his corral. I thought I'd give him a change of scenery, since I wasn't going far."

"Everything gets old, I guess. Most everything, anyway," she added with a faraway, wistful look in her eyes. She had an elderly horse of her own, that she might yet have to give away because it was hard to feed and keep him on her salary.

He dismounted and left George's reins on the ground to jump the fence and talk to her. "Did you see Kemp?" he asked.

"Yes. He said you phoned him."

"I asked a few questions and got some uncomfortable answers," he said, coming around the truck to stand beside her. His big lean hands went to her waist and he lifted her down close to him. Too close. She could smell his shaving lotion and feel the heat off his body under the Western cut long-sleeved shirt. In her simple, jacketed suit, she felt overly dressed.

"You don't look too bad when you fix up," he commented, approving her light makeup and the gray suit that made her eyes look greener than they were.

"You don't look too bad when you don't," she replied. "What uncomfortable answers are you getting?"

His eyes were solemn. "I think you can guess. I don't like the idea of you and Curt alone in that house with her."

"We have a shotgun somewhere. I'll make a point of buying some shells for it."

He shook her by the waist gently. "I'm not teasing. Can you lock your bedroom door? Can Curt?"

"It's an old house, Jordan," she faltered. "None of the bedroom doors have locks."

"Tell Curt I said to get bolts and put them on. Do it when she's not home. In the meantime, put a chair under the doorknob."

"But why?" she asked uncertainly.

He drew a long breath. His eyes went to her soft bow of a mouth and he studied it for several seconds before he spoke. "There's one very simple way to cause a heart attack. You can do it with a hypodermic syringe filled with nothing but air."

She couldn't speak for a moment. "Could they...tell that if they did an autopsy on my father?"

"I'm not a forensic specialist, despite the fact that there are half a dozen shows on TV that can teach you how to think you are. I'll ask somebody who knows," he added.

She hated the thought of disinterring her father. But it would be terrible if he'd met with foul play and it never came out.

He tilted her face up to his narrow dark eyes. "You're worrying. Don't. I'm as close as your phone, night or day."

She smiled gently. "Thanks, Jordan."

His thumbs moved on her waist while he looked down at her. His face hardened. His eyes were suddenly on her soft mouth, with real hunger.

The world stopped. It seemed like that. She met his searching gaze and couldn't breathe. Her body felt achy. Hungry. Feverish. She swallowed, hoping it didn't show.

"If you play your cards right, I might let you kiss me," he murmured.

Her heart skipped. "Excuse me?"

One big shoulder lifted and fell. "Where else are you going to get any practical experience?" he asked. "Duke Wright is a candidate for the local nursing home, after all…"

"He's thirty-six!" she exclaimed. "That isn't old!"

"I'm thirty-two," he pointed out. "I have all my own teeth." He grinned to display them. "And I can still outrun at least two of my horses."

"That's an incentive to kiss you?" she asked blankly.

"Think of the advantages if you kiss me during a stampede," he pointed out.

She laughed. He was a case. Her eyes adored him. "I'll keep you in mind," she promised. "But you mustn't get your hopes up. This town is full of lonely bachelors who can't get women to kiss them. You'll have to take a number and wait."

"Wait until what?" he asked, tweaking her waist with his thumbs.

"I don't know. Christmas? I could kiss you as part of your present."

His eyebrows arched. "What's the other part?"

"It's not Christmas. Listen, I have to get home and make supper."

"I'll send Curt on down," he said.

She was seeing a new pattern. "To make sure I'm not left alone with Janet, is that right?"

"For my peace of mind," he corrected. "I've gotten… used to you," he added slowly. "As a neighbor," he added deliberately. "Think how hard it would be to break in another one, at my age."

"You just said you weren't old," she reminded him.

"Maybe I am, just a little," he confessed. He drew her up until she was standing completely against him, so close that she could feel the hard press of his muscular legs against her own. "Come on," he taunted, bending his head with a mischievous little smile. "You know you're dying to kiss me."

"I am?" she whispered dreamily as she studied the long, wide, firm curve of his lips.

"Desperately."

She felt his nose brushing against hers. Somewhere, a horse was neighing. A jet flew over. The wind ruffled leaves in a small tree nearby. She was deaf to any sound other than the throb of her own heartbeat. There was nothing in the world except Jordan's mouth, a scant inch from her own. He'd never kissed her. She wanted him to. She ached for him to.

His hands tightened on her waist, lifting her closer. "Come on, chicken. Give it all you've got."

Her hands were flat against his chest, feeling the warm muscles under his cotton shirt. She tasted his breath. Her arms slid up to his shoulders. He had her hypnotized. She wanted nothing more than to drown in him.

"That's it," he whispered.

She closed her eyes and lifted up on her tiptoes as she felt the slow, soft press of her own lips against his for the first time.

Her knees were weak. She didn't think they were going to support her. And still Jordan didn't move, didn't respond.

Frustrated, she tried to lift up higher, her arms circled his neck and pulled, trying to make his mouth firm and deepen above hers. But she couldn't budge him.

"Oh, you arro…!"

It was the opening he'd been waiting for. His mouth crushed down against her open lips and his arms contracted hungrily. Libby moaned sharply at the rush of sensation it caused in her body. It had never been like this in her life. She was burning alive. She ached. She longed. She couldn't get close enough….

"Hey, Jordan!"

The distant shout broke the spell. Jordan jerked his head around to see one of his men waving a wide-brimmed hat and gesturing toward a pickup truck that was driving right out into the pasture where Jordan was putting those pregnant heifers.

"It's the feed supplement I ordered," he murmured, letting her go slowly. "Damn his timing."

He didn't smile when he said that. She couldn't manage even a word.

He touched her softly swollen mouth with his fingertips. "Maybe you could take me on a date and we could get lost on some deserted country road," he suggested.

She took a breath and shook her head to clear it. "I do not seduce men in parked cars," she pointed out.

He snapped his fingers. "Damn!"

"He's waving at you again," she noted, looking over his shoulder.

"All right, I'll go to work. But I'll send Curt on home." He touched her cheek. "Be careful, okay?"

She managed a weak smile. "Okay."

He turned and vaulted the fence, mounting George with the ease of years of practice as a horseman. "See you."

She nodded and watched him ride away. Her life had just changed course, in the most unexpected way.

Chapter Three

But all Jordan's worry—and Libby's unease—was for nothing. When she got home, Janet's Mercedes was gone. There was a terse little note on the hall table that read, *Gone to Houston shopping, back tomorrow.*

Even as she was reading it, Curt came in the back door, bareheaded and sweaty.

"She's gone?" he asked.

She nodded. "Left a note. She's gone to Houston and won't be back until tomorrow."

"Great. It'll give me time to put locks on the bedroom doors," he said.

She sighed. "Jordan's been talking to you, hasn't he?" she asked.

"Yes, and he's been kissing you, apparently," he murmured, grinning. "Old Harry had to yell himself hoarse to get Jordan's attention when they brought those feed supplements out."

She flushed. She couldn't think of a single defense. But she hadn't heard Harry yelling, except one time. No wonder people were talking.

"Interested in you, is he?" Curt asked softly.

"He wanted me to ask him out on a date and get him lost on a dirt road," she said.

"And you said...?"

She moved restively. "I said that I didn't seduce men in parked cars on deserted roads, of course," she assured him.

He looked solemn. "Sis, we've never really talked about Jordan...."

"And we really don't need to, now," she interrupted. "I'm a big girl and I know all about Jordan. He's only teasing. I'm older and he's doing it in a different way, that's all."

Curt wasn't smiling. "He isn't."

She cleared her throat. "Well, it doesn't matter. He's not a marrying man and I'm not a frivolous woman. Besides, his tastes run to beauty queens and state senators' daughters."

He hesitated.

She smiled before he could say anything else. "Let it drop. We've got enough on our minds now without adding more to them. Let's rush to the hardware store and buy locks before she gets back."

He shrugged and let it go. There would be another time to discuss Jordan Powell.

When Libby got home from work Tuesday evening she was still reeling from the shocking news that a fed-up Violet had quit her job and gone to work for Dick Wright. Blake Kemp had *not* taken the news well. Her mood lifted when she found Jordan's big burgundy double-cabbed pickup truck sitting in her front yard. He was sitting on the side of the truck bed, whittling a piece of wood with a pocket knife, his broad-brimmed hat pushed way back on his head. He looked up at her approach and jumped down to meet her.

"You're late," he complained.

She got out of her car, grabbing her purse on the way. "I had to stay late and type up some notes for Mr. Kemp."

He scowled. "That's Violet's job."

"Violet's leaving," she said on a sigh. "She's going to work for Duke Wright."

"But she's crazy for Kemp, isn't she?" Jordan wondered.

She scowled at him. "You aren't supposed to know that," she pointed out.

"Everybody knows that." He looked around the yard. "Janet hasn't shown up. Curt said she'd gone to Houston."

"That's what the note said," she agreed, walking beside him to the front porch. "Curt put the locks on last night."

"I know. I asked him."

She unlocked the door and pushed it open. "Want some coffee?"

"I'd love some. Eggs? Bacon? Cinnamon toast?" he added.

"Oh, I see," she mused with a grin. "Amie's gone and you're starving, huh?"

He shrugged nonchalantly. "She didn't have to leave. I only yelled a little."

"You shouldn't scare her. She's old."

"Dirt's old. Amie's a spring chicken." He chuckled. "Anyway, she was shopping for antique furniture on the Internet and she found a side table she couldn't live without in San Antonio. She drove up to look at it. She said she'd see me in a couple of days."

"And you're starving."

"You make the nicest scrambled eggs, Libby," he coaxed. "Nice crisp bacon. Delicious cinnamon toast. Strong coffee."

"It isn't the time of day for breakfast."

"No law that you can't have breakfast for supper," he pointed out.

She sighed. "I was planning a beef casserole."

"It won't go with scrambled eggs."

She put her hands on her hips and gave him a considering look. "You really are a pain, Jordan."

He moved a step closer and caught her by the waist with two big lean hands. "If you want me to marry you, you have to prove that you're a good cook."

"Marry…?"

Before she could get another word out, his mouth crushed down over her parted lips. He kissed her slowly, tenderly, his big hands steely at her waist, as if he were keeping them there by sheer will when he wanted to pull her body much closer to his own.

Her hands rested on his clean shirt while she tried to decide if he was kidding. He had to be. Certainly he didn't want to marry anybody. He'd said so often enough.

He lifted his head scant inches. "Stop doing that."

She blinked. "Doing what?"

"Thinking. You can't kiss a man and do analytical formulae in your head at the same time."

"You said you'd never marry anybody…."

His eyes were oddly solemn. "Maybe I changed my mind."

Before she could answer him, he bent his head and kissed her again. This time it wasn't a soft, teasing sample of a kiss. It was bold, brash, invasive and possessive. He enveloped her in his hard arms and crushed her down the length of his powerful body. She felt a husky groan go into her mouth as he grew more insistent.

Against her hips, she felt the sudden hardness of his body. As if he realized that and didn't like having her feel it, he moved away a breath. Slowly, he lifted his hard mouth from her swollen lips and looked down at her quietly, curiously.

"This is getting to be a habit," she said breathlessly. Her body was throbbing, like her heart. She wondered if he could hear it.

His dark eyes fell to the soft, quick pulsing of her heart, visible where her loose blouse bounced in time with it.

Beneath it, two hard little peaks were blatant. He saw them and his eyes began to glitter.

"Don't look at me like that," she whispered gruffly.

His eyes shot up to catch hers. "You want me," he said curtly. "I can see it. Feel it."

Her breath was audible. "You conceited...!"

His hands caught her hips and pushed them against his own. "It's mutual."

"I noticed!" she burst out, jerking away from him, red-faced.

"Don't be such a child," he chided, but gently. "You're old enough to know what desire feels like."

Her face grew redder. "I will not be seduced by you in my own kitchen over scrambled eggs!"

His eyebrows arched. "You're making them, then?" he asked brightly.

"Oh!" She pushed away from him. "You just won't take no for an answer!"

He smiled speculatively. "You can put butter on that," he agreed. His eyes went up and down her slender figure while she walked through to the kitchen, leaving her purse on the hall table as she went. "Not going to change before you start cooking?" he drawled, following her in. "I don't mind helping."

She shot him a dark glare.

He held up both hands. "Just offering to be helpful, that's all."

She laughed helplessly. "I can dress myself, thanks."

"I was offering to help you *un*dress," he pointed out.

She had to fight down another blush. She was a modern, independent woman. It was just that the thought of Jordan's dark eyes on her naked body had an odd, pleasurable effect on her. Especially after that bone-shaking kiss.

"You shouldn't go around kissing women like that unless you mean business," she pointed out as she got out a big iron skillet to cook the bacon in.

"What makes you think I didn't mean it?" he probed, straddling a kitchen chair to watch her work.

"You? Mr. I'll-Never-Marry?"

"I didn't say that. I said I didn't want to get married."

"Well, what's the difference?" she asked, exasperated.

His dark eyes slid down to her breasts with a boldness that made her uncomfortable. "There's always the one woman you can't walk away from."

"There's no such woman in your life."

"Think so?" He frowned. "What are you doing with that?" he asked as she put the skillet on the burner.

"You're the one who wanted bacon!" she exclaimed.

"Bacon, yes, not liquid fat!" He got up from the chair, pulled a couple of paper towels from the roll and pulled a plate from the cabinet. "Don't you know how to cook bacon?"

He proceeded to show her, layering several strips of bacon on a paper-towel coated plate and putting another paper towel on top of it.

She was watching with growing amusement. "And it's going to cook like that," she agreed. "Uh-huh."

"It goes in the microwave," he said with exaggerated patience. "You cook it for…"

"What's wrong?"

He was looking around, frowning, with the plate in one big hand. He opened cupboards and checked in the china cabinet. "All right, I'll bite. Where is it?"

"Where is what?"

"Your microwave oven!"

She sighed. "Jordan, we don't have a microwave oven."

"You're kidding." He scowled at her. "Everybody's got a microwave oven!"

"We haven't got one."

He studied her kitchen and slowly he put the plate back on the counter with a frown. The stove was at least ten years old. It was one of the old-fashioned ones that still had knobs instead of buttons. She didn't even have a dishwasher. Everything in the kitchen was old, like the cast-iron skillet she used for most every meal.

"I didn't realize how hard things were for you and Curt," he said after a minute. "I thought your father had all kinds of money."

"He did, until he married Janet," she replied. "She wanted to eat out all the time. The stove was worn out and so was the dishwasher. He was going to replace them, but she had him buy her a diamond ring she wanted, instead."

He scowled angrily. "I'm sorry. I'm really sorry."

His apology was unexpected and very touching. "It's all right," she said gently. "I'm used to doing things the hard way. Really I am."

He moved close, framing her oval face in his big warm hands. "You never complain."

She smiled. "Why should I? I'm healthy and strong and able to do anything that needs doing around here."

"You make me ashamed, Libby," he said softly. He bent and kissed her with aching tenderness.

"Why?" she whispered at his firm mouth.

"I'm not really sure. Do that again."

He nibbled her upper lip, coaxing her body to lean heavily against his. "This is even better than dessert," he murmured as he deepened the pressure of his mouth. "Come here!"

He lifted her against him and kissed her hungrily, until her mouth felt faintly bruised from the slow, insistent pressure. It was like flying. She loved kissing Jordan. She hoped he was never going to stop!

But all at once, he did, with a jerky breath. "This won't do," he murmured a little huskily. "Curt will be home any minute. I don't want him to find us on the kitchen table."

Her mouth flew open. "Jordan!"

He shrugged and looked sheepish. "It was heading that way. Here." He handed her the plate of bacon. "I guess you'd better fry it. I don't think it's going to cook by itself."

She smiled up at him. "I'll drain it on paper towels and get rid of some of the grease after it's cooked."

"Why are you throwing those away?" he asked when she put the bacon on to fry and threw away the paper towels it had laid on.

"Bacteria," she told him. "You never put meat back on a plate where it's been lying, raw."

"They teach you that in school these days, I guess?"

She nodded. "And lots of other stuff."

"Like how to use a prophylactic…?" he probed wickedly.

She flushed. "They did not! And I'll wash your mouth out with soap if you say that again!" she threatened.

"Never mind. I'll teach you how to use it, when the time comes," he added outrageously.

"I am not using a prophylactic!"

"You want kids right away, then?" he persisted.

"I am not having sex with you on my kitchen table!"

There was a sudden stunned silence. Jordan was staring over her shoulder and his expression was priceless. Grimacing, she turned to find her older brother standing there with his mouth open.

"Oh, shut your mouth, Curt," she grumbled. "It was a hypothetical discussion!"

"Except for the part about the prophylactic," Jordan said with a howling mad grin. "Did you know that they don't teach people how to use them in school?"

Curt lost it. He almost doubled over laughing.

Libby threw a dish towel at him. "Both of you, out of my kitchen! I'll call you when it's ready. Go on, out!"

They left the room obediently, still laughing.

Libby shook her head and started turning the bacon.

"Hasn't Janet even phoned to say if she was coming back today?" Jordan asked the two siblings when they were seated at the kitchen table having supper.

"There wasn't anything on the answering machine,"

Libby said. "I checked it while the bacon was cooking. Maybe she thinks we're on to something and she's running for it."

"No, I don't think so," Curt replied at once. "She's not about to leave this property to us. Not considering what it would be worth to a developer."

"I agree," Jordan said. "I've given Kemp the phone number of a private detective I know in San Antonio," he added. "He's going to look into the case for me."

"We'll pay you back," Curt promised, and Libby nodded.

"Let's cross our bridges one at a time," Jordan replied. "First order of business is to see if we can find any proof that she's committed a crime in the past."

"Mabel said she was suspected in a death at a nursing home in Branntville," she volunteered.

"So Kemp told me," Jordan said. "This is good bacon," he added.

"Thanks," she said with a smile.

"Violet's father was another one of her victims," Libby added.

Jordan nodded while Curt scowled curiously at both of them. "But they can't prove that. Not unless there's enough evidence to order an exhumation. And, considering the physical condition of Violet's mother," he added, "I'm afraid she'd never be able to agree to it. The shock would probably kill her mother."

Libby sighed. "Poor Violet. She's had such a hard life. And now to have to change jobs…"

"She works for Kemp, doesn't she?" Curt asked.

"She did. She quit today," Libby replied. "She's going to work for Duke Wright."

"Oh, Sherry King's going to *love* that," Curt chuckled.

"She doesn't own Duke," Libby said. "He doesn't even like her."

"She's very possessive about men she wants."

"More power to her if she can put a net over him and lock him in her closet."

Jordan chuckled. "He's not keen on the thought of a second wife."

"He's still trying to get custody of his son, isn't he?" Curt asked. "Poor guy."

"He won't be the first man who lost a woman to a career," Jordan reminded him. "Although it's usually the other way around." He glanced at Libby. "Just for the record, I think you're more important than a new bull, no matter what his ancestry is."

"Gee, thanks," she replied, tongue-in-cheek.

"It never hurts to clear up these little details before they become issues," he said wryly. "On the other hand, it would be nice if you'd tell me if you have plans to go to law school and move to a big city to practice law?"

"Not me, thanks," she replied. "I'm very happy where I am."

"You don't know any other life except this one," he persisted. "What if you regret not spreading your wings further on down the road?"

"We can't see into the future, Jordan," she replied thoughtfully. "But I don't like cities, although I'm sure they're exciting for some people. I don't like parties or business and I wouldn't trade jobs with Kemp for anything on earth. I'm happy looking up case precedents and researching options. I wouldn't like having to stand up in a courtroom and argue a case."

"You don't know that," he mused, and a shadow crossed his face. "What if you got a taste of it one day and couldn't live without it but it was too late?"

"Too late?"

"What if you had kids and a husband?" he prompted.

"You're thinking about Duke Wright," she said slowly.

He drew in a hard breath, aware that Curt was watching him curiously. "Yes," he told her. "Duke's wife was a secretary. She took night courses to get her law degree and then got pregnant just before she started practice. While Duke was giving bottles and changing diapers, she was climbing the ladder at a prestigious San Antonio law firm, living there during the week and coming home on weekends. Then they offered her a job in New York City.''

Libby couldn't quite figure out the look on his face. He was taking it all quite seriously and she'd thought he was teasing.

"So you see," he continued, "she didn't know she wanted a career until it was too late. Now she's making a six-figure annual income and their little boy's in her way. She doesn't want to give him up, but she doesn't have time to take care of him properly. And Duke's caught in the middle.''

"I hadn't realized it was that bad," she confessed. "Poor Duke.''

"He had a choice," he told her. "He married her thinking she wanted what he did, a nice home and a comfortable living, and kids." He drew a breath. "But she was very young," he added, his eyes studying her covertly. "Maybe she didn't really know what she wanted. Then.''

"I suppose some women don't," she replied. "It's a new world. Maybe it took her a long time to realize the opportunities and then it was too late to go back.''

He lowered his eyes to his boots. "That's very possible.''

"But it's Duke's problem," she added, smiling. "Want some pie? I've got a cherry one that I made yesterday in the refrigerator.''

He shook his head. "Thanks. But I won't stay." He got to his feet. "I'll tell Kemp to let you know what the private detective finds out. Meanwhile," he added, glancing at Curt, "not a word to Janet. Okay?''

They both nodded.

"Thanks, Jordan," Curt added.

"What are neighbors for?" he replied, and he chuckled. But his eyes didn't quite meet Libby's.

* * *

"Jordan was acting very oddly tonight, wasn't he?" Libby asked her brother after they'd washed the dishes and put them away.

"He's a man with a lot on his mind," he replied. "Calhoun Ballenger's making a very powerful bid for that senate seat that old man Merrill's had for so many years. They say old man Merrill's worried and so's his daughter, Julie. You remember, she's been pursuing Jordan lately."

"But he and Calhoun have been friendly for years," she said.

"So they have. There's more. Old man Merrill got pulled over for drunk driving by a couple of our local cops. Now Merrill's pulling strings at city hall to try and make the officers withdraw the charges. Merrill doesn't have a lot of capital. Jordan does."

"Surely you don't think Jordan would go against Cash Grier, even for Julie?" she wondered, concerned.

He started to speak and then thought better of it. "I'm not sure I really know," he said.

She rubbed at a clean plate thoughtfully. "Do you suppose he's serious about her? She and her father are very big socially and they have a house here that they stay in from time to time. She has a college degree. In fact, they say she may try her hand at politics. He was talking about marriage and children to us—like he was serious about it." She frowned. "Does that kind of woman settle down? Or was that what he meant, when he said some women don't know what they want until they find it?"

"I don't know that he's got marriage on his mind," Curt replied slowly. "But he's spent a good deal of time with Julie and the senator just lately."

That hurt. She bit her lower lip, hard, and forced her mind away from the heat and power of Jordan's kisses. "We've got a problem of our own. What are we going to do about Janet?"

"Kemp's working on that, isn't he? And Jordan's private detective will be working with him. They'll turn up some-

thing. She isn't going to put us out on the street, Libby,''
he said gently. "I promise you she isn't."

She smiled up at him. "You're sort of nice, for a
brother."

He grinned. "Glad you noticed!"

She didn't sleep all night, though, wondering about Jordan's odd remarks and the way he'd looked at her when
he asked if she had ambitions toward law practice. She
really didn't, but he seemed to think she was too young to
know her own mind.

Well, it wasn't really anything to worry about, she assured herself. Jordan had no idea of marrying *her,* regardless of her ambition or lack thereof. But Curt had said he
was seeing a lot of Julie Merrill. For some unfathomable
reason, the thought made her sad.

Chapter Four

It was late afternoon before Janet came back, looking out of sorts. She threw herself onto the sofa in the living room and lit a cigarette.

"You'll stink up the place," Libby muttered, hunting for an ashtray. She put it on the table.

"Well, then, you'll have to invest in some more air freshener, won't you, darling?" the older woman asked coldly.

Libby stared at her angrily. "Where have you been for three days?"

Janet avoided looking at her. "I had some business to settle."

"It had better not have been any sales concerning this property," Libby told her firmly.

"And who's going to stop me?" the other woman demanded hotly.

"Mr. Kemp."

Janet crushed out the cigarette and got to her feet. "Let him try. You try, too! I own everything here and I'm not letting you take it away from me! No matter what I have to do," she added darkly. "I earned what I'm getting, putting up with your father handling me like a live doll. The repulsive old fool made my skin crawl!"

"My father loved you," Libby bit off, furious that the awful woman could make such a remark about her father, the kindest man she'd ever known.

"He loved showing me off, you mean," Janet muttered. "If he'd really loved me, he'd have given me the things I asked him for. But he was so cheap! Well, I'm not being cheated out of what's mine," she added, with a cold glare at Libby. "Not by you or your brother. I have a lawyer, too, now."

Libby felt sick. But she managed a calm smile. "We have locks on our bedroom doors, by the way," she said out of the blue. "And Mr. Kemp is having a private detective check you out."

Janet looked shocked. "W-what?"

"Violet who works in my office thinks you might have known her father— Mr. Hardy from San Antonio?" she added deliberately. "He had a heart attack, just like Daddy…?"

Janet actually went pale. She jumped to her feet as if she'd been stung.

"Where are you going?" Libby asked seconds later, when the older woman rushed from the room.

Janet went into her bedroom and slammed the door. The sound of objects bouncing off walls followed in a furious staccato.

Libby bit her lip. She'd been warned not to do anything to make Janet panic and make a run for it, but the woman had pricked her temper. She wished she hadn't opened her mouth.

With dark thoughts, she finished baking a ham and made potato salad to go with it, along with homemade rolls. It gave her something to do besides worry.

But when Curt came home to eat, he was met by Janet with a suitcase, going out the door.

"Where are you off to?" he asked her coolly.

She threw a furious glance at the kitchen. "Anywhere I don't have to put up with your sister!" she snarled. "I'll get a motel room in town. You'll be hearing from my attorney in a day or so."

Curt's eyebrows lifted. "Funny. I was just about to tell you the same thing. I had a phone call from Kemp while I was at work. His private investigator has turned up some *very* interesting information about your former employment at a nursing home in Branntville...?"

Janet brushed by him in a mad rush toward her Mercedes. She threw her case in and jumped in behind it, spraying dirt as she spun out of the driveway.

"Well, that's clinched it," Curt mused as he joined his troubled sister in the kitchen. "She won't be back, or I'll miss my bet."

"I don't think it was a good idea to run her off," she commented as she set the table. "I'd already opened my big mouth and mentioned the locks on our bedroom doors and Violet's father to her."

"It's okay," Curt said gently. "I'm doing what Kemp told me to. I put her on the run."

"Mr. Kemp said to do that?"

He nodded, tossing his hat onto a side table and pulling out a chair. "Any coffee going? We've been mucking out line cabins all day. I'm beat!"

"Mucking out line cabins, not stables?"

"The river ran out of its banks right into that cabin on the north border," he said heavily. "We've been shoveling mud all afternoon. Crazy, isn't it? We had drought for four years, now it's floods. God must really be mad at somebody!"

"Don't look at me, I haven't done a single thing out of line."

He smiled. "When have you ever?" He studied her as she put food on the table. "Jordan says he's taking you out to a movie next week...watch it!"

Her hands almost let go of the potato salad bowl. She caught it and put it down carefully, gaping at her brother. "Jordan's taking *me* to a movie?"

"It's what usually happens when men start kissing women," he said philosophically, leaning back in his chair with a wicked grin. "They get addicted."

"How did you know he was kissing me last night?"

He grinned wickedly. "I didn't."

She cleared her throat and turned away, reddening as she remembered the passionate kiss she and Jordan had shared before the supper he'd coaxed her to cook for him. She hadn't slept well all night thinking about it. Or about what Curt had said, that Jordan was spending a lot of time with Julie Merrill. But he couldn't be interested in the woman, if he wanted to take Libby out!

"You never got addicted to any women," she pointed out.

He shrugged. "My day will come. It just hasn't yet."

"What were you telling Janet about a private investigator and the nursing home?"

"Oh, yes." He waited until she sat down and they said grace before he continued, while piling ham on his plate. "I'm not sure how much Kemp told you already but it seems that Janet has changed her legal identity since she worked in the nursing home. Also her hair color. She was under suspicion for the death of that elderly patient who liked to play the horses. She was making off with his bank account when it seems she was paid a visit by a gentleman representing a rather shadowy figure who was owed a great deal of money by the deceased. She left everything and ran for her life." He smiled complacently. "You see, there were more debts than money left in the elderly gentleman's entire estate!"

Libby was listening intently.

"There's more." He took a bite of ham. "This is nice!" he exclaimed when he tasted it.

"Isn't it?" She smiled. "I got it from Duke Wright. He's

sidelining into a pork products shop and he's marketing on the Internet. He's doing organic bacon and ham."

"Smart guy."

She nodded. "There's more, you said?"

"Yes. They've just managed to convince Violet's mother that her husband might have been murdered. She's agreed to an exhumation."

"But they said the shock might be fatal!"

"Mrs. Hardy loved her husband. She never believed it was a heart attack. He'd had an echocardiogram that was misread, leading to a heart catheterization. They found nothing that would indicate grounds for a heart attack."

"Poor Violet," Libby said sadly. "It's going to be hard on her, too." She glanced up at her brother. "I still can't believe she quit and is going to work for Duke Wright."

"I know," he said. "She was crazy about Kemp!"

She nodded sadly. "Serves him right. He's been unpleasant to her lately. Violet's tired of eating her heart out for him. And who knows. It might prompt Mr. Kemp to do some soul searching."

"More than likely he'll just hire somebody else and forget all about her. If he wanted to be married, he could be," he added.

"He doesn't date anybody, does he?" she asked curiously.

He shook his head. "But he's not gay."

"I never thought he was. I just wondered why he keeps so much to himself."

"Maybe he's like a lot of other bachelors in Jacobsville, he's got a secret past that he doesn't want to share!"

"We're running out of bachelors," she retorted. "The Hart boys were the last to go and nobody ever thought they'd end up with families."

"Biscuits were their downfall," he pointed out.

"Jordan doesn't like biscuits," she mused. "I did ask, you know."

He chuckled. "Jordan doesn't have a weakness and he's

never lacked dates when he wanted them." He eyed her over his coffee cup. "But he may be at the end of his own rope."

"Don't look at me," she said, having spent too much time lately thinking about Jordan's intentions toward her. "I may be the flavor of the week, but Jordan isn't going to want to marry down, if you see what I mean."

His eyes narrowed. "We may not be high society, but our people go back a long way in Jacobs County."

"That doesn't put us in monied circles, either," she reminded him. Her eyes were dreamy and faraway. "He's got a big, fancy house and he likes to keep company with high society. Maybe that's why he's been taking Senator Merrill's daughter around. It gets him into places he was never invited to before. We'd never fit. Especially me," she added in a more wistful tone than she realized.

"That wouldn't matter."

She smiled sadly. "It would and you know it. He'll need a wife who can entertain and throw parties, arrange sales, things like that. Most of all, he'll want a woman who's beautiful and intelligent, someone he'll be proud to show off. He might take me to a movie. But believe me, he won't take me to a minister."

"You're sure of that?"

She looked up at him. "You said it yourself— Jordan has been spending a lot of time with the state senator's daughter. He's running for re-election and the latest polls say that Calhoun Ballenger is almost tied with him. He needs all the support he can get, financial and otherwise. I think Jordan's going to help him, because of Julie."

"Then why is he kissing you?"

"To make her jealous?" she pondered. "Maybe to convince himself that he's still attractive to women. But it's not serious. Not with him." She looked up. "And I don't have affairs, whether it's politically correct or not."

He sighed. "I suppose we all have our pipe dreams."

"What's yours, while we're on the subject?"

He smiled. "I'd like to start a ranch supply company. The last one left belonged to Ted Regan's father-in-law. When he died, the store went bust, and then his daughter Corrie married Ted Regan and didn't need to make her own living. The hardware store can order most supplies, but not cattle feed or horse feed. Stuff like that."

She hadn't realized her brother had such ambitions. "If we weren't in such a financial mess, I'd be more than willing to co-sign a loan with the house as collateral."

He stared at her intently. "You'd do that for me?"

"Of course. You're my brother. I love you."

He reached out and caught her hand. "I love you, too, Sis."

"Pipe dreams are nice. Don't you give yours up. Eventually we'll settle this inheritance question and we might have a little capital to work with." She studied him with pride. "I think you'd make a great success of it. You've kept us solvent, up until Janet's unexpected arrival."

"She'll be out for blood. I should probably call Kemp and update him on what's happened."

"That might not be a bad idea. Maybe we should get a dog," she added slowly.

"Bad idea. We can hardly afford to feed old Bailey, your horse. We'd have to buy food for a dog, too, and it would break us."

She saw his eyes twinkle and she burst out laughing, too.

Janet's attorney never showed up and two days later, Janet vanished, leaving a trail of charges to the Collinses for everything from clothes to the motel bill.

"You won't have to pay that," Kemp told Libby when he'd related the latest news to her. "I've already alerted the merchants that she had no authority to charge anything to you or Curt, or the estate."

"Thanks," she said with relief. "What do we do now?"

"I've got the state police out looking for her," he replied, his hands deep in his slacks' pockets. "On suspicion of murder. You won't like what's coming next."

"What?"

"I want to have your father exhumed."

She ground her teeth together. "I was afraid of that."

"We'll be discreet. But we need to have the crime lab check for trace evidence of poisoning. You see, we know what killed the old man at the nursing home where she worked. I believe she did kill him. Poisoners tend to stick to the same routine."

"Poor Daddy," she said, feeling sick. Now she wondered if they might have saved him, if they'd only realized sooner that Janet was dangerous.

"Don't play mind games with yourself, Libby," Kemp said quietly. "It does no good."

"What a terrible way to go."

"The poison she used was quick," he replied. "Some can cause symptoms for months and the victim dies a painfully slow death. That wasn't the case here. It's the only good news I have for you, I'm afraid. But after they autopsy Mr. Hardy, there may be more forensic evidence to make a case against her. We've found a source for the poison."

"But the doctor said that Daddy died of a heart attack," she began.

"He might have," Kemp had to admit. "But he could as easily have died of poison or an air embolism."

"Jordan mentioned that," she recalled.

He smiled secretively. "Jordan doesn't miss a trick."

"But Janet's gone. What if they discover that Daddy's death was foul play and then they can't find her?" Libby pointed out. "She's gotten away with it at least two times, by being cagey."

"Every criminal eventually makes a mistake," he said absently. "She'll make one. Mark my words."

She only nodded. She glanced at Violet's empty desk and winced.

"I have an ad in the paper for a new secretary," he said coldly. "Meanwhile, Mabel's going to do double duty," he added, nodding toward Mabel, who was on the phone taking notes.

"It's going to be lonely without her," she said without thinking.

Kemp actually ground his teeth, turned on his heel and went back into his office. As an afterthought, he slammed the door.

Libby lost it. She laughed helplessly. Mabel, off the phone now and aware of Kemp's shocking attitude, laughed, too.

"It won't last long," Mabel whispered. "Violet was the only secretary he's ever had who could make and break appointments without hurting people's feelings. She was the fastest typist, too. He's not going to find somebody to replace her overnight."

Libby agreed silently. But it promised to be an interesting working environment for the foreseeable future.

Libby didn't even notice there was a message on the answering machine until after supper, when she'd had a lonely sandwich after Curt had phoned and said he was eating pizza with the other cowboys over at the Regan place for their weekly card game.

Curious, Libby punched the answer key and listened to the message. In a silken tone, the caller identified himself as an attorney named Smith and said that Mrs. Collins had hired him to do the probate on her late husband's will. He added that the children of Riddle Collins would have two weeks to vacate the premises.

Libby went through the roof. Her hands trembled as she tried to call Kemp and failing to reach him, she punched in Jordan's number.

It took a long time for him to answer the phone and when he finally did, there was conversation and music in the background.

"Yes?" he asked curtly.

Libby faltered. "Am I interrupting? I can call you another time..."

"Libby?" His voice softened. "Wait a minute." She heard muffled conversation, an angry reply, and the sound of a door closing. "Okay," he said. "What's wrong?"

"I can't get Mr. Kemp," she began urgently, "and Janet's attorney just called and said we had two weeks to get out of the house before they did the probate!"

"Libby," he said softly, "just sit down and use your mind. Think. When has anybody ever been asked to vacate a house just so that probate papers could be filed?"

She took a deep breath and then another. Her hands were still cold and trembling but she was beginning to remember bits and pieces of court documents. She was a paralegal. For God's sake, she knew about probate!

She sighed heavily. "Thanks. I just lost it. I was so shocked and so scared!"

"Is Curt there?"

"No, he went to his weekly card game with the cowboys over at Ted Regan's ranch," she said.

"I'm sorry I can't come over and talk to you. I'm having a fund-raising party for Senator Merrill tonight."

Merrill. His daughter Julie was the socialite. She was beautiful and rich and...socially acceptable. Certainly, she'd be at the party, too.

"Libby?" he prompted, when she didn't answer him.

"That's...that's okay, Jordan, I don't need company, honest," she said at once. "I just lost my mind for a minute. I'm sorry I bothered you. Really!"

"You don't have to apologize," he said, as if her statement unsettled him.

"I'll hang up now. Thanks, Jordan!"

He was still talking when she put the receiver down, very quickly, and put the answering machine back on. If he called back, she wasn't answering him. Janet's vicious tactics had unsettled her. She knew Janet had gotten someone to make that phone call deliberately, to upset Riddle's children.

It was her way of getting even, no doubt, for what Libby and Curt had said to her. She wondered if there was any way they could trace a call off an answering machine? A flash of inspiration hit her. Before Jordan would have time to call and foul the connection, she jerked up the phone and pressed the *69 keys. It gave her the number of the party who'd just phoned and she wrote it down at once, delighted to see that it was not a local number. She'd give it to Kemp the next morning and let his private investigator look into it.

Feeling more confident, she went back to the kitchen and finished washing up the few dishes. She couldn't forget Jordan's deep voice on the phone and the sound of a woman's voice arguing angrily when he went into another room to talk to Libby. It must be that senator's daughter. Obviously she felt possessive of Jordan and was wary of any potential rival. But Libby was no rival, she told herself. Jordan had just kissed her. That was all.

If only she could forget how it had felt. Then she remembered something else: Jordan's odd statements about Duke Wright's wife, and how young she was, and how she didn't quite know she wanted a career until she was already married and pregnant. He'd given Libby an odd, searching look when he said that.

The senator's daughter, Julie Merrill, was twenty-six, she recalled, with a degree in political science. Obviously she already knew what she wanted. She wanted Jordan. She was at his house tonight, probably hostessing the party there. Libby looked down at her worn jeans and faded blouse and then around her at the shabby but useful furniture in the old house. She laughed mirthlessly. What in the world would Jordan want with her, anyway? She'd been daydreaming. She'd better wake up, before she had her heart torn out.

* * *

She didn't phone Jordan again and he didn't call her back. She did give the telephone number of the so-called attorney to Mr. Kemp, who passed it along to his investigator.

Several days later, he paused by Libby's desk while she was writing up a precedent for a libel case, and he looked smug.

"That was quick thinking on your part," he remarked with a smile. "We traced the number to San Antonio. The man isn't an attorney, though. He's a waiter in a high-class restaurant who thinks Janet is his meal ticket to the easy life. We, uh, disabused him of the idea and told him one of her possible futures. We understand that he quit his job and left town on the next bus to make sure he wasn't involved in anything she did."

She laughed softly. "Thank goodness! Then Curt and I don't have to move!"

Kemp glared at her. "As if I'd stand by and let any so-called attorney toss you out of your home!"

"Thanks, boss," she said with genuine gratitude.

He shrugged. "Paralegals are thin on the ground," he said with twinkling blue-gray eyes.

"Callie Kirby and I are the only ones that I know of in town right now," she agreed.

"And Callie's got a child," he said, nodding. "I don't think Micah's going to want her to come back to work until their kids are in school."

"I expect not. She's got Micah's father to help take care of, too," she added, "after his latest stroke."

"People die," he said, and his eyes seemed distant and troubled.

"Mabel called in sick," she said reluctantly. "She's got some sort of stomach virus."

"They go around every spring," he agreed with a sigh. "Can you handle everything, or do you want to get a temp? If you do, call the agency. Ask if they've got somebody who can type."

She gave him her most innocent look. "Of course I can do the work of three women, sir, and even make coffee…"

He laughed. "Call the agency."

"Yes, sir."

He glowered. "It's Violet's fault," he muttered, turning. "I'll bet she's cursed us. We'll have sick help from now on."

"I'm sure she'd never do that, Mr. Kemp," she assured him. "She's a nice person."

"Imagine taking offense at a *look* and throwing in the towel. Hell, I look at people all the time and they don't quit!"

She cleared her throat and nodded toward the door, which was just opening.

A lovely young woman with a briefcase and long blond hair came in. "I'm Julie Merrill," she said with a haughty smile. "Senator Merrill's daughter? You advertised for a secretary, I believe."

Libby could not believe her eyes. Jordan's latest love and she turned up here looking for work! Of all the horrible bad luck…

Kemp stared at the young woman without speaking.

"Oh, not me!" Julie laughed, clearing her throat. "Heavens, I don't need a job! No, it's my friend Lydia. She's just out of secretarial school and she can't find anything suitable."

"Can she type?"

"Yes! Sixty words a minute. And she can take shorthand, if you don't dictate too fast."

"Can she speak?"

Julie blinked. "I beg your pardon?"

Kemp gave her a scrutiny that would have stopped traffic. His eyes became a wintry blue, which Libby knew from experience meant that his temper was just beginning to kindle.

"I don't give jobs through third persons, Miss Merrill,

and I don't give a damn who your father is," he said with a cool smile.

She colored hotly and gaped at him. "I...I...just thought...I mean, I could ask...!"

"Tell your friend she can come in and fill out an application, but not to expect much," he added shortly. "I have no respect for a woman who has to be helped into a job through favoritism. And in case it's escaped your attention," he added, moving a step closer to her, "nobody works for me unless they're qualified."

Julie shot a cold glare at Libby, who was watching intently. "I guess you think she's qualified," she said angrily.

"I have a diploma as a trained paralegal," Libby replied coolly. "It's on the wall behind you, at my desk."

Kemp only smiled. It wasn't a nice smile.

Julie set her teeth together so hard that they almost clicked. "I don't think Lydia would like this job, anyway!"

Kemp's right eyebrow arched. "Was there anything else, Miss Merrill?"

She turned, jerking open the door. "My father will not be happy when I tell him how you've spoken to me."

"By all means, tell him, with my blessing," Kemp said. "One of his faults is a shameful lack of discipline with his children. I understand you've recently expressed interest in running for public office in Jacobs County, Miss Merrill. Let me give you a piece of advice. Don't."

Her mouth fell open. "How dare you...!"

"It's your father's money, of course. If he wants to throw it away, that's his concern."

"I could win an election!"

Kemp smiled. "Perhaps you could. But not in Jacobs County," he said pleasantly. His eyes narrowed and became cold and his voice grew deceptively soft. "Closet skeletons become visible baggage in an election. And no one here has forgotten your high-school party. Especially not the Culbertsons."

Julie's face went pale. Her fingers on the briefcase

tightened until the knuckles showed. She actually looked frightened.

"That was…a terrible accident."

"Shannon Culbertson is still dead."

Julie's lower lip trembled. She turned and went out the door so quickly that she forgot to close it.

Kemp did it for her, his face cold and hard, full of repressed fury.

Libby wondered what was going on, but she didn't dare ask.

Later, of course, when Curt got home from work, she couldn't resist asking the question.

He scowled. "What the hell did Julie want in Kemp's office? Lydia doesn't need a job, she already has a job—a good one—at the courthouse over in Bexar County!"

"She said Lydia wanted to work for Mr. Kemp, but she was giving me the evil eye for all she was worth."

"She wants Jordan. You're in the way."

"Sure I am," she laughed coldly. "What about that girl, Shannon Culbertson?"

Curt hesitated. "That was eight years ago."

"What happened?"

"Somebody put something in her drink—which she wasn't supposed to have had in the first place. It was a forerunner of the date-rape drug. She had a hidden heart condition. It killed her."

"Who did it?"

"Nobody knows, but Julie tried to cover it up, to save her father's senate seat. Kemp dug out the truth and gave it to the newspapers." He shook his head. "A vindictive man, Kemp."

"Why?" she asked.

"They say Kemp was in love with the girl. He never got over it."

"But Julie's father won the election," she pointed out.

"Only because the leading lights of the town supported him and contributed to his reelection campaign. Most of those old-timers are dead or in nursing homes and the gossip around town is that Senator Merrill is already over his ears in debt from his campaign. Besides which, he's up against formidable opposition for the first time in recent years.''

Chapter Five

So that was Kemp's secret, Libby thought. A lost love. "Yes, I know," she said. "Calhoun Ballenger has really shaken up the district politically. A lot of people think he's going to win the nomination right out from under Merrill."

"I'm almost sure he will," Curt replied. "The powers that be in the county have changed over the past few years. The Harts have come up in the world. So have the Tremaynes, the Ballengers, Ted Regan, and a few other families. The power structure now isn't in the hands of the old elite. If you don't believe that, notice what's going on at city hall. Chief Grier is making a record number of drug busts and I don't need to remind you that Senator Merrill was arrested for drunk driving."

"That never was in the paper, you know," she said with a wry smile.

"The publisher is one of his cronies—he refused to run the story. But Merrill's up to his ears in legal trouble. So he's trying to get the mayor and two councilmen who owe him favors to fire the two police officers who made the arrest and discredit them. The primary election is the first week of May, you know."

"Poor police," she murmured.

"Mark my words, they'll never lose their jobs. Grier has contacts everywhere and despite his personal problems, he's not going to let his officers go down without a fight. I'd bet everything I have on him."

She grinned. "I like him."

Curt chuckled. "I like him, too."

"Mr. Kemp said they traced the lawyer's call to San Antonio," she added, and told him what was said. "Why would she want us out of the house?"

"Maybe she thinks there's something in it that she hasn't gotten yet," he mused. "Dad's coin collection, for instance."

"I haven't seen that in months," she said.

"Neither have I. She probably sold it already," he said with cold disgust. "But Janet's going to hang herself before she quits." He gave his sister a sad look. "I'm sorry about the exhumation. But we really need to know the truth about how Dad died."

"I know," she replied. The pain was still fresh and she had to fight tears. She managed a smile for him. "Daddy wouldn't mind."

"No. I don't think he would."

"I wish we'd paid more attention to what was going on."

"He thought he loved her, Libby," he said. "Maybe he did. He wouldn't have listened to us, no matter what we said, if it was something bad about her. You know how he was."

"Loving her blindly may have cost him his life."

"Try to remember that he died happy. He didn't know what Janet was. He didn't know that she was cheating him."

"It doesn't help much."

He nodded. "Nothing will bring him back. But maybe

we can save somebody else's father. That would make it all worthwhile."

"Yes," she agreed. "It would."

That evening while they were watching television, a truck drove up. A minute later, there was a hard knock on the door.

"I've got it," Curt said, leaving Libby with her embroidery.

There were muffled voices and then heavy footsteps coming into the room.

Jordan stared at Libby curiously. "Julie came to your office today," he said.

"She was looking for a job for her friend Lydia," Libby said in a matter-of-fact tone.

"That's not what she said," Jordan replied tersely. "She told me that you treated her so rudely that Kemp made her leave the office."

Libby lifted both eyebrows. "Wow. Imagine that."

"I'm not joking with you, Libby," Jordan said, and his tone chilled. "That was a petty thing to do."

"It would have been," she agreed, growing angry herself, "if I'd done it. She came into the office in a temper, glared at me, made some rude remarks to Mr. Kemp and got herself thrown out."

"That's not what she told me," he repeated.

Libby got to her feet, motioning to Curt, who was about to protest on her behalf. "I don't need help, Curt. Stay out of it, that's a nice brother." She moved closer to Jordan. "Miss Merrill insinuated that Mr. Kemp had better offer Lydia a job because of her father's position in the community. And he reminded her about her high-school graduation party where a girl died."

"He what?" he exploded.

"Mr. Kemp doesn't take threats lying down," she said, uneasy because of Jordan's overt hostility. "Miss Merrill was very haughty and very rude. And neither of us can understand why she'd try to get Lydia a job at Kemp's office, because she's already got one in San Antonio!"

Jordan didn't say anything. He just stood there, silent.

"She was with you when I phoned your house, I guess, and she got the idea that I was chasing you," she said, gratified by the sudden blinking of his eyelids. "You can tell her, for me," she added with saccharine sweetness, "that I would not have you on a hot dog bun with uptown relish. If she thinks I'm the competition, all she has to do is look where I live." Her face tautened. "Go ahead, Jordan, look around you. I'm not even in your league, whatever your high-class girlfriend thinks. You're a kind neighbor whom I asked for advice and that's all you ever were. Period," she lied, trying to save face.

He still wasn't moving or speaking. But his eyes were taking on a nasty glitter. Beside his lean hips, one of his hands was clenched until the knuckles went white. "Ever?" he prodded, his tone insinuating things.

She knew what he meant. She swallowed hard, trying not to remember the heat and power of the kisses they'd shared. Obviously, they'd meant nothing to him!

"Ever," she repeated. "I certainly wasn't trying to tie you down, Jordan. I'm not at all sure that I want to spend the rest of my life in Jacobsville working for a lawyer, anyway," she added deliberately, but without looking at him. "I've thought about that a lot, about what you said. Maybe I do have ambitions."

He didn't speak for several seconds. His eyes became narrow and cold.

"If you'd like to show your Julie that I'm no competition, you can bring her down here and show her how we live," she offered with a smile. "That would really open her eyes, wouldn't it?"

"Libby," Curt warned. "Don't talk like that."

"How should I talk?" she demanded, her throat tightening. "Our father is dead and it looks like our stepmother killed him right under our noses! She's trying to take away everything we have, getting her friends to call and threaten and harass us, and now here's Jordan's goody-two-shoes girlfriend making me out to be a man-stealer, or somebody. How the hell should I talk?!''

Jordan let out a long breath. ''I thought you knew what you wanted,'' he said after a minute.

''I'm young. Like you said,'' she said cynically. ''Sorry I ever asked you for help, Jordan, and made your girlfriend mad. You can bet I'll never make that mistake twice.''

She turned and went into the kitchen and slammed the door behind her. She was learning really bad habits from Mr. Kemp, she decided, as she wiped tears away with a paper towel.

She heard the door open behind her and close again, firmly. It was Curt, she supposed, coming to check on her.

''I guess I handled that badly,'' she said, choking on tears. ''Has he gone?''

Big, warm hands caught her shoulders and turned her around. Jordan's eyes glittered down into hers. ''No, he hasn't gone,'' he bit off.

He looked ferocious like that. She should have been intimidated, but she wasn't. He was handsome, even bristling with temper.

''I've said all I have to say,'' she began.

''Well, I haven't,'' he shot back, goaded. ''I've never looked down on you for what you've got and you know it.''

''Julie Merrill does,'' she muttered.

His hands tightened and relaxed. He looked vaguely embarrassed. His dark eyes slid past her to the worn calendar on the wall. ''You know how I grew up,'' he said heavily. ''We had nothing. I was never invited to parties. My parents were glorified servants in the eyes of the town's social set.''

She drew in a short breath. ''And now Julie's opening the doors and inviting you in and you like it.''

He seemed shocked by the statement. His eyes dropped to meet hers. "Maybe."

"Can't you see why?" she asked quietly. "You're rich now. You made something out of nothing. You have confidence, and power, and you know how to behave in company. But there's more to it than that, where the Merrills are concerned."

"That's not your business," he said shortly.

She smiled sadly. "They need financial backing. Their old friends aren't as wealthy as they used to be. Calhoun Ballenger has the support of the newer wealthy people in Jacobsville and they don't deal in 'good old boy' politics."

"In other words, Julie only wants me for money to run her father's re-election campaign."

"You know better than that," she replied, searching his hard face hungrily. "You're handsome and sexy. Women adore you."

One eyebrow lifted. "Even you?"

She wanted to deny it, but she couldn't. "Even me," she confessed. "But I'm no more in your class, really, than you're in Julie's. They're old money. It doesn't really matter to them how rich you get, you'll never be one of them."

His eyes narrowed angrily. "I am one of them," he retorted. "I'm hobnobbing with New York society, with Kentucky thoroughbred breeders, with presidential staff members—even with Hollywood producers and actors!"

"You could do that on your own," she said. "You don't need the Merrills to make you socially acceptable. And in case you've forgotten, Christabel and Judd Dunn have been hobnobbing with Hollywood people for a year. They're not rich. Not really."

He was losing the argument and he didn't like it. He glared down at her with more riotous feelings than he'd entertained in years. "Julie wants to marry me," he said, producing the flat statement like a weapon.

She managed not to react to the retort, barely. Her heart was sinking like lead in her chest as she pictured Julie in a designer wedding gown flashing diamonds like pennies on her way to the altar.

"*She* doesn't want a career," he added, smiling coldly.

Neither did Libby, really. She liked having a job, but she also liked living in Jacobsville and working around the ranch. She'd have liked being Jordan's wife more than anything else she could think of. But that wasn't going to happen. He didn't want her.

She tried to pull away from Jordan's strong hands, but he wasn't budging.

"Let me go," she muttered. "I'm sure Julie wouldn't like this!"

"Wouldn't like what?" he drawled. "Being in my arms, or having you in them?"

"Are you having fun?" she challenged.

"Not yet," he murmured, dropping his gaze to her full lips. "But I expect to be pretty soon…"

"You can't…!"

But he could. And he was. She felt the warm, soft, coaxing pressure of his hard mouth before she could finish the protest. Her eyes closed. She was aware of his size and strength, of the warmth of his powerful body against hers. She could feel his heartbeat, feel the rough sigh of his breath as he deepened the kiss.

He hadn't really meant to do this. He'd meant it as a punishment, for the things she'd said to him. But when he had her so close that he could feel her heart beating like a wild thing against him, nothing else seemed to matter except pleasing her, as she was pleasing him.

He drew her up closer, so that he could feel the soft, warm imprint of her body on the length of his. He traced her soft mouth with his lips, with the tip of his tongue. He felt her stiffen and then lift up to him. He gathered her completely against him and forgot Julie, forgot the argument, forgot everything.

She felt the sudden ardor of his embrace grow unmanageable in a space of seconds. His mouth was insistent on hers, demanding. His hands had gone to her hips. They were pressing her against the sudden rigidity of his powerful body. Even as she registered his urgent hunger for her, she felt one of his big, lean hands seeking between them for the soft, rounded curve of her breast...

She pulled away from him abruptly, her mouth swollen, her eyes wild. "N-no," she choked.

He tried to pull her back into his arms. "Why not?" he murmured, his eyes on her mouth.

"Curt," she whispered.

"Curt." He spoke the name as if he didn't recognize it. He blinked. He took a deep breath and suddenly realized where they were and what he'd been doing.

He drew in a harsh, deep breath.

"You have to go home," she said huskily.

He stood up straight and stared down his nose at her. "If you will keep throwing yourself into my arms, what do you expect?" he asked outrageously.

She gaped at him.

"It's no use trying to look innocent," he added as he moved back another step. "And don't start taking off your blouse, it won't work."

"I am not...!" she choked, crossing her arms quickly.

He made a rough sound in his throat. "A likely story. Don't follow me home, either, because I lock my doors at night."

She wanted to react to that teasing banter that she'd enjoyed so much before, but she couldn't forget that he'd taken Julie's side against her.

She stared at him coldly. "I won't follow you home. Not while you're spending all your free time defending Julie Merrill, when I'm the one who was insulted."

He froze over. "The way Julie tells it, you started on her first."

"And you believe her, of course. She's beautiful and rich and sophisticated."

"Something no man in his right mind could accuse you

of,'' he shot back. With a cold glare, he turned and went out the door.

He didn't pause to speak to Curt, who was just coming in the front door. He shot him a look bare of courtesy and stormed outside. He was boiling over with emotion, the strongest of which was frustrated desire.

Libby didn't explain anything to her brother, but she knew he wasn't blind or stupid. He didn't ask questions, either. He just hugged her and smiled.

She went to bed feeling totally at sea. How could an argument lead to something so tempestuous that she'd almost passed out at Jordan's feet? And if he really wanted Julie, then how could he kiss Libby with such frustrated desire? And why had he started another fight before he left?

She was still trying to figure out why she hadn't slapped his arrogant face when she fell asleep.

The tension between Jordan and his neighbors was suddenly visible even to onlookers. He never set foot on their place. When he had a barbecue for his ranch hands in April, to celebrate the impressive calf sale he'd held, Curt wasn't invited. When Libby had a small birthday party to mark her twenty-fourth birthday, Jordan wasn't on the guest list. Jacobsville being the small town it was, people noticed.

"Have you and Jordan had some sort of falling out?" Mr. Kemp asked while his new secretary, a sweet little brunette fresh out of high school named Jessie, was out to lunch.

Libby looked up at him with wide-eyed innocence. "Falling out?"

"Julie Merrill has been telling people that she and Jordan have marriage plans," he said. "I don't believe it. Her father's in financial hot water and Jordan's rich. Old man Merrill is going to need a lot of support in today's political climate. He made some bad calls on the budget and education and the voters are out to get him.''

"So I've heard. They say Calhoun Ballenger's just pulled ahead in the polls.''

"He'll win,'' Kemp replied. "It's no contest. Regardless of Jordan's backing.''

"Mr. Kemp, would they really use what happened at Julie's party as a weapon against her father?'' she asked carefully.

"Of course they would!'' he said shortly. "Even in Jacobs County, dirty laundry has a value. There are other skeletons in that closet, too. Plenty of them. Merrill has already lost the election. His way of doing business, under the table, is obsolete. He's trying to make Cash Grier fire those arresting officers and swear they lied. It won't happen. He and his daughter just don't know it and she refuses to face defeat.''

"She's at Jordan's house every day now,'' she said on a sigh that was more wistful than she knew. "She's very beautiful.''

"She's a tarantula,'' Kemp said coldly. "She's got her finger in a pie I can't tell you about, but it's about to hit the tabloids. When it does, her father can kiss his career goodbye.''

"Sir?''

He lifted both eyebrows. "Can you keep a secret?''

"If I can't, why am I working for you?'' she asked pertly.

"Those two officers Grier's backing, who caught the senator driving drunk—'' he said. "They've also been investigating a house out on the Victoria road where drugs are bought and sold. That's the real reason they're facing dismissal. Merrill's nephew is our mayor.''

"And he's in it up to his neck, I guess?'' she fished.

He nodded. "The nephew and Miss Merrill herself. That's where her new Porsche came from.''

Libby whistled. "But if Jordan's connected with her…" she said worriedly.

"That's right," he replied. "He'll be right in hot water with her, even though he's not doing anything illegal. Mud not only sticks, it rubs off."

She chewed her lower lip. "You couldn't warn him, I guess?"

He shook his head. "We aren't speaking."

She stared at him. "But you're friends."

"Not anymore. You see, he thinks I took your side unjustly against Miss Merrill."

She frowned. "I'm sorry."

He chuckled. "It will all blow over in a few weeks. You'll see."

She wasn't so confident. She didn't think it would and she hated the thought of seeing Jordan connected with such an unsavory business.

She walked down to Barbara's Café for lunch and ran right into Julie Merrill and Jordan Powell, who were waiting in line together.

"Oh, look, it's the little secretary," Julie drawled when she saw Libby in line behind them. "Still telling lies about me, Miss Collins?" she asked with a laugh.

Jordan was looking at Libby with an expression that was hard to classify.

Libby ignored her, turning instead to speak to one of the girls from the county clerk's office, who was in line behind her.

"Don't you turn your back on me, you little creep!" Julie raged, attracting attention as she walked right up to Libby. Her eyes were glazed, furious. "You told Jordan that I tried to throw my weight around in Kemp's office and it was a lie! You were just trying to make yourself look good, weren't you?!"

Libby felt sick at her stomach. She was no good at dealing with angry people, despite the fact that she had to watch

Kemp's secretaries do it every day. She wasn't really afraid of the other girl, but she was keenly aware of their differences on the social ladder. Julie was rich and well-known and sophisticated. Libby was little more than a rancher's daughter turned legal apprentice.

"Jordan can't stand you, in case you wondered, so it's no use calling him up all the time for help, and standing at his door trying to make him notice you!" Julie continued haughtily. "He wouldn't demean himself by going out with a dirty little nobody like you!"

Libby pulled herself up and stared at the older girl, keenly aware of curious eyes watching and people listening in the crowded lunch traffic. "Jordan is our neighbor, Miss Merrill," she said in a strained tone. Her legs were shaking, but she didn't let it show. "Nothing more. I don't want Jordan."

"Good. I'm glad you realize that Jordan's nothing more than a neighbor, because you're a nuisance! No man in his right mind would look at you twice!"

"Oh, I don't know about that," Harley Fowler said suddenly, moving up the line to look down at Julie Merrill with cold eyes. "I'd say her manners are a damned sight better than yours and your mouth wouldn't get you into any decent man's house in Jacobsville!"

Julie's mouth fell open.

"I wouldn't have her on toast!" one of the Tremaynes' cowboys ventured from his table.

"Hey, Julie, how about a dime bag?" some anonymous voice called. "I need a fix!"

Julie went pale. "Who said that?!" she demanded shakily.

"Julie, let's go," Jordan said curtly, taking her by the arm.

"I'm hungry!" she protested, fighting his hold.

Libby didn't look up as he passed her with Julie firmly at his side. He didn't look at her, either, and his face was white with rage.

As she went out the door, there was a skirl of belligerent

applause from the patrons of the café. Julie made a rude gesture toward them, which was followed by equally rude laughter.

"Isn't she a pain?" The girl from the clerk's office laughed. "Honestly, Libby, you were such a lady! I'd have laid a chair across her thick skull!"

"Me, too," said another girl. "Nobody can stand her. She thinks she's such a debutante."

Libby listened to the talk with a raging heartbeat. She was sick to her stomach from the unexpected confrontation and glad that Jordan had gotten the girl out of the room before things got ugly. But it ruined her lunch. It ruined her whole day.

It didn't occur to Libby that Jordan would be upset about the things that Julie had said in the café, especially since he hadn't said a word to Libby at the time. But he actually came by Kemp's office the next day, hat in hand, to apologize for Julie's behavior.

He looked disappointed when Kemp was sitting perched on the edge of Libby's desk, as if he'd hoped to find her alone. But he recovered quickly.

He gave Kemp a quick glare, his gaze returning at once to Libby. "I wanted to apologize for Julie," he said curtly. "She's sorry she caused a scene yesterday. She's been upset about her father facing drunk-driving charges."

"I don't receive absentee apologies," Libby said coldly. "And you'll never convince me that she *would* apologize."

Kemp's eyebrows collided. "What's that?"

"Julie made some harsh remarks about me in Barbara's Café yesterday," Libby told him, "in front of half the town."

"Why didn't you come and get me?" Kemp asked. "I'd have settled her hash for her," he added, with a dangerous look at Jordan.

"Harley Fowler defended me," Libby said with a quiet

smile. "So did several other gentlemen in the crowd," she added deliberately.

"She's not as bad as you think she is," Jordan said grimly.

"The hell she's not," Kemp replied softly. He got up. "I know things about her that you're going to wish you did and very soon. Libby, don't be long. We've got a case first thing tomorrow. I'll need those notes," he added, nodding toward the computer screen. He went to his office and closed the door.

"What was Kemp talking about?" Jordan asked Libby curiously.

"I could tell you, but you wouldn't believe me," she said sadly, remembering how warm their relationship had been before Julie Merrill clouded the horizon.

He drew in a long breath and moved a little closer, pushing his hat back over his dark hair. He looked down at her with barely contained hunger. Mabel was busy in the back with the photocopier and the girl who was filling in for Violet had gone to a dental appointment. Mr. Kemp was shut up in his office. Libby kept hoping the phone would ring, or someone would come in the front door and save her from Jordan. It was all she could do not to throw herself into his arms, even after the fights they'd had. She couldn't stop being attracted to him.

"Look," he said quietly, "I'm not trying to make an enemy of you. I like Julie. Her father is a good man and he's had some hard knocks lately. They really need my help, Libby. They haven't got anybody else."

She could just imagine Julie crying prettily, lavishing praise on Jordan for being so useful, dressing up in her best—which was considerably better than Libby's best—and making a play for him. She might be snippy and aggressive toward other women, but Julie Merrill was a practiced seducer. She knew how to wind men around her finger. She was young and beautiful and cultured and rich.

She knew tricks that most men—even Jordan—wouldn't be able to resist.

"Why are you so attracted to her?" Libby wondered aloud.

Jordan gave her an enigmatic look. "She's mature," he said without thinking. "She knows exactly what she wants and she goes after it wholeheartedly. Besides that, she's a woman who could have anybody."

"And she wants you," she said for him.

He shrugged. "Yes. She does."

She studied his lean, hard face, surprising a curious rigidity there before he concealed it. "I suppose you're flattered," she murmured.

"She draws every man's eye when she walks into a room," he said slowly. "She can play the piano like a professional. She speaks three languages. She's been around the world several times. She's dated some of the most famous actors in Hollywood. She's even been presented to the queen in England." He sighed. "Most men would have a hard time turning up their noses at a woman like that."

"In other words, she's like a trophy."

He studied her arrogantly. "You could say that. But there's something more, too. She needs me. She said everyone in town had turned their backs on her father. Calhoun Ballenger is drawing financial support from some of the richest families in town, the same people who promised Senator Merrill their support and then withdrew it. Julie was in tears when she told me how he'd been sold out by his best friends. Until I came along, he actually considered dropping out of the race."

And pigs fly, Libby thought privately, but she didn't say it. The Merrills were dangling their celebrity in front of Jordan, a man who'd been shut out of high society even though he was now filthy rich. They were offering him entry into a closed community. All that and beautiful Julie as well.

"Did you hear what she said to me in Barbara's Café?" she wondered aloud.

"What do you mean?" he asked curiously.

"You stood there and let her attack me, without saying a word."

He scowled. "I was talking to Brad Henry while we stood in line, about a bull he wanted to sell. I didn't realize what was going on until Julie raised her voice. By then, Harley Fowler and several other men were making catcalls at her. I thought the best thing to do would be to get her outside before things escalated."

"Did you hear her accuse me of chasing you? Did you hear her warn me off you?"

He cocked his head. "I heard that part," he admitted. "She's very possessive and more jealous of me than I realized. But I didn't like having her insult you, if that's what you mean," he said quietly. "I told her so later. She said she'd apologize, but I thought it might come easier from me. She's insecure, Libby. You wouldn't think so, but she really takes things to heart."

A revelation a minute, Libby was thinking. Jordan actually believed what he was saying. Julie had really done a job on him.

"She said that you wouldn't waste your time on a nobody like me," she persisted.

"Women say things they don't mean all the time." He shrugged it off. "You take things to heart, too, Libby," he added gently. "You're still very young."

"You keep saying that," she replied, exasperated. "How old do I have to be for you to think of me as an adult?"

He moved closer, one lean hand going to her slender throat, slowly caressing it. "I've thought of you like that for a long time," he said deeply. "But you're an addiction I can't afford. You said it yourself—you're ambitious. You won't be satisfied in a small town. Like the old-timers used to say, you want to go and see the elephant."

She was caught in his dark eyes, spellbound. She'd said

that, yes, because of the way he'd behaved about Julie's insults. She'd wanted to sting him. But she didn't mean it. She wasn't ambitious. All she wanted was Jordan. Her eyes were lost in his.

"The elephant?" she parroted, her gaze on his hard mouth.

"You want to see the world," he translated. But he was moving closer as he said it and his head was bending, even against his will. This was stupid. He couldn't afford to let himself be drawn into this sweet trap. Libby wanted a career. She was young and ambitious. He'd go in headfirst and she'd take off and leave him, just as Duke Wright's young wife had left him in search of fame and fortune. He'd deliberately drawn back from Libby and let himself be vamped by Julie Merrill, to show this little firecracker that he hadn't been serious about those kisses they'd exchanged. He wasn't going to risk his heart on a gamble this big. Libby was in love with love. She was attracted to him. But that wasn't love. She was too young to know the difference. He wasn't. He'd grabbed at Julie the way a drowning man reaches for a life jacket. Libby didn't know that. He couldn't admit it.

While he was thinking, he was parting her lips with his. He forgot where they were, who they were. He forgot the arguments and all the reasons he shouldn't do this.

"Libby," he growled against her soft lips.

She barely heard him. Her blood was singing in her veins like a throbbing chorus. Her arms went around his neck in a stranglehold. She pushed up against him, forcing into his mouth in urgency.

His arms swallowed her up whole. The kiss was slow, deep, hungry. It was invasive. Her whole body began to throb with delight. It began to swell. Their earlier kisses had been almost chaste. These were erotic. They were... narcotic.

A soft little cry of pleasure went from her mouth into

his and managed to penetrate the fog of desire she was drowning him in.

He jerked back from her as if he'd been stung. He fought to keep his inner turmoil from showing, his weakness from being visible to her. His big hands caught her waist and pushed her firmly away.

"I know," she said breathlessly. "You think I've had snakebite on my lip and you were only trying to draw out the poison."

He burst out laughing in spite of himself.

She swallowed hard and backed away another step. "Just think how Julie Merrill would react if she saw you kissing me."

That wiped the smile off his face. "That wasn't a kiss," he said.

"No kidding?" She touched her swollen mouth ironically. "I'll bet Julie could even give you lessons."

"Don't talk about her like that," he warned.

"You think she's honest and forthright, because you are," she said, a little breathless. "You're forgetting that her father is a career politician. They both know how to bend the truth without breaking it, how to influence public opinion."

"Politics is a science," he retorted.

"It can be a horrible corruption, as well," she reminded him. "Calhoun Ballenger has taken a lot of heat from them, even a sexual harassment charge that had no basis in fact. Fortunately, people around here know better, and it backfired. It only made Senator Merrill look bad."

His eyes began to glitter. "That wasn't fiction. The woman swore it happened."

"She was one of Julie's cousins," she said with disgust.

He looked as if he hadn't known that. He scowled, but he didn't answer her.

"Julie thinks my brother and I are so far beneath her that we aren't even worth mentioning," she continued, folding her arms over her chest. "She chooses her friends by their social status and bank accounts. Curt and I are losers in her book and she doesn't think we're fit to associate with you. She'll find a way to push you right out of our lives."

"I don't have social status, but I'm welcome in their home," he said flatly.

"There's an election coming up, they don't have enough money to win it, but you do. They'll take your money and make you feel like an equal until you're not needed anymore. Then you'll be out on your ear. You don't come from old money, Jordan, even if you're rich now…"

"You don't know a damned thing about what I come from," he snapped.

The furious statement caught her off guard. She knew Jordan had made his own fortune, but he never spoke about his childhood. His mother worked as a housekeeper. Everybody knew it. He sounded as if he couldn't bear to admit his people were only laborers.

"I didn't mean to be insulting," she began slowly.

"Hell! You're doing your best to turn me against Julie. She said you would," he added. "She said something else, too—that you're involved with Harley Fowler."

She refused to react to that. "Harley's sweet. He defended me when Julie was insulting me."

That was a sore spot, because Jordan hadn't really heard what Julie was saying until it was too late. He didn't like Harley, anyway.

"Harley's a nobody."

"Just like me," she retorted. "I'd much rather have Harley than you, Jordan," she added. "He may be just a working stiff, but he's got more class than you'll ever have, even if you hang out with the Merrills for the next fifty years!"

That did it. He gave her a furious glare, spit out a word that would have insulted Satan himself and marched right out the door.

"And stay out!" she called after it slammed.

Kemp stuck his head out of his office door and stared at

her. "Are you that same shy, introverted girl who came to work here last year?"

She grinned at him through her heartbreak. "You're rubbing off on me, Mr. Kemp," she remarked.

He laughed curtly and went back into his office.

Later, Libby was miserable. They'd exhumed her father's body and taken it up to the state crime lab in Austin for tests.

Curt was furious when she told him that Jordan had been to her office to apologize for the Merrill girl.

"As if she'd ever apologize to the likes of us," he said angrily. "And Jordan just stood by and let her insult you in the café without saying a word!"

She gaped at him. "How did you know that?"

"Harley Fowler came by where I was working this morning to tell me about it. He figured, rightly, that you'd try to keep it to yourself." He sank down into a chair. "I gave Jordan notice this afternoon. In two weeks, I'm out of there."

She grimaced. "But, Curt, where will you go?"

"Right over to Duke Wright's place," he replied with a smile. "I already lined up a job and I'll get a raise, to boot."

"That's great," she said, and meant it.

"We'll be fine. Don't worry about it." He sighed. "It's so much lately, isn't it, Sis? But we'll survive. We will!"

"I know that, Curt. I'm not worried."

But she was. She hated being enemies with Jordan, who was basically a kind and generous man. She was furious with the Merrills for coming between them for such a selfish reason. They only wanted Jordan's money for the old man's reelection campaign. They didn't care about Jordan. But perhaps he was flattered to be included in such high society, to be asked to hang out with their friends and acquaintances.

But Libby knew something about the people the Merrills associated with that, perhaps, Jordan didn't. Many of them were addicts, either to liquor or drugs. They did nothing for the community; only for themselves. They wanted to know the right people, be seen in the right places, have money that showed when people looked. But to Libby, who loved her little house and little ranch, it seemed terribly artificial.

She didn't have much but she was happy with her life. She enjoyed planting things and watching them grow. She liked teaching Vacation Bible School in the summer and working in the church nursery with little children. She liked cooking food to carry to bereaved families when relatives died. She liked helping out with church bazaars, donating time to the local soup kitchen. She didn't put on airs, but people seemed to like her just the way she was.

Certainly Harley Fowler did. He'd come over to see her the day after Julie's attack in the café, to make sure she was all right. He'd asked her out to eat the following Saturday night.

"Only to Shea's," he chuckled. "I just paid off a new transmission for my truck and I'm broke."

She'd grinned at him. "That's okay. I'm broke, too!"

He shook his head, his eyes sparkling as he looked down at her with appreciation. "Libby, you're my kind of people."

"Thanks, Harley."

"Say, can you dance?"

She blinked. "Well, I can do a two-step."

"That's good enough." He chuckled. "I've been taking these dance courses on the side."

"I know. I heard about the famous waltz with Janie Brewster at the Cattleman's Ball last year."

He smiled sheepishly. "Well, now I'm working on the

jitterbug and I hear that Shea's live band can play that sort of thing.''

"You can teach me to jitterbug, Harley," she agreed at once. "I'd love to go dancing with you."

He looked odd. "Really?"

She nodded and smiled. "Really."

"Then I'll see you Saturday about six. We can eat there, too."

"Suits me. I'll leave supper for Curt in the refrigerator. That was really nice of you to go to bat for him with your boss, Harley," she added seriously. "Thanks."

He shrugged. "Mr. Parks wasn't too pleased with the way Powell's sucking up to the Merrills, either," he said. "He knows things about them."

"So do I," she replied. "But Jordan doesn't take well-meant advice."

"His problem," Harley said sharply.

She nodded. "Yes, Harley. It's his problem. I'll see you Saturday!" she added, laughing.

When she told Curt about the upcoming date, he seemed pleased. "It's about time you went out and had some fun for a change."

"I like Harley a lot," she told her brother.

He searched her eyes knowingly. "But he's not Jordan."

She turned away. "Jordan made his choice. I'm making mine." She smiled philosophically. "I dare say we'll both be happy!"

Chapter Six

Libby and Harley raised eyebrows at Shea's Roadhouse and Bar with their impromptu rendition of the jitterbug. It was a full house, too, on a Saturday night. At least two of the Tremayne brothers were there with their wives, and Calhoun Ballenger and his wife, Abby, were sitting at a table nearby with Leo Hart and his wife, Janie.

"I'm absolutely sure that Calhoun's going to win the state senate seat," Harley said in Libby's ear when they were seated again, drinking iced tea and eating hamburgers. "It looks like he's going to get some support from the Harts."

"Is Mr. Parks in his corner, too?" she asked.

He nodded. "All the way. The political landscape has been changing steadily for the past few years, but old man Merrill just keeps going with his old agenda. He hasn't got a clue what the voters want anymore. And, more important, he doesn't control them through his powerful friends."

"You'd think his daughter would be forward-thinking," she pointed out.

He didn't say anything. But his face was eloquent.

"Somebody said she was thinking of running for public office in Jacobsville," she began.

"No name identification," Harley said at once. "You have to have it to win an office. Without it, all the money in the world won't get you elected."

"You seem to know something about politics," she commented.

He averted his eyes. "Do I?" he mused.

Harley never talked about his family, or his past. He'd shown up at Cy Parks' place one day and proved himself to be an exceptional cowboy, but nobody knew much about him. He'd gone on a gigantic drug bust with Jacobsville's ex-mercenaries and he had a reputation for being a tough customer. But he was as mysterious in his way as the town's police chief, Cash Grier.

"Wouldn't you just know they'd show up and spoil everything?" Harley said suddenly, glaring toward the door.

Sure enough, there was Jordan Powell in an expensive Western-cut sports coat and Stetson and boots, escorting pretty Julie Merrill in a blue silk dress that looked simple and probably cost the earth.

"Doesn't she look expensive?" Harley mused.

"She probably is," Libby said, trying not to look and sound as hurt as she really was. It killed her to see Jordan there with that terrible woman.

"She's going to find out, pretty soon, that she's the equivalent of three-day-old fish with this crowd," Harley predicted coolly, watching her stick her nose up at the Ballengers as she passed them.

"I just hope she doesn't drag Jordan down with her," Libby said softly. "He started out like us, Harley," she added. "He was just a working cowboy with ambition."

Jordan seated Julie and shot a cool glance in Harley and Libby's direction, without even acknowledging them. He sat down, placing his Stetson on a vacant chair and motioned a waiter.

"Did you want something stronger to drink?" Harley asked her.

She grinned at him. "I don't have a head for liquor, Harley. I'd rather stick to iced tea, if you don't mind."

"So would I," he confided, motioning for a waiter.

The waiter, with a fine sense of irony, walked right past Jordan to take Harley's order. Julie Merrill was sputtering like a stepped-on garden hose.

"Two more iced teas, Charlie," Harley told the waiter. "And thanks for giving us preference."

"Oh, I know who the best people are, Harley," the boy said with a wicked grin. And he walked right past Jordan and Julie again, without even looking at them. A minute later, Jordan got up and stalked over to the counter to order their drinks.

"He'll smolder for the rest of the night over that," Harley mused. "So will she, unless I miss my guess. Isn't it amazing," he added thoughtfully, "that a man with as much sense as Jordan Powell can't see right through that debutante?"

"How is it that you can?" Libby asked him curiously.

He shrugged. "I know politicians all too well," he said, and for a moment, his expression was distant. "Old man Merrill has been hitting the bottle pretty hard lately," he said. "It isn't going to sit well with his constituents that he got pulled over and charged with drunk driving by Jacobsville's finest."

"Do you think they'll convict him?" she wondered aloud.

"You can bet money on it," Harley replied. "The world has shifted ten degrees. Local politicians don't meet in parked cars and make policy anymore. The sunshine laws mean that the media get wind of anything crooked and they report it. Senator Merrill has been living in the past. He's going to get a hell of a wake-up call at the primary election, when Calhoun Ballenger knocks him off the Democratic ballot as a contender."

"Mr. Ballenger looks like a gentleman," Libby commented, noticing the closeness of Calhoun and his brunette wife Abby. "He and his wife have been married a long time, haven't they?"

"Years," Harley said. "He and Justin are honest and hardworking men. They came up from nothing, too, although Justin's wife Shelby was a Jacobs before she married him," he reminded her. "A direct descendant of Big John Jacobs. But don't you think either of the Ballenger brothers would have been taken in by Julie Merrill, even when they were still single."

She paused to thank the waiter, who brought their two glasses of tall, cold iced tea. Jordan was still waiting for his order at the counter, while Julie glared at Libby and Harley.

"She's not quite normal, is she?" Libby said quietly. "I mean, that outburst in Barbara's Café was so…violent."

"People on drugs usually are violent," Harley replied. "And irrational." He looked right into Libby's eyes. "She's involved in some pretty nasty stuff, Libby. I can't tell you what I know, but Jordan is damaging himself just by being seen in public with her. The campaigns will get hot and heavy later this month and some dirty linen is about to be exposed to God and the general public."

Libby was concerned. "Jordan's a good man," she said quietly, her eyes going like homing pigeons to his lean, handsome face.

He caught her looking at him and glared. Julie, seeing his attention diverted, looked, too.

Once he returned to the table Julie leaned over and whispered something to Jordan that made him give Libby a killing glare before he started ignoring her completely.

"Watch your back," Harley told Libby as he sipped his iced tea. "She considers you a danger to her plans with Jordan. She'll sell you down the river if she can."

She sighed miserably. "First my stepmother, now Julie,"

she murmured. "I feel like I've got a target painted on my forehead."

"We all have bad times," Harley told her gently, and slid a big hand over one of hers where it lay on the table. "We get through them."

"You, too?" she wondered aloud.

"Yeah. Me, too," he replied, and he smiled at her.

Neither of them saw the furious look on Jordan Powell's face, or the calculating look on Julie's.

The following week, when Libby went to Barbara's Café for lunch, she walked right into Jordan Powell on the sidewalk. He was alone, as she was, and his expression made her feel cold all over.

"What's this about you going up to San Antonio for the night with Harley last Wednesday?" he asked bluntly.

Libby couldn't even formulate a reply for the shock. She'd driven Curt over to Duke Wright's place early Wednesday afternoon and from there she'd driven up to San Antonio to obtain some legal documents from the county clerk's office for Mr. Kemp. She hadn't even seen Harley there.

"I thought you were pure as the driven snow," Jordan continued icily. His dark eyes narrowed on her shocked face. "You put on a good act, don't you, Libby? I don't need to be a mind-reader to know why, either. I'm rich and you and your brother are about to lose your ranch."

"Janet hasn't started probate yet," she faltered.

"That's not what I hear."

"I don't care what you hear," she told him flatly. "Neither Curt nor I care very much what you think, either, Jordan. But you're going to run into serious problems if you hang out with Julie Merrill until her father loses the election."

He glared down at her. "He isn't going to lose," he assured her.

She hated seeing him be so stubborn, especially when

she had at least some idea of what Julie was going to drag him down into. She moved a step closer, her green eyes soft and beseeching. "Jordan, you're an intelligent man," she began slowly. "Surely you can see what Julie wants you for…"

A worldly look narrowed his eyes as they searched over her figure without any reaction at all. "Julie wants me, all right," he replied, coolly. "That's what's driving you to make these wild comments, isn't it? You're jealous because I'm spending so much time with her."

She didn't dare let on what she was feeling. She forced a careless smile. "Am I? You think I don't know when a man is teasing me?"

"You know more than I ever gave you credit for and that's the truth," he said flatly. "You and Harley Fowler." He made it sound like an insult.

"Harley is a fine man," she said, defending him.

"Obviously you think so, or you wouldn't be shacking up with him," he accused. "Does your brother know?"

"I'm a big girl now," she said, furious at the insinuation.

"Both of you had better remember that I make a bad enemy," he told her. "Whatever happens with your ranch, I don't want to have a subdivision full of people on my border."

He didn't know that Libby and Curt had already discussed how they were going to manage without their father's life insurance policy to pay the mortgage payments that were still owed. Riddle had taken out a mortgage on the ranch to buy Janet's Mercedes. Janet had waltzed off with the money and the private detective Jordan had recommended to Mr. Kemp had drawn a blank when he tried to dig into Janet's past. The will hadn't been probated, either, so there was no way Riddle Curtis's children could claim any of their inheritance with which to pay bills or make that huge mortgage payment. They'd had to let their only helper—their part-time cowboy—go, for lack of funds to pay him. They only had one horse left and they'd had to sell off most of their cattle. The only money coming in right now was what Curt and Libby earned in their respective jobs, and it wasn't much.

Of course, Libby wasn't going to share that information with a hostile Jordan Powell. Things were so bad that she and Curt might have to move off the ranch anyway because they couldn't make that mortgage payment at the end of the month. It was over eight hundred dollars. Their collective take-home pay wouldn't amount to that much and there were still other bills owing. Janet had run up huge bills while Riddle was still alive.

Jordan felt sick at what he was saying to Libby. He was jealous of Harley Fowler, furiously jealous. He couldn't bear the thought of Libby in bed with the other man. She wasn't even denying what Julie had assured him had happened between them. Libby, in Harley's arms, kissing him with such hunger that his toes tingled. Libby, loving Harley…

Jordan ached to have her for himself. He dreamed of her every night. But Libby was with Harley now. He'd lost his chance. He couldn't bear it!

"Is Harley going to loan you enough money to keep the ranch going until Janet's found?" he wondered aloud. He smiled coldly. "He hasn't got two dimes to rub together, from what I hear."

Libby remembered the mortgage payments she couldn't make. Once, she might have bent her pride enough to ask Jordan to loan it to her. Not anymore. Not after what he'd said to her.

She lifted her chin. "That's not your business, Jordan," she said proudly.

"Don't expect me to lend it to you," he said for spite.

"Jordan, I wouldn't ask you for a loan if the house burned down," she assured him, unflinching. "Now, if you'll excuse me, I'm using up my lunch hour."

She started to go around him, but he caught her arm and marched her down the little alley between her office and the town square. It was an alcove, away from traffic, with no prying eyes.

While she was wondering what was on his mind, he backed her up against the cold brick and brought his mouth down on her lips.

She pushed at his chest, but he only gave her his weight, pressing her harder into the wall. His own body was almost as hard, especially when his hips shifted suddenly, and lowered squarely against her own. She shivered at the slow caress of his hands on her ribcage while the kiss went on and on. She couldn't breathe. She didn't want to breathe. Her body ached for something more than this warm, heady torment. She moaned huskily under the hard, furious press of his mouth.

He lifted his head a bare inch and looked into her wide green eyes with possession and desire. It never stopped. He couldn't get within arm's length of her without giving in to temptation. Did she realize? No. She had no idea. She thought it was a punishment for her harsh words. It was more. It was anguish.

"You still want me," he ground out. "Do you think I don't know?"

"What?" she murmured, her eyes on his mouth. She could barely think at all. She felt his body so close that when he breathed, her chest deflated. Her breasts ached at the warm pressure of his broad chest. It was heaven to be so close to him. And she didn't dare let it show.

"Are you trying to prove something?" she murmured, forcing her hands to push instead of pull at his shoulders.

"Only that Harley isn't in my league," he said in a husky, arrogant tone, as he bent again and forced her mouth open under the slow, exquisite skill of his kisses. "In fact," he bit off against her lips, "neither are you, cupcake."

She wanted to come back with some snappy reply. She really did. But the sensations he was arousing were hypnotic, drugging. She felt him move one long, powerful jean-clad leg in between both of hers. It was broad daylight, in the middle of town. He was making love to her against a wall. And she didn't care.

She moved against him, her lips welcoming, her hands spreading, caressing, against his ribcage, his chest. There was no tomorrow. There was only Jordan, wanting her.

Her body throbbed in time with her frantic heartbeat. She was hot all over, swelling, aching. She wanted relief. Anything…!

Voices coming close pushed them apart when she would have said that nothing could. Jordan stepped back, his face a rigid mask. She looked up at him, her crushed mouth red from the ardent pressure, her eyes soft and misty and dazed.

Her pocketbook was on the ground. He reached down and handed it back to her, watching as she put the strap over her shoulder and stared up at him, still bemused.

She wanted to tell him that Harley was a better lover, to make some flip remark that would sting him. But she couldn't.

He was in pretty much the same shape. He hated the very thought of Harley. But even through the jealousy, he realized that Libby's responses weren't those of any experienced woman. When Julie kissed him, it was with her whole body. She was more than willing to do anything he liked. But he couldn't take Julie to bed because he didn't want her that way. It was a source of irritation and amazement to him. And to Julie, who made sarcastic remarks about his prowess.

It wasn't a lack of ability. It was just a lack of desire. But he raged with it when he looked at Libby. He'd never wanted a woman to the point of madness until now and she was the one woman he couldn't have.

"Women and their damned ambitions," he said under his breath. "Damn Harley. And damn you, Libby!"

"Damn you, too, Jordan," she said breathlessly. "And don't expect me to drag you into any more alleys and make love to you, if that's going to be your attitude!"

She turned and walked away before he had time to realize what she'd said. He had to bite back a laugh. This was no laughing matter. He had to get a grip on himself before Libby realized what was wrong with him.

After their disturbing encounter, she wondered if she and Curt wouldn't do better to just move off their property and live somewhere else. In fact, she told herself, that might not be a bad idea.

Mr. Kemp didn't agree.

"You have to maintain a presence on the property," he told Libby firmly. "If you move out, Janet might use that against you in court."

"You don't understand," she groaned. "Jordan is driving me crazy. And every time I look out the window, Julie's speeding down the road to Jordan's house."

"Jordan's being conned," he ventured.

"I know that, but he won't listen," Libby said, sitting down heavily behind her desk. "Julie's got him convinced that I'm running wild with Harley Fowler."

"That woman is big trouble," he said. "I'd give a lot to see her forced to admit what she did to the Culbertson girl at that party."

"You think it was her?" she asked, shocked.

He shrugged. "Nobody else had a motive," he said, his eyes narrow and cold. "Shannon Culbertson was running against her for class president and Julie wanted to win. I don't think she planned to kill her. She was going to set her up with one of the boys she was dating and ruin Shannon's reputation. But it backfired. At least, that's my theory. If this gets out it's going to disgrace her father even further."

"Isn't he already disgraced enough because of the drunk-driving charges?" she asked.

"He and his cronies at city hall are trying desperately to get those charges dropped, before they get into some newspaper whose publisher doesn't owe him a favor," Kemp replied, perching on the edge of her desk. "There's a disciplinary hearing at city hall next month for the officers involved. Grier says the council is going to try to have the police officers fired.''

She smiled. ''I can just see Chief Grier letting that happen.''

Kemp chuckled. ''I think the city council is going to be in for a big surprise. Our former police chief, Chet Blake, never would buck the council, or stand up for any officer who did something politically incorrect with the city fathers. Grier isn't like his cousin.''

''What if they fire him, too?'' she asked.

He stood up. ''If they even try, there will be a recall of the city council and the mayor,'' Kemp said simply. ''I can almost guarantee it. A lot of people locally are fed up with city management. Solid waste is backing up, there's no provision for water conservation, the fire department hasn't got one piece of modern equipment, and we're losing revenue hand over fist because nobody wants to mention raising taxes.''

''I didn't realize that.''

''Grier did.'' He smiled to himself. ''He's going to shake up this town. It won't be a bad thing, either.''

''Do you think he'll stay?''

Kemp nodded. ''He's put down deep roots already, although I don't think he realizes how deep they go just yet.''

Like everyone else in Jacobsville, Libby knew what was going on in Cash Grier's private life. After all, it had been in most of the tabloids. Exactly what the situation was between him and his houseguest, Tippy Moore, was anybody's guess. The couple were equally tight-lipped in public.

''Could I ask you to do something for me, sir?'' she asked suddenly.

''Of course.''

''Could you find out if they've learned anything about… Daddy at the state crime lab and how much longer it's going to be before they have a report?'' she asked.

He frowned. "Good Lord, I didn't realize how long it had been since the exhumation," he said. "Certainly. I'll get right on it, in fact."

"Thanks," she said.

He shrugged. "No problem." He got to his feet and hesitated. "Have you talked to Violet lately?" he asked reluctantly.

"She's lost weight and she's having her hair frosted," she began.

His lips made a thin line. "I don't want to know about her appearance. I only wondered how she likes her new job."

"A lot," she replied. She pursed her lips. "In fact, she and my brother are going out on a date Saturday night."

"Your brother knows her?" he asked.

She nodded. "He's working for Duke Wright, too…"

"Since when?" he exclaimed. "He was Jordan's right-hand man!"

She averted her eyes. "Not anymore. Jordan said some pretty bad things about me and Curt quit."

Kemp cursed. "I don't understand how a man who was so concerned for both of you has suddenly become an enemy. However," he added, "I imagine Julie Merrill has something to do with his change of heart."

"He's crazy about her, from what we hear."

"He's crazy, all right," he said, turning back toward his office. "He'll go right down the tubes with her and her father if he isn't careful."

"I tried to tell him. He accused me of being jealous."

He glanced back at her. "And you aren't?" he probed softly.

Her face closed up. "What good would it do, Mr. Kemp? Either people like you or they don't."

Kemp had thought, privately, that it was more than liking on Jordan's part. But apparently, he'd been wrong right down the line.

"Bring your pad, if you don't mind, Libby," he said. "I

want you to look up a case for me at the courthouse law library.''

''Yes, sir,'' she said, picking up her pad. It was always better to stay busy. That way she didn't have so much time to think.

She was walking into the courthouse when she met Calhoun Ballenger coming out of it. He stopped and grinned at her.

''Just the woman I was looking for,'' he said. ''On the assumption that I win this primary election for the Democratic candidate, how would you like to join my campaign staff in your spare time?''

She caught her breath. ''Mr. Ballenger, I'm very flattered!''

''Duke Wright tells me that you have some formidable language skills,'' he continued. ''Not that my secretaries don't, but they've got their hands full right now trying to get people to go to the polls and vote for me in May. I need someone to write publicity for me. Are you interested?''

''You bet!'' she said at once.

''Great! Come by the ranch Saturday about one. I've invited a few other people as well.''

''Not…the Merrills or Jordan Powell?'' she asked worriedly.

He glowered at her. ''I do not invite the political competition to staff meetings,'' he said with mock hauteur. He grinned. ''Besides, Jordan and I aren't speaking.''

''That's a relief,'' she said honestly.

''You're on the wrong side of him, too, I gather?''

She nodded. ''Me and half the town.''

''More than half, if I read the situation right,'' he said with a sigh. ''A handful of very prominent Democrats have changed sides and they're now promoting me.'' He smiled. ''More for our side.''

She smiled back. "Exactly! Well, then, I'll see you Saturday."

"I've already invited your boss and Duke Wright, but Duke won't come," he added heavily. "I invited Grier, and Duke's still browned off about the altercation he had with our police chief."

"He shouldn't have swung on him," she pointed out.

"I'm sure he knows that now," he agreed, his eyes twinkling. "See you."

She gave him a wave and walked into the courthouse lobby. Jordan Powell was standing there with a receipt for his automobile tag and glaring daggers at Libby.

"You're on a friendly basis with Calhoun Ballenger, I gather?" he asked.

"I'm going to work on his campaign staff," she replied with a haughty smile.

"He's going to lose," he told her firmly. "He doesn't have name identification."

She smiled at him. "He hasn't been arrested for drunk driving, to my knowledge," she pointed out.

His eyes flashed fire. "That's a frame," he returned. "Grier's officers planted evidence against him."

She glared back. "Chief Grier is honest and openhanded," she told him. "And his officers would never be asked to do any such thing!"

"They'll be out of work after that hearing," he predicted.

"You swallow everything Julie tells you, don't you, Jordan?" she asked quietly. "Maybe you should take a look at the makeup of our city council. Those were people who once owned big businesses in Jacobsville and had tons of money. But their companies are all going downhill and they're short of ready cash. They aren't the people who have the power today. And if you think Chief Grier is going to stand by and let them railroad his employees, you're way off base."

Jordan didn't reply at once. He stared at Libby until her face colored.

"I never thought you'd go against me, after all I've done for you and Curt," he said.

She was thinking the same thing. It made her ashamed to recall how he'd tried to help them both when Janet was first under suspicion of murder and fraud. But he'd behaved differently since he'd gotten mixed up with Senator Merrill's daughter. He'd changed, drastically.

"You have done a lot for us," she had to agree. "We'll always be grateful for it. But you took sides against us first, Jordan. You stood by with your mouth closed in Barbara's Café and let Julie humiliate me."

Jordan's eyes flashed. It almost looked like guilt. "You had enough support."

"Yes, from Harley Fowler. At least someone spoke up for me."

He looked ice cold. "You were rude to Julie first, in your own office."

"Why don't you ask Mr. Kemp who started it?" she replied.

"Kemp hates her," he said bluntly. "He'd back your story. I'm working for Senator Merrill and I'm going to get him reelected. You just side with the troublemakers and do what you please. But don't expect me to come around with my hat in my hand."

"I never did, Jordan," she said calmly. "I'm just a nobody around Jacobsville and I'm very aware of it. I'm not sophisticated or polished or rich, and I have no manners. On the other hand, I have no aspirations to high society, in case you wondered."

"Good thing. You'd never fit in," he bit off.

She smiled sadly. "And you think you will?" she challenged softly. "You may have better table manners than I do—and more money—but your father was poor. None of your new high-class friends is ever going to forget that. Even if you do."

He said something nasty. She colored a little, but she didn't back down.

"Don't worry, I know my place, Mr. Powell," she replied, just to irritate him. "I'm a minor problem that you've put out beside the road. I won't forget."

She was making him feel small. He didn't like it.

"Thank you for being there when we needed you most," she added quietly. "We aren't going to sell our land to developers."

"If you ever get title to it," he said coldly.

She shrugged. "That's out of our hands."

"Kemp will do what he can for you," he said, feeling guilty, because he knew that she and Curt had no money for attorneys. He'd heard that Janet was still missing and that Kemp's private detective had drawn a blank when he looked into her past. Libby and Curt must be worried sick about money.

"Yes, Mr. Kemp will do what he can for us." She studied his face, so hard and uncompromising, and wondered what had happened to make them so distant after the heated promises of those kisses they'd exchanged only weeks before.

"Curt likes working for Wright, I suppose?" he asked reluctantly.

She nodded. "He's very happy there."

"Julie had a cousin who trains horses. He's won trophies in steeplechase competition. He's working in Curt's place now, with my two new thoroughbreds."

"I suppose Julie wants to keep it all in the family," she replied.

He glared down at her. "Keep all what in the family?"

"Your money, Jordan," she said sweetly.

"You wouldn't have turned it down, if I'd given you the chance," he accused sarcastically. "You were laying it on thick."

"Who was kissing whom in the alley?" she returned huskily.

He didn't like remembering that. He jerked his wide-brimmed hat down over his eyes. "A moment of weakness. Shouldn't have happened. I'm not free anymore."

Insinuating that he and Julie were much more than friends, Libby thought correctly. She looked past Jordan to Julie, who was just coming out of the courthouse looking elegant and cold as ice. She saw Libby standing with Jordan and her lips collided furiously.

"Jordan! Let's go!" she called to him angrily.

"I was only passing the time of day with him, Julie," Libby told the older woman with a vacant smile.

"You keep your sticky hands to yourself, you little liar," Julie told her as she passed on the steps. "Jordan is mine!"

"No doubt you mean his money is yours, right?" Libby ventured.

Julie drew back her hand and slapped Libby across the cheek as hard as she could. "Damn you!" she raged.

Libby was shocked at the unexpected physical reply, but she didn't retaliate. She just stood there, straight and dignified, with as much pride as she could muster. Around the two women, several citizens stopped and looked on with keen disapproval.

One of them was Officer Dana Hall, one of the two police officers who had arrested Senator Merrill for drunk driving.

She walked right up to Libby. "That was assault, Miss Collins," she told Libby. "If you want to press charges, I can arrest Miss Merrill on the spot."

"Arrest!" Julie exploded. "You can't arrest me!"

"I most certainly can," Officer Hall replied. "Miss Collins, do you want to press charges?"

Libby stared at Julie Merrill with cold pleasure, wondering how it would look on the front page of Jacobsville's newspaper.

"Wouldn't that put another kink in your father's reelection campaign?" Libby ventured softly.

Julie looked past Libby and suddenly burst into tears.

She threw herself into Jordan Powell's arms. "Oh, Jordan, she's going to have me arrested!"

"No, she's not," Jordan said curtly. He glanced at Libby. "She wouldn't dare."

Libby cocked her head. "I wouldn't?" She glared at him. "Look at my cheek, Jordan."

It was red. There was a very obvious handprint on it.

"She insulted me," Julie wailed. "I had every right to hit her back!"

"She never struck you, Miss Merrill," Officer Hall replied coldly. "Striking another person is against the law, regardless of the provocation."

"I never meant to do it!" Julie wailed. She was sobbing, but there wasn't a speck of moisture under her eyes. "Please, Jordan, don't let them put me in jail!"

Libby and Officer Hall exchanged disgusted looks.

"Men are so damned gullible," Libby remarked with a glare at Jordan, who looked outraged. "All right, Julie, have it your way. But you'd better learn to produce tears as well as broken sobs if you want to convince another *woman* that you're crying."

"Jordan, could we go now?" Julie sobbed. "I'm just sick…!"

"Not half as sick as you'll be when your father loses the election, Julie," Libby drawled sweetly, and walked up the steps with Officer Hall at her side. She didn't even look at Jordan as she went into the courthouse.

Chapter Seven

Calhoun Ballenger's meeting with his volunteer staff was a cheerful riot of surprises. Libby found herself working with women she'd known only by name a few months earlier. Now she was suddenly in the cream of society, but with women who didn't snub her or look down their noses at her social position.

Libby was delighted to find herself working with Violet, who'd come straight from her job at Duke Wright's ranch for the meeting.

"This is great!" Violet exclaimed, hugging Libby. "I've missed working with you!"

"I've missed you, too, Violet," Libby assured her. She shook her head as she looked at the other woman. "You look great!"

Violet grinned. She'd dropped at least two dress sizes. She was well-rounded, but no longer obese even to the most critical eye. She'd had her brown hair frosted and it was waving around her face and shoulders. She was wearing a low-cut dress that emphasized the size of her pretty breasts, and her small waist and voluptuous hips, along with high heels that arched her small feet nicely.

"I've worked hard at the gym," Violet confessed. She was still laughing when her eyes collided with Blake Kemp's across the room. The expression left her face. She averted her eyes quickly. "Excuse me, won't you, Libby? I came with Curt. You, uh, don't mind, do you?" she added worriedly.

"Don't be silly," Libby said with a genuine smile. "Curt's nice. So are you. I think you'd make a lovely couple…"

"Still happy with Duke Wright, Miss Hardy?" came a cold, biting comment from Libby's back.

Blake Kemp moved into view, his pale eyes expressive on Violet's pretty figure and the changes in the way she dressed.

"I'm…very happy with him, Mr. Kemp," Violet said, clasping her hands together tightly. "If you'll excuse me…"

"You've lost weight," Kemp said gruffly.

Violet's eyes widened. "And you actually noticed?"

The muscles in his face tautened. "You look…nice."

Violet's jaw dropped. She was literally at a loss for words. Her eyes lifted to Kemp's and they stood staring at each other for longer than was polite, neither speaking or moving.

Kemp shifted restlessly on his long legs. "How's your mother?"

Violet swallowed hard. "She's not doing very well, I'm afraid. You know…about the exhumation?"

Kemp nodded. "They're still in the process of evaluating Curt and Libby's father's remains, as well, at the crime lab. So far, they have nothing to report."

Violet looked beside him at Libby and winced. "I didn't know, Libby. I'm so sorry."

"So am I, for you," Libby replied. "We didn't want to do it, but we had to know for sure."

"Will they really be able to tell anything, after all this time?" Violet asked Kemp, and she actually moved a step closer to him.

He seemed to catch his breath. He was looking at her oddly. "I assume so." His voice was deeper, too. Involuntarily, his lean fingers reached out and touched Violet's long hair. "I like the frosting," he said reluctantly. "It makes your eyes look...bluer."

"Does it?" Violet asked, but her eyes were staring into his as if she'd found treasure there.

With an amused smile, Libby excused herself and joined her brother, who was talking to the police chief.

Cash Grier noticed her approach and smiled. He looked older somehow and there were new lines around his dark eyes.

"Hi, Chief," she greeted him. "How's it going?"

"Don't ask," Curt chuckled. "He's in the middle of a controversy."

"So are we," Libby replied. "We're on the wrong side of the election and Jordan Powell is furious at us."

"We're on the right side," Cash said carelessly. "The city fathers are in for a rude awakening." He leaned down. "I have friends in high places." He paused. "I also have friends in *low* places." He grinned.

Libby and Curt burst out laughing, because they recognized the lines from a country song they'd all loved.

Calhoun Ballenger joined them, clapping Cash on the back affectionately. "Thanks for coming," he said. "Even if it is putting another nail in your coffin with the mayor."

"They mayor can kiss my..." Cash glanced at Libby and grinned. "Never mind."

They all laughed.

"She's lived with me all her life," Curt remarked. "She's practically unshockable."

"How's Tippy?" Calhoun asked.

Cash smiled. "Doing better, thanks. She'd have come, too, but she's still having a bad time."

"No wonder," Calhoun replied, recalling the ordeal Tippy had been through in the hands of kidnappers. It had been in all the tabloids. "Good thing they caught the culprits who kidnapped her."

"Isn't it?" Cash said, not giving away that he'd caught them, with the help of an old colleague. "Nice turnout, Calhoun," he added, looking around them. "I thought you invited Judd."

"I did," Calhoun said at once, "but the twins have a cold."

"Damn!" Cash grimaced. "I told Judd that he and Crissy needed to stop running that air conditioner all night!"

"It wasn't that," Calhoun confided. "They went to the Coltrains' birthday party for their son—his second birthday—and that's where they got the colds."

Cash sighed. "Poor babies."

"He's their godfather," Calhoun told Libby and Curt. "But he thinks Jessamina belongs to him."

"She does," Cash replied haughtily.

Nobody mentioned what the tabloids had said—that Tippy had been pregnant with Cash's child a few weeks earlier and lost it just before her ordeal with the kidnapping.

Libby diplomatically changed the subject. "Mr. Kemp said that you can put up campaign posters in our office windows," she told Calhoun, "and Barbara's willing to let you put up as many as you like in her café," she added with a grin. "She said she's never going to forgive Julie Merrill for making a scene there."

Calhoun chuckled. "I've had that sort of offer all week," he replied. "Nobody wants Senator Merrill back in office, but the city fathers have thrown their support behind him and he thinks he's unbeatable. What we really need is a change in city government as well. We're on our second mayor in eight months and this one is afraid of his own shadow."

"He's also Senator Merrill's nephew," Curt added.

"Which is why he's trying to make my officers back down on those DWI charges," Cash Grier interposed.

"I'd like see it. Carlos Garcia wouldn't back down from anybody," Calhoun mused. "Or Officer Dana Hall, either."

"Ms. Hall came to my assistance at the courthouse this week," Libby volunteered. "Julie Merrill slapped me. Officer Hall was more than willing to arrest her, if I'd agreed to press charges."

"Good for Dana," Cash returned. "You be careful, Ms. Collins," he added firmly. "That woman has poor impulse control. I wouldn't put it past her to try and run somebody down."

"Neither would I," Curt added worriedly. "She's already told Jordan some furious lies about us and he believes her."

"She can be very convincing," Libby said, not wanting to verbally attack Jordan even now.

"It may get worse now, with all of you backing me," Calhoun told the small group. "I won't have any hard feelings if you want to withdraw your support."

"Do I look like the sort of man who backs away from trouble?" Cash asked lazily, with a grin.

"Speaking of Duke Wright," Libby murmured dryly, "he's throwing his support to Mr. Ballenger, too. But he had, uh, reservations about coming to the meeting."

Cash chuckled. "I don't hold grudges."

"Yes, but he does," Calhoun said on a chuckle. "He'll get over it. He's got some personal problems right now."

"Don't we all?" Cash replied wistfully, and his dark eyes were troubled.

Libby and Curt didn't add their two cents' worth, but they exchanged quiet looks.

The campaign was winding down for the primary, but all the polls gave Calhoun a huge lead over Merrill. Printed materials were ordered, along with buttons, pencils, bumper stickers and keychains. There was enough promotional matter to blanket the town and in the days that followed, Calhoun's supporters did exactly that in Jacobs County and the surrounding area in the state senatorial district that Merrill represented.

Julie Merrill was acting as her father's campaign manager and she was coordinating efforts for promotion with a group of teenagers she'd hired. Some of them were delinquents and there was a rash of vandalisms pertaining to the destruction of Calhoun's campaign posters.

Cash Grier, predictably, went after the culprits and rounded them up. He got one to talk and the newspapers revealed that Miss Merrill had paid the young man to destroy Calhoun's campaign literature. Julie denied it. But the vandalism stopped.

Meanwhile, acting mayor Ben Brady was mounting a fervent defense for Senator Merrill on the drunk-driving charges and trying to make things hot for the two officers. He ordered them suspended and tried to get the city council to back him up.

Cash got wind of it and phoned Simon Hart, the state's attorney general. Simon phoned the city attorney and they had a long talk. Soon afterward, the officers were notified that they could stay on the job until the hearing the following month.

Meanwhile, the state crime lab revealed the results of its report to Blake Kemp. He walked up to Libby's desk while she was on the phone and waited impatiently for her to hang up.

"They can't find any evidence of foul play, Libby," he said at once.

"And if there was any, they would?" she asked quickly.

He nodded. "I'm almost certain of it. The crime lab verified our medical examiner's diagnosis of myocardial infarction. So Janet's off the hook for that one, at least."

Libby sat back with a long sigh and closed her eyes.

"Thank God. I couldn't have lived with it if she'd poisoned Daddy and we never knew."

He nodded. "On the other hand, they hit paydirt with Violet's father," he added.

She sat up straight. "Poison?"

"Yes," he said heavily. "I'm not going to phone her. I'm going over to Duke Wright's place to tell her in person. Then I'll take her home to talk to her mother. She'll need someone with her."

Yes, she would, and Libby was secretly relieved that Kemp was going to be the person. Violet would need a shoulder to cry on.

"I'll phone Curt and tell him," she said.

"Libby, give me half an hour first," he asked quietly. "I don't want him to tell Violet."

She wondered why, but she wasn't going to pry. "Okay."

He managed a brief smile. "Thanks."

"What about Janet?" she wondered miserably. "They still haven't found her."

"They will. Now all we need is a witness who can place her with Mr. Hardy the night of his death, and we can have her arrested and charged with murder," he replied.

"Chance would be a fine thing, Mr. Kemp," she said heavily.

"Don't give up hope," he instructed. "She's not going to get away with your inheritance. I promise."

She managed a smile. "Thanks."

But she wasn't really convinced. She went home that afternoon feeling lost and alone. She'd told Curt the good news after Violet had gone home with Kemp. Curt had been as relieved as she had, but there was still the problem of probate. Everything was in Janet's name, as their father had instructed. Janet had the insurance money. Nobody could do anything with the estate until the will was probated and

Janet had to sign the papers for that. It was a financial nightmare.

There was a message on the answering machine when Libby got home. She pushed the Play button and her heart sank right to her ankles.

"This is the loan officer at Jacobsville Savings and Loan," came the pleasant voice. "We just wanted to remind you that your loan payment was due three days ago. Please call us if there's a problem." The caller gave her name and position and her telephone number. The line went dead.

Libby sat down beside the phone and just stared at it. Curt had told her already that they weren't going to be able to make the payment. Jordan had assured her that he wasn't going to loan her the money to pay it. There was nobody else they would feel comfortable asking. She put her face in her hands and let the tears fall. The financial establishment would repossess the ranch. It wouldn't matter where Janet was or what state the probate action was in. They were going to lose their home.

She went out to the barn and ran the curry comb over Bailey, her father's horse. He was the last horse they had.

The barn leaked. It was starting to rain and Libby felt raindrops falling on her shoulder through a rip in the tin roof from a small tornado that had torn through a month earlier. The straw on the floor of the barn needed changing, but the hay crop had drowned in the flooding. They'd have to buy some. Libby looked down at her worn jeans, at the small hand resting on them. The tiger eye ring her father had given her looked ominous in the darkened barn. She sighed and turned back to the horse.

"Bailey, I don't know what we're going to do," she told the old horse, who neighed as if he were answering her.

The sound of a vehicle pulling up in the yard diverted her. She looked down the long aisle of the barn to see Jordan's pickup truck sitting at the entrance. Her heart skipped as he got out and came striding through the dirty straw, his cotton shirt speckled with raindrops that had escaped the wide brim of his white straw hat.

"What do you want?" she asked, trying to ignore him to finish her grooming job on the horse.

"My two new thoroughbreds are missing."

She turned, the curry comb suspended in her small hand. "And you think we took them?" she asked incredulously. "You honestly think we'd steal from you, even if we were starving?"

He averted his face, as if the question had wounded him.

"Please leave," she said through her teeth.

He rammed his hands into his pockets and moved a step closer, looking past her to Bailey. "That horse is useless for ranch work. He's all of twenty."

"He's my horse," she replied. "I'm not getting rid of him, whatever happens."

She felt his lean, powerful body at her back. "Libby," he began. "About that bank loan…"

"Curt and I are managing just fine, thanks," she said without turning.

His big, strong hands came down heavily on her shoulders, making her jump. "The bank president is a good friend of the Merrills."

She pulled away from him and looked up, her unspoken fears in her green eyes. "They can't do anything to us without Janet," she told him. "She has legal power of attorney."

"Damn it, I know that!" he muttered. "But it's not going to stop the bank from foreclosing, don't you see? You can't make the loan payment!"

"What business is that of yours?" she asked bitterly.

He drew in a slow breath. "I can talk to the president of the Jacobsville Merchant Bank for you," he said. "He might be willing to work out something for the land. You and Curt can't work it, anyway, and you don't have the capital to invest in it. The best you could do is sell off your remaining cattle and give it up.''

She couldn't even manage words. She had no options at all and he had to know it. She could almost hate him.

"We can't sell anything," she said harshly. "I told you, Janet has power of attorney. And she was named in Daddy's will as the sole holder of the property. We can't even sell a stick of furniture. We're going to have to watch the bank foreclose, Jordan, because Janet has our hands tied. We're going to lose everything Daddy worked for, all his life..."

Her lower lip trembled. She couldn't even finish the sentence.

Jordan stepped forward and wrapped her up tight in his arms, holding her while she cried. "Damn, what a mess!"

She beat a small fist against his massive chest. "Why?" she moaned. "Why?"

His arms tightened. "I don't know, baby," he whispered at her ear, his voice deep and soothing. "I wish I did."

She nuzzled closer, drowning in the pleasure of being close to him. It had been so long since he'd held her.

His chest rose and fell heavily. "Kemp's detective hasn't tracked her down yet?"

"Not yet. But she didn't...kill Daddy. The autopsy showed that he died of a heart attack."

"That's something, I guess," he murmured.

"But Violet's daddy was poisoned," she added quietly, her eyes open as they stared past Jordan's broad chest toward his truck parked at the front of the barn. "So they'll still get her for murder, if they can ever find her."

"Poor Violet," he said.

"Yes."

His hand smoothed her hair. It tangled in the wavy soft strands. "You smell of roses, Libby," he murmured deeply, and the pressure of his arms changed in some subtle way.

She could feel the sudden tautness of his lean body against her, the increasing warmth of his embrace. But he'd taken Julie's side against her and she wasn't comfortable being in his arms anymore.

She tried to pull away, but he wouldn't let her.

"Don't fight me," he said gruffly. "You know you don't want to."

"I don't?"

He lifted his head and looked down into her misty and wet green eyes. His voice was deep with feeling. "You haven't stopped wanting me."

"I want hot chocolate, too, Jordan, but it still gives me migraine, so I don't drink it," she said emphatically.

His dark eyebrows lifted. "That's cute. You think you convinced me?"

"Sure," she lied.

He laughed mirthlessly, letting his dark eyes fall to her lips. "Let's see."

He bent, drawing his lips slowly, tenderly, across her mouth in a teasing impression of a kiss. He was lazy and gentle and after a few seconds of imitating a plank of wood, her traitorous body betrayed her.

She relaxed into the heat of his body with a shaky little sigh and found herself enveloped in his arms. He kissed her again, hungrily this time, without the tenderness of that first brief exchange.

She moaned and tried to protest the sudden crush of his lean hand at the base of her spine, rubbing her body against him. But he didn't give her enough breath or strength to protest and the next thing she knew, she was on her back in a stall of fresh hay and his body was completely covering hers.

"No, Jordan," she protested weakly.

"Yes," he groaned. His long leg slid lazily against hers, and between them, while his big, warm hands smoothed blatantly over her ribcage, his thumbs sliding boldly right over her breasts. "Don't think," he whispered against her parted lips. "Just give in. I won't hurt you."

"I know that," she whispered. "But..."

He nibbled on her lower lip. His thumbs edged out gently and found her nipples. They moved lazily, back and forth, coaxing the tips into hard little nubs. She shivered with unexpected pleasure.

He lifted his head and looked into her eyes while he did it again. If she was used to this sort of love play, it certainly didn't show. She was pliable, yielded, absolutely fascinated with what he was doing to her body. She liked it.

That was all he needed to know. His leg became insistent between hers, coaxing them to move apart, to admit the slow, exquisite imprint of his hips between her long legs. It was like that day in the alley beyond her office, when she hadn't cared if all of Jacobsville walked by while he was pressing her aching body against the brick wall. She was drowning in pleasure.

Surely, she thought blindly, it couldn't be wrong to give in to something so sweet! His hands on her body were producing undreamed of sensations. He was giving her pleasure in hot, sweeping waves. He touched her and she ached for more. He kissed her and she lifted against him to find his mouth and coax it into ardor. One of her legs curled helplessly around his powerful thigh and she moaned when he accepted the silent invitation and moved into near intimacy with her.

He was aroused. He was powerful. She felt the hard thrust of him against her body and she wanted to rip off her clothes and invite his hands, his eyes, his body, into complete surrender with her. She wanted to feel the ecstasy she knew he could give her. He was skilled, masterful. He knew what she needed, what she wanted. He could give her pleasure beyond bearing, she knew it.

His lean hands moved under her blouse, searching for closeness, unfastening buttons, invading lace. She felt his fingers brush tenderly, lovingly, over her bare breasts in an intimacy she'd never shared with anyone.

Her dreams of him had been this explicit, but she'd never thought she would live them in such urgent passion. As he touched her, she arched to help him, moved to encourage him. Her mouth opened wide under his. She felt his tongue suddenly thrust into it with violent need.

She moaned loudly, her fingertips gripping the hard muscle of his upper arms as he thrust her blouse and bra up to her throat and bent at once to put his mouth on her breasts.

The warm, moist contact was shattering. She stiffened with the shock of pleasure it produced. He tasted her in a hot, feverish silence, broken only by his urgent breathing and the rough sigh of her own voice in his ear.

"Yes," he groaned, opening his mouth. "Yes, Libby. Here. Right here. You and me. I can give you more pleasure than damned Harley ever dreamed of giving you!"

Harley. Harley. She felt her body growing cold. "Harley?" she whispered.

He lifted his head and looked down at her breasts with grinding urgency. "He's had you."

"He has not!" she exclaimed, shocked.

He scowled, in limbo, caught between his insane need to possess her and his jealousy of the other man.

She took advantage of his indecision by jerking out of his arms and pulling her blouse down as she dragged herself out of the stall. She groped for fastenings while she flushed with embarrassment at what she'd just let him do to her.

She looked devastated. Her hair was full of straw, like her clothes. Her green eyes were wild, her face flushed, her mouth swollen.

He got to his feet, still in the grip of passion, and started toward her. His hat was off. His hair was wild, from her searching fingers, and his shirt was half-open over hair-matted muscle.

"Come back here," he said huskily, moving forward.

"No!" she said firmly, shivering. "I'm not standing in for Julie Merrill!"

The words stopped him in his tracks. He hesitated, his brows meeting over turbulent dark eyes.

"Remember Julie? Your girlfriend?" she persisted shakily. Throwing his lover in his face was a way to cover her hurt for the insinuation he'd made about her and Harley. "What in the world would she think if she could see you now?"

He straightened, but with an effort. His body was raging. He wanted Libby. He'd never wanted anyone, anything, as much as he wanted her.

"Julie has nothing to do with this," he ground out. "I want you!"

"For how long, Jordan?" she asked bitingly. "Ten minutes? Thirty?"

He blinked. His mind wasn't working.

"I am nobody's one-night stand," she flashed at him. "Not even yours!"

He took a deep breath, then another one. He stared at her blankly while he tried to stop thinking about how sweet it was to feel her body under his hands.

"I want you to leave, now," she repeated, folding her arms over her loose bra. She could feel the swollen contours of her breasts and remembered with pure shame how it felt to have him touching and kissing them.

"That isn't what you wanted five minutes ago," he reminded her flatly.

She closed her eyes. "I'm grass-green and stupid," she said curtly. "It wouldn't be the first time an experienced man seduced an innocent girl."

"Don't make stupid jokes," he said icily. "You're no innocent."

"You believe what you like about me, Jordan, it doesn't matter anymore," she interrupted him. "I've got work to do. Why don't you go home?"

He glared at her, frustrated desire riding him hard. He cursed himself for ruining everything by bringing up Harley Fowler. "You're a hard woman, Libby," he said. "Harder than I ever realized."

"Goodbye, Jordan," she said, and she turned away to pick up the curry comb she'd dropped.

He gave her a furious glare and stormed out of the barn to his truck. Bailey jumped as Jordan slammed the door and left skid marks getting out of the driveway. She relaxed then, grateful that she'd managed to save herself from that masterful seduction. She'd had a close call. She had to make sure that Jordan never got so close to her again. She couldn't trust him. Not now.

Chapter Eight

Janet was still in hiding before the primary election and probate hadn't begun. But plenty had changed in Jacobsville. Libby and Curt had been forced to move out of the farmhouse where they'd grown up, because the bank had foreclosed.

They hadn't said a word to Jordan about it. Curt moved into the bunkhouse at the Wright ranch where he worked. Libby moved into a boardinghouse where two other Jacobsville career women lived.

Bailey would have had to be boarded and Libby didn't have the money. But she worked out a deal with a dude ranch nearby. Bailey would be used for trail rides for people who were nervous of horses and Libby would help on the weekends. It wasn't the ideal solution, but it was the only one she had. It was a wrench to give up Bailey, even though it wasn't going to be forever.

Jordan and Julie Merrill were apparently engaged. Or so Julie was saying, and she was wearing a huge diamond on her ring finger. Her father was using every dirty trick in the book to gain his party's candidacy.

Julie Merrill was vehemently outspoken about some un-named dirty tactics being used against her father in the primary election campaign, and she went on television to make accusations against Calhoun Ballenger.

The next morning, Blake Kemp had her served as the defendant in a defamation lawsuit.

"They're not going to win this case," Julie raged at Jordan. "I want you to get me the best attorney in Austin! We're going to put Calhoun Ballenger right in the gutter where he belongs, along with all these jump-up nouveau riche that think they own our county!"

Jordan, who was one of those jump-ups, gave her a curious look. "Excuse me?" he asked coolly.

"Well, I'm not standing by while Ballenger talks my father's constituents into deserting him!"

"You're the one who's been making allegations, Julie," Jordan said quietly. "To anyone who was willing to listen."

She waved that away. "You have to do that to win elections."

"I'm not going to be party to anything dishonest," Jordan said through his teeth.

Julie backed down. She curled against him and sighed. "Okay. I'll tone it down, for your sake. But you aren't going to let Calhoun Ballenger sue me, are you?"

Jordan didn't know what he was going to do. He felt uneasy at Julie's temperament and her tactics. He'd taken her side against Kemp when she told him that one of the boys at her graduation party had put something in the Culbertson girl's drink and she couldn't turn him in. She'd cried about Libby Collins making horrible statements against her. But Libby had never done such a thing before.

He'd liked being Julie's escort, being accepted by the social crowd she ran around with. But it was getting old and he was beginning to believe that Julie was only playing up to him for money to put into her father's campaign.

Libby had tried to warn him and he'd jumped down her throat. He felt guilty about that, too. He felt guilty about a lot of things lately.

"Listen," he said. "I think you need to step back and take a good look at what you're doing. Calhoun Ballenger isn't some minor citizen. He and his brother own a feedlot that's nationally known. Besides that, he has the support of most of the people in Jacobsville with money."

"My father has the support of the social set," she began.

"Yes, but Julie, they're the old elite. The demographics have changed in Jacobs County in the past ten years. Look around you. The Harts are a political family from the roots up. Their brother is the state attorney general and he's already casting a serious eye on what's going on in the Jacobsville city council, about those police officers the mayor's trying to suspend."

"They can't do anything about that," she argued.

"Julie, the Harts are related to Chief Grier," he said shortly.

She hesitated. For the first time, she looked uncertain.

"Not only that, they're related to the governor and the vice president. And while it isn't well-known locally, Grier's people are very wealthy."

She sat down. She ran a hand through her blond hair. "Why didn't you say this before?"

"I tried to," he pointed out. "You refused to listen."

"But Daddy can't possibly lose the election," she said with a child's understanding of things. "He's been state senator from this district for years and years."

"And now the voters are looking for some new blood," he told her. "Not only in local government, but in state and national government. You and your father don't really move with the times, Julie."

"Surely, you don't think Calhoun can beat Daddy?" she asked huskily.

"I think he's going to," he replied honestly, ramming his hands into his pockets. "He's way ahead of your father in the polls. You know that. You and your father have made some bad enemies trying to have those police officers fired. You've gotten on the wrong side of not only Cash Grier, but the Harts as well. There will be repercussions. I've already heard talk of a complete recall of the mayor and the city council.''

''But the mayor is Daddy's nephew. How could they…?''

''Don't you know anything about small towns?'' he ground out. ''Julie, you've spent too much time in Austin with your father and not enough around here where the elections are decided.''

''This is just a hick town,'' she said, surprised. ''Why should I care what goes on here?''

Jordan's face hardened. ''Because Jacobs County is the biggest county in your father's district. He can't get re-elected without it. You've damaged his campaign by the way you've behaved to Libby Collins.''

''That nobody?'' she scoffed.

''Her father is a direct descendant of old John Jacobs,'' he pointed out. ''They may not have money and they may not be socially acceptable to you and your father, but the Collinses are highly respected here. The reason Calhoun's got such support is because you've tried to hurt Libby.''

''But that's absurd!''

''She's a good person,'' he said, averting his eyes as he recalled his unworthy treatment of her—and of Curt—on Julie's behalf. ''She's had some hard knocks recently.''

''So have I,'' Julie said hotly. ''Most notably, having a lawsuit filed against me for defamation of character by that lawyer Kemp!'' She turned to him. ''Are you going to get me a lawyer, or do I have to find my own?''

Jordan was cutting his losses while there was still time. He felt like ten kinds of fool for the way he'd behaved in the past few weeks. ''I think you'd better do that yourself,'' he replied. ''I'm not going against Calhoun Ballenger.''

She scoffed. ''You'll never get that Collins woman to

like you again, no matter what you do," she said haughtily. "Or didn't you know that she and her brother have forfeited the ranch to the bank?"

He was speechless. "They've what?"

"Nobody would loan them the money they needed to save it," she said with a cold smile. "So the bank president foreclosed. Daddy had a long talk with him."

He looked furious. His big fists clenched at his hips. "That was low, Julie."

"When you want to win, sometimes you have to fight dirty," she said simply. "You belong to me. I'm not letting some nobody of a little dirt rancher take you away from me. We need you."

"I don't belong to you," he returned, scooping up his hat. "In fact, I've never felt dirtier than I do right now."

She gaped at him. "I beg your pardon! You can't talk to me like that!"

"I just did." He started toward the door.

"You're no loss, Jordan," she yelled after him. "We needed your money, but I never wanted you! You're one of those jump-ups with no decent background. I'm sorry I ever invited you here the first time. I'm ashamed that I told my friends I liked you!"

"That makes two of us," he murmured icily, and he went out the door without a backward glance.

Kemp was going over some notes with Libby when Jordan Powell walked into the office without bothering to knock.

"I'd like to talk to Libby for a minute," he said solemnly, hat in hand.

Libby stared at him blankly. "I can't think what you have to say," she replied. "I'm very busy."

"She is," Kemp replied. "I'm due in court in thirty minutes."

"Then I'll come back in thirty minutes," Jordan replied.

"Feel free, but I won't be here. I have nothing to say to

you, Jordan," she told him bluntly. "You turned your back on me when I needed you the most. I don't need you now. I never will again."

"Listen," he began impatiently.

"No." She turned back to Kemp. "What were you saying, boss?"

Kemp hesitated. He could see the pain in Jordan's face and he had some idea that Jordan had just found out the truth about Julie Merrill. He checked his watch. "Listen, I can read your writing. Just give me the pad and I'll get to the courthouse. It's okay," he added when she looked as if he were deserting her to the enemy. "Really."

She bit her lower lip hard. "Okay."

"Thanks," Jordan said stiffly, as Kemp got up from the desk.

"You owe me one," he replied, as he passed the taciturn rancher on the way out the door.

Minutes later, Mabel went into Kemp's office to put some notes on his desk, leaving Jordan and Libby alone.

"I've made some bad mistakes," he began stiffly. He hated apologies. Usually, he found ways not to make them. But he'd hurt Libby too badly not to try.

She was staring at her keyboard, trying not to listen.

"You have to understand what it's been like for me," he said hesitantly. He sat down in a chair next to her desk, with his wide-brimmed hat in his hands. "My people were like yours, poor. My mother had money, but her people disinherited her when she married my dad. I never had two nickels to rub together. I was that Powell kid, whose father worked for wages, whose mother was reduced to working as a housekeeper." He stared at the floor with his pride aching. "I wanted to be somebody, Libby. That's all I ever wanted. Just to have respect from the people who mattered in this town." He shrugged. "I thought going around with Julie would give me that."

"I don't suppose you noticed that her father belongs to

a group of respectable people who no longer have any power around here,'' she said stiffly.

He sighed. "No, I didn't. I had my head turned. She was beautiful and rich and cultured, and she came at me like a hurricane. I was in over my head before I knew it."

Libby, who wasn't beautiful or rich or cultured, felt her heart breaking. She knew all this, but it hurt to hear him admit it. Because it meant that those hungry, sweet kisses she'd shared with him meant nothing at all. He wanted Julie.

"I've broken it off with her," he said bluntly.

Libby didn't say anything.

"Did you hear me?" he asked impatiently.

She looked up at him with disillusioned eyes. "You believed her. She said I was shacking up with Harley Fowler. She said I attacked her in this office and hurt her feelings. You believed all that, even though you knew me. And when she attacked me in Barbara's Café and on the courthouse steps, you didn't say a thing."

He winced.

"Words don't mean anything, Powell," she said bitterly. "You can sit there and apologize and try to smooth over what you did for the rest of your life, but I won't listen. When I needed you, you turned your back on me."

He drew in a long breath. "I guess I did."

"I can understand that you were flattered by her attention," she said. "But Curt and I have lost everything we had. Our father is dead and we don't even have a home anymore."

He moved his hat in his hands. "You could move in with me."

She laughed bitterly. "Thanks."

"No, listen," he said earnestly, leaning forward.

She held up a hand. "Don't. I've had all the hard knocks I can handle. I don't want anything from you, Jordan. Not anything at all."

He wanted to bite something. He felt furious at his own

stupidity, at his blind allegiance to Julie Merrill and her father, at his naivete in letting them use him. He felt even worse about the way he'd turned on Libby. But he was afraid of what he'd felt for her, afraid of her youth, her changeability. Now he only felt like a fool.

"Thanks for the offer and the apology," she added heavily. "Now, if you'll excuse me, I have to get back to work."

She turned on the computer, brought up her work screen and shut Jordan out of her sight and mind.

He got up slowly and moved toward the door. He hesitated at it, glancing back at her. "What about the autopsy?" he asked suddenly.

She swallowed hard. "Daddy died of a heart attack, just like the doctors said," she replied.

He sighed. "And Violet's father?"

"Was poisoned," she replied.

"Riddle had a lucky escape," he commented. "So did you and Curt."

She didn't look at him. "I just hope they can find her, before she kills some other poor old man."

He nodded. After a minute, he gave her one last soulful glance and went out the door.

Life went on as usual. Calhoun's campaign staff cranked up the heat. Libby spent her free time helping to make up flyers and make telephone calls, offering to drive voters to the polls during the primary election if they didn't have a way to get to the polls.

"You know, I really think Calhoun's going to win," Curt told Libby while they were having a quick lunch together on Saturday, after she got off from work.

She smiled. "So do I. He's got all kinds of support."

He picked at his potato chips. "Heard from Jordan?"

She stiffened. "He came by the office to apologize a few days ago."

He drew in a long breath. "Rumor is that Julie Merrill's courting Duke Wright now."

"Good luck to her. He's still in love with his wife. And he's not quite as gullible as Jordan."

"Jordan wasn't so gullible," he defended his former boss. "When a woman that pretty turns up the heat, most normal men will follow her anywhere."

She lifted both eyebrows. "Even you?"

He grinned. "I'm not normal. I'm a cowboy."

She chuckled and sipped her iced tea. "They're still looking for Janet. I've had an idea," she said.

"Shoot."

"What if we advertise our property for sale in all the regional newspapers?"

"Whoa," he said. "We can't sell it. We don't have power of attorney and the will's not even in probate yet."

"She's a suspected murderess," she reminded him. "Felons can't inherit, did you know? If she's tried and convicted, we might be able to get her to return everything she got from Daddy's estate."

He frowned, thinking hard. "Do you remember Dad telling us about a new will he'd made?"

She blinked. "No."

"Maybe you weren't there. It was when he was in the hospital, just before he died. He could hardly talk for the pain and he was gasping for breath. But he said there was a will. He said he put it in his safest place." He frowned heavily. "I never thought about that until just now, but what if he meant a *new* will, Libby?"

"It wouldn't have been legal if it wasn't witnessed," she said sadly. "He might have written something down and she found it and threw it out. I doubt it would stand up in court."

"No. He went to San Antonio without Janet, about two days before he had the heart attack," he persisted.

"Who did he know in San Antonio?" she wondered aloud.

"Why don't you ask Mr. Kemp to see if his private detective could snoop around?" he queried softly.

She pursed her lips. "It would be a long shot. And we couldn't afford to pay him...."

"Dad had a coin collection that was worth half a million dollars, Libby," Curt said. "It's never turned up. I can't find any record that he ever sold it, either."

Her lips fell open. In the agony of the past few months, that had never occurred to her. "I assumed Janet cashed it in...."

"She had the insurance money," he reminded her, "and the property—or so she assumed. But when we were sorting out Dad's personal belongings, that case he kept the coins in was missing. What if—" he added eagerly "—he took it to San Antonio and left it with someone, along with an altered will?"

She was trying to think. It wasn't easy. If they had those coins, if nothing else, they could make the loan payment.

"I can ask Mr. Kemp if he'll look into it," she said. "He can take the money out of my salary."

"I can contribute some of mine," Curt added.

She felt lighter than she had in weeks. "I'll go ask him right now!"

"Finish your sandwich first," he coaxed. "You've lost weight, baby sister."

She grimaced. "I've been depressed since we had to leave home."

"Yeah. Me, too."

She smiled at him. "But things are looking up!"

She found Kemp just about to leave for the day. She stopped him at the door and told him what she and Curt had been discussing.

He closed the door behind them, picked up the phone, and dialed a number. Libby listened while he outlined the case to someone, most likely the private detective he'd hired to look for Janet.

"That's right," he told the man. "One more thing, there's a substantial coin collection missing as well. I'll ask." He put his hand over the receiver and asked Libby for a description of it, which he gave to the man. He added a few more comments and hung up, smiling.

"Considering the age of those coins and their value, it wouldn't be hard to trace them if they'd been sold. Good work, Libby!"

"Thank my brother," she replied, smiling. "He remembered it."

"You would have, too, I expect, in time," he said in a kindly tone. "Want me to have a talk with the bank president?" he added. "I think he might be more amenable to letting you and Curt back on the property with this new angle in mind. It might be to his advantage," he added in a satisfied tone.

"You mean, if we turn out to have that much money of our own, free and clear, it would make him very uncomfortable if we put it in the Jacobsville Municipal Bank and not his?"

"Exactly."

Her eyes blazed. "Which is exactly where we *will* put it, if we get it," she added.

He chuckled. "No need to tell him that just yet."

Her eyebrows lifted. "Mr. Kemp, you have a devious mind."

He smiled. "What else is new?"

Libby was furious at herself for not thinking of her father's impressive coin collection until now. She'd watched those coins come in the mail for years without really noticing them. But now they were important. They meant the difference between losing their home and getting it back again.

She sat on pins and needles over the weekend, until Kemp heard from the private detective the following Monday afternoon.

He buzzed Libby and told her to come into the office.

He was smiling when she got there. "We found them," he said, chuckling when she made a whoop loud enough to bring Mabel down the hall.

"It's okay," Libby told her coworker, "I've just had some good news for a change!"

Mabel grinned and went back to work.

Libby sat down in the chair in front of Kemp's big desk, smiling and leaning forward.

"Your father left the coins with a dealer who locked them in his safe. He was told not to let Janet have them under any circumstances," he added gently. "Besides that, there was a will. He's got that, too. It's not a self-made will, either. It was done by a lawyer in the dealer's office and witnessed by two people who work for him."

Libby's eyes filled with tears. "Daddy knew! He knew she was trying to cut us out of the will!"

"He must have," he conceded. "Apparently she'd made some comments about what she was going to do when he died. And she'd been harassing him about his health, making remarks about his heart being weak, as well." His jaw clenched. "Whatever the cause, he changed the will in your favor—yours and Curt's. This will is going to stand up in a court of law and it changes the entire financial situation. You and Curt can go home and I'll get the will into probate immediately."

"But the insurance…"

He nodded. "She was the beneficiary for *one* of his insurance policies." He smiled at her surprise. "There's another one, a half-a-million dollar policy, that he left with the same dealer who has the will. You and Curt are co-beneficiaries."

"He didn't contact us!" she exclaimed suddenly.

"Yes, and that's the interesting part," he said. "He tried to contact you and Janet told him that you and Curt were out of the country on an extended vacation. She planned to go and talk to him the very day you made the remarks about

Violet's father and having locks put on your bedroom doors. She ran for her life before she had time to try to get to the rest of your inheritance." He chuckled. "Maybe she had some idea of what the seller was guarding and decided that the insurance policy would hold her for a while without risking arrest."

"Oh, thank God," she whispered, shivering with delight. "Thank God! We can go home!"

"Apparently," he agreed, smiling. "I'm going to drive up to San Antonio today and get those documents and the coin collection."

She was suddenly concerned. "But what if Janet hears about it? She had that friend in San Antonio who called and tried to get us off the property…" She stopped abruptly. "That's why they were trying to get us out of the house! They knew about the coin collection!" She sat back heavily. "But they could be dangerous…."

"Cash Grier is going with me."

She pursed her lips amusedly. "Okay."

He chuckled. "Nobody is going to try to attack me with Grier in the car. Even if he isn't armed."

"Good point," she agreed.

"So call your brother and tell him the news," he said. "And stop worrying. You're going to land on your feet, Libby."

"How's Violet?" she asked without thinking.

He stood up, his hands deep in his pockets. "She and her mother are distraught, as you might imagine. They never realized that Mr. Hardy had been the victim of foul play. I've tried to keep it out of the papers, but when Janet's caught, it's going to be difficult."

"Is there anything I can do?"

He smiled. "Take them a pizza and let Violet talk to you about it," he suggested. "She misses working here."

"I miss her, too."

He shifted, averting his gaze. "I offered to let her come back to work here."

"You did?" she asked, enthused.

"She's going to think about it," he added. "You might, uh, tell her how short-handed we are here, and that the temporary woman we got had to quit. Maybe she'll feel sorry for us and come back."

She smiled. "I'll do my best."

He looked odd. "Thanks," he said stiffly.

Chapter Nine

The very next day, Kemp came into the office grinning like a lottery winner. He was carrying a cardboard box, in which was a mahogany box full of rare gold coins, an insurance policy, a few personal items that had belonged to Riddle Collins and a fully executed new will.

Libby had to sit down when Kemp presented her with the hard evidence of her father's love for herself and Curt.

"The will is legal," he told her. "I'm going to take it right to the courthouse and file it. It will supercede the will that Janet probably still has in her possession. You should take the coins to the bank and put them in a safe-deposit box until you're ready to dispose of them. The dealer said he'll buy them from you at market value any time you're ready to sell them."

"But I'll have to use them as collateral for a loan to make the loan payment..."

"Actually, no, you won't," Kemp said with a smile, drawing two green-covered passbooks out of the box and handing them to her.

"What are these?" she asked blankly.

"Your father had two other bank accounts, both in San Antonio." He smiled warmly. "There's more than enough there to pay off the mortgage completely so that the ranch is free and clear. You'll still have a small fortune left over. You and your brother are going to be rich, Libby. Congratulations."

She cried a little, both for her father's loving care of them even after death and for having come so close to losing everything.

She pulled a tissue out of the pocket of her slacks and wiped her red eyes. "I'll take these to the Jacobsville Municipal Bank right now," she said firmly, "and have the money transferred here from San Antonio. Then I'll have them issue a cashier's check to pay off the other bank," she added with glee.

"Good girl. You can phone the insurance company about the death benefit, too. How does it feel, not to have to worry about money?"

She chuckled. "Very good." She eyed him curiously. "Does this mean you're firing me?"

"Well, Libby, you won't really need to work for a living anymore," he began slowly.

"But I love my job!" she exclaimed, and had the pleasure of watching his high cheekbones go ruddy. "Can't I stay?"

He drew in a long breath. "I'd be delighted if you would," he confessed. "I can't seem to keep a paralegal these days."

She smiled, remembering that Callie Kirby had been one, until she'd married Micah Steele. There had been two others after her, but neither had stayed long.

"Then it's settled. I have to go and call Curt!"

"Go to the bank first, Libby," he instructed with a grin.

"And I'll get to the courthouse. Mabel, we're going to be out of the office for thirty minutes!"

"Okay, boss!"

They went down the hall together and they stopped dead.

Violet was back at her desk, across from a grinning Mabel, looking radiant. "You said I could come back," she told Kemp at once, looking pretty and uncertain at the same time.

He drew in a sharp breath and his eyes lingered on her. "I certainly did," he agreed. "Are you staying?"

She nodded.

"How about making a fresh pot of coffee?" he asked.

"Regular?" she asked.

He averted his gaze to the door. "Half and half," he murmured. "Caffeine isn't good for me."

He went out the door, leaving Violet's jaw dropped.

"I told you he missed you," Libby whispered as she followed Kemp out the door and onto the sidewalk.

Libby and Curt were able to go home the next morning. But their arrival was bittersweet. The house had been ransacked in their absence.

"We'd better call the sheriff's office," Curt said angrily, when they'd ascertained that the disorder was thorough. "We'll need to have a report filed on this for insurance purposes."

"Do we even have insurance?"

He nodded. "Dad had a homeowner's policy. I've been keeping up the payments, remember?"

She righted a chair that had been turned over next to the desk her father had used in his study. The filling cabinet had been emptied onto the floor, along with a lot of other documents pertaining to the ranch's business.

"They were looking for that coin collection," Curt

guessed as he picked up the phone. ''I'll bet anything Janet knew about it. She must be running short of cash already!''

''Thank God Mr. Kemp was able to track it down,'' she said.

''Sheriff's department?'' Curt said into the telephone receiver. ''I need you to send someone out to the Collins ranch. That's right, it's just past Jordan Powell's place. We've had a burglary. Yes. Okay. Thanks!'' He hung up. ''I talked to Hayes. He's going to come himself, along with his investigator.''

''I thought he was overseas with his army unit in Iraq,'' she commented.

''He's back.'' He glanced at her amusedly. ''You used to have a case on him, just before you went nuts over Jordan Powell.''

She hated hearing Jordan's name mentioned. ''Hayes is nice.''

''So he is.'' He toyed with the telephone cord. ''Libby, Jordan's having some bad times lately. His association with the Merrills has made him enemies.''

''That was his choice,'' she reminded her brother.

''He was good to us, when Dad died.''

She knew that. It didn't help. Her memories of Jordan's betrayal were too fresh. ''Think I should do anything before they get here?''

''Make coffee,'' he suggested dryly. ''Hayes's investigator is Mack Hughes, and he lives on caffeine.''

''I'll do that.''

Sheriff Hayes Carson pulled up at the front steps in his car, a brightly polished black vehicle with all sorts of antennae sticking out of it. The investigator, Mack Hughes, pulled up beside it in his black SUV with a deck of lights on the roof.

"Thanks for coming so quickly," Curt said, shaking hands with both men. "You remember my sister, Libby."

"Hello, Elizabeth," Hayes said with a grin, having always used her real first name instead of the nickname most people called her by. He was dashing, with blond hair and dark eyes, tall and muscular and big. He was in his midthirties; one tough customer, too. He and Cash Grier often went head-to-head in disputes, although they were good colleagues when there was an emergency.

"Hi, Hayes," she replied with a smile. "Hello, Mack."

Mack, tall and dark, nodded politely. "Let's see what you've got."

They ushered the law enforcement officers inside and stood back while they went about searching for clues.

"Any idea who the perpetrators were?" Hayes murmured while Mack looked around.

"Someone connected to our stepmother, most likely," Libby commented. "Dad had a very expensive coin collection and some secret bank accounts that even we didn't know about. If that's what they were looking for, they're out of luck. Mr. Kemp tracked them to San Antonio. Everything's in the bank now and a new will we recovered is in the proper hands."

Hayes whistled softly. "Lucky for you."

There was a sudden commotion in the front yard, made by a truck skidding to a stop between the two law enforcement vehicles. A dusty, tired Jordan Powell came up the steps, taking them two at a time, and stopped abruptly in the living room.

"What's happened?" he asked at once, his eyes homing to Libby with dark concern.

"The house was ransacked," Hayes told him. "Have you seen anything suspicious?"

"No. But I'll ask my men," Jordan assured them. He looked at Libby for a long time. "You okay?"

"Curt and I are fine, thanks," she said in a polite but reserved tone.

Jordan looked around at the jumble of furniture and paper on the floor, along with lamps and broken pieces of ceramic items that had been on the mantel over the fireplace.

"This wasn't necessary," Jordan said grimly. "Even if they were looking for something, they didn't have to break everything in the house."

"It was malicious, all right," Hayes agreed. He moved just in front of Libby. "I heard from Grier that you've had two confrontations with Julie Merrill, one of them physically violent. She's also been implicated in acts of vandalism. I want to know if you think she might have had any part in this."

Libby glanced at Jordan apprehensively.

"It could be a possibility," Jordan said, to her dismay. "She was jealous of Libby and I've just broken with Julie and her father. She didn't take it well."

"I'll add her to the list of suspects," Hayes said quietly. "But I have to tell you, she isn't going to like being accused."

"I don't care," Curt replied, answering for himself as well as Libby. "Nobody has a right to do something like this."

"Boss!" Mack called from the back porch. "Could you ask the Collinses to come out here, please?"

Curt stood aside to let Libby go first. On the small back stoop, Mack was squatting down, looking at a big red gas can. "This yours?" he asked Curt.

Curt frowned. "We don't have one that big," he replied. "Ours is locked up in the outbuilding next to the barn."

Mack and Hayes exchanged curious looks.

"There's an insurance policy on the house," Libby remarked worriedly. "It's got Janet, our stepmother, listed as beneficiary."

"That narrows down the suspects," Hayes remarked.

"Surely she wouldn't…" Libby began.

"You've made a lot of trouble for her," Jordan said grimly. "And now she's missed out on two savings accounts and a will that she didn't even know existed."

"How did you know that?" Libby asked belligerently.

"My cousin owns the Municipal Bank," Jordan said nonchalantly.

"He had no business telling you anything!" Libby protested.

"He didn't, exactly," Jordan confessed. "I heard him talking to one of his clerks about opening the new account for you and setting up a safe-deposit box."

"Eavesdropping should be against the law," she muttered.

"I'll make a note of it," Hayes said with a grin.

She grinned back. "Thanks, Hayes."

He told Mack to start marking evidence to be collected. "We'll see if we can lift any latent prints," he told the small group. "If it was Janet, or someone she hired, they'll probably have been wearing gloves. If it was Julie Merrill, we might get lucky."

"I hope we can connect somebody to it," Libby said wearily, looking around. "If for no other reason than to make them pay to help have this mess cleaned up!"

"I'll take care of that," Jordan said at once, and reached for his cell phone.

"We don't need—!" Libby began hotly.

But Jordan wasn't listening. He was talking to Amie at his ranch, instructing her to phone two housekeepers she knew who helped her with heavy tasks and send them over to the Collins place.

"You might as well give up," Hayes remarked dryly.

"Once Jordan gets the bit between his teeth, it would take a shotgun to stop him. You know that."

She sighed angrily. "Yes. I know."

Hayes pushed his wide-brimmed hat back off his forehead and smiled down at Libby. "Are you doing anything Saturday night?" he asked. "They're having a campaign rally for Calhoun's supporters at Shea's."

"I know, I'm one of them," she replied, smiling. "Are you going to be there?"

He shrugged. "I might as well. Somebody'll have a beer too many and pick a fight, I don't doubt. Tiny the bouncer will have his hands full."

"Great!" she said enthusiastically.

Jordan was eavesdropping and not liking what he heard. He wanted to tell Hayes to back off. He wanted to tell Libby what he felt. But he couldn't get the words out.

"If you two are moving back in," Hayes added, "I think we'd better have somebody around overnight. I've got two volunteer deputies in the Sheriff's Posse who would be willing, I expect, if you'll keep them in coffee."

She smiled. "I'd be delighted. Thanks, Hayes. It would make me feel secure. We've got a shotgun, but I don't even know where it is."

"You could both stay with me until Hayes gets a handle on who did this," Jordan volunteered.

"No, thanks," Libby said quietly, trying not to remember that Jordan had already asked her to do that. No matter how she felt about the big idiot, she wasn't going to step into Julie Merrill's place.

"This is our home," Curt added.

Jordan drew in a long, sad breath. "Okay. But if you need help…"

"We'll call Hayes, thanks," Libby said, turning back to the sheriff. "I need to tidy up the kitchen. Is it all right?"

Hayes went with her into the small room and looked

around. There wasn't much damage in there and nothing was broken. "It looks okay. Go ahead, Libby. I'll see you Saturday, then?"

She grinned up at him. "Of course."

He grinned back and then rejoined the men in the living room. "I'm going to talk to my volunteers," he told Curt. "I'll be in touch."

"Thanks a lot, Hayes," Curt replied.

"Just doing my job. See you, Jordan."

"Yeah." Jordan didn't offer to shake hands. He glared after the other man as he went out the front door.

"I can clean my own house," Libby began impatiently.

Jordan met her eyes evenly. "I've made a lot of mistakes. I've done a lot of damage. I know I can't make it up to you in one fell swoop, but let me do what I can to make amends. Will you?"

Libby looked at her brother, who shrugged and walked away, leaving her to deal with Jordan alone.

"Some help you are," Libby muttered at his retreating back.

"I don't like the idea of that gas can," Jordan said, ignoring her statement. "You can't stay awake twenty-four hours a day. If Janet is really desperate enough to set fire to the house trying to get her hands on the insurance money, neither you nor Curt is going to be safe here."

"Hayes is getting us some protection," she replied coolly.

"I know that. But even deputies have to use the bathroom occasionally," he said flatly. "Why won't you come home with me?"

She lifted her chin. "This is my place, mine and Curt's. We're not running anymore."

He sighed. "I admire your courage, Libby. But it's misplaced this time."

She turned away. "I've got a lot to do, Jordan. Thanks anyway."

He caught her small waist from behind and held her just in front of him. His warm breath stirred the hair at the back of her head. "I was afraid."

"Of…what?" she asked, startled.

His big hands contracted. "You're very young, even for a woman your age," he said stiffly. "Young women are constantly changing."

She turned in his hold, curious. She looked up at him without understanding. "What has that got to do with anything?"

He reached out and traced her mouth with his thumb. He looked unusually solemn. "You really don't know, do you?" he asked quietly. "That's part of the problem."

"You aren't making any sense."

"I am. You're just not hearing what I'm saying." He bent and kissed her softly beside her ear, drawing away almost at once. "Never mind. You'll figure it out one day. Meanwhile, I'm going to do a better job of looking after you."

"I can—"

He interrupted at once. "If you say 'look after myself,' so help me, I'll…!"

She glared at him.

He glared back.

"You're up against someone formidable, whoever it is," he continued. "I'm not letting anything happen to you, Libby."

"Fat lot you cared before," she muttered.

He sighed heavily. "Yes, I know. I'll eat crow without catsup if it will help you trust me again."

"Julie's very pretty," she said reluctantly.

"She isn't a patch on you, butterfly," he said quietly.

She hesitated. But she wasn't giving in easily. He'd hurt

her. No way was she going to run headfirst into his arms the first time he opened them.

She watched him suspiciously.

His broad chest rose and fell. "Okay. We'll do it your way. I'll see you at Shea's."

"You're the enemy," she pointed out. "You're not on Calhoun's team."

He shrugged. "A man can change sides, can't he?" he mused. "Meanwhile, if you need me, I'll be at the house. If you call, I'll come running."

She nodded slowly. "All right."

He smiled at her.

Curt came back in. He was as cool to Jordan as his sister. The older man shrugged and left without another word.

"Now he's changed sides again," Libby told Curt when Jordan was gone.

"Jordan's feeling his age, Libby," Curt told her. "And some comments were made by his cowboys about that kiss they saw."

Her eyebrows arched. "What?"

He sighed. "I never had the heart to tell you. But one of the older hands said Jordan was trying to rob the cradle. It enraged Jordan. But it made him think, too. He knows how sheltered you've been. I think he was trying to protect you."

"From what?"

"Maybe from a relationship he didn't think you were ready for," he replied. "Julie was handy, he'd dated her a time or two, and she swarmed all over him just about the time he was drawing back from you. I expect he was flattered by her attention and being invited into that highbrow social set that shut out his mother after she was disinherited because she married his father. The local society women just turned their backs on her. She was never invited anywhere ever again. Jordan felt it keenly, that some of his playmates weren't allowed to invite him to their houses.''

''I didn't know it was so hard on him. He's only told me bits and pieces about his upbringing.''

''He doesn't advertise it,'' he added. ''She gave up everything to marry his father. She worked as a housekeeper in one of the motels owned by her father's best friend. It was a rough upbringing for Jordan.''

''I can imagine.'' She sighed, unable to prevent her heart from thawing.

Shea's was filled to capacity on Saturday evening. Cash Grier got a lot of attention because he brought Tippy with him. She looked good despite her ordeals, except for the small indications of healing cuts on her lovely face. She was weak and still not totally recovered and it showed. Nevertheless, she was still the most beautiful woman in the room. But she had eyes only for Cash and that showed, too.

When they got on the dance floor together, Libby was embarrassed to find herself staring wistfully at them. Tippy melted into Cash's tall body as if she'd found heaven. He looked that way as well. They clung together to the sound of an old love song. And when she looked up at him, he actually stopped dancing and just stared at her.

''They make a nice couple,'' Jordan said from behind her.

She glanced up at him. He looked odd. His dark eyes were quiet, intent on her uplifted face.

''Yes, they do,'' she replied. ''They seem to fit together very well.''

He nodded. ''Dance with me,'' he said in a deep voice, and drew her into his arms.

She hesitated, but only for a few seconds. She'd built dreams on those kisses they'd shared and she thought it was all over. But the way he was holding her made her knees weak. His big hand covered hers against his chest and pressed it hard into the warm muscle.

"I've been an idiot," he said at her ear.

"What do you mean?" she wondered aloud, drugged by his closeness.

"I shouldn't have backed off," he replied quietly. "I got cold feet at the very worst time."

"Jordan…"

"…mind if I cut in?" Hayes Carson asked with a grin.

Jordan stopped, his mind still in limbo. "We were talking," he began.

"Plenty of time for that later. Shall we, Libby?" he asked, and moved right in front of Jordan. He danced Libby away before she had a chance to stop him.

"Now that's what I call a jealous man," Hayes murmured dryly, glancing over her shoulder at Jordan. "No need to ask about the lay of the land."

"Jordan doesn't feel that way about me," Libby protested.

"He doesn't?"

She averted her eyes to the crowded dance floor. "He isn't a marrying man."

"Uh-huh."

She glanced up at Hayes, who was still grinning.

She flushed at the look in his eyes.

Across the room, Jordan Powell saw that flush and had to restrain himself from going over there and tearing Libby out of Hayes's embrace.

"What the devil are you doing here?" Calhoun Ballenger asked abruptly.

Jordan glanced at him wryly. "Not much," he murmured. "But I came to ask if you needed another willing ally. I've, uh, changed camps."

Calhoun's eyebrows went up almost to his blond hairline.

"I do like to be on the winning side," Jordan drawled.

Calhoun burst out laughing. "Well, you're not a bad diplomat, I guess," he confessed, holding out his hand. "Welcome aboard."

"My pleasure."

Jordan contrived to drive Libby and Curt home, but he was careful to let Curt go into the ranch house before he cut off the engine and turned to Libby.

"There's been some news," he said carefully.

"About Janet?" she exclaimed.

"About Julie," he corrected. He toyed with a strand of her hair in the dim light of the car interior. "One of Grier's men saw her with a known drug dealer earlier today. She's put her neck in a noose and she doesn't even know it."

"She uses, doesn't she?" she asked.

He shrugged. "Her behavior is erratic. She must."

"I'm sorry. You liked her..."

He bent and kissed her hungrily, pulling her across his lap to wrap her up in his warm, strong arms. "I like you," he whispered against her mouth. "More than I ever dreamed I could!"

She wanted to ask questions, but she couldn't kiss him and breathe at the same time. She gave up and ran her arms up around his neck. She relaxed into his close embrace and kissed him back until her mouth grew sore and swollen.

He sighed into her throat as he held her and rocked her in his arms in the warm darkness.

"Libby, I think we should start going out together."

She blinked. "You and me?"

He nodded. "You and me." He drew back and looked down at her possessively. "I could give up liver and onions, if I had to. But I can't give you up."

"Listen, I don't have affairs..."

He kissed her into silence. "Neither do I. So I guess maybe we won't sleep together after all."

"But if we go out together…" she worried.

He grinned. "You have enough self-restraint for both of us, I'm sure," he drawled. "You can keep me honest."

She drew back a little and noted the position of his big lean hands under her blouse. She looked at him intently.

He cleared his throat and drew his hands out from under the blouse. "Every man is entitled to one little slip. Right?" His eyes were twinkling.

She laughed. "Okay."

He touched her mouth with his one last time. "In that case, you'd better rush inside before I forget to be honest."

"Thanks for bringing us home."

"My pleasure. Lock the doors," he added seriously. "And I'm only a phone call away if you need me. You call me," he emphasized. "Not Hayes Carson. Got that?"

"And since when did I become your personal property?" she asked haughtily.

"Since the minute you let me put my hands under your blouse," he shot right back, laughing. "Think about it."

She got out of the vehicle, dizzy and with her head swimming. In one night, everything had changed.

"Don't worry," he added gently, leaning out the window. "I have enough restraint for both of us!"

Before she could answer him, he gunned the engine and took off down the road.

Chapter Ten

For the next few days, Jordan was at Libby's house more than at his own. He smoothed over hard feelings with her brother and became a household fixture. Libby and Curt filed the insurance claim, paid off the mortgage, and started repurchasing cattle for the small ranch.

Janet was found a couple of days later at a motel just outside San Antonio, with a man. He turned out to be the so-called attorney who'd phoned and tried to get Libby and Curt out of their home. She was arrested and charged with murder in the death of Violet's father. There was DNA evidence taken from the dead man's clothing and the motel room that was directly linked to Janet. It placed her at the motel the night Mr. Hardy died. When she realized the trouble she was in, she tried to make a deal for a reduced sentence. She agreed to confess to the murder in return for a life sentence without hope of parole. But she denied having a gas can. She swore that she never had plans to burn down Riddle Collins's house with his children in it. Nobody paid her much attention. She'd told so many lies.

It was a different story for Julie Merrill. She continued

to make trouble, and not only for Calhoun Ballenger. She was determined that Jordan wasn't going to desert her for little Libby Collins. She had a plan. Two days before the hearing to decide the fate of the police officers who'd arrested her father— Saturday, she put it into practice.

She phoned Libby at work and apologized profusely for all the trouble she'd caused.

"I never meant to be such a pain in the neck," she assured Libby. "I want to make it up to you. You get off at one on Saturdays, don't you? Suppose you come over here for lunch?"

"To your house?" Libby replied warily.

"Yes. I've had our cook make something special," she purred. "And I can tell you my side of the story. Will you?"

Dubious, Libby hesitated.

"Surely you aren't afraid of me?" Julie drawled. "I mean, what could I do to you, even if I had something terrible in mind?"

"You don't need to feed me," Libby replied cautiously. "I don't hold grudges."

"You'll come, then," Julie persisted. "Today at one. Will you?"

It was against her better judgment. But it wasn't a bad idea to keep a feud going, especially now that Jordan seemed really interested in her.

"Okay," Libby said finally. "I'll be there at one."

"Thanks!" Julie said huskily. "You don't know how much I appreciate it! Uh, I don't guess you'd like to bring your brother, too?" she added suddenly.

Libby frowned. "Curt's driving a cattle truck for Duke Wright up to San Antonio today."

"Well, then, another time, perhaps! I'll see you at one." Julie hung up, with a bright and happy note in her voice.

Libby frowned. Was she stupid to go to the woman's home? But why would Julie risk harming her now, with the primary election so close? It was the following Tuesday.

She phoned Jordan. "Guess what just happened?" she asked.

"You've realized how irresistible I am and you're rushing over to seduce me?" he teased. "Shall I turn down the covers on my bed?"

"Stop that," she muttered. "I'm serious."

"So am I!"

"Jordan," she laughed. "Julie just called to apologize. She invited me to lunch."

"Did she?" he asked. "Are you going?"

"I thought I might." She hesitated. "Don't you think it's a good idea, to mend fences, I mean?"

"I don't know, Libby," he replied seriously. "She's been erratic and out of control lately. I don't think it's a good idea. I'd rather you didn't."

"Are you afraid she might tell me something about you that I don't know?" she returned, suspicious.

He sighed. "No. It's not that. She wasn't happy when I broke off with her. I don't trust her."

"What can she do to me in broad daylight?" she laughed. "Shoot me?"

"Of course not," he scoffed.

"Then stop worrying. She only wants to apologize."

"You be careful," he returned. "And phone me when you get home. Okay?"

"Okay."

"How about a movie tonight?" he added. "There's a new mystery at the theater. You can even have popcorn."

"That sounds nice," she said, feeling warm and secure.

"I'll pick you up about six."

"I'll be ready. See you then."

She hung and pondered over his misgivings. Surely he was overreacting. He was probably afraid Julie might make up a convincing lie about how intimate they'd been. Or perhaps she might be telling the truth. She only knew that she had to find out why Julie wanted to see her in person. She was going.

But something niggled at the back of her mind when she drove toward Julie's palatial home on the Jacobs River. Julie might have wanted to invite Libby over to apologize, but why would she want Curt to come, too? She didn't even know Curt.

Libby's foot lifted off the accelerator. Her home was next door to Jordan's. Julie was furious that Jordan had broken off with her. If the house was gone, Libby and Curt would have to move away again, as they had before…!

Libby turned the truck around in the middle of the road and sped toward her house. She wished she had a cell phone. There was no way to call for help. But she was absolutely certain what was about to happen. And she knew immediately that her stepmother hadn't been responsible for that gas can on the porch.

The question was, who had Julie convinced to set that fire for her? Or would she be crazy enough to try and do it herself?

Libby sped faster down the road. If only there had been state police, a sheriff's deputy, a policeman watching. She was speeding. It was the only time in her life she'd ever wanted to be caught!

But there were no flashing lights, no sirens. She was going to have to try and stop the perpetrator all by herself. She wasn't a big woman. She had no illusions about being able to tackle a grown man. She didn't even have a weapon. Wait. There was a tire tool in the boot! At least, she could threaten with it.

She turned into the road that led to the house. There was no smoke visible anywhere and no sign of any traffic. For the first time, she realized that she could be chasing make-believe villains. Why would she think that Julie Merrill would try to burn her house down? Maybe the strain of the past weeks was making her hysterical after all.

She pulled up in front of the house and got out, grabbing the tire tool out of the back. It wouldn't hurt to look around, now that she was here.

She moved around the side of the house, her heart beating wildly. Her palms were so sweaty that she had to get a better grip on the tire tool. She walked past the chimney, to the corner, and peered around. Her heart stopped.

There was a man there. A young, dark man. He had a can of gasoline. He was muttering to himself as he sloshed it on the back porch and the steps.

Libby closed her eyes and prayed for strength. There was nobody to help her. She had to do this alone.

She walked around the corner with the tire tool raised. "That's enough, you varmint! You're trespassing on private property and you're going to jail. The police are right behind me!"

Startled, the man dropped the gas can and stared wild-eyed at Libby.

Sensing an advantage, she started to run toward him, yelling at the top of her lungs.

To her amazement, he started running down a path behind the house, with Libby right on his heels, still yelling.

Then something happened that was utterly in the realm of fantasy. She heard an engine behind her. An accomplice, she wondered, almost panicking.

Jordan Powell pulled up right beside her in his truck and threw open the passenger door. "Get in!" he called.

She didn't need prompting. She jumped right in beside him, tire tool and all, and slammed the door. "He was dousing the back porch with gas!" she panted. "Don't let him get away!"

"I don't intend to." His face was grim as he stood down

on the accelerator and the truck shot forward on the pasture road, which was no more than tracks through tall grass.

The attempted arsonist was tiring. He was pretty thick in the middle and had short legs. He was almost to a beat-up old car sitting out of sight of the house near the barn when Jordan came alongside him on the driver's side.

"Hold it in the ruts!" he called to Libby.

Just as she grabbed the wheel, he threw open the door and leaped out on the startled, breathless young man, pinning him to the ground.

By the time Libby had the truck stopped, Jordan had the man by his shirt collar and was holding him there.

"Pick up the phone and call Hayes," he called to Libby.

Her hands were shaking, but she managed to dial 911 and give the dispatcher an abbreviated account of what had just happened. She was told that they contacted a deputy who was barely a mile away and he was starting toward the Collins place at that moment.

Libby thanked her nicely and cut off the phone.

"Who put you up to this?" Jordan demanded of the man. "Tell me, or so help me, I'll make sure you don't get out of prison until you're an old man!"

"It was Miss Julie," the young man sobbed. "I never done nothing like this in my life. My daddy works for her and he took some things out of her house. She said she'd turn him over to the police if I didn't do this for her."

"She'd have turned him over anyway, you fool," Jordan said coldly. "She was using you. Do you have any idea what the penalty is for arson?"

He was still sobbing. "I was scared, Mr. Powell."

Jordan relented, but only a little. He looked up as the sound of a siren was heard coming closer.

Libby opened the door of the truck and got out, just as a sheriff's car came flying down the track and stopped just behind the truck.

The deputy was Sammy Tibbs. They both knew him. He'd been in Libby's class in high school.

"What have you got, Jordan?" Sammy asked.

"A would-be arsonist," Jordan told him. "He'll confess if you ask him."

"I caught him pouring gas on my back porch and I chased him with my tire tool. I almost had him when Jordan came along," Libby said with a shy grin.

"Whew," Sammy whistled. "I hope I don't ever run afoul of you," he told her.

"That makes two of us," Jordan said, with a gentle smile for her.

"I assume you'll be pressing charges?" Sammy asked Libby as he handcuffed the young man, who was still out of breath.

"You can bet real money on it," Libby agreed. "And you'll need to pick up Julie Merrill as well, because this man said she told him to do it."

Sammy's hands froze on the handcuffs. "Julie Merrill? The state senator's daughter?"

"That's exactly who I mean," Libby replied. "She called and invited me over to lunch. Since she doesn't like me, I got suspicious and came home instead, just in time to catch this weasel in the act."

"Is this true?" the deputy asked the man.

"Mirandize him first," Jordan suggested. "Just so there won't be any loopholes."

"Good idea," Sammy agreed, and read the suspect his rights.

"Now, tell him," Libby prodded, glaring at the man who'd been within a hair of burning her house down.

The young man sighed as if the weight of the world was sitting on his shoulders. "Miss Merrill had something on my daddy, who works for her. She said if I'd set a fire on Miss Collins's back steps, she'd forget all about it. She just wanted to scare Miss Collins is all. She didn't tell me to burn the whole place down.''

"Arson is arson," Sammy replied. "Don't touch anything," he told Libby. "I'll send our investigator back out there and call the state fire marshal. Arson is hard to prove, but this one's going to be a walk in the park."

"Thanks, Sammy," Libby said.

He grinned. "What for? You caught him!"

He put the scared suspect in the back of his car and sped off with a wave of his hand.

"That was too damned close," Jordan said, looking down at Libby with tormented eyes. "I couldn't believe it when I saw you chasing him through the field with a tire iron! What if he'd been armed?"

"He wasn't," she said. "Besides, he ran the minute I chased him, just like a black snake."

He pulled her into his arms and wrapped her up tight. There was a faint tremor in those strong arms.

"You brave idiot," he murmured into her neck. "Thank God he didn't get the fire started first. I can see you running inside to grab all the sentimental items and save them. You'd have been burned alive."

She grimaced, because he was absolutely right. She'd have tried to save her mementos of her father and mother, at any cost.

"Libby, I think we'd better get engaged," he said suddenly.

She was hallucinating. She said so.

He pulled back from her, his eyes solemn. "You're not hallucinating. If Julie realizes how serious this is between us, she'll back off."

"She's going to be in jail shortly, she'll have to," she pointed out.

"They can afford bail until her hearing, even so," he replied. "She'll be out for blood. But if she hears about the engagement, it might be enough to make her think twice."

"I'm not afraid of her," she said, although she really was.

"Humor me," he coaxed, bending to kiss her gently.

She smiled under the warm, comforting feel of his hard mouth on her lips. "Well…"

He nibbled her upper lip. "I'll get you a ring," he whispered.

"What sort?"

"What do you want?"

"I like emeralds," she whispered, standing on tiptoe to coax his mouth down again.

"An emerald, then."

"Nobody would know?"

He chuckled as he kissed her. "We might have to tell a few hundred people, just to make it believable. And we might actually have to get married, but that's okay, isn't it?"

She blinked. "Get…married?"

"That's what the ring's for, Libby," he said against her warm mouth. "Advance notice."

"But…you've always said you never wanted to get married."

"I always said there's the one woman a man can't walk away from," he added. He lifted his head and looked down at her, all the teasing gone. "I can't walk away from you. The past few weeks have been pure hell."

Her eyes widened with unexpected delight.

He traced her eyebrows with his forefinger. "I missed you," he whispered. "It was like being cut apart."

"You wanted Julie," she accused.

He grimaced. "I wanted you to think about what was happening. You've been sheltered your whole life. Duke Wright's wife was just like you. Then she married and had a child and got career-minded. That poor devil lives in hell because she didn't know what she wanted until it was too late!"

She searched his face quietly. "You think I'd want a career."

"I don't know, Libby," he bit off. He looked anguished. "I'm an all-or-nothing kind of man. I can't just stick my toe in to test the water. I jump in headfirst."

He...loved her. She was stunned. She couldn't believe she hadn't noticed, in all this time. Curt had seen it long before this. He'd tried to tell her. But she hadn't believed that a man like Jordan could be serious about someone like her.

Her lips fell apart with a husky sigh. She was on fire. She'd never dreamed that life could be so sweet. "I don't want a career," she said slowly.

"What if you do, someday?" he persisted.

She reached up and traced his firm, jutting chin with her fingertips. "I'm twenty-four years old, Jordan," she said. "If I don't know my own mind by now, I never will."

He still looked undecided.

She put both hands flat on his shirt. Under it, she could feel the muted thunder of his heartbeat. "Why don't we go to a movie?" she asked.

He seemed to relax. He smiled. "We could grab a hamburger for lunch and talk about it," he prompted.

"Okay."

"Then we'll go by the sheriff's department and you can write out a statement," he added.

She grimaced. "I guess I'll have to."

He nodded. "So will I." His eyes narrowed. "I wish I could see the look on Julie's face when the deputy sheriff pulls up in her driveway."

"I imagine she'll be surprised," Libby replied.

Surprised was an understatement. Julie Merrill gaped at the young man in the deputy sheriff's uniform.

"You're joking," she said haughtily. "I...I had nothing to do with any attempted arson!"

"We have a man in custody who'll swear to it," he replied. "You can come peacefully or you can go out the door in handcuffs," he added, still pleasant and respectful. "Your choice, Miss Merrill."

She let out a harsh breath. "This is outrageous!"

"What's going on out here?" Her father, the state senator, came into the hall, weaving a little, and blinked when he saw the deputy. "What's he doing here?" he murmured.

"Your daughter is under arrest, senator," he was told as the deputy suddenly turned Julie around and cuffed her with professional dexterity. "For conspiracy to commit arson."

"Arson?" The senator blinked. "Julie?"

"She sent a man to burn down the Collins place," he was told. "We have two eyewitnesses as well."

The senator gaped at his daughter. "I told you to leave that woman alone," he said, shaking his finger at her. "I told you Jordan would get involved if you didn't! You've cost me the election! Everybody around here will go to the polls Tuesday and vote for Calhoun Ballenger! You've ruined me!"

"Oh, no, sir, she hasn't," the deputy assured him with a grin. "Your nephew, the mayor, did that, by persecuting two police officers who were just doing their jobs." The smile faded. "You're going to see Monday night just how much hot water you've jumped into. That disciplinary hearing is going to be remembered for the next century in Jacobsville."

"Where are you taking my daughter?" the senator snorted.

"To jail, to be booked. You can call your attorney and arrange for a bail hearing whenever you like," the deputy added, with a speaking glance at the older man's condition. "If you're able."

"I'll call my own attorney," Julie said hotly. "Then I'll sue you for false arrest!"

"You're welcome to try," the deputy said. "Come along, Miss Merrill."

"Daddy, do try to sober up!" Julie said scathingly.

"What would be the point?" the senator replied. "Life was so good when I didn't know all about you, Julie. When I thought you were a sweet, kind, innocent woman like your mother…" He closed his eyes. "You killed that girl!"

"I did not! Think what you're saying!" Julie yelled at him.

Tears poured down his cheeks. "She died in my arms…"

"Let's go," the deputy said, tugging Julie Merrill out the door. He closed it on the sobbing politician.

Julie Merrill was lodged in the county jail until her bail hearing the following Monday morning. Meanwhile, Jordan and Libby had given their statements and the would-be arsonist was singing like a canary bird.

The disciplinary hearing for Chief Grier's two police officers was Monday night at the city council meeting.

It didn't take long. Within thirty minutes, the Council had finished its usual business, Grier's officers were cleared of any misconduct, and the surprise guests at the hearing had Jacobsville buzzing for weeks afterward.

Chapter Eleven

Jordan drove Libby to his house in a warm silence. He led her into the big, elegant living room and closed the door behind them.

"Want something to drink?" he asked, moving to a pitcher of iced tea that Amie had apparently left for them, along with a plate of homemade cake, covered with foil. "And a piece of pound cake?"

"I'd love that," she agreed.

He poured tea into two glasses and handed them to her, along with doilies to protect the coffee table from spots. He put cake onto two plates, with forks, and brought them along. But as he bent over the coffee table, he obscured Libby's plate. When he sat down beside her, there was a beautiful emerald solitaire, set in gold, lying on her piece of cake.

"Look at that," he exclaimed with twinkling dark eyes. "Why, it's an engagement ring! I wonder who could have put it there?" he drawled.

She picked it up, breathless. "It's beautiful."

"Isn't it?" he mused. "Why don't you try it on? If it fits," he added slyly, "you might turn into a fairy princess and get your own true prince as a prize!"

She smiled through her breathless delight. "Think so?"

"Darlin', I can almost guarantee it," he replied tenderly. "Want to give it a shot?"

He seemed to hold his breath while he waited for her reply. She had to fight tears. It was the most poignant moment of her entire life.

"Why don't you put it on for me?" she asked finally, watching him lift the ring and slide it onto her ring finger with something like relief.

"How about that?" he murmured dryly. "It's a perfect fit. Almost as if it were made just for you," he added.

She looked up at him and all the humor went out of his face. He held her small hand in his big one and searched her eyes.

"You love emeralds. I bought this months ago and stuck it in a drawer while I tried to decide whether or not it would be suicide to propose to you. Duke Wright's situation made me uncertain. I was afraid you hadn't seen enough of the world, or life, to be able to settle down here in Jacobsville. I was afraid to take a chance."

She moved a step closer. "But you finally did."

He cupped her face in his big, warm hands. "Yes. When I realized that I was spending time with Julie just to keep you at bay. If she'd been a better sort of person, it would have been a low thing to do. I was flattered at her interest and the company I got to keep. But I felt like a traitor when she started insulting you in public. I was too wrapped up in my own uncertainties to do what I should have done."

"Which was what?" she asked softly.

He bent to her soft mouth. "I should have realized that if you really love someone, everything works out." He kissed her tenderly. "I should have told you how I felt and given you a chance to spread your wings if you wanted to. I could have waited while you decided what sort of future you wanted."

She still couldn't believe that he didn't know how she felt. "I was crazy about you," she whispered huskily. "Everybody knew it except you." She reached up and linked her arms around his neck. "Duke's wife wasn't like me, Jordan," she added, searching his dark eyes. "She lived with a domineering father and a deeply religious mother. They taught her that a woman's role in life was to marry and obey her husband. She'd always done what they told her to do. But after she married Duke, she ran wild, probably giving vent to all those feelings of suffocated restriction she'd endured all her life. Getting pregnant on her wedding night was a big mistake for both of them, because then she really felt trapped." She took a deep breath. "If Duke hadn't rushed her into it, she'd have gone off and found her career and come back to him when she knew what she really wanted. It was a tragedy in the making from the very beginning."

"She didn't love him enough," he murmured.

"He didn't love her enough," she countered. "He got her pregnant, thinking it would hold her."

He sighed. "I want children," he said softly. "But not right away. We need time to get to know each other before we start a family, don't we?"

She smiled. "See? You ask me about things. You don't order me around. Duke was exactly the opposite." She traced his mouth with her fingertips. "That's why I stopped going out with him. He never asked me what I wanted to do, even what I wanted to eat when we went out together. He actually ordered meals for me before I could say what

I liked.'' She glowered. ''He ordered me liver and onions and I never went out with him again.''

He lifted an eyebrow and grinned. ''Darlin', I swear on my horse that I will *never* order you liver and onions.'' He crossed his heart.

He was so handsome when he grinned like that. Her heart expanded like a balloon with pure happiness. ''Actually,'' she whispered, lifting up to him. ''I'd even eat liver and onions for you.''

''The real test of love,'' he agreed, gathering her up hungrily. ''And I'd eat squash for you,'' he offered.

She smiled under the slow, sweet pressure of his mouth. Amie said he'd actually dumped a squash casserole in the middle of the living room carpet to make the point that he never wanted it again.

''This is nice,'' he murmured, lifting her completely off the floor. ''But I can do better.''

''Can you really?'' she whispered, biting softly at his full lower lip. ''Show me!''

He laughed, even though his body was making emphatic statements about how little time there was left for teasing. He was burning.

He put her down on the sofa and crushed her into it with the warm, hard length of his body.

''Jordan,'' she whispered breathlessly when he eased between her long legs.

''Don't panic,'' he said against her lips. ''Amie's a scream away. Lift up.''

She did, and he unfastened the bra and pushed it out of the way under her blouse. He deepened the kiss slowly, seductively, while his lean hands discovered the soft warmth of her bare breasts in a heated silence.

Her head began to spin. He was going to be her husband. She could lie in his arms all night long. They could have children together. After the tragedy of the past few months, it was like a trip to paradise.

She moaned and wrapped her long legs around his hips, urging him even closer. She felt the power and heat of him intimately. Her mouth opened, inviting the quick, hard thrust of his tongue.

"Oh, yes," she groaned into his hard mouth. Her hips lifted into his rhythmically, her breath gasping out at his ear as she clung to him. "Yes. That feels…good!"

A tortured sound worked out of his throat as he pressed her down hard into the soft cushions of the sofa, his hands already reaching for the zipper in the front of her slacks, so far gone that he was mindless.

The sound of footsteps outside the door finally penetrated the fog of passion that lay between them. Jordan lifted his head. Libby looked up at him, dazed and only half aware of the sound.

"Amie," Jordan groaned, taking a steadying breath. "We have to stop."

"Tell her to go away," she whispered, laughing breathlessly.

"You tell her," he teased as he got to his feet. "She gets even in the kitchen. She can make squash look just like a corn casserole."

"Amie's Revenge?"

He nodded. "Amie's Revenge." Jordan paused. "I want to marry you," he said quietly. "I want it with all my heart."

She had to fight down tears to answer him. "I want it, too."

He drew her close, over his lap, and when he kissed her, it was with such breathless tenderness that she felt tears threatening again.

She slid her arms around his neck and kissed him back with fervent ardor. But he put her gently away.

"You don't want to ravish me?" she exclaimed. "You said once that you could do me justice in thirty minutes!"

"I lied," he said, chuckling. "I'd need two hours. And Amie's skulking out in the hall, waiting for an opportunity to congratulate us," he added in a whisper. "We can't possibly shock her so soon before the wedding."

She hesitated. "So soon...?"

"I want to get married as quickly as possible," he informed her. "All we need is the blood tests, a license, and I've already got us a minister. Unless you want a formal wedding in a big church with hundreds of guests," he added worriedly.

"No need, since you've already got us a minister," she teased.

He relaxed. "Thank God! The idea of a morning coat and hundreds of people..."

She was kissing him, so he stopped talking.

Just as things were getting interesting, there was an impatient knock at the door. "Well?" Amie called through it.

"She said yes!" Jordan called back.

The door opened and Amie rushed in, grinning from ear to ear.

"She hates squash," he said in a mock whisper.

"I won't ever make it again," Amie promised.

He hugged her. After a minute, Libby joined them. She hugged the housekeeper, too.

"Welcome to the family!" Amie laughed.

And that was the end of any heated interludes for the rest of the evening.

The next few days went by in a blur of activity. When the votes were counted on Tuesday at the primary election,

Senator Merrill lost the Democratic candidacy by a ten-to-
one margin. A recall of the city fathers was announced,
along with news of a special election to follow. Councilman
Culver and the mayor were both implicated in drug traf-
ficking, along with Julie Merrill. Julie had managed to get
bail the day before the primary, but she hadn't been seen
since. She was also still in trouble for the arson conspiracy.
Her father had given an impressive concession speech, in
front of the news media, and congratulated Calhoun Ballenger with sincerity. It began to be noticed that he im-
proved when his daughter's sins came to light. Apparently
he'd been duty-bound to try and protect her, and it had
almost killed his conscience. He'd started drinking heavily,
and then realized that he was likely to lose his state senate
seat for it. He'd panicked, gone to the mayor, and tried to
get the charges dropped.

One irresponsible act had cost Senator Merrill everything. But, he told Calhoun, he still had his house and his
health. He'd stand by his daughter, of course, and do what
he could for her. Perhaps retirement wouldn't be such a
bad thing. His daughter could not be reached for comment.
She was now being hunted by every law enforcement officer in Texas and government agents on the drug charges,
which were formidable. Other unsavory facts were still
coming to light about her doings.

Jordan finally understood why Libby had tried so hard
to keep him out of Julie's company and he apologized profusely for refusing to listen to her. Duke Wright's plight
had made him somber and afraid, especially when he realized how much he loved Libby. He was afraid to take a
chance on her. He had plenty of regrets.

Libby accepted his apology and threw herself into politics as one of Calhoun's speechwriters, a job she loved.
But, she told Jordan, she had no desire to do it for a pro-

fession. She was quite happy to work for Mr. Kemp and raise a family in Jacobsville.

On the morning of Libby's marriage to Jordan, she was almost floating with delight. "I can't believe the things that have happened in two weeks," Libby told her brother at the church door as they waited for the music to go down the aisle together. "It's just amazing!"

"For a small town, it certainly is," he agreed. He grinned. "Happy?"

"Too happy," she confessed, blushing. "I never dreamed I'd be marrying Jordan."

"I did. He's been crazy about you for years, but Duke Wright's bad luck really got to him. Fortunately, he did see the light in time."

She took a deep breath as the first strains of the wedding march were heard. "I'm glad it's just us and not a crowd," she murmured.

He didn't speak. His eyes twinkled as he opened the door.

Inside, all the prominent citizens of Jacobsville were sitting in their pews, waiting for the bride to be given away by her brother. Cash Grier was there with Tippy. So were Calhoun Ballenger and Abby, Justin Ballenger and Shelby Jacobs Ballenger. And the Hart brothers, all five of them including the attorney general, with their wives. The Tremaynes. Mr. Kemp, with Violet! The Drs. Coltrain and Dr. Morris and Dr. Steele and their wives. Eb Scott and his wife. Cy Parks and his wife. It was a veritable who's who of the city.

"Surprise," Curt whispered in her ear, and tugged her along down the aisle. She was adorned in a simple white satin gown with colorful embroidery on the bodice and puffy sleeves, a delicate veil covering her face and shoulders. She carried a bouquet of lily of the valley and pink roses.

Jordan Powell, in a soft gray morning coat and all the trappings, was waiting for her at the altar with the minister. He looked handsome and welcoming and he was smiling from ear to ear.

Libby thought back over the past few agonizing weeks and realized all the hardships and heartache she'd endured made her truly appreciate all the sweet blessings that had come into her life. She smiled through her tears and stopped at Jordan's side, her small hand searching blindly for his as she waited to speak her vows. She'd never felt more loved or happier than she was at that moment. She only wished her parents had lived to see her married.

Just after the wedding, there was a reception at the church fellowship hall, catered by Barbara's Café. The wedding cake was beautiful, with a colorful motif that exactly matched the embroidery on Libby's wedding gown.

She and Jordan were photographed together cutting the cake and then interacting with all their unexpected guests. The only sticky moment was when handsome Hayes Carson bent to kiss Libby.

"Careful, Hayes," Jordan said from right beside him. "I'm watching you!"

"Great idea," Hayes replied imperturbably and grinned. "You could use a few lessons."

And he kissed Libby enthusiastically while Jordan fumed.

When they were finally alone, hours later in Galveston, Jordan was still fuming about that kiss.

"You know Hayes was teasing," she said, coaxing him into her arms. "But I'm not. I've waited twenty-four years for this,'' she added with a wry smile. "I have great expectations."

He drew her close with a worldly look. "And I expect to satisfy them fully!"

"I'm not going to be very good at this, at first," she said breathlessly, when he began to undress her. "Is it all right?"

He smiled tenderly. "You're going to be great at it," he countered. "The only real requirement is love. We're rich in that."

She relaxed a little, watching his dark eyes glow as he uncovered the soft, petal-pink smoothness of her bare skin. She was a little nervous. Nobody had seen her undressed since she was a little girl.

Jordan realized that and it made him even more gentle. He'd never been with an innocent, but he knew enough about women that it wasn't going to be a problem. She loved him. He wanted nothing more than to please her.

When she was standing in just her briefs, he bent and smoothed his warm mouth over the curve of her breasts. She smelled of roses. There was a faint moisture under his lips, which he rightly attributed to fear.

He lifted his head and looked down into her wide, uncertain eyes. "Women have been doing this since the dawn of time," he whispered. "If it wasn't fun, nobody would want to do it. Right?"

She laughed nervously. "Right."

He smiled tenderly. "So just relax and let me drive. It's going to be a journey you'll never forget."

Her hands went to his tie. "Okay. But I get to make suggestions," she told him impishly, and worked to unfasten the tie and then his white shirt. She opened it over a bronzed chest thick with dark, soft hair. He felt furry. But under the hair was hard, warm muscle. She liked the way he felt.

He kissed her softly while he coaxed her hands to his belt. She hesitated.

"Don't agonize over it," he teased, moving her hands aside to unfasten it himself. "We'll go slow."

"I'm not really a coward," she whispered unsteadily. "It's just uncharted territory. I've never even looked at pictures…"

He could imagine what sort of pictures she was talking about. He only smiled. "Next time, you'll be a veteran and it won't intimidate you."

"Are you sure?" she asked.

He bent to her mouth again. "I'm sure."

His warm lips moved down her throat to her breasts, but this time they weren't gently teasing. They were invasive and insistent as they opened on the hard little nubs his caresses had already produced. When his hands moved her hips lazily against the hard thrust of his powerful body, she began to feel drugged.

She'd thought it would be embarrassing and uncomfortable to make love in the light. But Jordan was slow and thorough, easing her into an intimacy beyond anything she'd ever dreamed. He cradled her against him on the big bed, arousing her to such a fever pitch that when he removed the last bit of her clothing, it was a relief to feel the coolness of the room against her hot skin. And by the time he removed his own clothes, she was too hungry to be embarrassed. In fact, she was as aggressive as he was, starving for him in the tempestuous minutes that followed.

She remembered the first kiss they'd shared, beside her pickup truck at his fence. She'd known then that she'd do anything he wanted her to do. But this was far from the vague dreams of fulfillment she'd had when she was alone.

She hadn't known that passion was like a fever that nothing could quench, that desire brought intense desperation. She hadn't known that lovemaking was blind, deaf, mute slavery to a man's touch.

"I would die for you," Jordan whispered huskily at her ear as he moved slowly into total possession with her trembling body.

"Will it...hurt?" she managed in a stranger's voice as she hesitated just momentarily at the enormity of what was happening to her.

He laughed sensuously as he began to move lazily against her. "Are you kidding?" he murmured. And with a sharp, deft movement, he produced a sensation that lifted her clear of the bed and against him with an unearthly little cry of pleasure.

From there, it was a descent into total madness. She shivered with every powerful thrust of his body. She clung to him with her arms, her legs, her soul. She moaned helplessly as sensation built on sensation, until she was almost screaming from the urgent need for satisfaction.

She heard her own voice pleading with him, but she couldn't understand her own words. She drove for fulfillment, her body demanding, feverishly moving with his as they climbed the spiral of passion together.

She felt suddenly as if she'd been dropped from a great height into a hot, throbbing wave of pleasure that began and never seemed to end. She clung to him, terrified that he might stop, that he might draw back, that he might pull away.

"Shh," he whispered tenderly. "I won't stop. It's all right. It's all right, honey. I love you...so much!"

"I love you, too!" she gasped.

Then he began to shudder, even as she felt herself move from one plane of ecstasy to another, and another, and another, each one deeper and more satisfying than the one before. At one point she thought she might actually die from the force of it. Her eyes closed and she let the waves wash over her in succession, glorying in the unbelievably sweet aftermath.

Above her, Jordan was just reaching his own culmination. He groaned harshly at her ear and shuddered one last time before he collapsed in her arms, dead weight on her damp, shivering body.

"And you were afraid," he chided in a tender whisper, kissing her eyes, her cheeks, her throat.

She laughed. "So that's how it feels," she said drowsily. "And now I'm sleepy."

He laughed with her. "So am I."

"Will you be here when I wake up?" she teased.

He kissed her swollen mouth gently. "For the rest of my life, honey. Until the very end."

Her arms curved around him and she curled into his powerful body, feeling closer to him than she'd ever felt to another human being. It was poignant. She was a whole woman. She was loved.

"Until the very end, my darling," she repeated, her voice trailing away in the silence of the room.

She slept in his arms. It was the best night of her life. But it was only the beginning for both of them.

* * * * *

Look for these Diana Palmer novels:

After Midnight - *Mira Books*
Once in Paris - *Mira Books*

and

Carrera's Bride *in Silhouette Special Edition in December 2005.*

WILD IN THE MOONLIGHT
by
Jennifer Greene

JENNIFER GREENE

lives near Lake Michigan with her husband and two children. Before writing full-time, she worked as a teacher and a personnel manager.

Ms Greene has written more than fifty romances, for which she has won numerous awards, including three RITA® Awards from the Romance Writers of America in the Best Short Contemporary Books category, and she entered RWA's Hall of Fame in 1998.

For Ryan and his bride—

Everyone thinks the romance happens
before you get married, but I promise you two—
the true excitement and wonder and magic come after.

One

Just as Violet Campbell limped inside the back door into the kitchen, she heard the front doorbell ring.

She simply ignored it. It wasn't as if she had a choice. Wincing from pain, tears falling from her eyes, she hopped over to the sink. After spending hours in the brilliant Vermont sun, her kitchen seemed gloomier than a tomb. It wasn't, of course. Her pupils simply hadn't adjusted to the inside light—either that, or the terrible severity of pain from the sting of a particularly ferocious bee was affecting her vision.

Someone rang her doorbell a second time.

Impatiently she yelled out, "Look! I can't come

to the door because I'm dying, so just chill out for a few minutes!''

Everyone in White Hills knew her, so if they wanted something from her, they were hardly going to wait for formal permission. Heaven knew why she bothered keeping the doorbell operational, anyway. People barged in at all hours without a qualm.

Gingerly she lifted herself onto the red tile counter, kicked off her sandal and carefully, carefully put her right foot in the sink. Her skirt got in the way. Ever since opening the Herb Haven, she'd had fun wearing vintage clothes—her oldest sister claimed she looked as if she shopped from a gypsy catalog. Today, though, she had to bunch up the swingy long skirt to even see her poor foot. An empty coffee cup was knocked over. A spoon fell to the floor. One of the cats—Nuisance? Devil?—assumed she was in the kitchen to provide a lap and some petting.

She petted the cat, but then got serious. Darn it, she needed to get her foot clean. Immediately.

Until that was done, she couldn't tackle the bee sting. She was positive that the stinger *had* to still be in there. Nothing else explained the intense, sharp, unrelenting hurt. Well, there was one other explanation. Friends and family had no idea she was a complete coward, but Violet had discovered three years before that there was one terrific advantage to being divorced and living alone. She could be a cry-baby and a wimp anytime she wanted to be.

And right now, for damn sure, she wanted to be. As far as Violet was concerned, a bee sting justified a sissy fit any day of the week. She dunked her foot under the faucet and switched on the tap. The rush of lukewarm water nearly made her pass out.

Possibly that was taking cowardice too far, but cripes. The whole situation was so unfair—and so ironic. Everything around her seemed to be heart-lessly, exuberantly reproducing. Plants. Cats. Socks in her dryer. Even the dust bunnies under the bed seemed to lasciviously multiply the instant the lights turned off at night.

Everybody seemed to be having sex and babies but her—and that sure as sunlight included the bees. Lately she could hardly wander anywhere on the farm without running into a fresh hive. Possibly hav-ing twenty acres of lavender coming into bloom might—*might*—have encouraged a few extra bees to hang out. But it's not as if she went close to the lavender. And her normal bees were *nice* bees. They liked her. She liked them.

Not this fella. Didn't male bees die after stinging someone? She hoped he did. She hoped his death was violent and painful and lingering.

The front doorbell rang yet *again*.

"For Pete's sake, could you lay off the doorbell?

I *can't* come to the door, so either come in or go away!''

Bravely gritting her teeth, she squirted antibacterial soap on the injured foot, then screeched when it touched the stinger spot, which was already turning bruisey red and throbbing like a migraine. She forced the foot under the tap water again.

The glass cabinet behind her head contained the box of first-aid supplies, but when she tried to stretch behind her, the movement sent more sharp shooting pains up her leg. The cat had been joined by another cat on the other side of the sink. Both knew perfectly well they weren't allowed on the kitchen counters. Both still sat, as if they were the supervisory audience over an audition she was failing. Her skirt hem kept getting wetter. Her forehead and nape were sticky-damp from the heat—if not from shock. And she noticed the nail polish on her middle toenail had a chip. She hated it when her nail polish chipped.

''Allo?''

The sudden voice made her head jerk up like a rabbit smelling a jaguar in her territory. This just wasn't a kitchen where jaguars prowled. After the divorce, she'd moved home primarily because it was available—her mom and dad had just retired to Florida, leaving the old Vermont homestead clean, ready for family gatherings at any time, but vacant.

She'd made it hers. Not that her mom hadn't had wonderful decorating taste, but she'd fiercely needed to create a private, safe nest after Simpson took off with his extraordinarily fecund bimbo. Now, at a glance, she reassured herself that the world was still normal, still safe, still hers. The old cabinets held a prize collection of red Depression glass. A pot-bellied stove sat on the old brick hearth; she'd angled an antique-rose love seat on one side, a cane rocker on the other—both of which made seats for more cats. Red-and-white chintz curtains framed the wide windows overlooking the monster maple in the back-yard. Potted plants argued for space from every light source. A crocheted heart draped the round oak table.

Everything was normal. Everything was fine... except that she heard the hurried, heavy clump of boots in her hall, coming toward the kitchen, at the same time she heard the jaguar's voice doing that "Allo, allo" thing again.

She didn't particularly *mind* if there was a stranger in her house. No one was a stranger in White Hills for long, and potential serial killers probably wouldn't call out a greeting before barging in. Still, she didn't know anyone who said "allo" instead of "hi" or "hello." It wasn't the odd accent that rustled her nerves but something else. There was something...spicy...about that voice. Something just a little too sexy and exotic for a somnolent June afternoon in a sleepy Vermont town. Something that made her knees feel buttery.

On the other hand, Violet knew perfectly well that

she was a teensy bit prone to being overdramatic, so it wasn't as if she felt inclined to trust her instincts. Reality was she was more likely stuck with a visitor—and right now she just had no patience with any more complications.

Without even looking up, she snapped out, "My God, you nearly scared me half to death. Whoever the hell you are, could you reach in the cupboard behind my head? Second shelf. I need tweezers. First-aid cream. And that skinny tube of ammonium stuff for stings. And the plastic bottle of purple stuff that you wash out wounds with, you know, what's it called? Or maybe hydrogen peroxide. Oh, cripes, just give me the whole darn box—"

The stranger interrupted her list of instructions with that quiet, dangerous voice of his. "First— where exactly are you hurt?"

Like she had time for questions. "I'm not just *hurt*. I'm in agonizing pain. And I always tell myself that I should stockpile pain pills and narcotics, only damn, I never take any. I don't suppose you carry any morphine on you?"

"Um, no."

"I suppose you think it's crazy, my talking this way to a stranger. But if you're going to rob me, just do it. Feel free. I don't even care. But get me the first-aid box first, okay?"

Silence. Not just on his part, but on hers. It was one thing to believe she was totally okay with a

The Reader Service™ — Here's how it works:

If offer card is missing write to: The Reader Service, PO Box 676, Richmond, TW9 1WU

NO STAMP
NEEDED!

THE READER SERVICE™
FREE BOOK OFFER
FREEPOST CN81
CROYDON
CR9 3WZ

NO STAMP
NECESSARY
IF POSTED IN
THE U.K. OR N.I.

stranger in her kitchen, and another to have said stranger suddenly show up between her legs—before they'd even been introduced yet.

She gulped.

Close up, the guy could have sent any woman's estrogen levels soaring. He seemed to cross the room so fast, and suddenly his blond head was bent over her foot in the sink. He was built long and sleek, with a daunting shoulder span and arm muscles that looked carved out of hickory. His feet alone looked bigger than boats. His hair was dark blond, disheveled, longish, as if he'd been outside in the hot breeze for hours. She couldn't see much of his face except for his profile—which amounted to one hell of a nose and skin with a deep tan. The khaki shirt and boots and canvas pants were practical, not fancy, and though he was lean, he looked strong enough to knock down walls for a living.

When he finally glanced at her face, she caught the snap and fire of light-blue eyes, and a narrow mouth that seemed determined not to laugh. "All that yelling," he said finally, patiently, "was about this sting?"

"Hey. It's not *just* a sting. You didn't see the bee. It was huge. Bigger than a horse. Practically bigger than an elephant. And it—"

"Are you allergic to bee stings?"

"No. Good grief, no. I'm not allergic to anything.

I'm totally healthy. But I'm telling you, this was a big bee. And I think the stinger's still in there.''

"Yeah, I can see it is." Again he lifted his head. Again she felt those amused blue eyes pounce on her face, and caught a better look at him. That shag of blond hair framed a long-boned face that looked carved by a French sculptor.

If she wasn't dying from misery, she might have let a shiver sneak up her spine. One look—and no matter how soggy her mind was from the pain—she was absolutely positive this guy wouldn't normally be running around White Hills, Vermont...or any other back-country town.

"For the record," she said, "you're lost."

"You think?" He shifted behind her, opened the cabinet and promptly hefted down her first-aid box. Well, actually, it was a shoe box. Filled to overflowing with herbal, natural, artificial and any other kind of first-aid supplies she'd accumulated over the past three years—and probably a few her mom had had around for the thirty years before that. He located the tweezers first.

The way the stranger held the tweezers made her nervous. Either that or something else did. Either way, she was really starting to get seriously nervous, not just pretend—and darn it, she hadn't been doing all that well before the exotic stranger barged in.

"You're lost," she repeated. "I'm Violet Campbell. I own the Herb Haven—the building and greenhouses on the other side of the yard. This is my house. If you'll tell me who you're trying to find, I'll be glad to—*eeeikes!*"

He lifted the tweezers to show her the stinger. "It looks like the stinger of a little sweat bee."

Violet pinched the skin between her brows. Another delightful advantage to being divorced, apart from removing the scoundrel from her life, was not having to put up with men's sick sense of humor. "Who are you looking for?" she repeated.

"You."

He lifted the brown bottle of hydrogen peroxide and started unscrewing the top. She suspected he was going to pour it on the wound. She also suspected that she was going to shriek when he did—and maybe even cry. But the way he said "you" in that sexy, exotic accent put so much cotton in her throat that the shriek barely came out a baby's gasp.

"See, that wasn't so bad, was it? The stinger's out. The spot's clean. Now you might want to take an antihistamine or put some ice on the spot for a few minutes—"

"You couldn't possibly want me," she interrupted. And then pinched the skin between her brows a second time. On any normal day she liked people. She liked interruptions. She even liked a hefty dose of chaos in her life. But there were men she felt comfortable with and men she didn't.

This one was definitely a "didn't." He made her

feel naked, which was pretty darn silly considering she was dressed in the ultramodest clothes of another era—except she suddenly realized her skirt was hiked up past her thighs. The point, though, was that she most certainly wasn't wearing male-attracting clothes. Her women customers got a kick out of her sense of style, but men almost always backed away fast.

That was how she wanted it. She liked guys, had always liked guys, but she'd been burned enough for a while. Maybe for a whole lifetime. Normally men noticed her clothes and immediately seemed to conclude that she was a little kooky and keep their distance, so God knew what was wrong with this stranger. He'd surely noticed the oddball long skirt and vintage blouse, but he was still looking her over as if she were meringue and he had a sweet tooth.

Momentarily, though, he went back to playing doctor, scrounging in her first-aid box until he found the ammonium wand for bites and stings. She winced even before he'd touched the spot. As if they were in the middle of a civilized conversation, he said, "You were expecting me."

"Trust me. I wasn't expecting you."

"I'm staying here for a few weeks. With you."

The wince was wasted. When he touched the wound with the ammonium wand, she sucked in every last dram of saliva her throat had left and released a screech. A totally unsatisfying screech. The

ammonium hissed and stung like—damn it. Like another bee sting. Only worse. Still, she'd somehow
easily managed to keep track of the conversation this
time. "Obviously, you're not staying here. I don't
even know you. Although I'm beginning to think
you're a complete maniac—"

Actually, she wasn't particularly afraid of maniacs.
She took credit for being one herself often enough.
But she'd lost the last of her usually voluble sense
of humor with that bite of ammonia. Good-looking
or not—sexy or not—she was really in no mood for
an emotional tussle with a stranger.

The man swooped everything back in the first-aid
box, then turned around and aimed for the freezer,
obviously to find some ice. "My name is Cameron
Lachlan."

"Great name. I'm happy for you."

He grinned, but he also kept moving. When she
motioned to a lower cupboard, he bounced down on
his heels and came up with small baggie for the ice.
"We definitely have some kind of strange screwup
going on here. You *do* have a sister named Daisy
Cameron, don't you?"

It wasn't often she got that thud-thud-thud thing
in her stomach, but her palm pressed hard on her
tummy now. "Yes, for sure. In fact, I have two sisters—"

"But it's Daisy who lives in France."

"Yes, for several years now—"

"The point being," he said patiently, "that your sister has been playing go-between for us for months. Or that's what I've understood. Because she was living right there, and because she knows my work and me personally, so you wouldn't have to be dealing with a stranger. You were supposed to be expecting me. You were supposed to have a place for me to stay for several weeks. You were supposed to know that I was arriving either today or tomorrow—"

"Oh my God. *You're* Cameron Lachlan?"

He scratched his chin. "I could have sworn I already mentioned that."

It came on so fast. The light-headedness. The stomach thudding. The way her kitchen suddenly blurred into a pale-green haze.

Granted, she was a coward and a wuss—but normally she had a cast-iron stomach. Now, though, when she pushed off the counter and tried to stand on both feet, her bee sting stabbed like hot fire and her stomach suddenly pitched. "Try not to take this personally, okay?" she said. "It's not that I'm not glad to see you. It's just that you'll have to excuse me a minute while I throw up."

Two

Once Violet disappeared from sight—presumably to find the nearest bathroom—Cameron leaned against the kitchen counter and clawed a hand through his hair. Talk about a royal mess. What the hell was he supposed to do now?

Nothing usually rattled him. Normally people got a higher education to earn a better living. Cameron had pursued a Ph.D so he could enjoy a footloose, vagabond lifestyle. He was used to jet lag. Used to time changes and strange beds. He had no trouble getting along with people of all different backgrounds and cultures.

But this blonde was doing something to his pulse.

"Be careful with my sister," Daisy had warned him—which, at the time, had struck him as a curious thing to say. His only interest in Violet Cameron was business. Still, whether he'd wanted to hear it or not, Daisy had filled in enough blanks for him to understand why she was so protective of her younger sister. Violet had apparently been married to a real, selfish creep. "Something happened in that marriage that I still don't know about. Something really bad in the last year. I still can't get her to talk about it," Daisy had told him. "But the point is, Violet was always extra smart, in school and life and everything else. It's just since the divorce that she's been…different. Fragile and nervous about men."

Since that conversation had at the time been none of his business—and none of his interest—Cameron had pretty much forgotten it. Still, he'd definitely imagined a shy, quiet, understated kind of woman. A true violet in personality as well as name.

Now he wondered if Vermont might secretly be an alternative universe. Granted, he'd only been in the state for a couple of hours—and on the Campbell property even less than that—but Daisy's description didn't match anything he'd noticed in reality so far. Violet was as shy as neon lights, as nervous as a lioness, and as far as IQ…well, maybe she was smart, even ultrasmart, but who could tell beneath all those layers of ditsiness?

He heard a door open and instinctively braced.

Seconds later Violet walked back in the kitchen. When she spotted him leaning against the counter, she seemed to instinctively brace, too.

Considering that Cameron had always gotten on well with women, it was a mighty blow to his ego to make one sick on sight. At the vast age of thirty-seven, though, he never expected to respond to a woman with a tumbly stomach of his own.

The old Vermont farmhouse seemed sturdy and serious. At first glance, he'd thought the base structure had to be at least two centuries old. The brick surface had tidy white trim and a shake roof; the plank floors were polished to a high shine. He'd been drawn to the place on sight; it looked practical and functional and solid, nothing frivolous.

Only, then there was her.

Standing with the light behind her, she could have been a fey creature from a fairy story. The first thing any breathing male was going to notice, of course, was her hair. It was blond, paler than sunlight, and even braided with a skinny silk scarf, it bounced halfway down her back…which meant it had to reach her fanny when it was undone. Her face was a valentine with warm, wide, hazel eyes, sun-kissed cheeks and a nose lightly peppered with freckles.

She wasn't exactly pretty. She just had that *something.* Some kinds of women just seemed born pure female. They were never as easy to get along with—much less understand—but they seemed to radiate that female thing from the inside out. Nothing about her was flashy or sexy, but she was sensual from that pale, shiny hair to her soft mouth to the rounded swell of her breasts.

She seemed to be wearing old clothes—not old, as in practical, but old, as in the stuff you'd find in a great-grandmother's attic trunk. The white blouse completely covered those delectable breasts, but the fabric seemed less substantial than a handkerchief. It was tucked into a long skirt swirling with bright colors. Crystal earrings dangled to her shoulders. A couple of skinny bangle bracelets glinted on her wrist. There was nothing immodest about the clothes; if anything, they seemed unnecessarily concealing for a sultry, ninety-degree afternoon. Cameron just wasn't sure what the vintage gypsy image was supposed to mean.

He also couldn't help but notice that she smelled.

Guys weren't supposed to mention that sort of thing, but smells were Cameron's business—and had helped him put away a sizable bank account—so scent tended to be a priority for him. In her case, she wasn't using the kind of perfume that came out of a bottle, but around her neck and wrists there was the sweet, vague scent of fresh flowers—as if she'd ambled into a garden with roses and lilac petals and maybe some lily of the valley.

He noticed the delicate scents—which helped him forget that he'd also noticed her spanking-orange underpants. Usually he knew a woman just a wee bit better before he'd gotten a look at her underwear, but when Violet had been on the counter, trying to wash her foot in the sink, she'd pushed up her skirts—no reason for her to have been thinking about modesty since she obviously hadn't been expecting company.

Hell. He hadn't planned on barging in without being asked, either, but when a woman yelled out that she was dying, he could hardly stand on her front porch and wait politely for further news bulletins.

Now, though, she frowned at him. "We seem to be in quite an uh-oh situation," she announced.

That wasn't quite how he'd have put it, but he sure agreed. "You'd better get your foot up before that sting swells up on you."

"I will."

"You're not still feeling sick to your stomach, are you?" He wanted to directly confront their obvious problem, but since she'd established—incontestably—that she was a hard-core sissy about the bee sting, it seemed wise to get her settled down. He sure as hell didn't want her keeling over on him.

"I think my stomach's fine now. It doesn't matter, anyway. What matters is that we have to figure this out. Your being here. What we're going to do with you."

"Uh-huh. You want me to get us a drink?"

"Yes. That'd be great." She sank into a chair at the oak table, as if just assuming he could find glasses and drinks. Which he could. He just didn't usually walk in someone's house and take over this way.

Being in the kitchen with her was like being assaulted with a rocket full of estrogen. It wasn't just that she was a girly-girl type of woman, but everything about the place. Cats roosted on every surface—one blinked at him from the top of the refrigerator; another was sprawled on some newspapers on the counter; a black-and-white polka-dotted model seemed determined to wind around his legs. Every spare wall space had been decorated within an inch of its life, with copper pots and little slogans over the door and wreaths and just *stuff*. From the basket of yarn balls to heart-shaped rag rugs, the entire kitchen was an estrogen-whew. The kind of a place where a guy might be allowed to sip some wine, but God forbid he chug a beer.

On the other hand, he found lemonade in the fridge in a crystal pitcher. Fresh squeezed. The refrigerator was stuffed with so many dishes that he really wanted to stand and stare—if not outright drool. Never mind if she was overdosed with sex appeal. He might get fed out of this deal. That reduced the importance of any other considerations…assuming either of them could figure out how to fix such a major screwup.

"I think we need to start over," he suggested. "You seemed to recognize my name? So I assume you also know that I'm the agricultural chemist from Jeunnesse?''

She immediately nodded at the mention of the French perfume company, so at least Cameron was reassured there was some cognition and sense of reality between her ears. But somehow she looked even more shaken up instead of less.

''I just can't believe this. I *did* know you were coming, Mr. Lachlan—''

''Cameron. Or Cam.''

''Cameron, then. What you said was very true. My sister's called and written me several times about this.'' She lifted her bee-stung foot to a chair and accepted the long, tall glass of lemonade he handed her. ''I'm just having a stroke, that's all. The timing completely slipped my mind.''

''You have twenty acres of lavender almost ready to be harvested, don't you?''

''Well, yes.''

Cameron took a long slow gulp of the lemonade. It seemed to him that it'd normally be a tad challenging to forget twenty acres of lavender in your backyard.

''You're supposed to want me here,'' he said tactfully.

''I do, I do. I just forgot.'' She raised a ring-spangled hand. ''Well, I didn't just *forget*. It's been unusually chaotic around here. Our youngest sister,

Camille, got married a couple weeks ago. She'd been here most of the spring, working on the lavender. And she left on her honeymoon. Only, then she came back to get the kids.''

Boy, that made a lot of sense.

''Cripes, I don't mean *her* kids. I mean her stepkids. Her new husband had twin sons from a previous marriage. And actually since Camille thinks of them as hers, I suppose it's okay to call them her sons directly, don't you think?''

Cameron took a breath. As thrilling as all this information was, it had absolutely nothing to do with him. ''About the lavender…'' he gently interrupted.

''I'm just trying to explain how I got so confused. I started the Herb Haven three years ago, when I moved back home, and it's done fine—but it was this spring that it really took off. I've been running full speed, had to hire two staff and I'm still behind. And then Camille needed me to do something with all their dogs and animals while the family was on the honeymoon— I mean, they got a few days to themselves, but after that they even invited the kids and his dad, can you believe it? And then this old farmhouse I try to keep up myself. And then there are the two greenhouses. And Daisy…well, you already know my older sister, so you know Daisy's genetically related to a steamroller.''

Finally she'd said something that Cameron could connect to. Daisy was no close personal friend, only a business connection, but he'd spent enough time to believe the oldest Campbell sister could manage a continent without breaking a sweat. Daisy was a take-charge kind of woman.

"Anyway, the point is, sometimes Daisy runs on—"

"*Daisy* runs on?" Cameron felt that point needed qualifying. As far as he was concerned, Daisy couldn't touch her younger sister for her ability to talk—extensively and incessantly.

Violet nodded. "And I just don't always listen to her that closely. Who could? Daisy always has a thousand ideas and she's always bossing Camille and me around. We gave up arguing with her years ago. When you've got a headstrong horse, you just have to let them run. Not that I ride. Or that Daisy's like a horse. I'm just trying to say that it's always been easier to tune out and just let her think that she's managing us—"

"About the lavender," Cameron interrupted again, this time a wee bit more forcefully.

"I'm just trying to explain why I forgot the exact time when you were coming." She hesitated. "I also seemed to have forgotten exactly what you're going to do."

Before he could answer, someone rapped on her front door. She immediately popped to her feet and hobbled quickly down the hall. Moments later she came back with her arms full of mail. "That was

Frank, the mailman. Usually he just puts it in the box at the road, but at this time of year, there can be quite a load—''

More news he couldn't use. And before he could direct her attention back to the lavender, her telephone rang. Actually, about a half dozen telephones rang. She must have a good number of receivers, because he could hear that cacophonic echo of rings through the entire downstairs.

She took the kitchen receiver—which enabled her to pet two cats at the same time. Possibly she was raising a herd, because he hadn't seen these long-haired caramel models before. The caller seemed to be someone named Mabel, who seemed to feel Violet could give her some herbal suggestions for hot flashes.

This took some time. Cameron finished one glass of lemonade and poured another while he got an earful about menopause—more than he'd ever wanted to know, and more than he could imagine a woman as young as Violet could know. What was she, thirty? Thirty-one? What in God's name was squaw root and flax seed oil?

She'd just hung up and turned back to face him when the sucker rang again. This time the caller appeared to be a man named Bartholomew. Although she seemed to be arguing with the guy, it was a stressless type of quarrel, because she sorted through her mail, petted more cats and put breakfast cups in the dishwasher during the conversation. A woman could hardly be ditsy to the bone if she could multitask, right? Then she hung up and started talking to him again.

"You see?" she asked, as if there was something obvious he should be seeing. "That's exactly why it's impossible for you to stay. Bartholomew Radcliffe is supposed to be putting a new roof on the cottage. The place where you were going to stay when you came in July."

"It *is* July," he felt compelled to tell her.

She made a fluttery motion with her hand, as if the date were of no import. Clearly there were several things in life that Violet Campbell considered inconsequential—dates, facts, contracts and possibly anything else in that generically rational realm. Because he was starting to feel exhausted, he rested his chin in his hand while she went on.

"That's exactly the thing about July. The roof was supposed to be done by now. It's just a little cottage. How long can it take to put a roof on one little cottage? And Bartholomew promised me it'd only take a maximum of two weeks, and he started it way back near the first of June. Only, I've never worked with roofers before."

"And this is relevant, why?"

"Because I had no idea how it was with them. Today he didn't come because there's a threat of rain." She motioned outside to the cloudless sky.

"He doesn't come on Fridays because Friday apparently isn't a workday. And then there's fishing. If the fishing's good, he takes off early. You see what I mean?"

What he saw was that Violet Campbell was a sexy, sensual, unfathomable woman with gorgeous eyes and silky blond hair and boobs that he'd really, really like to get to know. The only problem seemed to be the content under her hair. There was a slim possibility she could fill out an application at a nut house, and no one would be certain whether she wanted employment or an inmate's room.

"I don't suppose there's any chance you'd like to talk about the lavender crop." But by then, he should have realized that Violet couldn't be tricked, coaxed or bribed into staying on topic.

"We *are*. Basically. I mean, the issue is that when—if—you came, I assumed you could stay at the cottage. It's nice. It's private. It's comfortable. But it's quite a disaster right now because they had to take off the old roof to put on the new one. So there's dust and nails everywhere. And tar. That tar is really hot and stinky. So the place simply isn't livable. It will be— In fact, I can't believe it'll take him more than another week to finish it—"

"Depending on his fishing schedule, of course."

"Yes. Exactly."

"Well, I'm hearing you, chère. But it'd be a wee bit tricky for me to fly all the way back to France, just to wait out Bartholomew's fishing schedule. And although I understand your strain of lavender runs late, I absolutely have to be here for the first of the harvest.''

''Well, yes, that's all true, but I'm just confused what I can possibly do with you until I've got a place for you to stay.''

Maybe jet lag was getting to him. Maybe at the vast age of thirty-seven, he was no longer the easy-care, rootless vagabond he used to be. Maybe missed sleep and strange mattresses had finally caught up with him…but it seemed pretty damn obvious that Violet couldn't really be this flutter-brained. Something must be bothering her about his being here. He just had no idea what. Considering her older sister had okayed him, she couldn't be afraid of him, could she?

Nah. Cameron easily dismissed that theory almost before it surfaced. It wasn't as if all women liked him. They didn't. But he got along with most, and those women who related to him sexually generally were afraid that he'd have taken a fast powder by morning—no one was afraid of him in any other sense, that he could imagine.

So he slowly put down his lemonade glass and hunched forward, deliberately making closer eye contact. Not to elicit any sexual response, but to encourage an eye-to-eye honest connection. ''Violet,'' he said slowly and calmly.

"What?"

"Quit with the nonsense."

"What nonsense?"

"Sleeping arrangements are not a problem. I wouldn't mind sleeping outside on the ground. Actually, I like sleeping under the stars. Hell, I've roughed it on four continents. And if we get into some stormy weather, I'll find a hotel in town and commute. My finding a place to throw a pillow is no big deal. So is there some reason that you don't want me here that you haven't said?"

"Good heavens. Of course not—"

Again, he said slowly and carefully, "You are aware that my work with your lavender is potentially worth thousands of dollars to you? Potentially hundreds of thousands?"

She squeezed her eyes closed briefly—and when she opened them again, he read panic in their deep, dark, beautiful, hazel depths. "Oh God," she said, "I'm afraid I'm going to be sick again."

Three

"No, you're not going to be sick again," Cameron said emphatically.

Violet met his eyes. "You're right. I'm not," she said slowly, and took a long deep breath.

She had to get a grip. A serious grip. She wasn't really nauseous, she was just shook up. Her foot throbbed like the devil—that was for real. She'd been running all day in the heat even before the bee sting—that was for real, too. And normally men didn't provoke her into behaving like a scatterbrained nutcase—but there were exceptions.

Virile, highly concentrated packages of testosterone with wicked eyes and long, lanky strides were a justifiable exception.

Violet tried another deep, calming breath. Most blondes hated blonde jokes, but she'd always liked them. She knew perfectly well how she came across to most men. A guy who thought he was dealing with a ditsy, witless blonde generally ran for the hills at the speed of light, or at the very least, considered her hands-off—and that suited Violet just fine.

It was just sometimes hard to maintain the ditsy, witless persona. For one thing, sometimes she actually felt ditless and witsy. Or witless and ditsy. Or…oh, hell.

That man had eyes bluer than a lake. She did much, much better with old, ugly men. And she did really great with children. Not that those attributes were particularly helping her now.

But that grip she'd needed was finally coming to her. Those long, meditative breaths always helped. "I have an idea," she said to Cameron. "You've traveled a long way. You have to be hungry and tired—and I'm the middle of an Armageddon type of afternoon. Could you just…chill…for an hour or so? Feel free to walk around…or just put your feet up on my couch or on the front porch. I need to walk over to my Herb Haven, tell my employee what's happening, finish up the problems I was in the middle of, get closed up for the day."

"Is there anything I could help you with?"

"No. Honestly. I just need an hour to get my life back in order…and after that I've got more than enough in the fridge for dinner. I can't guarantee it's something you'll want to eat, but we could definitely talk in peace then—''

''That sounds great. But if there's running I could do for you, say. I know you can't want to be on that foot.''

''I won't be for long.''

It worked like a charm. She just couldn't concentrate with all those life details hanging over her head—and with an impossibly unsettling man underfoot. An hour and a half later, though, she was humming under her breath, back in her kitchen, her one foot propped on a stool and a cleaver in her hand big enough to inspire jealousy in a serial killer.

Not that any foolish serial killer would dare lay a hand on one of her prized possessions.

She angled her head—just far enough to peer around the doorway to check on her visitor again. There was no telling exactly when Cameron had decided to sit down, but clearly it was his undoing. He'd completely crashed. He wasn't snoring, but his tousled blond head was buried in the rose pillow on the couch, and one of his stockinged feet was hanging over the side. That man was sure *long*. One cat—either Dickens or Shakespeare—was purring on the couch arm, supervising his nap with a possessive eye.

Amazing how easy it was for her to relax when he was sleeping.

She went back to her chopping and sautéing and

mixing. Cooking was a favorite pastime—and a secret, since she certainly didn't want anyone getting the appalling idea that she was either domestic or practical. Tonight she couldn't exercise much creativity, because she already had leftovers that needed using up, starting with some asparagus soup—and somehow finding an excuse to eat the last of the grape sorbet.

Early evening, the temperature was still too sweltering to eat anything heavy, but it was no trouble to put together bruschetta and some spicy grilled shrimp for the serious part of the meal. The shrimp took some fussing. First seeding and slicing the hot chilies. Then slicing the two tall stalks of lemongrass. Then she had to grate the fresh ginger, crush the garlic, chop the cilantro and mix it with warmed honey and olive oil.

He'd probably hate it, she thought. Men tended to hate anything gourmet or fancy, but as far as Violet was concerned, that was yet another of the thrilling benefits to being divorced. She could cook fancy and wild all she liked—and garlic-up any dish to the nth degree—and who'd ever care?

She'd have belted out a rock-and-roll song, off-key and at the top of her lungs, if it wouldn't risk waking her visitor. She'd deal with him. But right now she was just seeping in some relaxation, and satisfaction. She'd kicked some real butt in the last hour, finished up the week's bookkeeping, made up four arrangements for birthday orders and fetched a van full of pots and containers from town. Even without the bee sting, it was a lot to do for a woman who was supposed to be a flutter-brained blonde, but then, when no one was watching she had no reason to be on her guard.

Her sisters thought she was afraid of getting hurt again because of Simpson. The truth was that her ex-husband had turned out to be a twerp, but she never held that against the other half of the species. She wasn't trying to avoid men. She was trying to help men avoid her—and for three years she'd been doing a great job at it, if she said so herself.

She was still humming when the telephone rang—naturally!—just when she was trying to coat the shrimp with the gooey mixture. She cocked the receiver between her ear and shoulder. "Darlene! Oh, I'm sorry, I forgot to call you back...and yes, you told me he was a Leo. Okay. Try a fritatta with flowers. Flowers, like the marigolds I sold you the other day, remember? I'm telling you, those marigolds are the best aphrodisiac...and you wear that peach gauze blouse tonight...uh-huh...uh-huh..."

Once Darlene Webster had been taken care of, she washed her hands and started stabbing the coated shrimp on skewers. Immediately the phone rang again. It was Georgia from the neighborhood euchre group. "Of course I can have it here, what's the dif-

ference? We'll just have it at your house next time.
Hope the new carpet looks terrific.''

After that Jim White called, who wanted to know
if he could borrow her black plastic layer. And then
Boobla called, who wanted to know if there was any
chance Violet could hire her friend Kari for the summer, because Kari couldn't find a job and they
worked really well together. Boobla could talk the
leaves off a tree. Violet finally had to interrupt.
''Okay, okay, hon. I've got enough work to take on
one more part-timer, but I can't promise anything
until I've met her. Bring her over Monday morning,
all right?''

She'd just hung up, thinking it was a wonder she
wasn't hoarse from the amount of time she got
trapped talking on the phone, when she suddenly
turned and spotted Cameron in the door.

Her self-confidence skidded downhill like a sled
with no brake.

It was so unfair. Cameron had been in a coma-
quality nap; she knew he had, so you'd think he'd
have woken up still sleepy. And he yawned from the
doorway, but she still felt his eyes on her face like
sharp, bright lasers. Interested. Scoping out the territory from her disheveled braid to her bare feet.

''You're a hell of a busy woman,'' he said. His
tone was almost accusing, as if she'd misled him into
thinking she was too scatterbrained to maintain any
kind of serious, busy life.

"I'm sorry if the phone woke you. It's been hell coming back to the town where I grew up, because everyone knows me." She added quickly, "Are you hungry? All I have to do is pop the shrimp on the grill and I'm ready—"

"I'll do it, so you can stay off that hurt foot."

Whenever *she* woke up from a nap, she had cheek creases and bed hair and a crab's mood until she got going again. He seemed to wake up just as full of hell and awareness as when he'd dropped off. There was no way she could like a man with that kind of personality flaw. Worse yet, he proved himself to be one of those easygoing guys, the kind who rolled with the punches and tended to fit in whatever kind of gathering they walked into. He started her grill before she could—and the barbecue was one that could make her mother swear; it *never* lit unless you begged it desperately. Then he found her silverware drawer and set the table without asking. Granted, it wasn't challenging to find anyone's silverware drawer, but for a man to make himself useful without praising him every thirty seconds? It was spooky.

There had to be a catch.

"What do you usually drink for dinner? Wine, water, what?"

"You can have wine if you want. I know I've got a couple open bottles on the second shelf—not fancy quality, but okay. For myself, though, this day has been too much of a blinger to do wine."

He grinned. The smile transformed his face, whipped off five years and made her think what a hellion he must have been as a little boy. "So you'd like to drink…?"

"Long Island iced tea," she said primly.

He burst out laughing. "I got it now. Cut straight to the hard stuff."

"It's been an exhausting day," she defended.

"You're not kidding."

The phone rang yet again—it was just another call, nothing that affected life or death—so after that she turned down the volume and let the answering machine pick up. She wasn't ready to fix the sun and the moon, but she *was* prepared to concentrate on the lavender deal.

Still, the instant they sat down to dinner, it was obvious they wouldn't be talking business for a bit longer. "You haven't eaten in days?" she inquired tactfully.

"Not real food. Not food someone's actually taken the time to make from scratch." It was impossible to eat her spicy shrimp without licking one's fingers. But when he licked his, he also met her eyes. "Would you marry me?"

She rolled her eyes. "I'll bet you say that to all the girls."

"Actually, I never say it. I figured out, from a very short, very bad marriage years ago, that I'm too footloose to be the marrying kind. But I'm more than willing to make an exception for you.''

''Well, thanks so much,'' she said kindly, ''but I'd only say yes to my worst enemy, and I don't know you well enough to be sure you could ever get on that list.''

He'd clearly been teasing, but now he hesitated, his eyes narrowing speculatively. He even stopped eating—for fifteen seconds at least. ''That's an interesting thing to say. You think you'd be so hard to be married to?''

''I don't think. I know.'' She hadn't meant to side-track down a serious road. It was his fault. Once he'd implied that he wasn't in the marriage market, she instinctively seemed to relax more. Now, though, she steered quickly back to lighter teasing. ''Never mind that. The point is that you might want to be careful making rash offers like that, at least until you know the woman a little better.''

''Normally, yeah. But in your case I know everything I need to know. I haven't had food like this since…hell. Maybe since never. Where the hell did you learn to cook?''

''My mom. Most of her family was French, and she loved to putter in the kitchen, let all three of us girls putter with her. My one older sister is downright fabulous. Give Daisy a grain of salt, and I swear she can make something of it. Me, though…I just like to mess around with food.''

"Well, I can cook okay. I even like to—when I've got a kitchen to play around in. But at my best, I never came up with dishes like this."

That was enough compliments. The cats were circling, which he didn't seem to mind. She'd never fed them from the table, but that didn't mean anything. Telling a cat not to do something was like waving a red flag in front of a bull, and they'd all smelled the shrimp cooking.

Outside, evening was coming on. The crickets hadn't started up yet, but the birds had already quieted, the last of the day's sultry wind died down. It was that pre-dusk time when a soft, intimate yellow haze settled a gentle blanket on everything.

He'd leveled one plate, filled another. She had no choice about piling on more food. God knew how the man stayed so lean, but it was obvious he'd been starved. He even ate her asparagus soup with gusto, and that took guts for a guy.

"I didn't see that much, driving up—but it looks like you've got a beautiful piece of land here," he remarked.

"It is. Been in my family since the 1700s. My dad's side was from Scotland. Lots of people with that background here. Maybe they felt at home with the rocky land and the slopes and the stern winters." She asked, "Sometimes I catch a little French accent when you talk...which I guess is obvious if you work at Jeunnesse. But it's not there all the time. Do you actually live in France?''

''Yes and no. I've worked for Jeunnesse for better than fifteen years now. I like them, like the work. But basically what I've always loved is traveling around the globe. So I've got a small apartment in Provence, but I've kept my American citizenship, have a cottage in upstate New York. Both are only places I hang my hat. I live for months at a time wherever Jeunnesse sends me.''

''So there's no place you really call home?''

''Nope. I think I was just born rootless.'' He said it as if wanting to make sure she really heard him. ''You're the opposite, aren't you? Everything in your family's land is about people who value roots.''

''Yes.'' She suspected women had chased him, hoping they'd be the one who could turn him around. It was so ironic. She was as root bound as a woman could be. All she'd ever wanted in life was a man to love and a house full of kids. Still, discovering they were such opposites reassured her totally that nothing personal was likely to happen between them. ''You've never had a hunger for kids?'' she asked him.

''I've got kids. Two daughters, Miranda and Kate.'' He leaned over and filled her glass. She wasn't sure whether she'd finished two or he just kept topping off her first one. Either way she knew she wouldn't normally be prying into a stranger's life without the help of some Long Island iced tea. "My ex-wife still lives in upstate New York—which is why I've kept a cottage up there—so that I can easily come back a few times a year to see the girls. Although, often enough as they've gotten older, they've come to see me. They didn't mind having a dad spring for tickets to Paris or Buenos Aires."

"But didn't you mind missing a lot of their growing-up years?"

He got up and served the grape sorbet—once he'd determined that was the one course he hadn't tried yet. "Yeah. I missed it. But I tried the suit-and-tie kind of life when I was married. Almost went out of my mind. She kicked me out, told me I was the most irresponsible son of a gun she'd ever laid eyes on. But I wasn't."

"No?"

"No. I never missed a day's work, never failed to bring home a paycheck. It was sitting still I couldn't handle. Everyone can't like the same music, you know?"

She knew, but she also suspected there had to be some kind of story in those lake-blue eyes. Maybe he was a vagabond, one of those guys who couldn't stand to be tied down. But maybe something had made him that way.

She stood up and hefted their plates. His life wasn't her business, of course, or ever likely to be.

"I'll pop the dishes in the dishwasher, and then we can talk outside."

"Nope." He stood up, too. "I'll pop the dishes in the dishwasher, and you can put your foot up outside."

She let him.

Once he called out, "Is it okay if I put the cats in the dishwasher, too?"

And she yelled back, "Why, sure. If you don't want to live until morning."

He banged around in there, whistling something that sounded like "Hard-Hearted Woman," occasionally scolding the cats, but eventually he finished up and pushed through the back screen door, carrying another pitcher, sweating cold and jammed with ice cubes.

She'd already settled on the old slatted swing, with her sore foot perched on the swing arm and her good foot braced against the porch rail to keep the swing moving at a lullaby speed. He took the white wicker rocker and poured two glasses. "Two iced teas. No alcohol involved."

"Good." It was time they talked seriously. She knew it as well as he did, but the screen door suddenly opened as if by a ghost hand, startling them both...only to see a flat-faced golden Persian nuzzle her way outside. As soon as Cameron settled back in the rocker, the thug-size cat leaped on his lap.

"Could you tell your damn cat it's hotter than

blazes, and I need a fur coat on my lap like I need poison ivy?''

"It's hard to hear over her purring, but honestly, if she's in your way, just put her down.''

"Get down," he told the cat, in a lover's croon. But that wasn't the voice he used with her. Maybe he was stroking the cat, but the eyes that met hers had turned cool and careful. "You think we've spent enough time getting comfortable with each other?''

"Enough to talk," she agreed, and settled one thing right off the bat. "You've spent hours traveling and it's too late now to find a place in White Hills. You can stay here tonight, no matter how we work out everything else.''

"I'll camp outside," he said.

"Fine." She wasn't making a big deal out of where he hung his hat. He'd won some trust from her. Not a ton. But if she didn't feel precisely *safe* around him, it wasn't because she feared he was a serial killer or criminal. The man had more character in his jaw bone than most men did in their whole bodies. "But it's your plan for my lavender that I want to hear about.''

"Okay. Then let's start back at the beginning. Apparently you've been developing some strains of lavender in your greenhouse. And over a year ago, you sent your sister Daisy a sample of a lavender you particularly liked.''

"I remember all that. I also remember her telling me that she'd passed it on to someone at Jeunnesse."

"That was me. And initially I thought your sister was the grower. That's why I talked directly with her instead of you."

Violet sighed in exasperation. "Honestly, Daisy wouldn't have deliberately lied to you. She's just had this thing about protecting me ever since I got divorced. So she probably just tried to keep me out of it until she was sure something good could come from a meeting."

"Well, the point is...you've been crossbreeding a variety of lavender strains and come up with several of your own."

"Yes," she concurred.

"Well, Jeunnesse has been making perfume for over a hundred years. They have thousands of acres of lavender under contract. You know the history? Provence was always known for its acres of lavender. It's breathtaking in the spring and summer, nothing like it on the planet."

Violet nodded. "I saw it twice as a girl. Our mom's family was from that area. We still have cousins there, and Mom always, always grew some lavender in the backyard to remind her of home. That's how I got my ideas to develop different strains."

Fluffball—her biggest cat, and the one with the brazen-honky-tonk-woman character—draped over his lap and exposed her entire belly for his long, slow stroking fingers. "Maybe you did it for fun, but it's more than fun to Jeunnesse. The lavender ground around Provence has become problematic for the perfume growers. It's not a matter of depleted soil or anything like that, because you can always add or subtract nutrients from a soil. But nematodes and diseases build up when the same crop is grown year after year, decade after decade. So now the company seeks to acquire long-term contracts with people across the world who have the right growing situation for lavender."

Before he could continue the educational lecture, she lifted a finger to interrupt. "Cameron. You don't have to talk to me as if I were quite that dumb. I know most of this," she said impatiently.

For a second she forgot how hard she'd worked to give him the impression she was a dotty flake, but he continued without a blink. "Then you also know that lavender isn't hard to grow. It doesn't need the pampering that lots of plants require. There are also already hundreds of strains of lavender across Europe and America and South America."

She knew that, too, but this time she didn't dare interrupt.

"So…now you come to my role in this. I'm one of Jeunnesse's agricultural chemists. What that amounts to is that I have a fancy degree that gives me a chance to travel and get my hands dirty at the same time. My job is to study new lavender strains. To evaluate how they work in a perfume equation. In fact, it literally took months for our lab to complete an analysis of the lavender you sent.''

''And—''

''And it's incomparable. It's sturdy. It's strong. The scent is strong and true, hardy. But more than all the growing characteristics I could test, your strain of lavender has the magic.''

''The magic?''

Cameron lifted his hands—annoying the cat when he stopped petting her. ''I don't know how else to explain it. There's a certain chemical ingredient and reaction in lavender that makes it critical to the fine perfumes. It's not the lavender smell that's so important. It's how the lavender works chemically with the other ingredients. To say it simplistically, I'd call it 'staying power.' And I can explain that to you in more depth another time. The point is that your lavender has it. We think. I think.''

She'd never grown the strains of lavender for profit. Or for a crop. Or for its perfume potential. She'd started puttering in the green houses after her divorce, when she'd first come home and had nowhere to go with all the anger, all the loss. Growing things had been renewing. But hearing Cameron talk, seeing the sunset glow on his face, feeling his steady, dark eyes as night came on, invoked a shiver of excitement and interest she'd never expected. "All right."

"Initially, Jeunnesse just wants to buy your crop. However you planned to harvest it, I'll either take charge or work alongside you, whichever you want. Obviously, your twenty acres are no big deal in themselves, it takes five hundred pounds of flowers to make an ounce of lavender oil. But I can easily get enough to analyze the quality and nature and characteristics of your lavender. Enough for me to extract some oil, my own way, under my own control, so we'll know for sure what we could have."

She'd stopped rocking. Stopped nursing her bee-stung foot. In fact, she'd completely forgotten about her bee-stung foot. "And then what happens?"

"Then, at the end of the harvest, we make some decisions. If your strain is as unique as I think it is, you have several choices. No matter what, you want to get started on patenting your strain. Then, if you want to grow it yourself—and can buy or rent the acreage to do it—then Jeunnesse would offer you a long-term contract. Another choice would be for you to sell the rights to Jeunnesse for a period of years. We're talking a long-term commitment, worth a great deal of money on both sides—that is, assuming your strain of lavender lives up to its potential. But we have to see what this mysterious strain of yours can do before making any promises."

Violet wasn't asking for promises—from him,

from Jeunnesse. When it came down to it, she wasn't asking for any promises from anyone anymore. She'd stopped believing in luck—or that anyone would be there for her—the day she'd caught Simpson in bed with his fertile little bimbo.

Now, though, she felt old, rusty emotions trying to emerge from her heart's cobwebs. For the lavender, she thought. It's not that she really believed she was suddenly going to get ridiculously lucky over something so chancy as her playing around in the greenhouse. It was just that there was no reason not to go along with Cameron's plan. Whether she got rich or not didn't matter. She had nothing to lose—and a lot of fun and interest to be had—just to see if this crazy thing came true.

For the lavender, she'd take a chance.

Not for the man.

But then, she'd never thought for a minute that Cameron Lachlan was a threat to her heart, so that wasn't even worth a millisecond's worry.

Four

The moonless night was silent as a promise. Cameron lay on his back on the open sleeping bag, trying to fathom why he felt so strangely moody and restless. He wasn't remotely moody by nature. Normally he'd have inhaled a special night like this. Clouds were building, stealing in from the west, concealing the moon but also bringing tufts of cooler air. God knew he was tired, and when he closed his eyes he could smell the sweet summer grass, the lavender in the distance, the blooms whispering out of Violet's garden.

The lights had gone off in the upstairs bedroom an hour ago. Vi had told him he could sleep inside—in the spare room, on the living room couch, on the porch, wherever he wanted. But Cam had sensed she was uncertain around him. If sleeping outside might make her feel safer, it was sure no hardship for him.

Any other time, he'd have treasured the night. He'd found some wild mint growing near her mailbox, rubbed it on his neck and arms, enough to chase off the mosquitoes and bugs. No dew tonight, so the grass was warm and dry. He heard the hoot of a barn owl, the cry of crickets. Fireflies danced as if Violet's long lawn were their personal ballroom.

He owned the world on nights like this—or that's how he'd always felt before. Instead the frown on his forehead seemed glued there. It made no sense. He loved his freedom, loved the smells and scents of a night this breathless, this private. He'd never been prey to loneliness. Something just seemed off with him lately. Especially tonight.

After Violet had gone inside, he'd walked all over her family farm. She had a pretty piece of land—but he'd seen pretty pieces of land before and never felt inclined to plunk down roots.

Cameron had long realized he had an allergy to roots, or any other possessions that could tie him down. His father had built up millions, running a company that—as far as Cam was concerned—had taken over his dad's life. Peter Lachlan had died before the age of fifty-five, with a son who never knew him, a wife who'd slept alone most of their marriage and fabulous possessions that didn't do much more than collect dust. Even as a young boy, Cameron had refused to follow in his father's footsteps. He'd carved his own, and if his independence and vagabond ways weren't everyone's choice, he'd loved his life.

It was just tonight that a weird, unsettled restlessness seemed to hem his mood, nipping at his consciousness, stealing his peace.

A sudden brisk wind brushed his hair. The cats, who'd been purring relentlessly at his side, stood up and shot toward the house. The black sky suddenly started moving, clouds being whipped like cake batter. The fireflies disappeared.

He felt the first drop of rain, didn't move. If the sky got serious, he'd move onto the porch, but it was still warmish. If anything, the sudden spin of damp wind brought out her farm's sweet scents. He told himself he was looking at the old red barn with the Dutch shingled roof, the rock fence, the rolling slope in front of him. But somehow his gaze kept straying to her house. Not the architecture of the sturdy old white farmhouse…but the shiny windows on the second story.

Specifically the window on the east. The one where the light had been switched off an hour before. The one with the filmy drift of white curtain at sill level. The one where he'd seen her unbraid that long, long pale hair and shake it free. The one where she'd reached behind her to unbutton her blouse—and then, damnation, disappeared from sight to take the rest of her clothes off.

He couldn't figure her out.

She was awfully bright for a batty woman.

She cooked better than a professional chef. Had more business pots going—the land, the house, the greenhouses, her herb and flower business—than any one person could normally take care of. She seemed to be emotionally and financially thriving on all that chaos, even if she did choose to dress like an old-fashioned spinster. She also seemed to make a point of acting as if she were witless, goofy, one of those fragile women who'd swoon if life put any stress on them.

As far as he could tell, she loved stress.

Most confusing of all, though, those soft eyes were studying him—then shying away—as if she were a young girl unfamiliar with the chemical pull between the sexes. She'd been married, for heaven's sakes. She'd surely had a hundred men react to her before. Besides which, he knew perfectly well when he sent off interested signals to a woman.

He *was* interested. Hell, she was sensual to her fingertips, complicated in personality and character, and he'd always liked complicated woman. But he needed to seriously work with her, and the instant they met, he picked up her wariness of him. So he'd sent out no signals, no vibes. He *knew* he hadn't. And he sure as hell wouldn't go near a woman when she made it clear she wasn't in the market for attention— at least not from him.

But damn. She was a handful of fascination.

Another raindrop plopped on his forehead. Then another.

From one breath to the next, a meandering drizzle suddenly turned into a noisy deluge. Skinny needles pelted down, warm and wet. He climbed to his feet quickly enough, but before he could scoop up the sleeping bag, he heard a warning growl of thunder...followed by a breathtaking crack of lightning that seemed to split open the sky.

Abruptly her back screen door slammed open. "Damn it! Get in here!"

For a second he had to grin, lightning or no lightning. Unquestionably the screech came from his delicate flower of a hostess. The one with the vintage clothes and the fluttery hands who made out as if stringing a whole thought in a single sentence was a difficult challenge for her.

A yard light slapped on. Ms. Violet—harridan— Campbell showed up on the porch steps, barefoot, her tank and boxer shorts looking distinctly unvintage-like. In fact, her boobs looked poured into that tank, making him pause for another moment in sheer respectful appreciation.

"Have you lost your mind? That's lightning, for God's sake! Didn't you hear the storm coming? I kept waiting and waiting for you to come inside, but obviously you've been living in France too long. In America, we know enough to get out of the rain.''

"I'm coming—"

"By the time you get around to coming in, we'll both be electrocuted. Look. I may not have welcomed the idea of your sleeping in the house—for God's sake, I don't *know* you. But a storm is a storm, for Pete's sake.

"Pete's sake, God's sake… I'm getting confused whose sake is involved here—"

"Lachlan! Move your butt!''

Well, he'd been planning on it, but while she was screaming at him, she was also getting rained on. Which meant that tank and boxers were getting wet. And so was that long silvery curtain of blond hair.

Maybe he was thirty-seven, but he hoped to hell he never got so mature he failed to appreciate a beautiful woman. Particularly a beautiful woman whose attributes were outlined delectably between the yard light and the rain and the lightning.

On the other hand, being electrocuted posed a threat to his long-term ability to appreciate much of anything, so he hustled to the door just behind her. The instant she opened the screen, four cats seemed to leap from nowhere, determined to cut inline. And then, in the blink of a second, her yard light went out.

"There goes the power,'' she muttered.

It was his instinct to take charge, especially when a woman was in trouble. He couldn't help it. It was how he'd been raised—not by his absentee father, but by his mom, who'd expected even small kids to step up when there was a problem. He'd never minded. He liked stepping up. But in this case, the image Violet projected of being scatterbrained and helpless was—he was coming to understand—totally misleading.

She moved around in the dark, apparently gathering up candles—not the pretty decorative candles she had strewn all over the place but the practical, no-drippers she apparently stashed for no-power circumstances like this.

The back door opened off her kitchen, where she lit two and put them on the oak table, then kept going. She put one lit candle into a hurricane lamp, placing it in the bathroom off the kitchen, then carried more into the living room.

The living room, he'd noticed before, seemed to be part of the original farmhouse. In the dark, a guy could kill himself on all the stuff, but basically it was one of those long narrow rooms, with long narrow windows, requiring a long narrow couch. She'd done it all in roses and pinks—in case anyone could conceivably doubt she was female to the bone. Wade past the estrogen, though, and there was a massive old-fashioned brick hearth—big enough to roast a boar or two—where she lit four more candles.

"Better?" she asked.

"Can practically see well enough to read," he said mildly, although that wasn't exactly true. No matter how many fat white candles she lit, they didn't lighten the shadows. Mostly they lit up her. Eyes darker than secrets flashed up to his face, but he didn't think she really noticed him. She was too frazzled to think. Too frazzled to notice how that damp, stretchy red tank top was cupping her breasts.

"I can't guarantee we'll have light or water before morning," she said unhappily.

"Well, hell. I expected you to shut off that storm and restore the power immediately. What's wrong with you?"

He'd thought to lighten her up. It didn't seem to work. "I mean...I'm not sure the toilets will work."

"Inconvenient for sure, but more for you than me. If I have to step behind a tree before morning, I can probably cope."

"I'm afraid there's no phone."

"Damn. There goes another opportunity to make friends by calling people after midnight."

"*Lachlan.* Would you quit being so damn nice!"

He didn't get it. She seemed to be chasing around, lighting more candles for no particular reason that he could fathom. It was the middle of the night. So there was a storm. It was a sturdy house, nothing threatened by a little thunder and lightning.

And accusing him of being nice was a low blow.

No self-respecting male liked to think of himself as
"nice." Yeah, he'd offered to sleep outside and
made a point of communicating that he was a here-
today-gone-tomorrow kind of guy, but that was just
so she wouldn't be afraid of his coming on to her. It
wasn't because he wanted her to think he was *nice*.
Sheesh, how insulting could she get?

"You want me to drive into town? Is that why
you're upset, because you feel stuck with me under
your roof?" he asked. "There's just no reason to get
your liver in an uproar. If I'm a problem for you, I'll
just take off, go find a hotel or motel—"

"Oh, don't be ridiculous," she said crossly.
"You're not taking off cross-country in the middle
of the night in a thunderstorm. I never heard of anything so stupid."

Well, hell. Somehow he had to find some way to
communicate with her a hell of a lot better than they
were doing so far. They hadn't even started to do
serious business, yet he seemed to invoke some kind
of strange response from her. She was running on
froth and emotional fumes. He needed her straight
and coherent.

So he snagged her arm when she tried to go flying
by—God knew where she was sprinting off to this
time, but apparently her goal was to find more candles, even though the living room already looked like
a witch's lair. She went stark still the instant his hand
closed on her wrist.

"What are you doing?" she asked. She didn't shout it. Or whisper. Only...asked.

He felt her pulse gallop. Felt the warmth of her skin. Felt her gaze shoot to his face as if compelled by their sudden closeness. "I'm confused what's going on here. Are you afraid of storms?"

"No. Heavens. I grew up here. We get blizzards in winter, thunderstorms in summer. Vermonters are sturdy people. Actually, I love the rain."

Typical for her, she offered a lot of talk but very little information. "So it's just me, then? I'm doing something to make you nervous?"

"I'm not nervous. I'm always goofy," she assured him. "Ask anyone."

He struggled not to laugh. If he'd laughed, of course, she would have diverted him from the problem. Which made him wonder if that was why she came across so scatterbrained—because it was such an effective defense for her. "I don't want to ask 'anyone.' You're right here, I'm asking you. If you want me out of here, I'll leave. Just say the word."

She still hadn't seemed to breathe, although his hand had immediately dropped from her wrist. "You're staying. As long as you don't mind staying with a batty woman."

"You're not batty."

"You don't know me. I know me.. And if I say I'm batty, I should know."

God. It was like trying to reason with a cotton

puff. Only she wasn't a cotton puff. In all that flickering candlelight her hair was drying, looking like silky silver. The pulse in her throat was beating hard. Her skin, her mouth, defined softness. And her eyes…she was still meeting his eyes. There was nothing goofy there, just the awareness between a man and a woman that carried enough heat to melt the Arctic.

He had no intention of kissing her. Maybe she was just figuring out the chemistry, but he'd known it since he first laid eyes on her. There was no explaining what drew a man and woman together—particularly when the two people were as contrarily opposite as they seemed to be—but Cameron didn't sweat problems he couldn't solve. When there was heat, there was heat. You didn't lie about it. You didn't pretend. You just faced the truth, whatever it was.

And the truth was, he didn't care if there was a combustible furnace of chemistry between them, he wasn't going to kiss her.

Yet suddenly he was.

He wanted to blame it on the moonlight…only there was none. In the dark candlelit room, with the growl of thunder and hiss of rain just outside, there seemed nothing alive but her and him. Nothing he could smell but her soft skin, the flower scents drifting from her hair, her throat. Nothing he could hear but the pounding of his own heart, in anticipation.

He didn't exactly remember how he reached for her, how his hands happened to curve on the swell of her shoulders, slide down, slide around her back to pull her into him. Yet he knew the exact moment, the exact sensation, when her hands reached up to lock behind his neck.

He could have sworn she'd been sending him keep-off, no-trespassing messages—yet if she didn't want to be kissed, she sure acted as if she did. Her arms swooped around his neck and she came up on tiptoe.

There was one more brief millisecond when he remembered all the reasons why this was a bad idea, but once she was that close, all rational bets were off. In a blink his mind turned to mush. Electric, excited mush.

He hadn't kissed anyone in a while. He hadn't kissed a woman this way in years. Hadn't wanted to. He thought it was long gone from his life, from his heart—that pull, that wonder, that wildness. He didn't know why it had to be her, didn't care.

She tasted like magic. Sweet, soft, alluring. Unforgettable. That pale-blond hair sifted through his fingers. Her head tilted back, accepting his kiss, inviting more than the graze of his mouth. Her lips asked to be taken. He answered.

One tentative kiss melted into another stronger one, another richer one, and then another that lost all track of time and space. His tongue found hers. Her heartbeat was suddenly racing, chasing, against his. Her arms nested tighter around his neck, and his hands molded down her spine, down to her fanny, pulling her closer to him.

Silver rain shivered down. Candles flickered. Shadows whispered of loneliness and old hurts and need. She'd been hurt. She'd been lonely. She needed. And maybe those were secrets she never meant to reveal to a stranger, but she didn't tell him anything. She just kissed him back, wildly, freely, intimately.

Cameron thought he was a man who took gutsy risks...but she was the brave one, the honest one, revealing so much. Something in her called him. Something in him answered her with a huge, name-less well of feeling that he'd never known he had.

He raised his head suddenly, feeling shocked and disoriented and unsettled. Her eyes were still closed, lashes lying like kitten whiskers on her cheeks, but when she finally looked at him, her eyes were lu-minous and her mouth wet and trembly.

"I never meant..." he started to say.

She gulped in a breath. "It's all right. I didn't think you did."

"It was the storm."

"I know."

"It was the moonlight."

"I know."

"I *need* you to know you can trust me. The last

thing in hell I wanted was to make you worried I'd—"

"I'm not worried. I'm thirty-four, Cameron. Too old to trust someone I barely know. But also way too old to make more of a kiss than what it was."

"You said it exactly. That was just a kiss." He added, "Right?"

"Right," she said firmly. "We'll just mark this down as a moment's madness and forget all about it."

Five

Violet's bedside telephone rang just after five in the morning. She jolted awake like a kicked colt. Mental images of her mom and dad or her sisters in an accident flashed through her mind in a panic as she fumbled for the phone. No one called this early unless there was a dire emergency—or unless someone had the sensitivity of an ox.

She clapped the receiver to her ear and recognized Simpson's voice.

Her pulse climbed back down from the worry stratosphere. Her ex-husband—like PMS and rain—could always be counted on to show up at the most inconvenient time. "Insensitive" should have been his middle name.

"Were you asleep?" he asked, his tone warmly ebullient.

"Me? Heavens, no." Why tell the truth? He wasn't worth it.

"Good. Because I didn't want to wake you. I just couldn't seem to resist calling. Vi, Livie had the baby."

As if someone slapped her, Violet instinctively braced against the headboard. "Congratulations."

"A son this time. We're going to name him John Edward, but Livie wants to call him Ed, after me."

"You got your son," she said.

"Yeah." Pride colored his booming baritone— pride that he'd never felt for her. Or with her. "Almost nine pounds. Twenty-two inches."

"He'll be playing football before you know it."

"Yeah, in fact—"

"I hope Livie's okay, and I'm happy you've got a son, Ed." She hung up, plunking down the receiver before he had a chance to continue the conversation.

For a second she had the oddest trouble catching her breath. The east window was open, letting in cool, rain-freshed air. Outside, nothing stirred in the pre-dawn light. Even the bugs were still snoozing. The sky was paler than smoke, the sunrise nothing more than a promise this early, but last night's violent storm had completely washed away.

Remembering the storm made her also remember how soundly she'd been dreaming until the telephone call. The dream pictures were still vivid in her mind…images of tumultuous kisses from a Scotsman named Lachlan, backdropped by Scottish lakes and moors and mist, her running naked and uninhibited through a moss-carpeted forest and Lachlan catching her.

The call from her ex-husband had certainly wilted *that* dream.

She pushed away the sheet and stood up, not awake yet—or wanting to be—but knowing she didn't have a prayer of going back to sleep. Not after *that* call. She tiptoed around the room, gathering clothes, not turning on a light, not wanting to wake Cameron down the hall.

It wasn't hard to navigate, even in the darkness. Unlike the rest of the house, which she'd jam-packed with girl stuff, she'd redone two of the upstairs bedrooms completely differently. One she'd turned into an office. For the other, her childhood bedroom, she'd bought a Shaker bed and dresser, painted the walls a virgin white, bought a plush white carpet, and called it quits.

Family and friends would find the decorating strange, she knew. All her life she'd gone for lots of color and oddball style and ''stuff,'' yet, especially right after the divorce, the barren room suited her in ways she'd never tried to explain—not to friends, not even to family.

Now, though, the point was that she could easily

find her way around the room even in the dark…at least, if it wasn't for the cats tripping her. On the rare occasions she woke up this early, the cats usually ignored her and continued sleeping, but maybe they sensed how suddenly rattled she felt—possibly because of remembering Cameron's totally unexpected and very real kisses the night before. Possibly because of her ex-husband's call.

Ed hadn't called out of meanness. Violet had figured out a long time ago that Ed was far too unimaginative to be deliberately mean. He undoubtedly believed she'd want to know that his second child had been born, the son he'd wanted so much. No one knew more than Violet how much he'd wanted a son.

Downstairs, lights were on all over the place—she'd forgotten about losing power the night before. Forgotten almost everything when that sassy upstart Scotsman had pulled her into his arms.

She pulled on mud boots, a patchwork light jacket over her long denim skirt. Her hair was hanging in a wild heap down her back, but she didn't care. She needed…something. Air. A slap of morning. Some way, somehow, to catch her breath. She hadn't been all that upset about those kisses from Cameron until her ex had called.

Now, she felt all churned up. A young rabbit hopped across the grass, trying to evade her bodyguard contingent of cats—none of whom could catch road kill, they were all so fat and lazy, but the baby bunny didn't know that.

Violet aimed for the front door of the Herb Haven, then changed her mind and headed for the greenhouses. There were two. The newest one she'd built herself, a couple years ago, but by this time in the summer, it was almost empty. Plants were all outside, either transported to the nursery or for sale in the business.

The original greenhouse, though, had been her mother's. It wasn't as high-tech as the new one, the heating and cooling and watering systems not even half as efficient. But her mom's sacred pruning shears were still hung on the wall, as was the old French apron she used to wear. Violet could remember the three sisters chasing up and down the aisles while Margaux potted and fussed with plants—her mom had always been the kind of mother who encouraged kids to get their hands dirty, to get *into* life, not just watch from the bleachers. Her sisters had often gone off with their dad into the fields. Not her.

She'd loved hanging out with her mom, loved watching Margaux nurturing and babying each flower, each herb, as if it alone were precious to her. She loved to dry the herbs, to watch her mom create artistic arrangements, to hear her mother insist that she needed to listen to each plant to understand what it needed. Her mom was a life lover, emotional about everything, an unrepentant romantic, a woman to the core. Margaux, in fact, was the only one who knew the real reason she'd divorced Simpson.

Of course, if Violet started remembering that ghastly memory, how Margaux had wrapped her up in a long, rocking hug and tried to soothe her like a child, she'd burst out crying. She didn't mind crying. She did it regularly, but it was just too darn early for that kind of heavy emotion, so she pushed up her sleeves and started puttering. In the heat of summer, there wasn't much left here in the greenhouse, either, but she still had some experiments going.

She plucked dry leaves, smelled the soil for health, and was just uncoiling a long skinny hose to mist-water her babies when she heard the door swing open. Cameron stood there, looking as devilish and sexy as he had the night before. In spite of the cool morning, his shirt was unbuttoned and he was wearing jeans so old and worn they cupped his bitsy butt and long, lean legs.

"Damn, did I wake you up? I tried to be quiet. After all your traveling, I figured you'd sleep most of the morning if you had a chance," she said.

"You didn't wake me up, but the phone did. A call that early usually means trouble. Everything okay?"

"Just hunky-dory," she said lightly. And then had to sniff fast. Tears welled in her eyes before she could possibly stop them—not that she would. When she was a young girl, she hated being so impulsive and emotional, but these days, she knew the power of it. Men got shook up when they saw tears. They backed away from an emotional woman. It all worked out fine. Usually.

"Hey." He saw the tears, and instead of looking frantic and freaked like any *normal* man, he walked slowly toward her. "What are we talking here? Bad news, bad morning, what?"

"An idiotic mood, that's all."

"Nobody died?"

"Nope."

"Some idiot dump you?"

"God, no."

"You hurt yourself? Another bee sting?"

"No. Nothing happened."

"Someone called," he persisted.

"Yeah. My ex-husband. To tell me that he and his wife had a baby. Their second. A son. They were very happy. And I'm very happy for them." Tears welled up again. Announcing her happiness and crying at the same time should *certainly* have ensured that Cameron thought she was a fruitcake.

Instead, as if unconcerned whether she made any sense or not, he ambled past her, squeezing her shoulder momentarily when he passed by. And then started snooping. Poking at her pots and plants. Sniffing. Tasting. Literally tasting.

How could she help but be diverted? "You usually eat dirt?"

"Yeah. I've tried every fancy chemical test known to man, but sometimes the senses seem to tell the most important truth. A taste'll tell me if the soil is highly acid or not." He moved on, doing more poking, more smelling, more snooping. "These are more of your lavender experiments?"

"Not just lavender." Because she was still feeling emotionally shaky, her tongue seemed to get loose. Not that her tongue needed an excuse to talk incessantly, but this time there was an actual reason. "Originally when I came home after the divorce, I didn't know what I wanted to do. Mom and Dad had retired south. This house was just left available for family. Dad wasn't ready to do anything else with it, thinking one of us girls could still want to live here. So it was perfect for me to move into…and I didn't have to rush getting a job, because I'd received a big settlement from the divorce. Partly there was a lot of money because he wanted the matrimonial house himself, and I didn't, so I got that share. But whatever. I thought of that settlement as guilt money."

"And was it?"

"Yeah. Big guilt on his part. But the point was, I came here and suddenly started remembering being a kid, trailing after my mom, all the pleasure we got out of growing things. Long term, I didn't have any idea what I was going to do for a career, but for a couple years the Herb Haven just hit me as right. A divorce is like…destroying something, you know?

So I wanted to create something. Grow things. Do something purposefully constructive instead of destructive.''

"You've got more than a green thumb," Cameron remarked.

"Yeah. It's kind of a joke in the family. Everything I touch seems to reproduce tenfold." Again she felt a round of tears threatening. "Come on," she said briskly. "I'll show you the lavender."

"First, I have to make you breakfast."

"Pardon?"

"Breakfast. You haven't had any. I haven't had any. And since you put me up, I'm cooking."

He made her crepes with blueberries. She sat at the table, lazy as a slug, letting him wait on her. It was another of the behaviors she'd taken up after Simpson—not kowtowing to men; acting like a spoiled princess. All normal men—certainly all Vermont men—steered way clear of an obviously high-maintenance woman, but Cameron...he just didn't seem to be normal.

If he remembered those potent kisses from the night before—or if they meant anything to him—he never let on.

If he found anything odd in a woman wearing dangling marquisite earrings and a patchwork jacket and rubber boots and uncombed hair, he never let on about that, either.

"I'm going to need a place to set up a minilab. If

I won't be in your way, I could use the potting room in your greenhouse—the old greenhouse we were in this morning. It seems perfect. It's got a sink and a longer counter for a work space, exactly what I need.''

"It'll be too hot there," she said.

"I'm not afraid of heat."

"You'll get interrupted—"

"I can work around noise and interruptions."

"There's no comfortable chair. I can't make it into any kind of good working environment—"

"I don't need everything perfect. In fact, I'm usually bored by perfection. Life's a hell of a lot more interesting if we take the road less traveled, yes? Wasn't it a Vermont man who said that?"

Well, yes, but Robert Frost was safely dead, which Cameron certainly wasn't. In fact, although Cam was talking about his work…he kept looking at her. At her eyes. At her unkempt hair. At her bare mouth. As if he were communicating that he liked complicated women. Uncomfortable, difficult women. Hot women. As if he'd pegged her as less than perfect, the kind of woman who interested him.

"Well, do what you want," she said crossly. She glanced at the clock and abruptly stood up. "Thanks for breakfast, but I really have to go. I should have already opened my Herb Haven. I'll catch up with you later—"

She started to turn away when he suddenly said her name, very quietly, very gently.

"What?"

"I just want to make sure we're clear. You're okay with me working here. Living here. Setting up here for now."

"Sure," she said.

"We need to sign some agreements."

She motioned, an exasperated gesture. "I don't care about legal stuff like that."

"Yeah, you do. Because it's about potential money for you and protecting your rights."

"Well, I don't have time now." She took off, leaving him with the dishes and her house. Leaving him, surely, with the impression that she was flaky and emotional and not the kind of woman he'd want to be involved with.

He'd readily established that he wasn't looking for involvement. But those kisses last night—she didn't trust them. It seemed wise to make absolutely sure there was a five-mile fence of emotional distance established between them...so there'd be no more kisses.

Not just for his sake. For hers. Because a man like Cameron reminded her of everything she couldn't have.

Cam always had an unspoken impression that small towns in Vermont were quiet, bucolic, peaceful.

Violet's place was as peaceful as JFK International Airport on a holiday.

He made a quick trek to view her twenty acres of lavender, but he swiftly returned to the yard. He couldn't be that close to the lavender without making himself crazy. The field was breathtaking. She had plants close to harvest, florets already starting to open up, a few that were just days away from the perfect time to extract oil from and test. But he didn't feel right about touching the lavender until they'd both signed some legal agreements. Violet could trust him not to take advantage of her, but of course, she had no way to know that.

Sometime that day he simply had to trap her alone and sit on her until he'd made all the contract issues clear for her.

Until then, he figured he could spend the morning setting up. His gaze kept wandering around the yard and house and property as he unpacked his car and started carting equipment into the old greenhouse. It was odd. Normally he didn't much care where he was. Every place was new and interesting and involved different challenges. But there was something about her place—the land, the buildings, the whole feeling here—that provoked the strangest feeling.

He'd never been drawn to a place, partly because he'd always been bulldog stubborn about not becoming dependent on physical possessions. But damn. Some of the buildings showed wear and tear, the original house showed generations of character and age, but all of it looked well loved. The property kept striking him as a spot where a man could come and find a place for himself, feel as if he belonged.

Cam had never belonged anywhere. Never known he even wanted to. Of course, maybe his immune system was down and he was catching some annoying bug that was messing with his mind. He kept working.

Unfortunately, he always had to travel heavy. His clothes could be stuffed easily enough into a duffel bag, but he had to cart enough equipment to set up a minilab, and although he'd deny it to the death, he was just a wee bit fussy about his equipment. His microscope had cost a fortune—and was worth every penny, because his testing chemicals had to be exactly right. And he couldn't possibly carry around a full-scale distillation process, but he'd created a small, efficient steam distiller so that he could extract oil from small amounts of lavender.

Strangers assumed his old Birks and practical khakis meant that he was a totally laid-back personality. And he was. He'd been determined to convince himself for years that he was—except for his work, where Cam figured he had a reasonable excuse to be a perfectionist.

Setting up should have been a piece of cake after

doing it around the world all these years, but this morning, it seemed, one humorous problem followed another. To begin with, Violet's cats—for some God unknown reason—decided to hang with him. The old greenhouse had a lot of character, with a brick base and brick walkways and a nice, long concrete slab for a work space. But six of her mammoth, hairy cats sat on the greenhouse counter next to the sink, supervising every move he made. Worse yet, they wanted the water turned on. Regularly. Not a gush of water. A skinny little thread. And after one took her time getting a drink, it seemed the next one wanted her turn.

The herd of cats seemed to get thirsty about every twenty minutes.

By ten o'clock he hadn't accomplished much of anything. He suddenly looked up and noticed a girl leaning in the doorway. She was a young teenager, somewhere around fourteen, he guessed. She looked younger than spring grass, with eyes big as beacons, frothy brown hair and shorts two sizes too tight.

"Hi. I'm supposed to get some twine from in here." She motioned to the old cupboards above the sink.

"Go for it," he invited her.

But she didn't. She took a few steps in and then just kind of hung there, pulling her ear, changing feet, looking at the equipment he'd started to lay out. "I'm Boobla. Actually my name is Barbara and I'm

sick to death of everyone calling me Boobla, but
that's what my little brother called me when he was
too little to say my whole name and then it stuck.
I'm so sick of it, I could cry.''

"Okay. Barbara it is," he said obligingly.

"I work for Violet. Actually I'm her assistant
manager.''

Cameron didn't raise his eyebrows, but this one
was barely in a bra. It seemed mighty doubtful that
she carried such a mighty title.

"I run the place when she's busy," Barbara offered further. "And Violet is really busy most of the
time. We have tons of customers. And she's really
nice, too. She said you were going to be here for a
few weeks.''

"That's the plan.''

"Well, we're probably going to hire my friend
Kari because we're so busy and all. But I'd still have
time to help you. If you need anything, you could
just yell in the shop for me.''

"That's really nice of you." He added carefully,
"Barbara.''

"I like perfume and all. *Good* perfume," she qual-
ified. "Not just the stuff you buy at discount stores.
I've smelled the real stuff. We go shopping at
Macy's every fall. Violet said you were a chemist.
You had to go to college for a long time to do that,
huh?''

Okay. So this morning he was doomed not to get

any work done. The kid eventually left, but cars and trucks zoomed in and out of the yard; he could hear the phone ringing both in Violet's house and the shop. Every time he carried something in from the car, someone else seemed to stop to talk to him. The mailman. A neighbor. A customer who assumed he'd know if Violet sold "Yerba mate", whatever that was.

He was annoyed, he told himself. He needed to get kicking, get serious, get into his job. But it seemed to be the kind of place where people took friendliness for granted. If you were in sight, you were fair game for conversation.

The sun poured down, heating up the day, making the cats want to snooze, bringing the irresistible scent of lavender wafting in from her east fields. Still, he tried to stay focused. Until he suddenly saw her striding out the back door of her Herb Haven, aiming for him.

Just like that, he felt a kick in the heart.

She was dressed just as goofy as the day before. Sandals today, paired with a sundress that wouldn't pass for work clothes anywhere he could imagine. The fabric was all sunflowers, matching long dangling sunflower earrings and a sunflower ring. She'd swished her long hair into a haphazard coil, to get the heat of it off her neck, he supposed, and her cheeks were flushed with heat and sunshine.

So were her eyes when she spotted him.

Or maybe the problem was his vision suddenly blurring when he spotted her. Those midnight kisses suddenly zoomed into his mind, sneakier than temptation, wilier than forbidden. Her mouth was naked this morning. Those same supple, plump lips asked to be kissed. Those same striking hazel eyes dared him to figure her out.

She was a complicated, contradictory woman, he told himself. There were a ton of signs that she was too much trouble. To begin with, she was obviously a home-and-hearth kind of female, which meant he had nothing in hell to offer her. And then there was the mystifying issue of how she could be so damned beautiful and yet totally unattached. On top of that, the woman acted like a complete flake sometimes and other times clearly had a tantalizing brain. Whatever secrets she was holding back, it seemed obvious that she didn't need a guy messing with her who wasn't serious. There was too much vulnerability in those huge eyes.

Too much vulnerability in those kisses.

Better that he should stay clear, knowing he was only going to be there for a short time.

"You have a few minutes, Cam? I can steal a half hour now, if you want to go look at the lavender."

"Ready," he said. But the minute she came close, he felt his world shift. It was nuts. He'd had tons of women shake his timbers and move his hormones. Her pulling his chain wasn't a new issue. He liked his chain pulled, for God's sake. But those eyes, that hair, that smile…

Be careful, his heart warned him.

Which was the craziest thing of all, because Cam never, never did uncareful things.

Six

Violet understood that she couldn't postpone dealing with the touchy lavender problem forever, but just then she was saved by the bell—or the ring, as it happened. Barbara yelled from the Herb Haven that there was an overseas telephone call for her. That meant Daisy had to be on the line—and there was no way she wanted to postpone a chance to talk with her sister.

She sent Cam up to the house for lunch. It was an easy way to get him out of listening range. Suggest food and men always moved. Once in her broom-closet-size office in the Herb Haven, she closed the door and listened to Daisy's perky greeting.

"So. He got there. What'd you think of him?"

Violet briefly held the phone away from her ear to stare at it, then clapped it back tight. "Wait a minute. What is this?"

"What's what?"

"You know what. What I think of *him* should have nothing to do with a lavender deal. His being here is supposed to be about oil. Lavender oil. And for the record, all the legal stuff sounds like a nightmare."

"It is," Daisy said cheerfully. "But don't worry about it. Just leave all that junk to Cam. He's straight as an arrow. With any luck, you're going to make a fortune, kiddo. And in the meantime, you'll have a chance to forget that bubble-brain you finally got divorced from."

Violet closed her eyes and prayed for patience. She loved both her sisters, even if both of them could be total pains. Camille was the youngest, though, so she was more easily suckered. If Violet wanted Camille to do something, she just nurtured and fed and mothered until Camille either gave in or begged for mercy. Getting Daisy to behave was a far tougher challenge.

Daisy was the beauty of the family. God knew how Mom had named her for the common flower, when she was the exotic tropical blossom of the clan, with a model's figure and that kind of style and élan. Daisy also had guts—enough guts to take off for France and live a wild, free lifestyle like everybody dreamed of but nobody ever really did. Unfortunately nobody could bully Daisy. Daisy could exhaust the whole family with her sneaky, take-charge, bossy ways.

"Something smells really, really rotten here," Violet said darkly. "How long have you been planning this? You didn't send Cameron Lachlan over here just for the lavender. You were thinking about setting me up. Damn it, you twerp. You didn't think I'd fall for Cameron, did you?"

"Come on. He's adorable."

"He's a lot of things, but adorable isn't one of them. Good-looking, yeah. Rough and tough, yeah. Independent, yeah. Great eyes, yeah. But adorable is a word for boys."

"Exactly. You don't need any more *boys* in your life. About time you had a man scale your walls."

"I beg your pardon."

"I don't know for sure what that bozo did to you, and neither does Camille. But we both know something was bad at the end. So, fine. Broken bones take six weeks in a cast. Broken hearts taken longer. But you were made to be married, Vi. It's time to take another chance."

"You're out of your mind. And I'm going to tell Mom you did this to me."

"Are you kidding? Mom's in on it."

"You're low. Lower than a skunk. Lower than an

earthworm. I thought you were my favorite sister, but not anymore.''

''Uh-huh.'' Daisy yawned through this threat. All three sisters regularly pulled the ''favorite sister'' jealousy thing on each other. But something happened then. As clear as the connection to France was, something seemed different—as if Daisy put her hand over the mouthpiece—and when she suddenly came back on, her voice changed. The real humor in her tone now sounded forced. ''Listen, you, it's your turn for some happiness. You don't have to tell me what happened before the divorce—''

''What's wrong?'' Violet said.

''Nothing's wrong.''

Violet wasn't the maternal sister for nothing. Her job in the family was to be the caretaker, the one who made chicken soup when the other two were dumped, the one who cleaned up their scrapes and listened to stuff they couldn't tell their mother. ''The last four times you've called, something hasn't been right in your voice. Is the romance fading with Monsieur Picasso? You tired of living in France?''

''What could be wrong? The romantic French countryside, a hot summer sun, bougainvillea outside my window, breezes off the Mediterranean, freedom, a country where men really know how to appreciate a woman—''

Now Violet started to get really worried. ''Quit with the horse spit. He hasn't hurt you, has he?''

"No. And quit turning the subject around. We're talking about you. You and love. You and sex. You and Cameron. Just think about it, would you? He's not the marrying kind. But he's a good man. The kind who'll be honest. And good to you. A good guy to get your feet wet in the love pool again, without having to make any major risky dives. Besides which, he really is an answer for your lavender problem."

When Violet hung up, she thought, what's wrong with me has nothing to do with lavender. And it can't be fixed.

She hustled to the house to grab some lunch—but there was no further serious talking with Cameron, because he was the one to get a phone call that time. One of his daughters kept his ear pinned for almost a half hour.

She was dying to ask him some questions about that conversation, but about the time he hung up, she saw the roofer's truck bounce into the yard. Par for the course, the roofers were late, so she ran over to the cottage to raise hell.

Just when she tried to track down Cameron again, the lady from the *White Hills Gazette* showed up with her sunny face and her legal pad—Violet remembered the interview, didn't she? No, she hadn't remembered, and she hadn't had time to put on lipstick in hours now, but publicity for the Herb Haven was too important to pass up.

An hour later, she glanced up to see Cameron in the doorway, listening to her rant on about the events and products and courses she'd scheduled for the summer. He lifted his hand in the air, showing her what looked to be an oatmeal raisin cookie. Thank God. If she didn't get some sugar and junk food soon, she was probably going to fade out altogether.

After the interview, she leveled the plate of cookies he'd brought—but he'd disappeared by then. She searched until she found him on her back porch, talking with Filbert Green.

Filbert was the farmer her father had hired to caretake the farm after her parents retired to Florida. The idea was for Filbert to put in corn and soybeans or whatever, to keep the land in shape, until one of the Campbell daughters realized how much they belonged on the Vermont homestead and settled down to have some kids.

Camille had just gotten married, but she had no need for the land, and heaven knew when or if Daisy was coming back from France. So when Violet had limped home after the divorce, the house had been empty and everyone happy she was going to stay there. She'd let Filbert go. She wanted to wallow on the land in peace and quiet. Now, though, she saw Filbert hunkered down on her porch with Cam hunkered down next to him, both of them drawing plans with sticks like two smudge-nosed boys in a sandbox. They were talking about her lavender. Talking about the harvest. What needed doing, who'd do it, how. She needed to listen, needed to actively participate, only, damnation if there wasn't another interruption.

Kari was the interruption, and actually it occurred to Violet by then that the girl had been shadowing her around for some time. A job interview, she recalled. Kari wanted a job, and God knew Violet was so behind she could barely catch her own tail. The girl was hardly out of diapers, but damn, she could talk spreadsheets like a true computer geek.

"Okay. These are the rules. Take 'em or leave 'em. I don't give a damn what you wear, as long as you don't show up naked. I don't care if you're late or early as long as the work gets done. But you have to like cats. And I need accurate records. I can't work with someone who's careless with numbers. So. Are we square or not?"

Kari of the shy smile and hopelessly baby blue eyes suddenly turned shrewd. "How much you gonna pay me?"

"How much you want?"

"Ten bucks an hour. I'm worth it."

"This is your first job. Don't you think that's a little high?"

"Beats me. That's what my dad told me to ask for, first try."

"Okay, then you got it, first try. I love guts in a girl."

Once she put the girl on the payroll, by a miracle, she caught a thirty-second break. In those thirty seconds, she remembered those kisses of Cameron's from last night, how she'd felt—how he'd felt—and whether she dared entertain the extraordinary fantasy of making love with him.

Cripes, it was one of those days when she could barely find time to pee, so considering a love affair seemed the height of lunacy. But her sister's phone call had helped promote the lunacy. Daisy had pointed out that Cameron had a uniquely perfect qualification for a lover—he didn't want to settle down.

For another woman, that would obviously be a disadvantage. But for her... For three years now, she'd been afraid of attracting a man who'd want a normal, married type of life with her. Cameron was the first guy where she was dead sure he wouldn't want something from her that she couldn't give.

On top of which, she couldn't even remember feeling this level of lust and longing for a man she'd barely met. There was something dangerous about that man. Something wicked. Something that made her dream about dumb things she knew she couldn't have.

Thankfully, the insane day just kept getting worse. There were no more thirty-second breaks. Around four, she gulped down two glasses of water before she keeled over from heat exhaustion, remembered she had a killer bee sting, babied it with some honey, then abruptly heard raised voices from inside the shop.

She hiked out to find Boobla near tears, being railed on by an unsatisfied customer. Wilhelmena wanted a cure for age. There wasn't one. It seemed she'd bought some chamomile and clover and mint and parsley and primrose a few weeks ago, believing the combination of products would clear up her wrinkles and fix her dry skin, and now she wanted a refund because they didn't work.

Violet gently stepped in front of her clerk. "Those are all good ideas for dry skin, but I don't know why you had the impression they'd fix wrinkles."

"Because your girl told me it would."

Violet didn't have to ask Boobla to know the teenager never said any such thing. "If you don't want the products, you can bring them back. I'll give you a partial refund."

"That isn't good enough."

Violet's gaze narrowed. She knew Wilhelmena. Hell's bells, every shopkeeper in three counties knew Wilhelmena. "I'm afraid you'll have to sue me then, hon, because that's as far as I'm going."

The woman railed a little while longer. For anyone else, she'd have gone the long mile, but not for a complainer—and then there was the principle of backing up her staff. Boobla was still a baby, which was precisely the point. This was her first job. Violet wasn't about to let anyone browbeat her just because she was a kid.

More customers came and went. In the meantime, orders for baskets still had to be filled, plants needed watering, the grass mowed. Even after hours, the phone kept ringing and a delivery truck came in.

The next time Violet looked up, somehow it was well past seven. The kids had both gone home, the closed sign was parked in the window, and Cameron was standing in the Herb Haven doorway with the fading sun behind him.

"What the hell kind of place are you running here, chère?" he murmured.

"What do you mean?"

"I mean you're doing the work of four men and then some. You barely had time to grab half a sandwich at lunch, and I know you had a couple of cookies. But have you had anything serious to eat since breakfast?"

Who knew? Who cared? She had no idea how long he'd been standing there, but the silence suddenly coiled around her nerves like velvet ribbons. He looked like such a shout of male next to all the flower sights and smells and fuss, especially with his leg cocked forward and his broad shoulders filling the doorway. When she met his gaze, there was no instant thunderclap, just more of those itchy-soft velvet nerves. She was just so aware that no one else was in sight or sound but her and Cam and all that golden dusk.

But then she recalled his question. He sounded as if he were accusing her of being an effective manager, so Violet instinctively defended herself. "I really don't work very hard. All my running around is just an act—to fool people into thinking I have a head for business. I'd be in real trouble if the customers ever realized I don't have a clue what I'm doing."

"Sure," Cam said, but there was a wicked glint in his eyes. She had a bad feeling he was on to her flutter-brained routine—which was a foolish fear, since every guy in the neighborhood and surrounding county had been convinced for years she was a hardcore ditz. He distracted her, though, when he lifted a white paper bag and shook it.

She smelled. "Food?"

"Don't get your hopes up. It's nothing like what you cook. But I made a trek into White Hills and picked up some fresh deli sandwiches, drinks, dessert. By midafternoon I figured that I'd never get you out to the lavender to talk unless I somehow wooed you away from the phone and the business. I thought you must be hungry by now."

She wasn't. Until she looked at him. And then realized there seemed to be something hollow inside her that had been aching for a long time.

"I don't have long," she said.

He nodded, as if expecting that answer, too—but shook the bag again, so she could catch the scent of a kosher dill and corned beef on rye.

"I don't usually eat red meat," she said twenty minutes later, as she was wolfing down her second sandwich.

"I can see you're not into it."

"And I never eat chips. They're terrible for you."

"Uh-huh," he said, as he opened the second bag of chips and spilled them onto a napkin.

She wasn't exactly sure how he'd conned her into this picnic, but he seemed to have pulled a Pied Piper routine—his carrying an old sheet to use as a tablecloth, and the food and his car keys and strapping her into the front seat and his driving—while she did nothing but follow the scent of food. By the time he'd unfurled the sheet to sit on, on the crest of the east hill overlooking the lavender, she'd already been diving in.

He had a kind side, she had to give him that, because he didn't say a word when she gobbled down the second helping of chips. All that salt. All that fat. She tasted guilt with every bite, but, man, were they good. "You really ate ahead of time?" she insisted again.

"Sure did," he said.

But she wasn't convinced. He'd brought enough for two. She'd assumed he was diving in when she was, until she suddenly glanced up and noticed that he was mounding his food on her plate. "I never eat this much. You must think I'm a greedy pig."

"Yeah. I've always admired greed in a woman. Always admired meanness, too, and you've got an unusually mean streak. I was watching how you treated those two kids who work for you. They both think you're a goddess."

"Are you making fun of me?"

"Are you kidding? I'm in awe, chère." When she finally finished enough to please him, he reopened the bag and emerged with more goodies. "Almond cookies. And there's a little more raspberry iced tea. Although I only bought a few cookies. I had no idea you were going to need three or four dozen just to fill you up on a first round."

The darn man was so comfortable and fun to be with that she had to laugh…but then, of course, reality caught up with her. She couldn't be feeling comfortable. Not here.

It wasn't that she never came out to this stretch of the farm. She'd planted the twenty acres of lavender over the past few years, after all. Still, she avoided this view if she could help it. She wasn't the one who'd tended it—her younger sister Camille had, when she'd come home early in the spring, yelling the whole time about how crazy Violet had become to neglect anything like this.

And the craziness was true. Obviously, she knew she was coming out here with Cameron; they had to get the harvest business settled. But for whole long stretches of time, she forgot how traumatically symbolic the lavender was for her.

A knot filled her throat as she gazed at the stretching, rolling sweep of lavender. Until Camille had come home, the long rows of lavender bushes had been an unkempt, overgrown thatchy mess. They still weren't perfect, yet Violet—who had always nurtured and mothered everything and everyone—had thrown these plants in the ground and just left them.

Cameron suddenly said quietly, "Tell me what you originally planned to do with this?"

His voice was gentle, serious, nonjudgmental, but she couldn't speak for the lump in her throat—not for that moment.

The smell of lavender saturated the warm summer air. The buds were just barely coming on, because all the strains she'd put in were late types. Buds would keep coming from now through August, and by late summer the smell would be unbearable, invading everything, impossible to escape from—not that anyone would want to.

The plants were pale purple, soft in the evening light, and that first blush of bud smell was like nothing else—not at all heavy, but immeasurably light, a scent that was forever fresh and frisky and clean. There was nothing quite like it. No other flower, no other herb, had a scent even remotely related to lavender.

"Violet?"

When he prompted her, she motioned to the field without looking at him. "Our mom—her name was Margaux—always had lavender growing in the backyard. She's the one who taught me what I know. There are all kinds of lavender, but basically most strains fall in one of two camps. 'Hardy lavender' is what a lot of people call English lavender, even though it's not from England. And the 'tender lavenders' tend to grow around France and Spain."

Cameron leaned back. "Go on."

"Okay. The thing is…you get the finest oil—as far as perfume—from the hardy lavenders. Which I guess you obviously know, huh?"

"I may know just a little something about that, yeah. But keep talking, anyway. I want to know how you got into this, how you developed this strain."

There. She was starting to unchoke. Cameron surely knew all this stuff already if he was a chemist, but babbling was one of her best ways of covering up nerves. "Well…I knew from my mom that there are advantages to each type of lavender. The oil wasn't really my interest, because I already realized you needed some ridiculous amount—like 500 pounds of flowers—to get even ounces of the oil. But some lavenders are stronger in color and scent. Some are hardier as far as where they can grow."

She wasn't going to think about babies. She was just going to keep talking until she got a good grip and could look at Cameron with a smile again. "Anyway, after the divorce, I had time on my hands. And Daisy happened to send me some interesting strains of lavender, so then, for fun, I just started setting up some experiments in the greenhouse. I brought in some of my mom's favorite strains from her garden, then started collecting others from around the country. What I wanted to do was just... play...see if I could blend the best qualities of all my favorites."

"For what reason?" Cameron asked.

"Just for fun. Just to see if I could do it, if I could produce a lavender where the scent stayed truer than all the other types. I always loved puttering with plants, you know? And—" She stopped.

She was lying to him. Images spilled through her mind, mental pictures of the man she'd once married and believed was the love of her life. She'd learned everything she knew about sex from Simpson—particularly all the wrong things. Things like how guys needed to get off or they suffered. Things like how guys couldn't wait. Things like Real Women climaxed with no problem unless they were inhibited. Also, Real Women got pregnant as long as the guy was virile, and Simpson's sperm—he'd had that checked—were damn good swimmers.

She was the one with the skinny tubes.

"Violet, what's wrong?" Cameron asked quietly. She stared at the field until her eyes started to clear. "After the divorce...I just wanted to grow things. Reproduce things. Everybody thought I was crazy to let this field get so out of control. They were all right. But the truth, Cam, is that I didn't care if it was out of control."

"All right," he said.

"It was *mine* to love or lose. If I lost it, if I never made a dime, I didn't care. I don't need money from it. I can afford the loss. I don't really give a damn if anyone thinks I'm crazy or not."

"Hey," he said gently.

Tell him, her heart said. Just tell him. Then it's out on the table. You'll know if it's important to him or not.

But she knew it wasn't that simple. Cameron might have an already grown family; he might not want kids. But a lot of men thought a woman was less than a complete woman—less sexual, less feminine—if she was infertile.

"I just wanted to grow something. Of my own. I wanted to make something out of land that had been barren, because this slope was rocky and nothing ever grew well here before. So it was the challenge. To create something that hadn't existed before. It wasn't about making money. It was just about—"

"Whoa," Cameron whispered, and as if he had some cockamamie idea that he was dealing with a fragile woman on the verge of a big, noisy, crying jag, he swooped her into his arms.

Seven

The last thing Cameron intended to do was pull Violet into his arms.

Yeah, he'd dragged her off to the lavender field—and brought the picnic dinner—but that was only because he finally figured out the whole picture. Violet's herb business was chaotically busy. Unless he found some way to isolate her from the phone and her neighbors and all the other people noise, he figured they'd never get the contract details settled between them. That issue was critical. Even though the nature of her lavender strains were supposed to be harvested late, the huge heat wave was bringing on the crop at the speed of sound. Within days, they needed to start the harvest.

So he'd taken her to the one place where he knew he could talk to her privately, but not to seduce her. Not to even think about touching her. Nothing would have happened—Cameron really believed—if she hadn't suddenly looked so shaken up.

He couldn't stand it. Violet was so full of energy. For damn sure, she was a manipulative, confusing woman who seemed to mislead a guy about the truth of things. She was stubborn, independent to an exasperating degree, a woman who did exactly what she wanted on her own timetable. She was a tough cookie—even if for some reason she didn't want anyone to know it.

And that was exactly why it killed him to see her eyes fill up, suddenly so full of hurt and sadness. He'd *had* to grab her. He wasn't thinking of romance, he was just responding instinctively to a need to protect her, comfort her somehow.

Only a split second later, all his honest, sincere, chivalrous intentions went to hell.

The very instant his mouth came down on hers, the damn woman *responded*. Her lips were warm as sunshine, as soft as silver. Her head tipped back, willingly absorbing the pressure of his mouth and his first kiss…which gave him absolutely no choice but to follow through with a second kiss and then a third. Her eyelashes fluttered down and her slim fingers seemed to hesitate, then slowly climb his shoulders and curve around his neck.

When he felt her warm, supple body slide against his…something happened. Deep inside him, there was a silent whoosh, as if the rest of the world disappeared from sight, sound, touch. She was his reality. She, and all the senses she invoked.

He clutched her tighter. She clutched right back, and suddenly all that long, wild, silky hair was coming loose in his hands. Her bracelets jangled, one of her sandals slipped and tumbled down the slope; yet she never opened her eyes, never made out like there was a damn thing that mattered to her but him—and getting more of those sweet, dangerous, uninhibited kisses.

Maybe he was guilty of initiating that first kiss. Maybe he knew he shouldn't have, knew she was trouble. But how could he possibly, conceivably have guessed that she'd be *this* much trouble?

He'd tasted her before. It had been intense, but not like this. Whatever had shaken her seemed to act like some kind of trigger, as if something tight and trapped were suddenly freed from deep inside her. She not only kissed him back but dumped emotional rocket fuel on the flames. She didn't just yield but sought. She didn't just touch but invited, demanded, his touch.

Warm, damp skin slid against his. He smelled her hair, her ice-raspberry breath, the lick of scent on her skin. As the night dropped, with the moon showing up like a promise in the far sky, it seemed as if sud-

denly all those acres of lavender released a whole
song of scent. The lavender flowed all around them,
filling the air, filling their senses, teasing their sense
of taste and smell. The scent was so like her—wild
and fresh and elusive. Magical.

"Cam," she whispered, her voice barely a whisper, an ache of wonder.

He felt the same wonder, tried to steal more in
another kiss. His hand drifted down, shimmering
over her collarbone and then to her breast, snuggling
there. No matter how carefully, how reverently he
touched, his body groaned that it wasn't enough. Not
nearly enough.

Her blouse pushed up, pushed off fairly easily.

For a second he thought she wasn't wearing a
bra—but she was, it was just that the fabric was a
teensy scrap of lace. A front opener, though, easy
enough to unlatch. And then he had his warm cal-
lused hand on her immeasurably soft breast, the flesh
swelling for him, the nipple perking under his
palm—only that wasn't enough, either. Not even
close to enough. She groaned against his mouth, so
he bent down and delivered kisses down her throat,
down to her breasts, faster kisses now, rougher ones.

Somewhere he still had a functioning conscience—a murky conscience, but one stabbing him
with warning instincts. He knew he didn't understand
her. Knew she had some troubling deep waters that

she hid from sight. Knew she was a worrisome maze of contradictions.

He'd seen her supposed flaky side...yet he'd also seen how many balls she efficiently, effectively juggled, even on an average business day.

He'd also heard her claim more than once how she didn't care if the lavender had gotten out of control, yet that was impossibly contradictory, too, because no one accidentally experimented in a greenhouse to the tune of twenty acres of lavender.

And then there was her wildly estrogen-overdosed house, compared to that strange, contrary shock of her austere nun-like bedroom he'd only glimpsed.

He couldn't be sure of anything, not around her, except for the one obvious thing—that he was here for the lavender. And to do that business, they had to be able to trust each other. To seduce her before she could trust him was as foolhardy as betting on a lottery.

He'd never been foolhardy. Independent, yes. Self-centered, oh, yes. But never a fool.

"Cam," she whispered again, this time pleating his shirt open with her hands, pulling at it, reaching to touch his bare chest with her own.

His head promptly swelled with fool's thoughts, fool's needs, filled so full there was nothing else but her, her taste, her profile in the moonlight, her lavender-whispered skin, her winsome, demanding mouth.

He *had* to go back for more. This pull for her—he had to get a grasp of it. What he felt with her, for the land, for everything here was alien to the Cameron Lachlan he knew himself to be. He'd sworn never to become like his father, never to become attached to a place. He'd sworn never to let any place own him. Ever.

Yet there was something about her that made him feel this horrifying, embarrassing, stupid sense of belonging. She made him feel as if she needed him.

As if he needed her.

As if she wanted him—*just* him, not any man, not any guy, but only him.

He wanted her, only her—not just a woman to fill a sexual need or the lonely hours of the night, but something else, something more. Cameron kept getting the unnerving, frightening impression that he wanted her the way he'd wanted no other woman. That she alone could fill a hole inside him that he hadn't even known was there.

The night kept coming, bringing the privacy of darkness, intensifying the scents of verdant earth and lavender. The ache inside him felt part of the night, lonely and dark, hot and urgent. He knew it was crazy, yet the drumbeat of his pulse kept thrumming the same message, that he'd lose something irretrievable if he didn't love her, didn't have her, now, right now.

She lay back against the cool sheet he'd brought

as a picnic blanket, pulling him down to her, communicating how much she wanted the same thing. Him. Naked. Now. For whatever reasons, right or wrong, sane or crazy, this felt so right. *She* felt right.

His shirt peeled away as easily as her skirt. She made an exasperated sound, half sat up, peeled off a tangle of noisy jewelry from her wrists and ears, came back to him, damp soft skin intimately molding to his. He had to devour her with more kisses. Against the white sheet, her skin looked so golden dark, her eyes so shining, and all that wild silken hair kept tangling him closer. He thought she was naked, but it seemed she was still wearing see-through panties...panties he didn't discover until his mouth had trailed an intense, tender path from her breast to the hollow in her navel, down to the sweet roundness of her abdomen and finally lower.

Even in the dark, he could see through those filmy panties. Even in the dark, he could see the urgent rise and fall of her breasts, the pulse drumming in her throat, the heat in her eyes. And when those panties were gone, when there was nothing between them but anticipation, she said suddenly, wildly, "Cam... Cameron, I need to tell you something—"

"Birth control. You're not protected?"

For a millisecond she didn't answer, but then she said with absolute sureness, "No. That's not a problem."

"Then you'd better give me a very fast, very serious reason to stop, chère, or else I'm going to be very sure you want this as much as I do."

Again she hesitated for barely a millisecond, but once she answered him, her voice was strong and true. "I don't want to stop, not tonight, not with you. Take me, Cam. Make everything else go away. Make this night belong just to us."

Hell. That might just be an impossibly huge expectation to put on a lover...but a guy couldn't win what he didn't aspire to. So he tried. He concentrated five hundred percent of himself into every kiss, every caress. He tried tender, then rough. Tried an urgent, ardent rush, then the seductive frustration of slow hands and a lazy tongue.

Moonlight bathed her skin in silver. A nearby owl hooted, their only voyeur. And the scent of lavender kept seeping into his senses, into hers. When he finally swept her beneath him, his flesh seemed on fire, his muscles turgid and tight, drugged—crazy with her, for her.

She wrapped her long, slim legs around him even as he tested her soft center for moistness—as if she hadn't already told him in a thousand ways she was ready for him. Lips met and clung as he eased inside her, initially trying to be gentle, determined to be gentle. But she hissed his name in a fierce, frantic call, wooing him into her deeper, harder.

He plunged in then, burying his hands in her hair,

burying his lips in her lips, burying himself in the heart of her. It was crazy, totally crazy, but he had the sensation of belonging to her, belonging with her, in some emotional way he'd never even known existed before. This was about sex, he told himself. The best sex he'd ever had, but still, about sex.

The lie didn't last any longer than it took his mind to try it out. This was so *not* about sex it was shaking his world.

Or she was. She matched him, stroke for stroke, slamming heartbeat for slamming heartbeat, her lithe slick body tightening exactly when his did. She owned him at that moment. Or he owned her. Damned if he knew the difference—damned if he cared. The sky opened up in a shower of stars, or that's how he felt, as if he were flying over the moon with her, release pouring through him and into her.

For the briefest second he wished she hadn't answered his question about birth control, because this insane feeling of longing, belonging, owning was so compelling. He wanted his seed inside her, a child that came from the two of them. But that thought, like every other coherent thought, fled faster than moonbeams. They rode the crest together, then sank, both spent, in each other's arms.

Later…minutes later, hours later, Cameron opened his eyes. The moon was still up there, still framed in stars. The smells of earthy loam and lavender still pervaded his nostrils; somewhere a raccoon rustled and an owl hooted. He'd smelled the smells before, knew that moon. But he didn't know her; how it would feel to have her warm, vibrant body in his arms, still half-wrapped around him, her cheek nestled in the arch of his neck, her silky hair tickling his chin.

"Damn," he said.

She leaned back her head. "Uh-oh. That sounds like a man in the throes of regrets."

"Try again. I couldn't regret what just happened between us if my life were at stake." He bussed the top of her head, which made Charlie pop to attention again. He was too old to have Charlie pop to attention again this fast. It was her. Making him feel things, do things, want things that weren't *normal* for him.

He couldn't be in love with her. Not just because he barely knew the woman, but because his pull for her made no sense. She'd almost cried twice that day. Did he need a weepy woman? Did he need all those cats? For that matter, he'd seen Alps and ocean, so how could he possibly be drawn to some rocky land with red barns and stone fences and winding roads?

Perhaps more directly to the point, if he'd lost his mind, where the hell had it gone?

Was there a chance it could find its way home again?

"Cameron?" She twisted in his arms, not moving far away from him, just pushing back far enough that she could tilt her head and look at him face-to-face. Below, her fingers reached over and gently, playfully, entwined with his. "Tell me about your daughters."

He glanced down and watched their two hands blend together. Hell. Double hell. Teenagers held hands like this, not fully grown adults who were lying naked in the moonlight. But she didn't seem willing to sever all closeness yet, and neither was he.

The question about his daughters seemed to come from nowhere, but he was more than willing to answer it. Talk was better than the alternative—which was lying there, drinking in the scent of lavender and moonlight and wanting to make love to her again. So he talked. "Miranda's fifteen. Kate's sixteen." He hesitated. "For a long time it was totally clear cut that they belonged with their mom. It's not that I didn't want to be an active dad. I've always wanted that, always tried to be. I just traveled so much. Over the years, I always talked to them twice a week. We spend time together every holiday and school break. And I usually hang there at least a month every year to just be around them, part of their routine. Only lately…"

"Lately what?"

"Well, lately, they're fighting all the time with their mom. Most of it seems to be pretty standard teenage girl, mother stuff. Rules. Roles. But sometimes she's had it, and then I think…"

"You think what?"

"That if I lived in a more settled way, I could have them with me for a while. Most parents don't seem to like the teenage years, but for some strange reason, it doesn't bother me that they're being difficult and impossible. If anything, I feel like now I could be a better parent to them." Okay. He'd stripped naked some of his heart to tell her that. And left him hanging besides, so it was her turn now, he figured. "What about your ex?"

Her hand dropped away from his. She lay back, facing the stars. "Well...his name is Ed. Simpson, I always called him. Back in college, I took one look and just knew he was my first and only true love. He was a warm, family kind of guy, good sense of humor. Fun. I quit my last year of school to help him finish faster—he got his social work degree. He was always one to reach out to help someone else."

"Sounds like a saint," Cam said, and was briefly tempted to spit and paw the earth—but naturally he was too mature.

"Not exactly," she said wryly. "He's married to someone else now. In fact, they had their first child five months after the wedding. And he called me this morning to tell me about their newborn son."

"I don't understand why he'd call you." It wasn't hard for Cam to deduce that the creep had cheated on her, judging from the age of the first kid.

"Who would? I wouldn't take him back for a fortune, am over him in every way a woman can get over a man. For some reason he seems to still think I'm his friend. That we're still good friends.''

''So, are you?''

''No.''

''Then why on earth do you let him keep calling?''

''Because.'' She lifted a hand to the moonlight. ''Oh, cripes, I don't know why. In the beginning, I acted friendly out of pride because I never wanted to let on how much he'd hurt me. And then I just didn't seem to know how to cut him off. I know they've really been struggling to afford their growing family.''

''Struggling? I thought your ex was wealthy.''

She frowned. ''Why'd you think that?''

''Because…I thought you said or implied you'd gotten a pretty good settlement from the divorce. When you were talking about how you could afford to put up the greenhouses, not have to care if you lost money on the lavender, all that.''

''Oh. Well, I *did* get a good lump of money from the divorce—but not because Simpson gave me anything for free. We had a house together. He wanted to stay in the house to raise his kids, and I didn't need or want to stay there, so he owed me my share. Actually, I'd earned more than him back then. But the point was—''

It wasn't that hard to finish her sentence that time. ''You wanted to spend any money you got from the marriage. It felt like ugly money somehow. As if it could sabotage your luck if you used it in a relationship with someone else.''

"Yeah. And I know that thinking was superstitious.''

"It is. But I remember feeling that way after my divorce, too. Then it wasn't about money. I gave her all the money I could, wanted her to have it. She had the girls. But the 'stuff'—furniture, paintings, the *things* we'd split up that were part of the marriage— at the time, it didn't matter how valuable they were or how much I liked them or even needed them. I wanted all ties severed.''

"So you understand. Why'd you get divorced, Cam?''

"I told you. Because I couldn't settle in one place. I was too restless. Not responsible enough. Not mature enough to make any kind of husband, either,'' he said honestly. "And you?''

Her bare big toe had sneaked over and found his bare big toe. Now they were playing footsie, he realized. Both of them, like kids who couldn't stop touching each other. No matter what they were sure of and what they weren't.

There had to be something narcotic in the Vermont air. Something dangerous.

Maybe it was even in her big toe.

"Me, what?'' She seemed to be referring to some

question he'd asked, as if she'd lost track of the conversation.

Hell, so had he. "Why'd you get divorced? Because he cheated? Because you fell out of love? What?"

She didn't answer for a long time, and then finally she made a sound—like a wry little chuckle, only not so much humor in it. "We have a problem, Lachlan."

"What's that?"

"The problem is that I want to answer your question. I have this horrible feeling that you could turn out to be someone I could seriously trust. How weird is that?"

"Weird? You're not used to trusting people?"

She propped up on an elbow then. Moonlight draped the round of her shoulder, the edge of one plump, firm breast, the sweet soft curve of her hip and high. "Don't waste your time sounding surprised, Cam. You're no more used to trusting people than I am. You're a loner. Just like me."

He didn't know what to say, except that she didn't strike him as a natural loner in any conceivable way. She was an earth mother, a giving lover, a warm, nurturing woman right down to her toes. He said honestly, "I can well understand your needing time to get over a hurtful relationship, but in the long run it's impossible to imagine you living alone. Or not wanting to be in a marriage."

"I won't be climbing into another serious relationship," she said firmly.

He didn't believe her. But he said, "That's a relief, because I don't want to hurt you. And for darn sure, I won't lie to you. You know my work here's only temporary, that I'll be leaving soon. That's the way it has to be."

Again she smiled, at a moment when no other woman would have smiled at him. "And I'll be staying here. Because that's the way it has to be—for me. So we're both safe, right?"

"Safe?"

"Safe," she repeated. "You don't want to shake up my world. I don't want to shake up yours."

"Yes," he agreed.

"We do need to watch it, though," she said carefully. "I'm totally for casual sex. Especially with a man who's only going to be here for a short time, and who positively doesn't want anything serious from me. But we'll both get cranky if we start to seriously trust each other, so let's try not to, okay?"

She got up then. He didn't instantly understand that the conversation—and their lovemaking—was all done. In principle, they should have left an hour earlier at least. The night temperatures were dropping fast now, and the mosquitoes had come out to feast— still, he was shaking his head as he quickly gathered their gear together.

The woman he seemed to be falling for, very hard,

very fast, very irresponsibly, was walking toward his car completely naked in the moonlight. She didn't seem to find anything odd about that. She didn't seem to find anything odd about wanting to sleep with a man who wouldn't stick around for her, either.

But it bugged him.

It was never a good idea, to wake up the next morning without both people having agreed on what they needed from such an encounter. Only Violet's version of clearing the air had sure muddied his. Maybe most men would be happy to hear she was up for a short, passionate affair.

Maybe, even as early as last week, he'd have been ecstatic to hear a woman talk that way.

Only hearing Vi talk about casual sex and not wanting to trust him made him feel as edgy as if he'd sat on a porcupine. She deserved more than that. She should be demanding more from a man than that.

And damn it. He wanted to *be* more than that to her. Realizing how hard his heart was suddenly pounding, Cameron took a long, low, calming breath.

It had to be the moonlight. He just wasn't a man to think, or spell, a word as petrifying as commitment. Tomorrow—daylight—he'd get a grip on this whole thing. He just knew he would.

Eight

When Violet walked outside, the morning fog was magical. Pink dawn hues swirled in the mist. Drenched flowers and grass made the whole world sing with scent and color. It was her favorite kind of morning.

Today, though, she clumped toward her Herb Haven in mud boots and a scowl. She'd had hiccups twice already. Her stomach seemed to be doing a nonstop agitated jitterbug.

The Haven's parking lot already had four cars, even though it was barely seven. Customers were waiting for her. She gave an early class on Wednesday morning before the store opened, a class she normally loved to bits. But this morning her mind was entirely on the night before.

She'd never had casual sex before. It wasn't her fault. She'd always meant to fool around tons, but she'd fallen in love with Simpson young and there'd never been a chance. Now she was perfectly thrilled to throw her morals out the window, only it was all so awkward. She'd gone into her bedroom first last night, but she assumed Cameron would join her. Instead he'd gone into the spare room. And stayed there.

When you had mind-blowing fabulous sex with a lover, didn't you get to spend the night with him? What the hell were the rules to this deal, anyway? Cripes, it would resolve so many problems—and so much heartache—if she could just privately love someone and not have to worry about his caring about her long term.

Only, so far, this wasn't working at all. The sex part had been terrifyingly stunning. Only, she hadn't slept all night, first waiting for Cameron to come into her bed, and then worrying why he'd slept in the other room. And then there was that other tricky little problem.

She was crazy about the guy. More crazy than she could ever remember feeling before—even about Simpson. Cam was warm and funny and accepting and interesting and honest and everything she loved in a guy—not counting that naked-to-naked had been better than anything she'd ever dreamed of.

The *love* word had been on her mind even before they'd done the Deed. Making love had just made that worse.

She *knew* better than to let that *love* word enter the picture.

Glumly she opened the door to the Herb Haven. Lights were already on. Four women sat on the wooden table in the back, all talking at once and sipping her best coffee brew. They all knew where the key and coffeepot were; they knew the whole routine. Betsy and Harriet were farmers' wives; Roberta was a freshly divorced teacher; Dinah was a college student home for the summer with energy to burn. The women had nothing in common besides a history in White Hills—and wanting to make natural cosmetics at home.

"We're making cold cream today, right? Cold cream, aftershave and an herb bath." Violet heeled off her mud boots, plastered on a cheerful smile and charged in. Work would get her mind off Cam. It had to. "Did you ladies hear that Dora Ritter is pregnant? And everyone says it's Tom Johnson's, and his wife is pregnant at the same time."

"No!" Betsy said in delighted horror, and the women were off. Aprons were donned. Bowls and pots and measuring devices gathered from the cupboards, and then the core ingredients brought out.

Lanolin. Beeswax. Almond oil. Naturally Violet started making herb water first, and each of the women had chosen their favorite: lavender, rose, mint and lemon balm.

Smells pervaded the back room. Violet kept both the gossip and the work flowing, but no matter how fast she ran, her mind kept sneaking back to Cameron. She kept thinking, I want that man. I want to sleep with him. Love him. Laugh with him. And why shouldn't I? What's so wrong if two consenting adults both simply want to have a good time together?

"Violet, how long does this mess have to cook?" Betsy asked her.

Violet peered over the edge of the double boiler. "You're not trying to cook it. You just want the lanolin and beeswax to melt together. After that you add the almond oil."

"Gotcha."

"And at that point you call me, and I'll show you how we whisk in the herb water. You wanted the lemon balm, right?"

"Yeah, that was me. Harriet wanted the mint."

"Okay," she said, and thought: I can change. She didn't have to be a wife and mother. She could be an immoral, carefree lover who lived for today.

The more she thought about it, the more she realized how long she'd allowed the problem of her narrow fallopian tubes to get her down. So she'd been devastated to know she'd never likely conceive. So she'd been further crushed when Simpson had taken such a fast powder for another woman—a fertile woman—when Violet proved to be less than perfect.

I could do wicked, she figured. Obviously she'd have to work at it. She'd have to know the rules. She'd have to find someone she wanted to be wicked with—such as Cameron. In fact, specifically Cameron, since she'd never found anyone else she wanted to be wicked for...or with.

Turning into an amoral, immoral tramp would solve so many of her problems. Men were like perfume. Some had staying power. Some didn't. Counting on a guy to stick around just because he claimed to love you was the height of lunacy. It was far better to pick a guy from the get-go where you didn't have to feel bad about not being perfect.

"Hey, Violet. Come see how this is coming!"

Firmly, she turned her attention back to her class. Betsy, at the table's far end, was exuberantly slathering on her newly made almond cold cream. She'd come dressed today in a baseball cap, Jack Daniel's tee, and her favorite sequined tennis shoes. And then there was Harriet, who'd been married fifty-two years and could have starred in the infamous portrait of the two farmers carrying the pitchfork. Harriet had so many lines from the sun that the first three layers of cold cream seeped into the crevices and were never seen again. Roberta had been showing up for the classes ever since her divorce, wearing five pounds of mascara, a bra that pushed her boobs up to her throat, and fire-engine-red nail polish. And then there was Dinah.

"Hokay," Dinah drawled, "I think this aftershave lotion is finished. It was fun to make and all, but now I don't know what to do with it. Or how."

Harriet, ever wise, piped in, "Trust the one virgin in the group to make something for a man."

"Hey, who said I was a virgin?"

"The point, dear, is that we obviously need someone to test the aftershave on before you try giving it away as a present. Anyone have hairy legs? I mean, someone who's willing to admit it?"

Betsy, who always played Harriet's straight man, promptly burst out laughing. And because Betsy's laughter could make anyone laugh, within seconds the whole room was cracking up, holding stomachs and gasping guffaws and sputtering coffee—made worse as bare legs were lifted in the air as proof of their recent shaving—or lack thereof.

Silence fell as suddenly as a light switch. God knows how the rest of them realized there was a man in the room, but Violet sensed Cameron's sudden appearance from the instinctive change in her own heartbeat.

She whirled around to see him standing in the doorway, a steamy mug in one hand and a sheaf of papers in the other, looking wrinkled and sleepy and sexy. Wild. Wantable.

His eyes found hers as if there was no one else in the room. Last night suddenly danced between them—that surge of wanting, of urgency, of belonging, like she'd never felt for any man or anyone else. She'd never given herself that easily, that intimately.

And suddenly she wasn't so sure she could manage being as wicked and immoral as she wanted to be. Suddenly she sensed she could risk more with Cameron than she'd ever risked before—if she wasn't very, very careful.

The other women pounced on Cameron for entirely different reasons. "My God. He's the ideal test case," Dinah said.

Cameron tore his eyes off her and seemed to swiftly take in the others in the room. He may not have heard the gist of their earlier conversation, but he seemed to pick up fast that he was in trouble. He said, "No!" as if hoping that would cover everything.

"Now, there's nothing to worry about, dear. Come on. We just want to put a little bit of lotion on your cheek. It won't hurt. It's made of witch hazel and apple vinegar and lavender and sage—"

"Oh, my God. *No.*"

"It's supposed to make your skin feel really soft," Dinah assured him. "That's the whole point. To make it easier to shave—"

"Violet." His gaze swiveled back toward her. Desperately. "I just need to talk to you. About some business—"

Harriet said, "There now. Just sit down. You can do all the business you want with Violet and we can test our little aftershave recipe on you at the same time. You're not from Vermont, are you, but women here have been known to keep secrets for three and four centuries. No one will ever know you've been here, trust us. Don't be scared—"

He backed out of the doorway and took off like a bat out of hell.

She couldn't even try to catch up with him for several hours. She had to finish up the class and clean up, after which her two girls arrived to formally open the store for business. It was past ten before she could catch a five-minute stretch when the phone wasn't ringing or some customer asking for her.

Then, though, she had a hard time finding him. She looked in the house, in the yard, in the green-houses. His car was still parked by the barns, so he hadn't left the property, but she was mystified where he might have walked. Finally she located him at her great-grandmother's cottage.

Decades ago the cottage had been built to give Gram independence in a way that would keep her close to family. No one had lived there after Gram died until Camille had come home in the spring. The place had been fixed up then—except for the roof.

That was the infamous roof she'd hired to have fixed so Cameron would have a place to stay. The roofer was supposed to show up this morning, but just like most mornings in a week, he'd neither showed nor called.

It was Cameron on top of the roof with a hammer in his hand, a box of shingles next to him. He'd yanked off his shirt, undoubtedly because of the sun beating down with baking intensity. His skin looked oiled and bronzed. All six cats were up there with him—either trying to help, or just wanting to be around the sexiest guy in three counties.

She felt the same way, but she stood below with her hands on her hips. "So. You've decided to take up a new career as a roofer?"

He turned around on a heel and rubbed a wrist on his damp forehead. "More likely a new career as escape artist. Those women aren't still around, are they?"

"No." Maybe last night was between them like an elephant in their emotional living room, but she still had to grin. "You're safe."

Apparently he wanted more proof. "And you don't have any of that smelly aftershave concoction anywhere around, do you?"

"Why, Lachlan. The girls *did* scare you. Imagine, a big strong guy like you—"

"I'm not *scared*," he said testily. "I just happened to come across this half-finished roof because of your cats. *They* were scared. Ran out of the place faster than I did and led me to the nearest high place.''

"You expect me to believe that half-baked story?''

"Look. I'm sure they were nice women. In fact, if I ever get attacked in the middle of the night by a gang of cutthroats, I'd really like them on my side. Especially the one—'' he motioned vaguely ''—you know. The one who'd rearranged the shape of her—''

"Breasts.''

"Yeah. So that they looked like two oranges poking out right under her chin. And the one with the hairy legs—you know, the one who looked as if she had more wrinkles than a Shar Pei? Look, it's just a lot safer up here—''

"You're killing me.'' Damn man. They'd gotten into serious, deep waters last night. Mighty deep waters. Yet somehow he was making her comfortable, making her laugh.

He squinted down at her, his voice quieting. "Well, chère, it damn near killed me to sleep down the hall from you last night.''

Her pulse suddenly seemed to careen down a long, sleek hill. Who'd have guessed he would confront her hurt, confused feelings straight up? She took a breath. "Then why did you?''

"Because of the lavender. Because until we get some legal details discussed and agreed on, I'm representing Jeunnesse. That doesn't have to be a complication. But I don't want you worrying for even a minute that it could be." He lifted a sheaf of papers from his side. "Have you got fifteen minutes to look at these?"

"Cam, I *hate* legal mumbo-jumbo," she groused, but her pulse careened back up that long, sleek hill. So he hadn't slept in the other room because he hadn't wanted to be with her. And he was sure as hell still looking at her as if she were sugar and he was more than happy to take on the role of hummingbird.

"It won't hurt, I promise. And no one will find us out here, so without interruptions, we can get it done fast."

"I really don't have a bunch of time. I can't leave the girls alone for very long. They're both really young—"

He heard all her protests, but he still had them sitting together on the porch steps of the cottage and the papers whipped out faster than lightning. He might be determined to talk, but Violet couldn't seem to concentrate on his silly papers. His knee was grazing hers. She wasn't sure if the touch was accidental, or if he was deliberately keeping in physical contact. But knees had never struck her as an intimate, erogenous zone before. Still didn't. His knee was bony, his legs long and lanky and tanned, leading to sandals. Long feet. Very long. Really long big toes.

"...patent?" he asked.

"Hmm?"

"Patent, Violet. We're talking about your applying for a patent for the new breeds of lavender you developed."

"Okay."

He sighed. "One of us doesn't seem to be concentrating, because 'Okay' doesn't answer the question. The question is—did you apply for a patent?"

"Um, no, not exactly."

"In other words, no. All right. But listen seriously for a minute, okay? Because you need to know this. You want to patent both the product and the process. They're two separate things. So I'm going to apply for both those patents in your name. It takes forever before you actually get your patents, but just by applying and starting the process, you have some serious legal protections."

As boring and tedious as all this junk sounded, she started to feel guilty. "Cam, you don't have to do this. I'll get around to it, honestly."

"No, you won't. You've started yawning every time we started talking about this, and I can see the same suffering expression on your face now. So I'll get the applications started. But if anyone else tries this on you, you say no, hear me? Because you can't just go around trusting people."

"Did you think I was worried you were going to cheat me?"

"You should be worried," he said sternly.

"Gotcha." She tried to look more attentive, but he was so right about the subject being boring—and he wasn't. Besides which, his protectiveness was adorable, even if he did have knobby knees and really, really long big toes. His eyelashes were blond. Long and wonderful, but unless you were close enough to notice—which she was—you'd never realize they were so long and thick. And God, those eyes.

"You have to have a name for the strain of lavender you created. I don't suppose you might have one in mind?"

"Sure do!" At last, a question she had answer for. "Moonlight."

He paused. "*That's* the name you want? Moonlight lavender?"

"Yup. My lavender isn't as dark a purple as some strains, but it has a color that seems almost… translucent. A rich purple, almost as if the color seems lit from within. The way the light shines from the moon, you know?"

He looked as if he wanted to comment—possibly Moonlight wasn't too formal a botanical name? But whatever, he changed his mind about commenting, plugged a pencil behind his ear and went on.

And on.

And on.

Sheesh, all this serious stuff and information kept

pouring from his mouth. How Jeunnesse wanted to handle the lavender. What she could choose or not choose to be involved in. Exactly what he needed to put in motion over the next three weeks; what would happen after the harvest. What she would get for this, for that, for the next thing. How she was protected. What her choices were, but also how she shouldn't listen to him. The type of attorney and accountant she should call to help her understand the ramifications of her choices.

"All right," Cam said finally. "Now there's just one more thing before I can get this started."

"Shoot," she said, thinking that she just might curl up in his lap and snooze if they had to talk this kind of business much longer.

"Maybe you think I should take this answer for granted—but I can't. You *do* know what you did, right? You *can* reproduce it?"

"You mean, can I reproduce the strain of lavender I developed out there?" When he nodded in agreement, she lifted a hand. "Beats me. I don't know."

"Vi."

"What?"

"Quit with the blonde talk. I was only fooled the first day. You know more about this than a chemist any day of the week. In fact, you could probably teach classes at Harvard. So quit goofing off and tell me straight. Can you reproduce how you did this or not?"

"I'll have you know I'm as flaky as they come," she defended herself.

"You can do flaky," he agreed, obviously not wanting to insult her. "In fact, you could win an Oscar for how well you do flaky. But right now you're just talking to me. I'm not going to tell anyone you're brilliant if you want it kept a secret. But before we go any further with the patent process, or the harvest, I need to know. Could you go into another greenhouse and reproduce these strains? Or would we only be cloning the plants you have on the twenty acres out there?"

She was starting to feel miffed. Every guy in the neighborhood thought she was a ditsy blonde. It had been easy to fool them. Easy to fool the whole world—or at least the male half of it. So why did Cam have to be so damned different? "I'll answer the question only if you'll answer one for me."

"So go."

"All right. Then yes, I can recreate this nature of lavender anywhere. It took working with about four different strains and some specific growing techniques and conditions, but it wasn't a fluke. I planned the experiments. I knew what I was doing." She said firmly, "So now it's your turn to answer a question."

"Let's hear it."

"Is that really the reason you took off for the spare room last night? Because of some idiotic ethics thing?"

"Idiotic... What can I say? I'm sorry. I take ethics really seriously. It's a character flaw I've never completely been able to shake."

If he teased her anymore, she might just have to slap him. Instead, she asked him the crux of the question. "So. We did the ethics thing. Now what. Are we going to sleep together while you're here or not?"

"We are. We definitely are," he said, as if the question hadn't surprised him in the slightest. His tone was low, fervent and very, very clear. So was the way he looked at her. "And damn soon."

Nine

"**G**ood afternoon, ladies." Cameron walked into the kitchen. At least he was wearing a T-shirt this time, but after spending two solid weeks in the sun, his bronzed skin in shorts and sandals still made five pairs of eyes instantly swivel in his direction.

"Hi, Cameron!"

"Hi, Cameron, how's it going?"

"Good to see you, again, Cam!"

Violet rolled her eyes. Two weeks ago, Cameron would have broken out in an alpha-male sweat to see four women, sitting in bathrobes at the kitchen table, slathered in white-purple face masks and sipping wine. Now, he cheerfully fielded their greetings, reached in the refrigerator for a cold soda and promptly hiked back outside.

The tableful of women let out a collective sigh. Once a month, Violet put on a "pamperfest," not because she needed more to do, but because the products she used invariably brought more customers. Today's agenda had included a facial mask made from oatmeal and lavender, a foot soak and a conditioner for damaged hair. The conditioner was her own private recipe of geranium, lavender, sandalwood and rosewood, all diluted in vegetable oil, rubbed in the hair and covered in a towel for two hours.

At this point in the proceedings, all four women had the face masks on and the conditioner slathered in their hair. Originally she'd served a cooled herbal tea, but Maud Thrumble—typically—had slipped two bottles of wine onto the table before they'd even started.

"God, he's such a hulk," Maud said fervently.

"Hunk, not hulk," Mary Bell corrected her. "Quit trying to be cool when you don't know the terms. You're so old you'd probably have called him a dreamboat in your day."

"Whatever," Maud said. She and Mary Bell had never gotten along all that well. "He's to die for. That's the point. If only I hadn't been married for fifty years, I'll tell you, I'd give him a good run for his money."

The other two women hooted at this news, causing

a bowl of lavender-oatmeal goo to spill and Violet
to leap up for a rag.

"Aw, Violet, leave it be. We'll all clean it up
when we're through."

"It's all right," she said.

"No, it's not." Sally Williams frowned at her.
"You've been quiet all afternoon, not like yourself.
"What's wrong?"

"Not a thing. In fact, everything's hunky-dory.
Smooth as silk. Georgy-peachy. Totally copacetic."
In fact, if things got any better, she'd have to smash
her head into a door. Edgy as a wet cat, Violet
swiped at the spill on the floor, then aimed for the
sink. If a woman was going to make a mess, it was
her theory that a woman should make a good one.
Her entire kitchen looked like a witch's trash. Clay
and porcelain pots of herbs spilled over the counters.
Leaves and stems and flowers strewed from the door
to the sink. And the pot that mixed the oatmeal and
lavender—God knew how she was going to clean it.
"What's not to be happy? It's a gorgeous day. Life's
good—"

"Enough, already," Maud said. "It's that man
that's gotten you down, isn't it?"

"What man?" She'd never been less depressed,
Violet told herself. The last couple weeks had been
wonderful. Every day had been sunny. Her Herb Haven business was busier than a swarm of bees. Cameron had taken over the lavender harvest completely,

hiring Filbert Green, the local farmer who'd taken care of the land after the parents retired. At this very moment, in fact, there was a crew in the lavender, unseen, unheard, none of whom had bothered her for anything.

Family news had been just as peaceful. Camille had called to wax poetically on the wonders of honeymoons with teenagers. Her mom had called to convey that she and her dad had been going to vacation in Maine and somehow taken a wrong turn; they were headed for New Zealand. And Daisy hadn't called—which was yet another good thing—because when she connected with her oldest sister the next time, Violet planned to strangle her. Daisy was very good at getting her sisters embroiled with men, but when it came to revealing what she was doing herself, suddenly she took a powder, probably somewhere on the Riviera on a nude beach.

Violet opened the fridge, put the dish rag on the top shelf and closed it. When she turned around, the women were all staring at her.

"What? What?"

"Vi, you're just not yourself today," Sally repeated. "Sit down and have some wine, girl."

"It's four in the afternoon. If I have wine now, I'll be curled up on the floor before dinner."

"Well, something stronger then. How about a little strawberry daiquiri?" From nowhere, Mary Bell lifted a delicate sterling silver flask in the air. Sally promptly zoomed for the cupboard and brought down a glass, then cleared a seat of damp towels so Violet could sit down. "Speaking of alcohol—"

"I didn't think we were."

That was ignored. "It looks as if your houseguest is doing something illegal out there. At least in my daddy's day, we used to call that kind of device a still. He making moonshine on you?"

"No. He's making lavender oil…or 'lavender absolute' as it's properly called, I guess. It's kind of hard to explain the process." She stared at the glass of cherry daiquiri in front of her, then thought what the hell and took a sip. "First you have to pick the flowers when only two thirds of the florets are opened up. Then…well, come to think of it, the distilling process probably does have something in common with a bootlegger's still. You put water in one container and the flowers in another. You heat the water hot enough to make steam, and then that's pushed through a pipe under high pressure through the plant material. The steam works to separate or displace the water from the oil. The oil always…"

"Good grief," Maud said. "You're going to make our eyes cross. None of us give a holy damn about the still business, dear, we were just trying to get you talking. You haven't had a man near you since you came home after the divorce, and suddenly you've got this gorgeous hulk living with you—"

"Hunk," Mary Bell corrected.

"Whatever. The point is that your mother isn't here, but we all know she'd be hoping that you're taking advantage of the situation."

Violet gulped down another sip of daiquiri, feeling cornered. Furthermore, her cats had all hunkered on top of the refrigerator, away from the bawdy, noisy drinkers with their increasingly stiff facial masks. "He's not *living* with me. He's just living here. Until the roof for the cottage is done—which was supposed to have been finished a whole month ago. In fact, almost two months ago now. I can't make Bartholomew show up regularly for work to save my life."

"That's roofers, dear. I should know. I was married to one for twelve years. He only showed up on time for dinner twice, God rest his soul." Anne Blayton almost never spoke up, but she'd finished two glasses of wine now. Her mask was starting to crack like old parchment. "He sure was good between the sheets, though."

"Well, you've been through enough husbands, you should be a judge," Mary Bell said sweetly.

"The point," Maud said, "is not whether he's sleeping here or in the cottage, but where he's not sleeping when the lights go out. Are you deaf and blind, Violet Campbell? Last week, with that ghastly heat wave, I swear the only redeeming part of my day was to drive past here and see him walking in the yard, at least half the time without a shirt. Whooee."

"I hadn't noticed." Violet reached forward to pour a little wine into her now-empty glass.

"Violet, honey, you just added wine to your daiquiri," Mary Bell said kindly. "You're just not yourself."

"I am *too* myself."

The back door opened again. Cameron ambled in. "Hi, ladies. Looks like you're having fun." He deposited an empty can in the trash, smiled at the group, stroked three cats and ambled through to the other room.

Four women let out another collective sigh. All of them were smiling hard enough to crack their masks. "It's time we washed you all off," Violet said firmly.

That was at least three times he'd walked in this afternoon. Three times, when he'd laughed and joked with the women. It wasn't that long ago that he would have had a cow and a half over an estrogen-loaded event like this. He didn't run anymore. He didn't act terrified—or even surprised—if he wandered into the kitchen and found a roomful of masked women with their bare feet in buckets, sitting in bathrobes in the middle of the afternoon.

It just wasn't natural. He was beyond being the ideal guy—helping her with everything from dishes to chores, making the whole lavender thing look effortless, doing his own wash, never taking over the remote, bringing groceries in. He'd quit trying to finish the roof, but that was only because he'd completely run out of spare time. Normal men only helped out if they were harassed, blackmailed or wanted sex. Everybody knew that. Cameron seemed to think it was ordinary behavior to pitch in. More confusing yet, he took every damn thing in her life in stride, as if it were all very interesting, instead of the nature of stuff that should have given an alpha guy like him nightmares.

Instead, he'd been giving *her* nightmares.

As soon as the women were cleaned up and herded out, Violet piled dishes into the sink, added sudsy water and then turned on the dishwasher. A moment later she realized she'd turned the dishwasher on without any dishes in it, and thought she'd either had too much to drink…

Or too little Cameron.

She looked frantically around for the dish towel, but it seemed to have disappeared.

Two weeks ago he'd claimed he wanted to sleep with her. Intended to sleep with her. Imminently soon.

Only, they hadn't.

He'd been kissing her regularly. Over breakfast. Before lunch. In the middle of the day, if he found her in the Herb Haven with her hands filled with a dried-herb arrangement, he'd take a bite out of the back of her neck, cup her fanny. He'd walked with her in the moonlight. They'd hip-danced doing the dishes after dinner, barged in on each other coming out of the bathroom, fallen asleep watching horror movies on the same couch.

But the damn man hadn't done one thing about seriously seducing her. She was free! She was cheap! She was available. She had boobs. She wasn't asking him for a single thing! So what was the matter with the man?

Upstairs, she heard the pipes rattle. He was taking a shower. She opened the refrigerator for some God-unknown reason and found her dish towel. She held the cool towel to her pounding head. The man was turning her into a train wreck. She had to get her life back. She couldn't remember where her shoes were, her keys, her dishrags. She was starting to become ditsy for real.

Enough was enough. If Mohammed wasn't willing to come to the mountain, she was darn well going to have to try seducing the mountain herself.

Cameron walked into the kitchen and stopped dead. They'd been sharing KP duty over the past couple weeks, but after seeing the war zone caused by the women's group earlier, he'd put on clean khakis and a decent shirt, figuring that Violet would want to go out to dinner.

Instead, the women were gone and the kitchen cleaned to within an inch of its life—give or take the cats and cat hair. The old oak table had white quilted place mats, roses floating in a bowl, some kind of wild salad—smelled like lemon-pepper shrimp— puffed-up fresh rolls…

Violet whirled around. "We're having something I call come-to-Bahama wings. They're chicken wings without the bones. Kind of hot. A little lime juice, some rum, some honey, some hot peppers… I guess I should have asked you first, but you can handle hot, can't you, Lachlan?"

"Sure," he said, but the adrenaline was instantly pumping. Something was wrong. Worrisome wrong. The way she smiled at him raised the temperature in the kitchen twenty degrees. He saw the hot wings and the roses and heard the come-to-mama invitation in her voice.

Everywhere he looked, there were more land mines. And the more he looked, the more he recognized that she'd gone to a ton of trouble, laying all kinds of intricate, tricky traps.

She was barefoot, wearing a skirt that looked like a long, floaty handkerchief. Her midriff was bare, her long hair all scooped up and twisted and sedated with long clips off her neck. Said neck had been doused with some lethal scent—not her usual citrus soap, for damn sure, but something that reached his nostrils from the doorway. The perfume was a drug. That was all he was sure of.

Her lips had been coated with something shiny, and she was wearing a top that looked like another handkerchief. Only the top was actually about the size of a handkerchief this time, such a light fabric that he could clearly make out the plump swell of her breasts and the shape of her nipples.

"Whew, it's really hot tonight, isn't it?" she said with a grin.

His bloodstream shot his heart another dose of adrenaline. Yeah, he'd suspected that patience—and celibacy—would pay off eventually. But Violet was usually so warm and nurturing that he'd never figured she'd be the kind of woman to play mean.

This setup wasn't just mean; it was down and dirty.

"I figured you had such a swamped afternoon that you'd want to go out, pick up dinner. Hell, I'd have helped if I'd known you were going to all this trouble."

"No trouble," she said sweetly. "You've been working crazy long hours yourself. I decided that we both needed some real food and a relaxing evening for a change."

"Relaxing," he echoed, thinking that nothing about this setup was remotely relaxing. On the other hand, even in ninety-degree heat after putting out a ten-hour work day, his entire body was hard as stone. Hard, willing and high on anticipation.

However, he hadn't sucked it up and slept alone the past two weeks just to let her get off this easy. Yeah, he was willing to kiss her feet—and all the way up from there. But he hadn't deprived himself, or her, without reason. He smiled at her as if his blood wasn't pounding, ambled up behind her and dropped a soft, slow kiss on the drift of her nape. "What can I do to help?"

He felt her responsive shiver—but she recovered too darn fast. "Nothing but enjoy the feast. Or…how about if you pour the wine? It's red. I know you're supposed to have white wine with fish and chicken, but I didn't have any around…and red is so much more potent, don't you think?"

Another glossy, sultry smile, another tip of the lashes. He thought, I'll be lucky to make it through dinner without throwing her on the table and going for it. "Yeah, I like red better than white, too. Hey…"

"Yes?"

Somehow he had to buy some time. He was more than willing to let her have her way. But first he wanted to understand what had motivated all these sudden wicked tactics of hers—not that he wasn't enjoying them. Just that he figured a few minutes of distracting conversation was a good idea. "I was thinking how crazy it was that we've been together every day, yet I never asked you what you did. I mean, I know you moved here after a divorce and set up your herb business. But what kind of work did you do before that?"

"Work?" The question obviously startled her, because momentarily she forgot the sultry-smile, big-eye thing.

"Yeah. I mean, for a living. Were you into some kind of different career before this?"

There went the last of the provocative smile and the hip sashaying. It wasn't as if she didn't still look sexy as hell, and then some, but as if she stopped planning it.

She handed him dishes, one after the other, and he carted them to the table. Within minutes they were eating. A half hour later they were on the last bites and their second glass of wine.

"I was a physical therapist," she told him. "I didn't have any kind of formal specialty or anything fancy like that. But I mostly worked with kids. Kids who'd been in accidents, lost a limb or use of a limb. Tough road, to get a little one physically and emotionally prepared for life again, after going through a trauma to that extent."

Cameron shook his head, no longer stalling or playing games. He was fascinated by everything she'd been telling him. "Wow. I can't believe you never mentioned this before."

"There was no reason to. I'm not doing it now."

He hesitated. He could see in her face there was more here. He sensed Violet kept the "more" to herself for reasons he couldn't fathom. So he pressed. "You quit because you burned out on it?"

"No. Not exactly. Kids tend to hate physical therapy. Actually, adults do, too. It's not fun. It hurts and it's hard work. And especially for children who've been through a life-changing event, they feel confused and angry about what's happened to them. Anger, fear, frustration. I can't explain this, but that's exactly why I loved the work—at the time. Have some more wings, Cam."

"I couldn't eat another bite. So you really liked working with children, huh?"

She snapped her fingers and jumped up. "I'll bet I can coax you into eating one more thing. How about a little dish of vanilla-bean ice cream? With a little drizzle of raspberry rum sauce over it?"

"Whatever you can handle, I can handle," he said.

She shot him a look. By then the sun was skating down the horizon, turning the treetops a velvet green and the sky a silky azure. One cat opened her eye at the word *ice cream* but otherwise the herd was snoozing at a distance, too lazy to even beg.

"Well then, hon, I'll just dish you up a big dollop of trouble," Vi promised him.

As if she hadn't done that from the second he met her. Right then, though, Cameron wasn't willing to be completely diverted from the bone he was determined to pick. "So…why aren't you still doing the physical therapist thing?"

He saw a sudden flash in her eyes, the slightest stiffening in her shoulders. "Because when I came home, I started the Herb Haven."

Which didn't answer his question in the slightest. "And that's obviously gone great for you," he said smoothly, "but you weren't inclined to find work as a physical therapist in White Hills? Or weren't there any PT jobs here?"

"No. There's probably work. There's a good-size clinic in White Hills. I just—"

"You just what?" He smiled at her as he poured her another glass of wine.

"I just decided that maybe I should stop working with children for a while. Do something else. Everyone doesn't stay in the same job forever."

"No, they don't. In fact, I never got it, why people felt obligated to find one career and stick to it. What's so wrong about liking change? Wanting to do new things, see new horizons?"

"Exactly. People don't have just one dream," she said defensively.

"They sure don't." Yet he was almost sure that Vi still did have that one dream about working with kids. Not because he had extrasensory perception. But because there seemed a haunted unhappiness in her eyes, a tension.

"Change is fun," she agreed. "What's not to love about new challenges? Doesn't everybody need to stretch their minds? Not fall into a rut?"

"That's really true...but, damn, I have the hardest time imagining you falling into any kind of rut. You bring a sense of fun and adventure into everything you do. Other people get bored. You seem to find a spirit of fun in everything."

She glowed for a second, then jumped up on him again, all flustered. "All right. That's enough being nice to me. About time we talked about you. In fact, I've been wondering—"

"No," he said mildly, not responding to her words but to her actions. He suspected that she was about to make a deliberately catastrophic amount of noise, banging around the kitchen—an effective way to cut off any further serious conversation. "Let's leave the dishes for now. How about if we take the ice cream out on the porch swing and see if we can scout up a breeze?"

Typically, she was willing to do anything to get out of dishes so she agreed. She bought out the ice-cream dishes, not little dishes, like she'd claimed, but major masterpieces with her fancy sauce. The smell of rum was wildly sweet and strong, adding to the other nectar smells of the evening. He exclaimed over the dessert. She laughed. Yet it was Violet who spooned one bite and then put her dish on the ground.

Before he could ask another personal question— and, for damn sure, before he could get her to talk about her work with children again—she suddenly stole his dish, too. Set it on the ground in the sun, next to hers. And plopped in his lap.

A guy always hoped to win the lottery, but he didn't expect it. Her fanny nestled in his lap, as if seeking the exact weight and pressure that would drive him crazy. She found it easily. Before he could even breathe, her arms had swooped around his neck. For all that sudden impulsiveness, though, she leaned closer and only offered him a whisper of a kiss. The graze of her mouth against his was soft, light, silky.

"Hey," he whispered. "What's happening here?"

"You don't want me to kiss you?"

"Oh, yeah, I do." And all his control buttons snapped. The power outage of '03 had nothing on this moment. He'd waited and waited and waited to taste her again, and here she was, warm and willing and almost bare, obviously intent on inviting him to take what he'd been craving for the past two weeks.

So he let her test him with that teasing little kiss of hers and then came back, pirate fast, with another kind of kiss entirely. He didn't want her lips; he wanted her whole mouth, her tongue. He didn't want a sweet sample; he wanted saliva and combustible heat. He wanted her heart pounding. He wanted her eyes to open wide with awareness and worry—not *bad* worry, but he was definitely tired to hell of her thinking she was safe around him. He wanted her to know that she wasn't safe. And neither was he.

He got everything he wanted and then some. When her lashes shuttered open, she looked dazed and more than a little shook up. "Well," she said faintly, on the gust of a pale breath. "I guess you *did* want to kiss me."

But he couldn't come up with any more easy smiles. "You really thought I didn't?"

"You didn't seem to have any problem walking into your own room all these nights. You didn't even try to—"

"Seduce you?"

"I don't need to be *seduced,* Lachlan. I'm a grown woman. But I just didn't understand what the deal was."

"Neither did I, chère." He pushed back a strand of hair that had sneaked free from all those clips holding it back. "I knew I wanted you. I knew you were willing to make love with me. But I kept having the bad, bad feeling that you were going to regret it."

That startled her. "Why did you think I'd regret sleeping with you? I never said—"

"I know you 'never said' anything specific. But you only said you were willing to make love when you pegged me as the kind of man who wouldn't give a damn about you, wouldn't stick around." When she tried squirming and doing her flutter-the-hands thing, he gently cuffed her wrist. "The fact is, I do care. I do give a damn. And nothing I understand about you, sensed about you, made me believe you were being truthful. If you want a short fling, trust me, Vi, I'd be happy to give you one. But I can't buy it. That you're going to be okay to just hit the sheets and then go our different ways the next morning. Or the next week.''

She took a hard breath. Then pushed off his lap and stood. So did he. As if the porch had suddenly become unbearably claustrophobic, she suddenly vaulted down the porch steps and started walking. So did he. Restless or not, it was still tepid hot, still too humid to breathe. She didn't run any farther than the deep shade of the maple, and then she turned on him.

''You want to know the deal, Lachlan? It's that I have skinny tubes. That's the deal. The whole deal. The chance of my ever having kids is mighty unlikely.''

Aw, hell. The minute she blurted that out, Cameron wanted to slug himself. God knew how he'd missed it, because immediately he realized she'd given him a ton of clues. Her reproducing plants so wildly. Her endless herd of cats. Her not going back to a profession with children. The way she mothered the two girls who worked for her. He even remembered—now, too damn late—the funny look on her face when she'd first said she didn't need birth control. ''That's about as unfair as it gets, chère,'' he said softly.

''More than unfair. I never wanted fancy things. Forget the riches and jewels and all that. I just wanted a house and kids and a man to love.'' Her head shot up, her eyes jewel bright. ''And you're wondering what that has to do with our making love.''

"No. I wasn't wondering anything. I was just feeling bad for you.''

"Yeah, well. The thing is…maybe there was a time I wouldn't have been comfortable with casual sex. But that was then. And this is now. I've been alone since the divorce. That's three years.''

"Hey," he said gently. Hell's bells, those tears were welling up. And yeah, of course he knew she cried at the drop of a hat. Only, damn it, this time she had reason to cry, a terrible huge reason to cry, and that was way different from seeing her cry at a Kodak commercial. He scooped her close, stroking her back, feeling her shudder back a real sob, afraid that she was going to do it seriously to him this time—cry until they were both drenched.

"I don't want a husband," she said fiercely.

"You don't have to have a husband.''

"I've been trying to scare men away for three years. And doing a *great* job of it.''

"You're great at being ditsy," he reassured her, and stroked, stroked, stroked. "But maybe you don't have to work at it quite so hard. It's not like every man wants kids—''

"I *know* that. But I also had a husband who took off the minute he found out I was…flawed. Yes, he wanted kids. And so did I. But we could have made other choices—like adopting or fostering. That's when I realized it wasn't as simple as just being about kids. It was about his seeing me differently, seeing me as less of a woman. My feeling like less of a woman.''

He stopped stroking. ''Wait a minute. What kind of horse hockey is this?''

''It's not horse hockey, Lachlan. You asked me what the deal is, and I'm telling you. In the beginning I just didn't see a reason to get into all this. It wasn't your problem, wasn't your business. But you asked so I'm telling you. I want to get into casual sex. With you. I want to know for sure that you're leaving. That you're going back to your own life. That I don't have to worry about how you think about me as a woman, deep down. How you—''

Damned if he was going to let her finish another idiotic sentence. Enough was enough.

Ten

Violet felt completely bewildered when Cameron suddenly grabbed her. She'd been trying to seriously talk to him. She was all riled up and upset that the whole crappy story about her skinny tubes had come out. She'd never wanted Cam to know. It was fine the way it was. Good the way it was. He thought of her as a whole, sexy woman—she knew he did. She didn't want him to see her differently, and she'd been afraid all along that he would if he knew the whole blasted picture.

Yet suddenly his arms swept around her, tighter than a noose, and his mouth swooped down on hers, slapped hers, crushed hers…then almost immediately lightened. Slower than honey, a taking kind of kiss became a wooing kind of kiss. A coaxing, wooing kind of kiss suddenly became an ardent, Iwantyou needyou havetohaveyou kind of kiss. His tongue found hers. His hands sieved into her hair. She felt his long, hard body throb against hers, and suddenly she was trembling from the inside out.

He was going to take her. She knew it in the flash of an instinct, a burst of heat and fear and excitement streaking through her pulse. Right here, right now, right under the deep, dark shade of the maple. No one was around, and the sun was setting fast now, but heaven knew strangers and neighbors both drove by and drove in at all hours.

It was as if he didn't care. Didn't notice.

And then neither did she.

She'd never felt like this. As a young girl, she'd dreamed incessantly all that tedious stuff about the prince who'd find her, who'd make her the center of his world, who'd slay dragons for her. But obviously she'd grown up. There were no fairy tales, and she'd wanted a flesh-and-blood guy and not a fake prince anyway. But Cameron…oh, Cameron.

He pushed at clothes, buttons, zippers. Heeled off his shoes, lifted her out of hers. No one had ever swept her away like this. Made her feel as if he couldn't breathe without her breath, couldn't survive without touching her, couldn't live. Without having her.

His eyes were open on hers, intense, unrelenting. Yet his mouth kept coming, even as he swooped her down to the ground on their makeshift nest of clothes. A car went by, maybe saw them, maybe didn't.

Pagan kiss followed pagan kiss, each more fierce and wild than the last. A button dug into her spine. Grass tickled. Her hair tangled—her darn long hair was always tangling—yet only one thing mattered to her. Cam. And what they seemed to be creating together.

When he suddenly lifted his head, she tried to say something, but the way he looked at her dammed all the words in her throat and her heart was suddenly hammering, hammering. "I *love* you," he said roughly. "*Love,* Vi. Do you hear me?"

Again she tried to answer, but he moved so fast. One instant he was taking her mouth, the next he'd twisted around, all naked and bronzed and bare, and started over completely at the other end. He kissed her right foot, from arch to toe, then worked his way up. Kisses wreathed from ankle to knee to the inside of her thigh to the core of her, and when she was gasping for breath, he flipped her over. He kissed her fanny; bit softly, tenderly, then laved a silken path up her spine to the nape of her neck. Then flipped her again.

His tongue dove into her mouth, mated with hers, even as he reached down. He wrapped her legs around his waist, intimately tight, and then dove in, drove in, taking her high and tight and intimately. Desire suddenly developed sharp teeth. Need clawed at her, ached through her. The need for completion, but even more, the need to love. Him. To be loved. By him.

"Come with me," he rasped. The sun dropped so fast, as if understanding they needed privacy, yet the darkness so stealthily brought voyeurs. Crickets. Frogs. Lightning bugs. Cats. And then the moon.

Their moon.

She saw his face above her, so sharply honed, so full of passion and emotion, even as she could feel herself losing any last ounce of control. Love reeled through her, whipped through her senses and heart.

"*Now,* Vi," he said.

She came with him, feeling as if she were free-falling from the top of the sky. But not alone. She fell with Cam, wildly, from the heart. Even minutes later, even hours later, she couldn't shake the flushed, joyous sensation of feeling totally complete. Totally whole. As if she were the most powerful woman ever born, woman with a capital *W,* the woman she'd always wanted to be.

Cam's woman.

And at that moment she couldn't imagine feeling any other way.

Cameron couldn't sleep.

It had to be well past two in the morning. They'd

eventually made it to her bedroom, dozed for a while, wakened to make love all over again. Now, oddly, he was more wide awake than a hoot owl. She was lying in his arms, damp, warm, draped all over him— or he was draped all over her. Who cared who was doing the draping as long as every inch of his skin was touching every inch of hers?

His eyes were used to the darkness now. He kept staring at the silver moonlight flooding in the open window, the quiet stir of curtains, the pale light falling on that strangely austere bedroom. "Vi," he whispered.

"Hmm?"

He'd been pretty sure she was awake, just not positive. Her voice was sleepy, sated, content—but awake. "*Chère,* are you absolutely positive about the infertility?"

She didn't stiffen in his arms this time, which told Cameron that she was okay talking about the subject with him now. The trust was there. For him. For her. "Let's put it this way," she said with a wry touch of humor. "Originally I learned everything about sex from Simpson—which means that I learned almost everything wrong. From the time we were in high school, Simpson made me think that a guy had to get off or he suffered terribly. That guys couldn't wait. That sometimes girls made it and sometimes they didn't, but overall, that Real Women did."

"As in...it's the woman's fault if she doesn't have a climax?"

"Yup. I can't believe I swallowed a lot of the things Simpson used to tell me. And on the baby subject, he really believed that it must be the woman's fault if she couldn't get pregnant, if the guy was virile." She sighed. "Some things he didn't have completely wrong. He had his sperm checked. And they were all aggressive little swimmers. I was the one with the skinny tubes." She snuggled closer. "You know what?"

"What?"

"I didn't want to tell you about all this, but... somehow it's opened my eyes to just air it all out. It's obvious to me now what I was doing with the lavender. I needed to create something that was totally my own, something that came specifically from me. And I guess I did go a little batty with enthusiasm."

"A little?"

He heard her soft chuckle in the darkness. "Okay. So I went hog wild. But the thing is—I never thought all my experiments would take. I thought most of them would miscarry, you know? Why should they work? I was a novice at this, no more than a closet gardener. It just seemed to be luck, that everything I touched reproduced with no problem. It was so ironic."

"Ironic in what way?" He stroked that long hair,

knowing she'd be annoyed in the morning she hadn't braided it, but loving it loose.

"Ironic, because all I had to do was love it. And nurture it. And it thrived." She sighed. "Same with cats. I took in one stray barn cat three years ago. He was starved, crippled. I didn't think he had a chance of making it, and the next thing I knew, he'd miraculously turned into a she-cat and had kittens on me." She stroked his neck, as if somehow instinctively knowing where he liked being touched most. "My mom had this theory, raising kids."

"Which was?"

"Which was that everybody's powerful in some way. We just have to clue in to who we naturally are. My mom taught us girls that each of us had something in our nature that we needed to listen to, develop. For me, I thought it was to be a mother. To grow and raise and nurture. To feed. To caretake. That's part of what was so hard. Knowing I couldn't have kids. I'd just always been programmed to believe that was a natural part of me."

Cameron hesitated. He'd never been afraid of wading into touchy waters, but this time, he desperately wanted to say the right thing. It's not like he knew anything about infertility. Or that he had any way to make her loss any less painful. But he had to find something right to say. The jerk she'd married had made her feel less than a woman, as if she were less than whole because of those "skinny tubes."

"*Chère,* I think you were a born nurturer. Just like your mother said. But I don't think that's just about children. It's about everything and everyone around you. Always will be. Although…"

"Although what?"

"Although I think there's a definite danger you could get overrun by cats." There, he'd made her smile. "If you started adopting elephants…well, the potential problems boggle the mind."

And there. He'd made her really laugh now. Feeling high on those successes, he pressed toward touchier ground. "I'm relieved you went for the divorce," he murmured, and kissed her forehead. "I'm sorry that he was such a blind idiot and hurt you. But if he hadn't had all those stupid ideas, who knows, maybe you'd have stuck with him. And then I'd never have found you."

"You think it's fate we found each other when we did?"

Her voice was getting sleepier, her cheek rooting for just the right place on his shoulder. "Not fate," he said quietly, bluntly. "Love. The kind of love that's actually freeing for us both. I mean—I already have two kids, so I don't need to start a formal family all over again. This is perfect. I'm a free spirit. So are you. We can both do anything, go anywhere we want. There's nothing to hold us down. Nothing to hold us back."

She seemed to go very still when he said the

"love" word, but she didn't immediately answer. Moments later, he realized she'd fallen asleep.

That was okay, he told himself. He just wanted to reassure her that he loved her for *her*. Maybe he'd hoped she would say something to indicate she wanted him to stick around in her life. But she'd just revealed that huge hole in her heart. Rome wasn't built in a day. Maybe she needed to think about that "love" word for a while. They had time yet.

Surely they still had time yet.

"Girls. Could you keep quiet for a full three seconds?" Both girls whirled around in surprise at her sharp tone. She never yelled at them. She never yelled at anyone, but darn it, August had blown in on a hot, mean wind. A few days ago she'd picked up a stomach bug she couldn't seem to shake. The cats were crabby; she hadn't been sleeping; and the girls had been talking for hours about school coming, boys, clothes, boys and then more boys.

"We need to make some more insect repellent. Remember the recipe? Ten parts lavender, ten parts geranium, five parts clove—"

"Hey, I remember it, Vi, not to worry."

"All right then, if you two'll make up two dozen of those vial—" She tried to finish the sentence, couldn't. Suddenly every smell in the Herb Haven seemed to fill her nostrils. She loved those smells. Every single one of them. Always had, always would. But just then, she put a hand over her mouth and ran like a bat out of hell for the back bathroom.

Twenty minutes later she decided that she wouldn't die, even found the strength to fumble in the medicine cabinet for her spare toothbrush and toothpaste. She worked up a good foam as she stared in the mirror. Her cheeks were pinch-pink, her eyes bright, her hair wild as a witch's but certainly glossy and healthy. Yet over the past week, she'd found an excuse to cry every day and hurl at least once.

Of course, crying was nothing new. She cried for the national anthem and for dog food commercials. But usually her stomach was cast iron. Last night they'd had fish with a spinach sauce and peachy sweet potatoes. Nothing a normal man would eat, but Cameron, par for Cameron, ate anything she put in front of him and asked for seconds. For herself, they were old favorites, comfort foods, no matter how weird they might be for someone else. Nothing, for damn sure, to inspire an upset tummy.

If she didn't have those skinny tubes, she might fear she was pregnant.

"Hey, Violet." Barbara rapped on the bathroom door. "We think you should go up to the house. Just forget all this. We'll make up the vials and those sachet things and handle the customers."

"You just want to talk about boys."

"Yeah, so? Go on. Go lie down or something."

She didn't want to go home. Cameron was up

there packing. He wasn't leaving for another couple of days, but the lavender harvest was over and it was not as if he could get all his stuff ready in a second. Between her missed period and her upset tummy and the insanely radiant cheeks she kept seeing in the mirror, Violet kept finding the "pregnancy" word sneaking into her mind. But skinny tubes didn't suddenly disappear, so she figured she was simply emotionally upset about his leaving.

"I'm not leaving you two kids alone in the shop," she said firmly.

Barbara opened the door, took one look and popped a bubble. "Yeah, you are." She aimed her thumb at the house in a clear-cut order. "Go on. It's hot. Go drink some lemonade or something."

Violet winced. "Don't say lemonade. Don't even think it out loud."

That's it. They pushed her out. And the heat was too searing and sticky to just stand there, so she had to traipse up to the house. The back door was open, the phone ringing, but hell's bells, the phone was always ringing. She opened the refrigerator and then just leaned into the cold smoky air with a sigh.

"Oh, God. Let me waste some electricity along with you." Cameron suddenly appeared from the dining room, shirtless and shoeless, just wearing low-slung khaki shorts and carrying packing tape. Now, though, he tossed the tape and hiked over to the open refrigerator. Faster than lightning, he dropped a soft,

lingering kiss on her mouth. "Mmm. Fresh toothpaste. What an aphrodisiac."

"I hate to say this, Lachlan, but you could find an
aphrodisiac in a dust bunny." Oh, God. Even that
light kiss and she was not only fine again, but her
pulse was soaring like a hummingbird's. He'd
changed her so much. Healed her. Made her feel like
a whole woman again. And all because of those long,
wicked nights and wild, sneaky kisses. Because of
the way he loved her.

And the way she loved him back.

"Have you been out to our lavender? You know
how it needs to be cut back, hard, as soon as the
crop's taken. Well, old Filbert and the crew finished
an hour ago. She's all tied up and pretty again."

Bad news. She closed the refrigerator door—after
filling a cup full of ice—and headed for the couch in
the living room. It was too hot to stand up. Too hot
to hear bad news anywhere near that bright, happy
sunlight. "You talked to Jeunnesse?"

"Yup." He didn't sit on the couch, instead, pulled
up the old round ottoman and plunked down, facing
her. "You know what has to happen now. I've tested
all I can here. The rest has to happen in a bigger
lab."

"I know."

"The next part of the testing takes time. Perfumes
have a top note, a middle note and a base note.
Lavender is used for all three. But the top note is

usually the most volatile—the scent you pick up when you first put on perfume. And the base note—that's the scent that lingers even hours after you've been wearing the perfume.''

He was talking as if she didn't know these things. As if he believed he needed to carefully cover them again. He was looking at her as if she were some kind of fragile treasure. Searching her face the way he'd searched her face for days—even though she'd never told him, and never would, how strangely sick she'd been.

''The middle note in the perfume isn't so much about smell. It's about staying power. About chemistry. It's what makes one perfume last and another completely dissipate. It's what makes the best perfumes endure. And the right lavender is the key to that enduring power. It's what we're hoping your lavender has.''

She had no idea why he was telling her this. She knew it all. He knew it all. Somehow, though, every darn time Cam brought all this up again, all she could think of was how something was terribly wrong with her. Because unlike a good lavender, she seemed to have no enduring power for men. It wasn't just Simpson who'd left her.

Cam was leaving her now, too.

Simpson, she'd just loved. But Cameron was about to take her heart and soul with him. It was definitely some kind of flaw in her—she just seemed to attract men who didn't want to stay. For three years now, she'd blamed her infertility, but Cam had certainly proven that theory wrong, because he didn't care if she could have kids or not. He'd made it more than clear that he needed no more children.

"Vi, I *have* to go back to France. To the Jeunnesse labs."

"Of course you do." Because her voice sounded so hollow, she said more strongly, "I've known that from the start."

"There's a good staff of chemists there, and they can run most of the tests. But I know the lavender. I need to take charge of it."

"Cam, why are you telling me this? I've known from the beginning that you were only going to be here for a few weeks. We both knew."

"I just want to be sure you realize…that this isn't about wanting to leave you. It's just about the work." He waited, as if hoping she'd ask him something, say something.

And Violet knew exactly what he wanted to hear, so she put on her best ultraviolet smile and touched his cheek with love. "Didn't I tell you I never wanted ties?" she asked fiercely. "I love you, Cameron Lachlan. Just the way you are. Just the way we've been together. I wouldn't have given up a second of our summer for the world."

She saw his jaw clamp tight, and a light seemed to deaden in his eyes, but she couldn't fathom what else he might conceivably have wanted her to say. "There's no reason we can't see each other again," he said.

"I hope we do. But I don't want you worried about it." She couldn't tie him down. Wouldn't. Cam was who he was, a heart-free vagabond, a lover and a giver and a healer of women—but he'd tried marriage before, already had two daughters. He'd been terribly unhappy, and if there was one thing she wanted for this man who'd become her whole world, it was to love him. There was no way she'd ask him for anything he hadn't clearly offered.

"Have you picked a time to leave?" she asked lightly.

He nodded, then had to swallow as if something thick were stuck in his throat. "Tomorrow morning at daybreak. I can't wait longer than that."

So, Violet thought. Now I know the exact minute my heart's going to be broken for all time.

Eleven

Cameron watched his daughter's Jeep bounce out of his driveway. It had rained the last five days in September. His gravel driveway could have been renamed Mud Puddle Avenue. He waved another goodbye to Miranda and Kate.

The two girls were ecstatic he'd quit Jeunnesse and come home from France for good. They'd both asked about living with him—which could happen, if their mother agreed. He wasn't that sure what the girls really wanted or needed yet, but in the meantime he was less than two hours from their home. They could visit him anytime they wanted, especially now that Miranda had a driver's license.

When the car rounded the curve out of sight, he stuck his hands in his jeans pockets and aimed for the old shake-shingled cottage. The surrounding woods were starting to change color, picking up tips of gold and vermilion and bronze. The brook, at the back of the property, glistened in the sunlight. He took in a long clean breath, wanting to feel like he belonged here.

He didn't.

He wanted to. He'd loved the place when he bought it, even though at the time it was only to have a house close to his daughters for their visits here. And he'd quit Jeunnesse once he'd finished Violet's business and knew she was going to be set up any way she wanted to be in the future. At that point, though, he knew he no longer wanted to continue with that job. The work had been good to him and for him, but was nothing remotely what he wanted in his life anymore.

He'd thought—perhaps crazily—that he could recapture the feeling he had with Violet. He wanted that feeling of belonging. Of roots. He wanted a red barn and a stone fence. Rocks. Insane neighbors. A place private enough to make wild love in the moonlight with his one and only lover.

He stomped up the porch steps and pushed open the door, thinking darkly that he wanted a woman who cried at the drop of a hat, who made strange and wonderful food, who took in no end of cats and neighbors, who wore Victorian lace and neon-orange underpants.

Nothing but lonely silence greeted him in the house.

It was funny, but coming home, he'd made all kinds of foolish assumptions. For sure, he hadn't blindly assumed that Violet was ready to talk about wild, crazy things like *marriage*. But it was going to be so much easier to see her now, easier to talk, easier to be together. He'd planned to try a relentless romantic assault by courting her in all the old-fashioned ways.

It had never once occurred to him that she wouldn't answer his notes or phone calls.

In the brick kitchen he poured the last mug of coffee from this morning's pot. The brew was now thicker than mud, not that he cared.

One of the girls had left a pink sock, and a couple of teen girl magazines zooed up the pristine neatness of the place, but otherwise there was nothing inside but wood and a stone fireplace and big leather furniture and silence.

It was tough, accepting that he'd misunderstood everything that mattered. He'd *thought* he was ready to settle down. He'd *thought* he was ready to finally belong. He'd *thought* he'd finally come to terms with his father's legacy of fearing a place could own him instead of the other way around. Instead, he'd discovered that his lack of interest in a home had nothing to do with his father.

All this time, it had simply been about finding a woman he wanted to belong with.

He got it now. He got it all. Except, he couldn't seem to believe that he'd come this far, hurt this much, finally found himself—and found her—and then had to accept that he'd lost her.

The phone rang, a shock of sound that made him whip around and spill a few coffee drops from his mug. He grabbed the receiver and tucked it under his ear.

"Cameron Lachlan?"

He heard the woman's scream, and immediately recognized the voice as Daisy Campbell, Violet's oldest sister. He'd always liked her. She was breathtaking, an exotic beauty, fiercely independent, her own woman. She'd been living with some artist in the south of France, which was how she'd been in his "Jeunnesse neighborhood" these last years. But the thing was, they'd always gotten along well, so it was nearly impossible to connect the cool-eyed beauty with the woman yelling at him across the ocean.

"Lachlan, did I or did I not tell you that I'd kill you if you broke my sister's heart?!"

"What?"

"I *told* you she was vulnerable. I *told* you to be

good to her or to leave her alone. I thought you were a decent guy!''

''Um, I could have sworn I was, too—''

''Well, I'm leaving Provence for good and coming back across the Atlantic. And the very minute I get home, I'm going to kill you. I'm not sure how yet. I've never killed anything before. But where I grew up, buster, a man didn't get a woman pregnant and then take off.''

''*What?*'' This time he'd been lifting the mug to his mouth. Only, he dropped it. Sludgy hot coffee spattered all over the place. The ceramic mug broke in a half dozen pieces. ''What did you say?''

''Give me a break, Lachlan! I don't care whether she told you or not. If you weren't going to use some protection, you knew perfectly well you were taking a risk. You know damn well how babies are made!''

''But not for your sister.'' He couldn't seem to catch his breath, couldn't seem to think.

''What's that supposed to mean, not for my sister?''

He opened his mouth to answer but then couldn't. In a flash he realized that Violet had never told her family about the infertility, how her ex-husband had treated her, none of it. She loved her sisters, talked about them all the time. So it must have hurt more than she could bear to even try to share it.

Except with him.

She'd cared enough to share it with *him*. The

thought registered, but it was pretty hard to concentrate. Daisy was still winding up, and beauty or no beauty, she could yell like a drill sergeant. "Don't even try playing any stupid games with me, Lachlan. I've heard every excuse a man can make up for irresponsibility. I can smell them. I *told* you my sister was vulnerable. All I asked was that you be decent to her, be nice, be fair. If you two ended up in the sack...all right, I admit I thought you'd like each other. I even admit I thought an affair was a good idea for our Vi. But to get her pregnant, you scoundrel, you creep, you turkey, you unfeeling, revolting, irresponsible... Cameron, why the hell aren't you answering me?"

"Daisy, do me a favor and don't tell your sister that you called me."

For the first time since the phone call started, Daisy stopped frothing fire and brimstone. Confusion silenced her—although not for long. "Do you a favor? Do *you* a favor? Did you want me to do you that favor before or after I murder you?!"

He didn't mean to hang up on her. He just forgot she was there. Violet? Pregnant with his child? And once those wheels started spinning, they seemed to pick up speed nonstop.

He was in upstate New York, not Vermont. He had fresh food in the fridge, a coffeepot on, a load of clothes heaped in the washer, bills waiting to be paid on the counter, a dentist appointment two days from now. He couldn't just take off.

Fifteen minutes later he started the car.

If everything went perfectly—no pit or food stops, no construction zones—he could make the trip in four hours.

Naturally he ran into three construction zones and one minor accident. He combined a pit stop with a run on fast food and strong coffee. Even this early in fall, the sun dropped fast. By the time he crossed the border into Vermont, dusk had fallen. Blustery clouds stole the last of daylight, and then there was only that quiet blacktop and him.

He remembered the rolling hills. The stone fences. The white steepled churches in White Hills. The pretty red barns and winding roads. Every familiar sight heightened both his anticipation and his fear.

He pulled into her yard after nine, not realizing until then how long his heart had been pounding, or that the burger he'd wolfed down was still sitting in his stomach like a clunky ball. Yellow lights glowed in her windows. A cornstalk scarecrow sat at the bottom of her porch steps, keeping two of the cats company. A pair of giant pumpkins, still uncarved, framed her door. Pruning shears sat on the porch swing, not put away.

He vaulted the steps of the porch, hiked toward the door and then abruptly stopped. Faster than lightning, he tucked, buttoned, straightened. Then he realized that, hell, he hadn't brushed his hair since he could even remember. And he should have shaved. Still…he'd come this far, and God knew Violet had seen him in worse shape than in an old black sweater and cords. So he knocked.

Nothing. No answer.

He knocked again, louder this time.

Still, there was no response. So he poked his head in. Smells immediately swarmed his senses—apples and cinnamons and cloves. A bowl of mums nested on the hearth. A copper pot held long, tall grasses and reeds. Lavender—naturally—hung upside down from the kitchen beams. Two cats spotted him, remembered him for the sucker he was and leaped down from the rockers to get petted.

Still, there was no sight of Violet, only the sound of her. She was singing from somewhere upstairs, assuming one could call the sounds emanating from her throat "singing." Her sister Daisy could scream like a shrew, where Vi's singing voice, he thought tenderly, resembled steel scratching steel—at a high pitch.

"Violet?" He had to let her know he was there, didn't want to scare her. "Vi?"

The caterwauling stopped. A hesitant voice called down, "Cameron?" But then followed through with a swift, "Don't answer that. Obviously you can't be Cameron."

Oh, God. It was like coming home. Only his ditsy

Violet could make irrational comments like that, and maybe he was crazy, maybe he was risking his heart and his life, but he took the stairs three at a time and galloped down the hall. He wouldn't have known positively where that ghastly operatic voice had been coming from, if there hadn't been puffs of fragrant steam dancing out the open door of the master bath.

He leaned both arms against the doorjamb, trying to catch his breath. Yet almost immediately he realized that he would likely never catch his breath because his heart had completely stopped.

She was in the bathtub. No longer singing the blues, just sunken in the warm water to the tips of her nipples, her long hair twisted and clipped out of the way. Two cats sat on the porcelain rim, balanced precariously but acting the part of sentinels. The bathwater wasn't sudsy. In fact, he could see clearly to her pale white skin under the surface, the long slim legs, the white curve of her hip, the plump breasts. And the tummy.

His gaze fell on her tummy and his heart stopped all over again.

"Hi," she said, as if she regularly greeted strange men in her bathtub. Now, though, he knew her well. Doing the unpredictable, the ditsy, the flaky, was how she'd learned to protect herself—especially from men wanting to look too closely. He wasn't fooled anymore. He could hear the uncertainty in her voice and see the gamut of emotions in her eyes. Pain. Longing. Love.

How could he have missed that the love was there?

"Smells great in here," he murmured.

"It should. It's my personal recipe for a bath to take away your cares, no matter how heavy your heart is. It's got a little lavender, a little marjoram, a little peppermint and some secret ingredients I'll never tell anyone." She looked at him with those clear, soft, vulnerable eyes and then took a breath.

"Except you, Cam. I'll tell you. I mix a little lily of the valley and jasmine in there. That's my secret."

"Aha," he said. And heeled off his right shoe. Then his left. His black sweater peeled off by a miracle. It had to be a miracle, because he was too fumble-fingered to do it himself. "I like the tummy."

She glanced down. "I've really been on a milk-shake binge."

"I don't think that's the reason for the tummy."

"No?" She sucked in a breath when he peeled off his cords and shorts. "Um, Cameron. You're going to smell like flowers if you come in here."

"I'd care about that if I were a sissy. But I happen to be a tough guy. A tough guy always does what a tough guy has to do." The cats scattered when he stepped in. The water whooshed up to the top of the tub and splashed over. She didn't notice or look. She only looked at him, pulled her knees up.

"You couldn't get a bath closer to home?"

"Well, that's the problem, chère. It took me this long, not to take a bath, but to realize that this *is* home."

Total silence fell for a moment. He sank in, knee to knee, eye to eye, and reached out a hand. She folded her fingers with his. "I didn't think you wanted a home, Cameron Lachlan."

"I don't know if I ever told you about my dad. I loved him. He wasn't a bad guy, nothing like that. But he built his whole life around possessions. Things owned him instead of the other way around. He was never home for us. He never had time for us."

"I'm sorry."

"I don't want you to be sorry. I just needed you to understand how I turned into a vagabond. I just never wanted that to happen to me. I wanted people to matter, not things. I wanted the freedom to love people, not things." He laved her feet, since they were easy to reach. And her knees. He got her knees really, really clean. "And then I met you. And lost you. And realized I was doing exactly what he did wrong. Putting a barrier between myself and who I wanted to spend time with, who I wanted to love. Who I needed in my life."

He moved up from the knees, to those long, silky white thighs. Her phone rang. It seemed a measure of how well he knew her, and them, that neither even blinked or made any effort to answer it. Phones were always going to ring in this house. They'd wait.

"I quit Jeunnesse. Came back to my place in New York, saw my girls. But the whole time I kept thinking about making a whole different kind of life. I've got the money to buy the land, put in a big five-hundred acres of lavender. It'd be adventurous, challenging. Hard work, but still a lot of free traveling time in the winter. Time to be impulsive any way a couple might want to be. Of course, we have to find a house-sitter for the cats. And obviously it's not your usual life—it'd only work for people who really liked the land, got a charge out of getting their hands dirty—"

"So…you came back for the land, did you?"

"Nope." He could see that haunted look leaving her eyes. And she wasn't backing away from him. But she didn't move toward him.

"You always sounded so positive, Cam. That you didn't want to settle down."

"I don't want to settle down. I want to live with you and be your lover. Forever. I don't want to *settle* for anything. I want to create exactly the life that works for us. I was going to say for the two of us— but maybe for the three or four or five of us, if for any reason the family somehow grew."

Again she went still, seemed to even stop breathing. "Daisy called you, didn't she?"

He didn't directly answer that, because this wasn't

about her sister or anything her sister had said to him. It was about the two of them. And to make sure he had her attention, he took her warm, slippery hands in his. "I don't think it's a good idea for a woman to marry a guy who has nearly grown children…at least until you've met the children. I'm totally positive you'd get on with them like a house afire, but they *are* teenagers, which means they stay up nights trying to think up new ways to make adults' lives difficult. For myself, though, I've always liked kids. Nice kids, wild kids, difficult kids, doesn't matter to me. I'd love more."

"Lachlan, that isn't at all what you said before."

"I know, I know. I wasn't exactly lying before. But I was trying to make sure you know I loved you for *you*. That you were what mattered to me, not whether you could have kids or not. I love you first. I want you first."

Tears started to well up in her soft eyes, so he started talking faster.

"Violet, you're probably ten times more woman than I can handle, but I'd like to try. But I want you to absolutely know that my loving you has nothing to do with kids. If you want some, we can adopt or foster, or try working with those skinny tubes…hell, maybe we can just take in more cats. I don't know. I don't care. I just care that we work together to find choices that are right for us."

She took a long, shaky breath. "It's possible that this tummy isn't caused by too many milkshakes."

"I thought the skinny tubes were pretty much a for-sure problem."

"So did I. Every doctor I went to told me my chances of conception were minuscule." Her fingertips caressed his. Her gaze seemed to caress his face at the same time. "You must have awfully determined little seeds in there, Lachlan."

"I prefer to think of them as skillful. And smart enough to go after what they want." He wanted to draw her into his arms, right there, right then. They had a lifetime to finish all this talking business, and the old-fashioned tub was big, but not necessarily big enough for the rest of the night he had planned. Yet he had to say gently, "You should have told me you were pregnant, chère."

"I wanted to and I would have. But I had to think about how, Cam. I never wanted you to feel trapped. Nothing works when a person feels trapped. And I love you. Of everyone in the universe, Cameron Lachlan, I so want you to be happy. I want you to have what you need in your life."

There, now. He drew her on top of him. Warm water sloshed on the floor, but still he finally had her, breast to breast, tummy to tummy. Heart to heart. "That's easy, then, because what I need is you. In my life, all my life."

"That's a two-way street. I love you so much. And

I want you in my life, all my life,'' she whispered, and blessed him with an eyes-closed, drowning-defying, promise-invoking kiss. When they came up for air, his eyes were moist and hers were dry.

It was going to be a hell of a thing, if she turned him into an emotional kind of guy. Chemists were supposed to be rational, calm, cold types, but somehow Cameron didn't think that was going to work. Not anymore.

He'd always tried to be careful, not to let anything own him. Yet Violet owned his heart—and it was the best thing that had ever happened to him. Of course, that was just today.

They had a lifetime to explore all they could be together.

* * * * *

Watch for Daisy's story, coming soon from Silhouette Desire.

"How old are you?" he probed.

Delia sighed. "I'm twenty-three."

He glanced at her with an indulgent smile. "You're still a baby."

"Really?" she asked, slightly irritated.

"I'll be thrity-eight my next brithday." he said. "And I'm older than that in lots of ways."

She felt an odd pang of regret. He was handsome and very attractive. Her whole young body throbbed just being near him. It was a new and unexpected reaction. Delia had never felt those wild stirrings her friends talked about. She'd been a remarkably late bloomer.

"No comment?" he queried, lifting his eyes.

"You never told me your name." she countered.

"Carrera," he said, watching her face. "Marcus Carrera." He noted her lack of recognition. "You haven't heard of me have you?"

She hadn't, which he seemed to find amusing.

"Are you famous?" she ventured.

"*In*famous," he replied, studying her oval face, with those big green eyes and soft, creamy complexion. Her mouth was full and sweet looking. His eyes narrowed on it and he felt a sudden, unexpected surge of hunger. But he resisted the temptation.

It was unwise to start things he couldn't finish…

BOOK Offer Exclusive to Silhouette Romance Series

Buy this book and get another free! Simply indicate which series you are interested in by ticking the box and we'll send you a FREE book.
Please tick only one box

✂

Special Edition	❏	Superromance	❏
Sensation	❏	Intrigue	❏
Desire	❏	Spotlight	❏

Please complete the following:

Name _____

Address _____

_____ Postcode _____

Please cut out and return the above coupon along with your till receipt to:

**Silhouette Free Book competition,
Reader Service
FREEPOST NAT 10298, Richmond,
Surrey TW9 1BR**

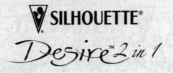

0105/SH/LC96

SILHOUETTE®

Desire™ 2 in 1

presents

DYNASTIES:
THE DANFORTHS

A family of prominence...tested by scandal,
sustained by passion!

January 2005 **The Cinderella Scandal** *by Barbara McCauley*
 Man Beneath the Uniform *by Maureen Child*

March 2005 **Sin City Wedding** *by Katherine Garbera*
 Scandal Between the Sheets *by Brenda Jackson*

May 2005 **The Boss Man's Fortune** *by Kathryn Jensen*
 Challenged by the Sheikh *by Kristi Gold*

July 2005 **Cowboy Crescendo** *by Cathleen Galitz*
 Steamy Savannah Nights *by Sheri WhiteFeather*

September 2005 **The Enemy's Daughter** *by Anne Marie Winston*
 The Laws of Passion *by Linda Conrad*

November 2005 **Terms of Surrender** *by Shirley Rogers*
 Shocking the Senator *by Leanne Banks*

Also look for DYNASTIES: SUMMER IN SAVANNAH
Barbara McCauley, Maureen Child and Sheri WhiteFeather
Available in June 2005

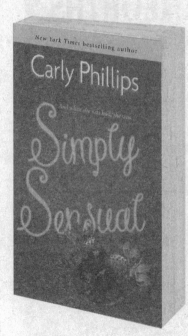

Coming soon from
Nora Roberts

DANGEROUS
20th May 2005
ISBN: 0 373 60157 3

SUSPICIOUS
15th July 2005
ISBN: 0 373 60158 1

MYSTERIOUS
18th November 2005
ISBN: 0 373 60273 1

0505/121/SH96

On sale 15th April 2005

Available at most branches of WHSmith, Tesco, ASDA, Martins, Borders, Eason, Sainsbury's and all good paperback bookshops.

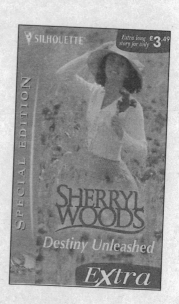

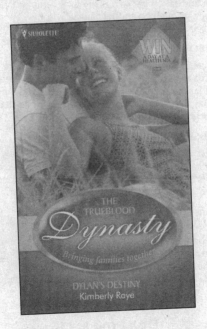

0305/01a

MILLS & BOON®

Live the emotion

Modern
romance™

POSSESSED BY THE SHEIKH by Penny Jordan

After being stranded in the desert, Katrina was rescued by
a Sheikh and taken back to his luxury camp. He decided to
marry her, though he thought her a whore. Then he
discovered – first hand – that she was a virgin...

THE DISOBEDIENT BRIDE by Helen Bianchin

Their marriage was perfect – and then billionaire Tyler
Benedict's wife left! Now he wants her back. Beautiful
Lianne Marshall can't refuse his deal – but this time she
won't play fair. However, Tyler is after more than a
business arrangement!

HIS PREGNANT MISTRESS by Carol Marinelli

Australian billionaire Ethan Carvelle left Mia Stewart years
ago. Now Mia's pregnant – claiming Ethan's late brother is
the father! Torn between duty and desire, he decides to
make her his mistress. But he knows nothing of the secret
Mia is hiding...

THE FUTURE KING'S BRIDE by Sharon Kendrick

Prince Gianferro Cacciatore is heir to the throne of
Mardivino and his father, the King, is dying. The pressure
is on Gianferro to find a wife and his heart is set on
English aristocrat Millie de Vere. But Millie hardly knows
the prince...

Don't miss out...

On sale 1st April 2005

MILLS & BOON®

Live the emotion

0305/01b

Modern
romance™

IN THE BANKER'S BED by *Cathy Williams*

When Melissa Lee works for Elliot Jay, she expects their relationship to be strictly business. He is seriously sexy, but he keeps his emotions in the deep freeze! Melissa is soon getting Elliot hot under the collar, and now he has a new agenda: getting her into his bed!

THE GREEK'S CONVENIENT WIFE by *Melanie Milburne*

When her brother's exploits leave Maddison Jones at the mercy of billionaire Demetrius Papasakis, the last thing she expects is a proposal. But Demetrius knows she has to agree to a marriage of convenience – and Maddison finds herself unable to resist!

THE RUTHLESS MARRIAGE BID by *Elizabeth Power*

Taylor's time as Jared Steele's wife was short, but not sweet. Within weeks she discovered that he had a mistress and that she was pregnant. She lost the baby *and* her marriage. Now she is stunned by Jared's return – and his claim that he wants her back!

THE ITALIAN'S SEDUCTION by *Karen van der Zee*

It sounded like heaven: an apartment in a small Italian town. But after a series of mishaps Charli Olson finds herself stranded – until gorgeous Massimo Castellini offers her a room in his luxurious villa. Though he's vowed never to love again, Massimo finds Charli irresistible.

Don't miss out...

On sale 1st April 2005

EXtra

Favourite, award-winning or bestselling authors. Bigger reads, bonus short stories, new books or much-loved classics. *Always* **fabulous reading!**

Don't miss:

EXTRA passion for your money! (March 2005)
Emma Darcy – Mills & Boon Modern Romance
NEW *Mistress to a Tycoon* and **CLASSIC** *Jack's Baby*

EXTRA special for your money! (April 2005)
Sherryl Woods – Silhouette Special Edition –
Destiny Unleashed. This **BIG** book is about a woman who is finally free to choose her own path…love, business or a little sweet revenge?

EXTRA tender for your money! (April 2005)
Betty Neels & Liz Fielding – Mills & Boon
Tender Romance – **CLASSIC** *The Doubtful Marriage*
and **BONUS,** *Secret Wedding*
Two very popular writers write two very different, emotional stories on the always-bestselling wedding theme.

THE TRUEBLOOD
Dynasty

*Isabella Trueblood made history reuniting people
torn apart by war and an epidemic. Now,
generations later, Lily and Dylan Garrett carry on
her work with their agency, Finders Keepers.*

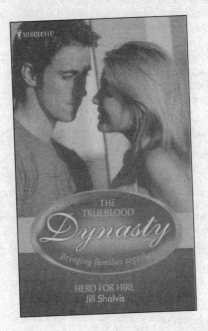

Book Thirteen available from 18th February

FREE!
2 Books
and a surprise gift!

We would like to take this opportunity to thank you for reading this Silhouette® book by offering you the chance to take TWO more specially selected titles from the Desire™ series absolutely FREE! We're also making this offer to introduce you to the benefits of the Reader Service™—

- ★ **FREE home delivery**
- ★ **FREE gifts and competitions**
- ★ **FREE monthly Newsletter**
- ★ **Exclusive Reader Service offers**
- ★ **Books available before they're in the shops**

Accepting these FREE books and gift places you under no obligation to buy, you may cancel at any time, even after receiving your free shipment. Simply complete your details below and return the entire page to the address below. You don't even need a stamp!

YES! Please send me 2 free Desire books, and a surprise gift. I understand that unless you hear from me, I will receive 3 superb new titles every month for just £4.99 each, postage and packing free. I am under no obligation to purchase any books and may cancel my subscription at any time. The free books and gift will be mine to keep in any case.

D5ZEF

Ms/Mrs/Miss/Mr .... Initials ....

BLOCK CAPITALS PLEASE

Surname ....

Address ....

....

.... Postcode ....

Send this whole page to:
UK: FREEPOST CN81, Croydon, CR9 3WZ